THE
COVEN

LIZZIE FRY

SPHERE

First published in Great Britain in 2021 by Sphere
This paperback edition published by Sphere in 2021

1 3 5 7 9 10 8 6 4 2

A CIP catalogue record for this book
is available from the British Library.

ISBN 978-0-7515-7794-5

Typeset in Garamond by M Rules
Printed and bound in Great Britain by
Clays Ltd, Elcograf S.p.A.

Papers used by Sphere are from well-managed forests
and other responsible sources.

Sphere
An imprint of
Little, Brown Book Group
Carmelite House
50 Victoria Embankment
London EC4Y 0DZ

An Hachette UK Company
www.hachette.co.uk

www.littlebrown.co.uk

To Laura,
<u>You</u> are The One.
Aunty L x

The Proclamation of the Elementals

We are all kernels in the earth. We are baptised by fire; fed by the water of life; powered by air. To us, we call The One: connect us through the chain of being and bring us liberation from the ties that bind us.

PART ONE

Friday, March 6th

PROLOGUE

Green light was leaking under the bedroom door.

The sight of it made Li stop in her tracks and back up, dropping the washing basket she'd been holding. Her brain attempted to push the realisation away in sluggish disbelief. She had prayed to the triple goddesses she would never have to deal with this. Her heartbeat thundered in her ears as anxiety crashed through her body.

The day Li had been putting off had finally arrived.

Until that moment, it had been a completely ordinary Friday in March. Li had been stripping the beds, her usual end-of-the-week routine, when Chloe had returned from college around midday, her lectures finished for the weekend. As usual, Li had asked her daughter how her day had been; as usual, Chloe had rebuffed her with that sneering way of hers. Li tried to not let it bother her. Since puberty had struck around the age of fourteen, Chloe had made it clear she had no time for her parents. At nineteen, almost twenty, she should have grown out of such juvenile power-plays, but Li understood it wasn't entirely her only child's fault.

Seeing the green light now, pooling on the floor like liquid, Li knew it was all hers.

Fear gripped her, guilt rushing up behind it. As if in a nightmare, her bones felt as heavy as concrete. She hesitated, unable to raise her arm to push the door and go inside. Blinking back the tears pricking her eyelids, she took her phone from her jeans pocket and pulled up her call log; DANIEL was first on the list. Bar the odd errand in town, Li saw only two people most days: Daniel and Chloe. Apart from a dozen Facebook and Twitter followers she spoke with online regularly, she had few real-life friends and worked from home. Her love of travel and a degree from a British university twenty years ago had led her to make a life for herself on the other side of the world. Too late, she realised she was isolated and alone when it really counted.

Li finally managed to press the button to call her husband.

'Hi.' Daniel's gravelly voice filtered down the line.

'You need to—'

The voicemail kicked in. He hadn't really answered at all. Keying off, Li swore in Mandarin, the sound of her native tongue discordant in her own ears. Her hands were shaking so much she almost dropped the phone. She redialled again with difficulty, irritation and fear clashing together. Daniel had to pick up this time. Had to. She couldn't deal with this alone. Not any more. She would tell him everything.

Chloe was not the type to go drinking or take drugs; Li had never worried about her coming home one day, pregnant. Some days, she wished it could be as simple as that. At least that way, they would be forced to confront their issues as a family and find a solution together. But Chloe's constant anger was seemingly without cause or purpose.

Through the years, Li had seen Chloe erupt over and over again. During these episodes, Chloe would scream in frustration, beating her fists against her head like she was trying to pound her brains from her skull. She would turn her hands into weapons and scratch at her eyes, her face, her arms. Li would have to wrestle Chloe's hands away, pinning her daughter's arms to her sides until they both collapsed on the floor together in shocked silence, leaving Chloe staring at the wall, unable to speak. She'd stay like that for at least an hour, sometimes longer if the attack had been particularly ferocious.

Each time Chloe disappeared inside herself, Li wondered if she would be able to make her way back. Li could see the fear and confusion in her daughter's eyes, yet was totally unable to help her. She and Daniel had sent Chloe to psychiatrists, counsellors, neuroscientists. They'd gone for second, even third and fourth opinions – before the money had run out. All of the professionals had subjected Chloe to rigorous tests and examinations. All had given Chloe a clean bill of health, labelling her attacks as 'growing pains' or 'behavioural issues'.

Li had been relieved with these verdicts, but not because there was nothing wrong with her child. She'd always known there was something very different about Chloe, from the moment the midwife had placed her on her chest. She'd felt it moving within her tiny muscles, as obvious as the blood pumping through her veins.

The phone rang and rang. Even behind the wood of the door, Li could see the green light was getting stronger, could sense its growing power. Her panicked thoughts shimmered through her mind like multiple reflections in a hall of mirrors. Had she really thought this day would never come? That she could put it off for ever?

The voicemail cut in again. As she was forced to wait until the recording came to an end, Li became aware of a loud humming noise behind Chloe's bedroom door. It had the intensity of an aeroplane engine, and was growing exponentially with every second. She could feel it in her belly, in the marrow of her bones.

Finally, on the end of the line: *beep*.

'... Daniel? Oh, Daniel. You have to come home, quick!'

With a sudden flush of bravery borne of fatalism, or perhaps bolstered by the distant comfort of being connected to Daniel's voicemail, Li pushed the door inwards to confront whatever was on the other side. The phone fell from her hand as she took in the sight before her.

Chloe sat on her bed, her face turned upwards, her eyes glazed with concentration. She was cross-legged, palms out in front of her, as if poised to catch a ball. Green light spiralled up out of her hands in a column. As it hit the ceiling the light crawled out across the plaster like a living thing. The window-pane rattled in its frame; books on the shelves fell over; a glass on Chloe's bedside cabinet exploded, sending water and shards of glass into the plaster of the wall beside it. Li could feel raw power swarm across the floor towards her, making her teeth chatter. As she looked on in horror, a realisation flowered in Li's brain, nineteen years too late.

She'd completely and utterly failed to keep her precious child safe.

'Chloe! Chloe, look at me!'

Li's voice was snatched by the noise enveloping Chloe. The air felt like it was splitting apart, just like the onset of a storm. Even though the distance from the bedroom door to Chloe's bed was just four or five feet, Li staggered as if she was walking against high winds, her daughter miles away. The smell of ozone, strong like chlorine, assaulted Li's nostrils and throat as she spoke, making her gag and her eyes water. Still Li forced one foot in front of the other. She had to make it. She had to try and reach Chloe, not only literally but also the real girl, lost deep inside herself right now.

Li made it to the bed. She pushed her arm through the space between them, grabbing Chloe by the shoulder. 'Chloe, lovely, don't! I'll explain ...'

Li's words died on her tongue as her daughter turned her head away from the vortex of green light. Repelled and in shock, Li let her hand drop away from Chloe's shoulder. Her daughter's eyes were black and shiny, like the carapace of a beetle. With no pupils, no whites at all, the look Chloe gave Li was devoid of all humanity.

'What have you done to me, *Mother*?' Chloe hissed.

The green light rushed in at Li like a tidal wave.

ONE

Texts, USA

C onsciousness came back to Adelita with the ferocity of an express train. She was out cold, then she was back. There was no in-between.

Her eyes snapped open and reality burst through her senses. Her surroundings took a little longer to come into focus. Polyester curtains fluttered in the windows as a silhouette passed by. She could hear the hum of a Coke machine outside and the sound of the ice dispenser as the silhouette collected ice in the bucket. She lay on a double bed with stained sheets, a cheap Formica cabinet beside it. She knew without looking there would be a Bible inside the top drawer. She was in a cheap back-road motel. How had she got here?

Adelita wasn't able to stand as fast as she'd come round. Fatigue was shot through her bones; her limbs were heavy with it. Ever the medic, she examined herself. Her arms and legs were scratched and bruised; several of her fingernails were bloodied. There was a tremor in her hands and shoulders. Her heart ricocheted around her ribcage.

She pinched the pulse point in her wrist: definitely more than one hundred beats a minute. There were bright spots floating before her eyes, despite the gloom of the room around her. If she didn't know any better, she would have thought she had gone on a two-day bender; that she was hung-over. But even with blank spots in her memory, Adelita knew she hadn't drunk liquor in a very long time. What the hell had happened to her?

'Son of a bitch!'

Who was *that*? Her heart made a pained, panicked thud in her chest. The voice was male, a low growl, and had come from the motel's en suite bathroom. From the bed, she couldn't see around the bathroom door to locate the voice's owner, nor could she even fathom whom the voice could belong to. Numerous faces, mostly female, flashed through her brain. Names swam up in her consciousness: *Elinor . . . Maddie . . . Claire . . . Yukio*. She'd been with these women, she'd known them. But how? Where? Thoughts clamoured through her brain as she tried to concentrate, but she was too exhausted to focus.

Adelita swung her bare feet over the side of the bed and took two or three tottering steps, like an hour-old foal. She looked around the room in search of something she could use as a weapon. She didn't have to look far; a Colt 1873 Single Action Army sat on the cheap-looking sideboard, its cold steel glinting in the lamplight. She snatched it up, feeling slightly better with the weight of it in her hands. Her father had favoured Colts, keeping one under the counter in his bodega, along with a shotgun. Ernesto Garcia had always told Adelita and her older twin sisters that guns should be outlawed in any civilised nation. As he also pointed out, the United States was very far from civilised. Ernesto insisted all his girls have shooting lessons.

Adelita checked it was loaded and staggered towards the bathroom to try and get a glimpse of the stranger in there before she revealed herself. Peering through the crack in the door, she could see another handgun, abandoned in the sink like a can of shaving foam. Next to the tap, where the soap should go, was an open bottle of Jack Daniel's, half the liquor gone.

A white guy sat on the side of the bath.

His back was to her but, even sitting down, Adelita could tell he wasn't particularly tall, maybe five nine or ten, just an inch or two taller than her. He was shirtless, lean and broad-shouldered. She could count his ribs and the muscles undulating under his skin. Whatever he lacked in height, he was strong, and young. Barely thirty – a good decade younger than her. His black pants were pulled down as low as they could go without exposing his ass. A black shirt, replete with gold insignia on the shoulders, lay abandoned on the floor. His boots, kicked off next to the toilet, were polished and shiny; his blond hair was closely cropped. Even half-dressed, Blondie had the unmistakable air of military about him.

He was Sentinel.

He twisted around so he might tend to the injury on his side near his hip. It looked like a bullet wound, a through-and-through. He was attempting to sew it up himself, but its location was making it difficult. Adelita knew from all the time she'd spent tending gunshot victims in the ER that Blondie had been lucky, though he probably didn't feel it. Even minor bullet wounds hurt like hell. He growled again and grabbed the bottle of JD off the sink, slugging it back with a grimace.

Adelita kicked the door open with her bare foot. 'Who the fuck are you?'

She raised the gun, just as he turned towards her. At the sight of his face, Adelita's memory flooded back against her will, assaulting her senses.

The blond Sentinel guard ran straight at her.

She let the gun fall to her side as she lurched towards the motel door frame to steady herself.

A feeling of being on fast-forward, like she was moving between two planes of existence, super-fast.

11

In the motel room, Blondie stepped forwards.

'Don't!'

Adelita uttered the warning too late, though he made no attempt for the gun. His gnarled hands grabbed her around the waist, steadying her. Bursts of imagery seared through her brain:

Her fist, glowing like a beacon.

Blondie, hit in the chest by a column of white light, going down as if by a battering ram.

Adelita pushed him away from her and raised the gun again, finger on the trigger. She took in the rivulets of dried blood from Blondie's ear, his split lip. She faltered as a realisation flowered in her brain.

'I did that to you.'

Blondie nodded.

'. . . I was in jail.'

'S'right. Our Lady of Nazareth, Texas.'

Adelita laughed at herself as clarity came to her. 'This is a prison break. I'm not your hostage, you're mine!'

Blondie pulled a face. 'Not really.'

'What's that supposed to mean?'

'If I really was your hostage, don't you think I could have left when you were asleep and brought back a bunch of Sentinel?'

Adelita's weary mind connected the dots. He was right.

'So, I escaped . . . and you came with me.'

'Yup.'

Blondie moved away from her, staggering a little – from the bourbon or the pain, Adelita wasn't sure. He leant over the sink with both hands, clearly exhausted. It still didn't make any sense. Why would a Sentinel escape a super-max prison with a witch? He was free. He could have walked out of the prison at the end of his shift. He didn't need to be here, with her.

'Don't move.' Adelita forced threat into her voice.

But Blondie held her gaze in the reflection of the bathroom

mirror. 'You and I both know you aren't going to shoot me. Thanks, by the way.'

Adelita stared back, wrong-footed. 'Er ... don't mention it?'

Adelita watched herself lower the gun in the mirror, catching sight of the fact that she was only in her underwear, practically naked. He didn't seem concerned about being half-dressed himself, either. They might have been spouses on a last-minute, budget road trip. One in which she blacked out and he got shot. There was a familiar air between them she could not explain. Even so, she needed to know one thing.

'Where the fuck are my clothes?'

The Sentinel raised both palms in mock surrender this time. 'Nothing to do with me. You took your prison uniform off in the passenger seat and threw it out the car window.'

Adelita considered this and let it pass. It seemed like something she might do. She'd hated the scratchy material of her uniform; the fact its purple colour marked her out as a witch from the women in orange, the 'Goodys'. Derived from the archaic 'goodwife' from colonial times, that label nowadays meant non-witches. Whatever the case, the word was a complete misnomer for the prisoners they had been locked up with. At Our Lady, she'd lived side by side with murderers and gang-bangers. Adelita's only crime had been her strong magical bloodline, her existence.

'What's the last thing you remember?'

Blondie rebuckled his belt and sat back down on the side of the bath. Before Adelita could answer, her brain solved the puzzle for her. Disjointed fragments of sound and vision rolled through her mind's eye. In the dust of the prison yard, under the punishing Texas sun: a pebble, a seam of quartz shot right through it. Adelita couldn't believe what she'd been seeing; the prison was swept daily for crystals, just in case. She had snatched it up.

13

'*Para ti, Madre*,' Adelita had whispered into her closed hand. *For you, Mother.*

Then white light had burst from her fist with the power of lightning.

She met the Sentinel's gaze. 'You left the crystal in the prison yard on purpose for me to find?'

He nodded again. *Guilty as charged.*

'How did you know it would work?'

He shrugged. 'I didn't. I hoped.'

'I would have got out of there by myself, eventually. Somehow.'

'I know.' He grinned at her. 'I just wanted to speed up the process . . . Kinda like the spark to your flywheel.'

Adelita's brow knitted in suspicion. 'Why? What do you get out of this?'

Blondie took another slug of JD and wiped his mouth with the back of his hand. 'I'm sick of living on the wrong side of history.'

Adelita picked over his words as she took in the Sentinel tattoo on his bare chest, depicting the Earth as the pupil in an eye surrounded by the Latin motto *Si vis pacem, para bellum.* If you want peace, prepare for war. That was how guys like him saw the world: as black and white; good and bad; winning and losing. He had been on the winning side. He must have changed his mind somewhere down the line.

'We should get our stuff together.'

'Where are we going?'

'Let me worry about that, for now.'

Adelita's mind flitted through everything that had happened, reaching for possibilities. What else could she do now? Where could she go? She came up with nothing. She had no money. No clothes. Her face would surely be circulated everywhere by now; there would almost certainly be a kill order on her. If she got taken back to Our Lady, her next destination

14

would be Yard B, where they barbecued the most troublesome witches. Just the thought sent her stomach into a spin cycle: she could not go back. She would never go back; something within her knew she'd die first. It was strange – and unnerving – that this guy seemed to want to help her; she couldn't think of a reason a Sentinel penal guard would purposely break a witch out of jail. She would have to take him at his word. For now, at least.

'You're doing a terrible job.' Adelita indicated the ragged stitches on his side. 'Let me. I'm a doctor – or, I was.'

Blondie grinned at her. 'Yeah?'

Adelita felt irritation crash through her. 'Why's that so surprising?'

'You have a lot of street smarts for an educated lady. I watched you on the prison CCTV. You didn't let anyone push you around in there.'

'Because women can be only one thing, right?'

'I didn't say that.'

Blondie sat down on the side of the bath while Adelita knelt beside him. He winced each time she unpicked one of his crappy stitches. It had been a long time since she'd been a junior doctor working in one of New York's busiest hospitals – coming up to two years since she'd practised for real – yet it came back naturally to her. Without warning, she grabbed the bourbon bottle and sloshed some on the wound. He yelped like a chihuahua and brought his fist down on the sink, gritting his teeth.

'So much for being a tough guy.'

'I never said I was a tough guy.'

Adelita smirked as she rethreaded the needle. 'I do neat, small stitches so it's gonna take a while. You might want to bite down on a bit of wood or something for this, *debilucho*.'

His face was pale and drawn in the mirror. 'I don't think much of your bedside manner.'

'I don't think much of your first aid kit. You know iodine is much cheaper than bourbon, right?'

She grinned, catching his eye in the mirror over the sink, but the bonhomie between them abruptly evaporated as she remembered herself. This stranger was – or at least had been – Sentinel, one of the men responsible for the turn her life had taken.

As if detecting her sudden tension, Blondie gave a strained smile. 'I'm Ethan, by the way.'

'Adelita.'

She didn't know what his game was. Her mother had always impressed on her and her sisters the need to act with caution around white men, and from experience she knew this to be true. Their favours rarely came without a price.

She returned to stitching.

TWO

Exeter, Devon, UK

Daniel Su had to get home. Now.

He was on autopilot, his body a permanent flux of reactivity. When he'd received Li's voicemail, his stomach had plummeted into his shoes. Li would be livid with him when he finally turned up as back-up for dealing with their wayward child. Daniel's usual method was to try to stay out of the conflict between his wife and daughter, but it sounded now like it had exploded right in his face.

As he raced towards his car in the university car park, Daniel wondered what Chloe had said or done this time to make Li sound so beside herself on the phone. All he knew was that it must have been something awful. How much time had passed since Li had called him . . . Five minutes? Ten? Twenty? Daniel couldn't tell. Panic had corrupted his sense of time.

Daniel finally found himself beside his car. He tapped his pocket with his palm in that nervous way of his, feeling for his car keys through the fabric. They were there. *Thank God.* Even though he was a theology professor (of perhaps because of it), Daniel didn't believe in any deity; he never had. It was just something he said, though the Sentinel insisted only their puritanical version of Jesus Christ was the one true God now. The triumvirate, or triple goddesses, were forbidden.

Daniel's gaze flicked towards the clock on the dashboard as he slid into his vehicle. It was almost quarter to six. Chloe only had lectures until midday on a Friday, and Li worked from home. They both had to be at the house. That was something, at least. Daniel was a very private man and found Chloe's public meltdowns the most difficult. He couldn't stand the judgemental stares of strangers, or, even worse, their pitying, averted gazes. Thankfully, it had only happened a few times over the years.

With both of his hands knuckle-white on the wheel, Daniel's small car careered down the hill that overlooked the city of Exeter. As he drove, passing the university's stock of conifers and hardwood trees, he barked a direction at his phone to 'call Li', before realising he didn't have the phone on him; he must have left it behind in his panic – along with his wallet and the notes he had been making for the non-fiction book he was writing. He pressed the brake as he approached the checkpoint, which blocked off the road up towards the Great Hall.

The barrier was never down, but everyone always slowed and stopped before receiving the go-ahead. It was the British way. Usually there was only one Sentinel guard on duty at Exeter University's checkpoint but today, on the way in, Daniel had noticed there had been two. The first one was in his fifties and clearly not a career soldier. His face was slack with age and dis-interest; a rounded paunch hung over his black combat trousers. The other was much younger, barely into his thirties. He was thin and feral, with wide eyes that darted everywhere like a cat's. Daniel eyed the red band at the top of his arm: a trainee sergeant, eager to prove himself.

Daniel wound down his window, ready to flash his lanyard so he could get out of there and get home. He had managed to still some of the panic quivering in his chest. But from their high

18

vantage point, both Sentinel were staring at something in the distance, across the city. Now irritated and exasperated as well as afraid, Daniel swivelled in his seat and stretched so he could see out the passenger window, towards Exeter below.

A column of black smoke rose vertically towards the middle of the city. A bomb? Surely not in sleepy Exeter. But there it was, larger than life, spiralling into the sky.

Right where Daniel and his girls lived.

'Oh no,' he breathed.

Daniel had spent his entire life in academia; he'd never been even close to a survival situation. Yet he knew in that moment, via animal instinct, his precious family was in mortal danger. He jammed his foot on the accelerator.

The shriek of tyres and the pulse pounding in his head obliterated everything else. Daniel was unaware of the shouts of the Sentinel after him, or the younger one calling in his transgression over the radio. He was laser-focused. The driver's window was still open. He could hear no sirens yet. Whatever had happened couldn't have taken place too long ago. Or maybe those budget cuts in the provinces meant the emergency services were taking an age to get there. He willed the first option to be true.

Daniel raced through Exeter, taking corners and back roads to try and avoid the gridlock of rush hour. As he got closer and closer to the source of the black smoke, increasing traffic and growing groups of gawking people slowed his advance. He narrowly avoided pedestrians near Exeter prison, then again outside the mosque. A group of older men dressed in their long thobes waved their fists at Daniel as he was forced to slow down. Daniel waved no apology, but merely turned onto the next road, out towards the Odeon.

Time had become an elastic concept, stretching then snapping back without warning. Despite every second feeling like an hour, Daniel blinked and he was at his destination. His brain reeled as he turned onto the small cul-de-sac where he, Li and Chloe had lived since Chloe was two. Their home was the end property, the most sought-after in a half-circle of new-build toy-town red-brick houses with sandstone surrounds on the windows.

The scene was not so idyllic now. Rounding the corner, the first thing Daniel noticed was that every single window in the vicinity was broken. Houses, car windows and windscreens. There was glass strewn on every surface: the tarmac of the roadside; the concrete pavements; grass in the gardens. It twinkled like deadly confetti in the late afternoon sunlight. Had a bomb gone off? *Oh no. Oh God no.* Daniel could hear the ringing of multiple car alarms. It was a deafening din, but none of their owners came running.

Instead they stood frozen outside their homes in the middle of the road, their eyes fixed in front of them.

There were no broken bricks or rubble. Nor was there any of the ominous white dust of Ground Zero that he'd seen on the news when the Twin Towers fell. The sight in front of him was clear, easy to pick out. Still Daniel's brain refused to process what he was seeing, just as no one standing either side of him could believe, either.

A vortex of black cloud spewed from the spot where Daniel's detached home had stood. It whirled around and around like a corkscrew yet stayed where it was; it didn't make sense. Underneath it, Daniel's house was reduced to rubble. No, scrub that.

His house was simply . . . *gone.*

Daniel's nostrils flared as he detected the powerful stink of magic. Green light enveloped his home like a deadly sphere. He could feel, rather than hear, its power; it thrummed through his body like a jet engine. Its power poured upwards, ripping the blue sky in two. Near where the kitchen had been, the tarmac bubbled, boiling tar sending off jets of steam. An incongruous image of Li at the sink surfaced in Daniel's mind. She'd watch cows and sheep grazing behind the house in the verdant English fields through the window, enjoying the green and pleasant land

and how it stood in stark contrast to the urban sprawl of hot, humid Beijing, where she'd grown up.

Daniel's body threatened to give up, to fall to its knees, yet his mind continued to catalogue his catastrophic loss. Where was Chloe? Had she been in her room, as usual? The driveway was cracked open, like an earthquake had hit it. Had she disappeared into it? In its middle, deep in the crack, rock liquefied, white hot like lava. Daniel whimpered at the thought of his girl burning; pain speared through his solar plexus like electricity.

Another rumble came from the smoky whirlwind, prompting everyone to stagger backwards, raised from their reverie at last.

'Get back!' someone yelled.

As the others retreated, he found himself rushing towards the house. It was a pointless endeavour; he was no fireproof superhero. His precious family inside were dust. He felt an intense blast of heat against his face, threatening to take his eyebrows, and his treacherous feet arrested his body's movements, seemingly against his will. He couldn't get any closer.

Then, without warning, the thunderous cyclone of heat and smoke stopped. It did not blow itself out. Instead it seemed to race backwards, like an old VHS tape rewound. The space where Daniel's home had been became clearer as the tumult of smoke and power grew smaller and smaller. Finally, it disappeared altogether.

Straight *into* the body of a young girl.

The crowd craned their necks; suspended in mid-air, a silhouette. The phenomenon defied physics, but no more so than what they'd already witnessed. She was shadowed against the setting sun, but Daniel knew her right away. He'd known her since he had placed his hand on his wife's bulging stomach and felt the tiny movements of limbs within.

'Chloe!'

Disbelief burst out of Daniel like the cyclone of destruction had moments earlier. He raced towards her, dodging the crack in the driveway which had abruptly cooled.

If Chloe heard her father, she gave no indication. She did not look like his daughter. Like many teen girls, Chloe prided herself on her appearance; she watched make-up and hair tutorials online daily. Now her hair was in disarray, her face smudged with soot. But most of all, it was her eyes: she stared at Daniel as if he were a stranger. She looked so threatening, her face dark with fury. Daniel slowed down, intimidated, as he reached her.

'... Chloe?'

His daughter floated downwards like a soap bubble. As her feet hit solid pavement, Chloe's expression changed. Her visage slackened; her eyes rolled back in her head. Her body went limp and she swooned like a Victorian lady with an attack of the vapours. Daniel caught her just in time, following her to the ground on his knees. A memory of seeing Li breaking their daughter's fall when Chloe had fainted after one of her previous attacks surfaced in his brain. Self-preservation kicked in and arrested the thought. He couldn't think about Li.

Not yet.

Instead, Daniel gathered Chloe to his chest, rocking her like she was a baby. He could barely speak, nor process what had happened. His shocked brain marvelled at the cold ground beneath them that moments earlier had been boiling. He was not ready to make the connection of what this meant.

But the watching crowd was way ahead of him, the realisation racing around the huddle surrounding Daniel and Chloe. Even if the forbidden word itself had been uttered, language was not necessary. Daniel could discern the truth reflected in their eyes as they looked to one another, then back at the catatonic girl in his arms. They had all seen his house, a dome of green light around it: earth magic.

Witch.

Chloe was Elemental.

DITCH
THE WITCH

This Public Service Announcement is brought to you by Sentinel HQ

THINK:

HAT  SPELLS

JEWELRY KIDS

THINK: HAT

Elementals are the most dangerous of all magical women. Accounting for less than 1% of witches, their magical flares are brightly colored. They access their magic via one of the four elements – air (yellow); water (blue); fire (red); or earth (green). When not using their flares, their magic colors can sometimes be seen in their hair or on their scalp. **BEWARE OF WOMEN WEARING HATS.**

THINK: JEWELRY

Crystal witches can only access their magic via crystals. Their flares are always white. They are approximately 5% of witches. They may hide their crystals or wear them in plain sight. **BEWARE OF WOMEN WITH LOTS OF NECKLACES, BRACELETS OR RINGS.**

THINK: SPELLS

Kitchen witches do not have innate magic. They need natural ingredients for their low-grade spells. Watch out for your neighbor women leaving the house at midnight on full moons, or on witchcraft holidays such as solstices or Samhain. When visiting another woman's home, look out for cauldrons, Books of Shadows and jars of dried goods or anything else that seems suspicious. **BE VIGILANT.**

THINK: KIDS

'Legacies' are girls without innate magic who are born to witches. NEVER harbor a Legacy in your home or help her escape the Sentinel. Penalty: ten years in prison. **REPORT ALL SUSPECTED LEGACIES TO SENTINEL HQ.**

SENTINEL HOTLINE:	TEXT:	EMAIL:
212 – 285 – 6906	555 – WITCH	witchreports@sentinelHQ.com

THREE

Exeter, Devon, UK

Exeter at least had the good grace to have an airport, so Sentinel Premier Agent Jake Pembroke's journey was not so long or as bad as he'd feared. The private jet touched down following an uneventful flight and, moments later, he was on British soil.

The call had come into Sentinel HQ at the Orchid Tower in New York almost as soon as the heat bloom had been detected by Operation Safeguard satellites. Within the hour, Jake had been in the air. When HQ's initial report came through, he'd been pissed at the thought of having going to Exeter, New Hampshire. When he'd realised he would have to fly to the Exeter in goddamn England, he was incandescent. But the Sentinel's Numero Uno had been in no mood to wait. Hell, Uno never waited for anything, spitting demands as easily as most people breathed.

'I'm counting on you, Scourge,' Uno had barked at him over the internal line.

Pride flooded through Jake's broad chest just like it always did when he heard the special handle Uno had bestowed upon him. *Scourge: a person or thing that causes great trouble or suffering.* Bringing retribution to those who deserved it was the Scourge's mission in life and no one deserved punishment more than witches. They were toxic bitches, unnatural ticking time bombs just waiting to go off. The Scourge would not be happy until the witch threat was eradicated from the face of the earth.

'It's The One, I just know it.'

'Satellite images are inconclusive, boss.' He knew better than to stoke Uno's excitement. If he speculated it was The One too, but it turned out to be a freak warm spot, Uno would go nuts and it would be the Scourge's head on the block.

'There's been zero developments for nearly three months on our special project.' Uno's rage had created crackles down the line. 'I haven't seen so much as a new halo on a Crystal witch in nearly twice that.'

The Scourge enjoyed his favoured position with the number one too much to jeopardise it. He also loved his job, period. Like most God-fearing Puritan men, he had no time for women who employed magic. He wanted to scrub those infidels from existence like that avenging angel, Azrael. With a halo and a glow-stick in his hand, the Scourge no longer feared magic-bearers like he had twenty-five years ago. He would never fear a woman again.

'I'll fly out tonight, boss.'

At Exeter airport, the Scourge rolled his head around his bull neck, enjoying the *crack* of his shoulders. He could already feel the onset of jet lag: the drumbeat of a headache in the back of his skull; the twinges of his stomach as acids swished around in there. Irritation knitted its way through the fibres of his muscles.

A woman was waiting for him on the runway. She was tall, in her mid-forties, would have been attractive a decade ago. She stood like a man, legs wide apart, her arms behind her back. She was dressed like one too: suit, jacket and tie. The Scourge knew without even asking that she was government. Her expression was aloof, yet watchful. MI6. Or maybe MI5. He could never remember the difference; not that he cared. There was only one security agency that really mattered now: the Sentinel.

She flashed some ID at him. 'Sir. I'm Agent Stephanie Ripley. I'm here to facilitate your stay and offer you the British government's assistance, as protocol demands in the Safeguard Initiative.'

The Scourge still couldn't believe they let Goodys into the security forces over here, but then the Limeys had always asked for trouble. If the Scourge had his way, he would not have just outlawed witchcraft and its associated myths and legends. He'd have ensured *all* women the world over were at home, a baby in their bellies. Where they belonged.

Wanting to unnerve her, the Scourge flicked his gaze up and down her body. 'I bet you are.'

Ripley did not react. She just met his gaze in that British passive-aggressive way of theirs. She could at least have had the grace to act intimidated. He would have invited her interest, at least. She should fear him or want him, preferably in that order. The Scourge was almost fifty but had the physique of a much younger man. He was six two and a hundred and fifteen kilograms; built like a human juggernaut in the signature dark suit all Sentinel agents wore. He had high cheekbones, blue eyes and silver hair. He was not conventionally handsome, more striking. Women had long let him know he was a regular panty-dropper.

'Where the fuck are my Sentinel officers?'

The woman's expression was still maddeningly impassive. 'Exeter has a population of less than one hundred and thirty thousand, sir. The surrounding area barely as many again. As per the agreements of the Safeguard Initiative with our government, there's one Sentinel per fifty thousand people.'

The Scourge did the maths in his head. As his jet lag kicked in, this was more difficult than he would like to admit. 'Wait. There's only *five* Sentinel in this godforsaken hole?'

'Yes, sir. They are all at the site of the heat bloom already.' Ripley's ice-maiden veneer cracked a little as she added, 'Plus *our* agents and police.'

The subtext was clear: *We don't need or want you, Yank.*

The Scourge looked around the small landing strip as she led him off the airfield. There were a couple of planes dotted about; a small glass-fronted building with EXETER INTERNATIONAL emblazoned on the front. The night skies seemed to stretch for ever beyond the concrete runway; no light pollution. He guessed there were fields nearby. He wrinkled his nose: was that cow shit? Jeez. They really were out in the boondocks.

He tried to keep his fatigued mind on the British agent's words as they clambered into the sleek black Bentley waiting for them. He liked cars; at least the Brits could do something right. As he studied the interior and breathed in its new-leather smell, she droned on and on.

'It's all in here, sir,' Ripley finished, handing him a folder of documents.

Sighing, he grabbed it from her outstretched hand. The Brits loved their bits of paper. He leafed through the file. More alarming reading. White British and White Irish populations in Exeter had been on the decline in the past twenty years. In stark contrast, the Chinese population had grown, as had other Asian ethnic groups, by an astonishing 400 per cent. The world really was going to hell in a handcart.

The Scourge threw the folder down on the seat as the car slowed down. They were at their destination. It was a previously banal British street, lined by well-to-do middle-class homes. Now it looked like a bombsite, broken glass strewn across the tarmac and smoke hanging over it like storm clouds.

'So, this is how it's going to play out.'

He delighted in the turnaround as Ripley stared at him, incredulous. She'd obviously not had to play chaperone to a senior Sentinel agent before. It wasn't much, but it was a small victory the Scourge savoured.

'The British government's lack of *real* engagement with the Safeguard Initiative in this case has been noted. I will be placing a call to Sentinel HQ at the American Embassy, requesting a proper contingent of my personnel. When they get here, you will call off your officers and your agents. You will not attempt to delay, obstruct, or even fucking come near me. Understood?'

Ripley cast her gaze at her shoes. 'Sir.'

The Scourge grinned. At last. 'Good dog.'

He manoeuvred his formidable bulk out of the vehicle, leaving Ripley behind, muttering into her radio. He found himself looking down at a much shorter and leaner fledgling Sentinel agent.

'Barnabas Carter, sir. Sentinel agent 905 of 42nd Infantry Division.'

Carter gave him the Sentinel salute with unmistakable gusto. He was just a young buck. A rookie sergeant at that, the tell-tale red band around his arm. Yet the Scourge immediately knew he had a kindred spirit in front of him. It was in his eyes. The boy had a steely, determined air about him; one that told him Carter would do anything on his way to the top. There was even a metal New Puritan button on his collar; an icon of two punching fists, shiny under the spotlights. Carter reminded the Scourge of himself when he first started.

'At ease, soldier. So, what the hell did you do to get stuck out here in the hinterlands?' The Scourge couldn't resist prodding him, seeing what came out.

To his credit, Carter didn't flinch. 'God works in mysterious ways, sir.'

'That he does, my man. What you got for me?'

'I think it's best if you just look, sir.'

'Copy that.'

Carter made to guide him around, but the Scourge ploughed straight through the police cordon. The young buck at his heels, he ignored the gathered crowds of white-faced neighbours and the British officers in their neon-yellow high-vis jackets. They had at least thought to erect floodlights as technicians worked in their hazmat suits. More of Ripley's spook brigade were standing around like headless chickens. For heaven's sake. No wonder this little island needed rescuing by its star progeny, the United States. Again.

The Scourge reached the end of the little cul-de-sac. The houses were red brick and sandstone, well-finished, desirable. The Brit version of McMansions. 'What am I looking at?'

'That's just it, sir. The house is literally gone.'

His mind caught up. 'Holy shit.'

The Scourge's unblinking gaze roamed around the space the house at the end had left. He took in the melted tarmac, the split across the sidewalk and what presumably would have been the driveway. It reached down into the earth about ten feet. He knelt down and touched it with two fingers. As he suspected, it was completely cold. It could have been caused by an earthquake.

Except every elementary school kid knows England does not have earthquakes of that size.

The Scourge had thought this was yet another wild goose chase. Now he could feel the stir of excitement in his chest. Maybe he would have something to report to the number one about their 'special project', after all.

Carter was breathless. 'Eyewitnesses said there was a girl here. Right in the middle of the destruction, but it didn't hurt her at all. Like she caused it.'

'You're telling me a *little girl* did this?'

The Scourge felt his excitement turn to nausea. The onset

30

of puberty for Elementals had been known to create accidents when females' magic came in at the same time. This could happen at any age, though usually between nine and fifteen. But previous outbursts had only resulted in flash burns for onlookers; or minor floods, gales or geysers; maybe small rockfalls or mini cyclones. Nothing like this.

Carter consulted his notebook. 'No. Witnesses reported it was Chloe Su, who lived in the house. She's nineteen years old.'

The Scourge felt his queasiness subside, a little. There was only one thing he hated more than Elementals and that was Elementals who were still children. They were almost impossible to control as they had no reasoning capability whatsoever. Unfortunately, Joe Public still saw them as kids, rather than potential weapons. The Scourge still hoped child witches would be included in Safeguard Laws. President Hopkins had launched the Pre-Emptive Strike legislation as soon as he'd made office in 2016, demanding the incarceration of Crystal witches and their Legacies over the age of eighteen. Not all of the Safeguard countries had agreed to jailing Legacies, but most had submitted to the Sentinel's plan for 'curing' Crystal witches of the magic coursing their veins by sending them to the angel caves. Too bad the cure didn't work, but the people at home didn't need to know that.

'Her parents?'

'Her father was seen outside the house. Her mother is missing, presumed . . . ' Carter looked at the space where the house had been, searching for the right word, 'disappeared.'

The Scourge clambered to his feet. 'Where is the girl now?'

'Gone. The girl's father spirited her away in his car, before Sentinel could arrive.' Carter waved a dismissive hand at the British presence, as if they were immaterial. Which they were.

'What time did it happen?' the Scourge enquired, still unable to tear his eyes from the split earth.

'Around five o'clock yesterday evening.'

The Scourge turned his wrist and looked at the face of his watch. It was coming up four a.m. His fugitives had nearly a twelve-hour head start.

'There's one other thing, sir.' Carter nodded towards a white tent that had been erected nearby. Unlike its British counterparts, this one bore the Sentinel crest: a giant eye watching, its pupil a globe. 'A Crystal witch was on site and helped them escape.'

The Scourge clapped his meaty palms together. 'Did she now?'

The Sentinel outside the white tent stood to attention the moment he arrived. The underling's body language crackled with alarm when he saw it was the Scourge. His reputation preceded him, even out here in the middle of fucking nowhere.

'David Moore, sir. Sentinel agent 657.'

The Scourge curled his lip. He couldn't be bothered to speak to Moore, a fat fuck with a beer belly. Sentinel postings were long, sometimes as long as two or three years. Moore had the soft body and attitude of someone who'd taken his eye off the ball. He could see a shiny gold band on the guard's left hand. Had he gone and married one of these English hillbillies? That could count as potentially fraternising with the enemy.

'I take it the Crystal witch was searched for gems?'

Crystal witches channelled their magic through their chosen crystals and gems, hence the name. They were not born naturally talented like their Elemental sisters. Instead they had to study for their otherwise dormant powers, but sometimes hard work trumped natural talent and they could be as dangerous as Elementals. It wasn't worth being complacent.

'Absolutely, sir.'

Pulling the canvas tent open, the Scourge ducked inside, Carter following him. He could barely stand inside, but it didn't matter. A large woman sat splay-legged in the middle of it, hands cable-tied in front of her. There was an air of lethargy, apathy to her. The Crystal witch's head was slumped to her chest, drool falling onto her generous cleavage from her slack mouth. The cause of her malaise: the Sentinel halo wrapped around her head. Its lights twinkled green, left to right, like emeralds on a deadly tiara.

'Rita Morrison, a neighbour.' Carter consulted his notebook. 'Caught her at Exeter St David's station, trying to flee.'

'Nice work, rookie.' The Scourge squatted down next to the apathetic woman. Her eyes were dull and misty. She was lost inside herself. 'It's disturbing how many of these Crystal bitches keep flying under the radar.'

The Scourge clicked his fingers and Carter handed over the halo's regulator. It was a small controller, with a selection of buttons. The two main buttons were red and green, with another, smaller, amber one in the middle. Without hesitation, the Scourge clicked the green button once with his thumb.

Rita inhaled. The mists in her eyes cleared and she focused on the two Sentinel in front of her. Perhaps her subconscious already knew where she was, because it took less than two seconds for her conscious brain to catch up. Furious anger took over her visage.

'Pigs!' She hocked up a gobful of phlegm and spat it at the Scourge.

It landed on his shoe. He did not react. He'd interrogated enough Crystal witches in his time to know how to deal with them. He pressed the regulator's red button twice, in quick succession. The halo's green lights flashed yellow as electricity was delivered straight to the witch's skull. Rita shrieked and grabbed for her head with her bound hands. As the pain receded, she flopped forwards, hands first. She leant on her palms, panting with the effort.

'That was only one hundred millijoules of static electricity.

One thousand, three hundred and fifty can kill you.' The Scourge smiled, though there was no warmth in it.

Rita raised her head with difficulty. She was still angry, but the Scourge was gratified to see fear in her eyes now, too. He turned the regulator over, so she might see the dial. It ran all the way up to fifteen hundred millijoules. He let that sink in.

'Are you ready to answer our questions, Rita?'

She pursed her lips, as if to prevent the words spilling out. The Scourge decided he would give her another chance to cooperate. He was not a monster.

'Tell me about the girl. What was her chosen element? I'm guessing fire. Though maybe air, to make the house disappear like that?'

Rita's own gaze was dark with fury. 'I. Don't. Know.'

'She's lying,' Carter declared, consulting the small leather-bound notebook in his hand. 'Other eyewitnesses report they saw green light welling up around the house.'

The Scourge tutted, like he was disappointed in Rita. Green flares signified Earth, the most feared of Elemental witches. He pressed the red button again. Rita screamed and thrashed, her eyes rolling back in her skull as it delivered a stronger current. He released the button. He did not let Rita recover before barking more questions at her.

'Did you know the girl was Elemental? Maybe her mother told you?'

Rita took deep breaths. 'No, I barely knew them.'

Carter interjected, his exasperation obvious. 'More lies. They lived across the road from you for nearly ten years.'

The Scourge shot a warning glance at Carter before he asked his next question.

'I don't believe you. I think you were all in a coven together – you, the girl, her mother. How many more are there here, in Exeter?'

'I told you. None.'

The Scourge leant in closer. He knew he was intimidating her; she was shaking. Tears tracked down her ruddy cheeks.

'You got daughters and granddaughters, Rita? How about sisters, nieces?'

She stood her ground. 'No. Only a son. Unmarried. No kids. Praise *the goddess*.'

The Scourge could still see too much defiance in the old broad for his liking. She must have sensed this too, because Rita proffered him a rictus grin, her teeth bloody. She'd bitten her tongue when he'd shocked her.

'Remember, Rita, the Sentinel has jurisdiction here, even on English land. Your guys can't save you.'

Still the woman said nothing. The Scourge sucked in a breath over his teeth. This was a dead end. He could never understand why these heathens were so stubborn. Didn't they realise they couldn't possibly win? He gave her one last chance.

'Your helping me means the difference between you living out the rest of your years in a British witch jail upcountry ... Or getting deported to one of our state-of-the-art angel caves over in the US.'

The Scourge delighted in seeing the wizened old hag's eyes bug out. She would have heard of the American 'angel caves', courtesy of the British tabloids. Haloed Crystal witches were incarcerated in far worse conditions in the USA than in Europe. British pussy prisons were well-known for going easy on their Crystal witches. Hell, they didn't even imprison Legacies over here, unless they were 'actively involved in the terror threat'. It's like the Limeys had never heard of the old adage *prevention is better than cure*. Assholes.

Yet Rita met his gaze, chin up and defiant. *'I am not alone, I am connected to all. Mother, guide me and protect me ...'*

'Oh, Rita.' The Scourge sighed as he heard her begin their

stupid Crystal witch prayer. The old woman was a lost cause. He pressed the button twice in quick succession again.

Rita shook with pain, but still managed to gasp: '... *I offer myself to the light!*'

The Scourge pressed the red button again.

President Michael Hopkins' emergency inauguration speech after the assassination of Dr Miriam Stone, April 2016 (Transcript)

These are dark days. My being on this podium was only made possible by catastrophic loss. I give thanks to my predecessor, Dr Miriam Stone, for her sacrifices. She gave everything – her whole life – to brokering peace between men, Goodys and witches. We may not have seen eye to eye on the best ways to do this . . .

(Loud HECKLES. Sentinel move forwards; Hopkins waves them back to their places on the stage behind him.)

No, no, that's fair. No one could say I was a fan of her methods; it would be a lie to pretend otherwise. And one thing I will never do is lie to you. Not now, when the stakes are so great and we have much work to do . . .

(WHOOPS from the crowd)

I've being praying to Our Savior for guidance. New Puritans like myself believe in logic; in paring back the unnecessary and exposing the vital truth within. In the course of my conversations with Our Lord, it has become clear to me we became complacent under Dr Stone's watch. We believed witches when they told us they were peaceful beings. Even when the Cursed Light exploded into being, showing us witchcraft was state-sanctioned terrorism, capable of mass destruction, we hung back, believing my colleague on the Left, Ms Geraldine NDeritu and her band of Legacies, when they told us we were prejudiced or small-minded.

(HUBBUB of agreement, some dejected HECKLING)

Our latest estimations suggest approximately fifty per cent of women have some form of magic—

(GASPS from the crowd)

Yes, yes, I know. These stats are frightening. But, my friends and followers, we must not be afraid, we must stand firm. We must remember that for the vast majority of that fifty per cent, their magic is not innate. It is mere female tradition: good luck spells; protection invocations and blessings on the house. There's a handful of men who may also engage in this unnatural practice too—

(YELLS from the crowd of 'CUCKS!')

Now, now. As Puritans, we must try to be understanding. These men may have been brought up with witches; they can't help being mistaken when it has been all they know. It is our job to show them all the way back, away from false idols such as the triumvirate. With all this in mind, then, these so-called 'Kitchen witches' are invited to submit to the Sentinel ... I tell them now, bring in your Books of Shadows, your cauldrons, your family spells to be destroyed. Attend our re-education classes and come to our churches. If you do, the New Puritans will have no further argument with you.

Next in witchcraft's Unholy Trinity, the Crystal Witches. Accounting for less than five per cent of witches, these women have latent, innate magic moving in their veins. They can access it with study and the help of crystals, hence their name. I hereby forbid the stocking and sale of crystals and propose an amnesty on such artifacts. Yes, this includes our old favorites such as diamonds, sapphires and rubies, I am sorry to say. But better safe than sorry!

Now, crystals are naturally occurring, so we must be vigilant. Look out for these godforsaken things in your yards and lands, bring them to the Sentinel whenever you find them. We must not put temptation in these women's way.

My message for the Crystal witches is this: come to us, we can cure you. Our state-of-the-art angel caves have the technology to ensure you don't have to live with the curse any longer. Like the Kitchen witches, if you do this and come in voluntarily, we will have no further argument with you. We will leave you and your daughters – the ones you call 'Legacies' – alone.

Thankfully, Elemental witches are very rare. Less than one per cent of witches are Elemental. That said, that's far too many such women in a country as large as the United States. You can rest assured my Sentinel scientists are working very hard to ensure we don't have to live with the Elemental threat any longer. The unnatural, toxic power they wield via their chosen elements of fire, water, air or earth can be monumental. Dr Miriam Stone lost her life because of her complacency about these dangerous women. We will not be making the same mistake!

(More HOOTS and JEERS)

So I say this, today. All women must give up their biological rites to practice magic or face the harshest of penalties. Our very civilization depends on it.

But how to undertake this heartbreakingly necessary work? Well, perhaps we must decide first what a witch truly is. It is not a case of simply singling out every woman as being a potential mischief-maker or worse. That would be absurd. I am a proud husband to the wonderful Marianne . . .

(She waves)

. . . and the father of daughters, my beautiful Regan and Alice.

(Both girls smile and curtsy)

So I recognize, like so many of you, that our Goody women can be powerful allies in this fight against the dark arts. They can help light the way and ensure every man, child and woman is safe. Let us consider five signifiers that make up our definition of a witch.

One: A witch is unnatural. They may claim to be born this

way, but they can choose to give up their toxic magic for the good of mankind.

Two: A witch threatens our community. Goodys and men are not safe when magic is tolerated. That much is clear now.

Three: A witch's traditions are heresy, an affront to our Lord and savior. We must learn a lesson from history.

Four: A witch is evil.

(Crowd GASPS)

Yes, I said it. I am not bound by politically correct snowflake claptrap and nor should any other God-fearing American. If we are to accept magic is not God-given, then we must conclude the magic in their veins was put there by Old Nick himself.

Lastly, number five: A witch must be resisted, by whatever means necessary. Note that last part. Whatever. Means. Necessary.

There will be hard decisions ahead. There will be penalties some will deem unfair or unreasonable. But we must not falter. We have been tolerant; we have been patient; we have been understanding. Instead of trying to work with us, witches have sent us death and destruction via the Cursed Light. They are toxic savages, terrorists. Enough is enough.

Who's with me?

(Crowd in joyful UPROAR)

FOUR

Somewhere off the North Devon Link Road, UK

Daniel's hands gripped the steering wheel, claw-like, for the second time that day. His foot pressed down on the accelerator, the engine of his small car whining as he ground the gears too harshly. He wasn't sure where he was going yet, but he knew he had to get his daughter far away from Exeter.

In the passenger seat next to him, Chloe muttered something unintelligible.

He took his eyes off the road momentarily, reached across the gearstick and grabbed Chloe's shoulder, shaking her. It didn't rouse her. She slumped forwards, hanging against her seatbelt, her eyes barely open. She looked like she was in a drunken stupor. Daniel wished it was as simple a problem as that.

You know what she is. We all do.

The woman's words had been low, barely murmured. She'd edged forwards from the rest of the shocked crowd, an older woman in her sixties. Daniel's fragmented thoughts had picked her out as one of their neighbours, Rita Something. She was the hippy type; bell sleeves and patchouli scent. She squatted down with some difficulty by Daniel and the barely conscious Chloe on the driveway of what had been their home.

'They'll be coming. Go.'

For a moment, Daniel had struggled to comprehend what the woman was talking about. Who was coming? Then his synapses fired a connection: *the Sentinel*. Still, a ridiculous hope prevented him from moving. He turned to look at his missing house. 'Li . . . '

Looking back at Rita, the pity in her eyes confirmed for Daniel what he already knew to be true.

Daniel had scooped Chloe up in his arms – not without difficulty – and carried her to his car, which stood where he'd abandoned it behind the gathered crowd. The group parted as Rita pulled a forbidden crystal from one of her voluminous sleeves and told them to stay back.

Now, as he drove without a destination in mind, Daniel realised he hadn't had time to thank Rita for the sacrifice she'd made for them, revealing herself like that. He'd barely spoken to the woman before, besides waving when he saw her as he left for work in the mornings. That had been enough. His old life had been enough. For him, at least.

But it had been a lie. Li had been keeping things from him.

His eyes strayed to the clock on the dashboard. He was sure that only blind luck had facilitated their escape; there was unlikely to be a full Sentinel team on the ground in Exeter like there were in the bigger towns and cities.

Through the windscreen of Daniel's car, green fields flashed by and disappeared in the gloaming as the sun retreated into the River Exe, turning the skies purple and orange. As he journeyed past South Molton, wind turbines cut their white blades through the night skies. A curious mix of grief and anger and helplessness surged through him.

Questions circled through his mind on an endless loop.

What had happened at the house? How had Chloe destroyed everything like that, and why? Like everyone else, he knew about the trinity of witches – Kitchen, Crystal and Elemental. Not everyone had got on board with various governments' attempts to curb the witch threat at first. Nearly forty young Elemental women between eighteen and twenty-five had been killed almost three years ago at Stonehenge, Salisbury. Before they'd died, the girls had killed nearly every single one of their Sentinel handlers. President Hopkins and the Sentinel had only just managed to turn the tide back in their own favour, reminding everyone Elementals might be after people's own family members next.

Daniel had been in class, taking his undergraduate students through their History of Early Christianities module, when phones had started to light up and vibrate in bags and pockets like dozens of swarms of angry bees. It was said in the past that every American remembered where they were when JFK had been assassinated; now every Brit recalled their exact whereabouts when they'd heard about Stonehenge. One of Daniel's students had snatched her mobile up, then shrieked in horror and rage, racing from the lecture hall as if someone had put a match under her. Others followed suit, while most of their male counterparts simply sat in their chairs, their expressions blank, unclear what to do. His hand forced, Daniel looked at his own handset and knew his next move immediately.

'Class dismissed.'

Post Safeguard, government leaflets posted through his letter box had reminded Daniel to watch out for possible witches amongst his neighbours; posters on campus urged him to report any signs of magic in female students to the Sentinel hotline. He was sure he had never seen an Elemental in the flesh before, convinced he would have sensed the phenomenal power an Elemental could wield. But today's events had proved how

43

wrong he was. He'd had no clue his own daughter was capable of such power.

Chloe remained asleep beside him in the passenger seat. He prodded at her again without hope.

'Chloe? . . . *Bǎobǎo*, come back to me.'

His daughter's eyes snapped open like steel traps. She sat bolt upright and screamed, high-pitched. It was the loudest sound Daniel had ever heard Chloe emit in her life. The windscreen spidered with cracks; so did all the other windows.

On instinct, Daniel attempted to take his hands off the wheel to cover his ears, but couldn't. It felt like his palms were glued in place, the wheel freezing cold under his hands. Just as this thought unfolded in his brain, that deep, cold sensation made its way into his arms. It travelled like electricity through his torso and into his right leg, making him jam his right foot on the accelerator.

'Chloe, don't!'

Daniel didn't know how he knew Chloe was responsible for what was happening. He just did. Horrified and completely helpless to fight it, he watched the speedometer approach one hundred miles per hour. The engine of the car roared; the cracked windows shook. Daniel's vision was compromised by the broken windscreen, but they were on a country road – anything and anyone could be coming the other way: tractors, hayricks, families returning home. None of them would get out of a head-on crash alive. He shouted again at Chloe, but she just stared ahead, unblinking.

'*Hui Yin*, you stop it right now!' he yelled.

The cold sensation in Daniel's veins and limbs lifted, as abrupt as it had come, and the car slowed right down. He turned the wheel, taking them towards the side of the road as the car eased to a halt altogether. Somehow, the name her mother had given her had brought Chloe back.

His daughter's lip wobbled as she processed her surroundings: the sight of the broken glass; the smoke spiralling from the bonnet of the car. Confused, she looked to him. Daniel could see she was clueless about how she'd got there, or why. She turned, looking into the empty back seats.

'Where's Mum?' Chloe whimpered.

Daniel's stomach went into free fall. How could he tell his only child she'd killed her mother?

But he didn't need to. Li's loss must have been written all over his face. Chloe's own expression crumpled. Sobs burst out of her. Daniel gathered her in his arms. Chloe rested her face on her father's shoulder, her tears soaking through his shirt. Time passed; Chloe's distress subsided a little.

'It's not your fault.' He wiped her tears away, kissed her forehead. He hadn't been so close to Chloe in years. He couldn't recall the last time she'd permitted him to so much as touch her arm, never mind embrace her. Even as this thought flowered, he could feel her putting her walls back up, pushing him away again.

Chloe's eyes were still wild with confusion. 'How could I have done this?'

Daniel had to play this carefully. Chloe was already agitated, grief-stricken and upset. He couldn't be her second casualty today. Then she would have no one to protect her.

'Sometimes, in periods of high emotion, Elementals have accidents. Not usually as big as this, but—'

Chloe let out a gasp as she interrupted him. '*Elemental?* Dad, I'm not Elemental. What are you talking about?'

Daniel's clamouring thoughts all connected together at once, like the end of a telescope adjusted into sharp focus. It was time to stop kidding himself. Li had never been just a Kitchen witch. Worst of all, his wife hadn't just been keeping Chloe's secret from him – she'd obviously been keeping it from Chloe, too.

Damn you, Li.

Daniel took a deep breath. 'I need to tell you something, *bǎobǎo.*'

FIVE

Texas, USA

O nce she'd stitched him up, the rogue Sentinel agent left the motel to find them some food and something for Adelita to wear. Stuck in the room alone, Adelita took the opportunity to rinse her old underwear, then got under the shower herself.

Her last shower had been taken in the company of four other women, all Legacies like herself, imprisoned simply for being female in a strong magical bloodline. They'd walked behind the blond Sentinel penal guard she now knew as Ethan, his gun slung across his body, as he led them to the shower block by following the painted white line on the floor, taking them past Our Lady's angel cave.

The Legacies behind Adelita had turned their faces away, determined not to look at the denigration of their sisters. But Adelita looked upon as many of them as she could: row after row of Crystal witches, all wearing haloes, their eyes dull, their faces downcast, their movements sluggish. She had felt it was only right to bear witness to their suffering. She had also been searching for her mother's face.

The rogue sentinel had muttered in her ear as they walked. 'Looking for someone?'

'Fuck you.'

Adelita had felt naked, like he'd seen into her very soul. She recalled the anger that had surged through her, replacing her shame at being caught out by a Sentinel.

She'd expected to find triumph on his face, but instead Ethan's expression had been impassive, scrutinising her.

'Fiery one,' he had mused. 'I heard witches need to feel strong emotions to access their magic. Hatred, fear, joy, love. That true?'

Adelita had met his gaze at last. 'I wouldn't know. I'm just a Legacy.'

'Oh, yeah. S'right. I forgot.'

A few metres on, down the dark corridor, he opened the door to a mouldering old shower block, gesturing them to get inside. They had all filed past him, obedient and wary.

Adelita was last. As she moved past Ethan, he'd grabbed her by the elbow.

'You willing to pay the price?'

'For what?' She'd heard of guards making deals with Legacies and sometimes even Crystal witches before. She could guess what he wanted, but she wanted him to spell it out.

'To get outta here.'

Oh, he was one of those. Dangling hope in front of incarcerated women, making them think he was on their side, because it made him feel powerful. That was worse than the creeps who wanted favours. At least they didn't pretend to be anything other than scum.

She stiffened under his grasp. 'Get off me, pig.'

Ethan had flinched, dropping his grasp from her arm. Pins and needles flooded down to her hand as the blood rushed back into her flesh. Adelita massaged her wrist. Ethan flashed her a disarming grin.

'That's all I needed to know.'

Adelita had turned her back on him, joining her Legacy sisters in the shower block. Ethan closed the door behind her, leaving them all alone.

In the motel bathroom, the walls were peeling; its tiles grimy. But it smelled sort of clean, the tang of old bleach permeating everything. The hundreds of small, black bugs that infested the communal showers back at Our Lady were nowhere to be seen and clean cotton towels were waiting for her. They were not balding and stiff, but fluffy and soft. There was even a bottle of liquid soap in the stall, as opposed to the slimy slivers she'd grown used to in prison. The water barely dribbled out but as the first hot shower she'd taken in eighteen months, it felt like bliss.

Back at Our Lady, Adelita and the other women had taken advantage of the lack of overt surveillance. They'd communicated their names to one other as finger-spelling, or by mouthing the words. *Yukio. Maddie. Elinor. Claire. Adelita. Pleased to meet you!* It felt audacious in a system that insisted prisoners be known only by their numbers. They were naughty children rebelling against a tyrant parent. As Legacies they'd had to stay vigilant, guarding their family histories from those in charge, or from their Goody peers in orange uniforms. Some Legacies had female relatives still on the run; or sons, husbands and brothers who might be murdered by vigilantes for having Legacy DNA. Non-witches were always listening, eager to exchange information for reduced sentences.

As one last act of defiance, they'd raised their middle fingers at the door, at the guards waiting behind it. Then they made the sign of the Goddess – three fingers and pumping their fists in the air, like their mothers had taught them. Adelita had never been interested in following the Path of Light, much to her mother Julia's chagrin, but she had still made the signs in honour of her:

Fuck the Sentinel! Praise the Goddess!

Hecate for ever!

In the motel, Adelita wiped tears from her eyes as she tied a towel under her arms. Ethan had been serious about getting out of there. She realised now what the rogue Sentinel had intuited in her: latent magic, moving in her veins. That's why he'd grabbed her arm on the way into the shower. He'd provoked her anger and felt its power. The low-grade pins and needles she'd felt flooding through her arm must have made their way into him, too, and confirmed his suspicions.

Adelita left her undergarments hanging up on the shower rail to dry. Now what? She had seen only the same four walls of Our Lady for twenty-four months. It was time to find out where she was now. The clock on the TV read just after midnight. Unable to resist, she took a chance and peeked out of the polyester curtains. She was on the top floor of a low-rise building. A flickering neon MOTEL sign reached up into the night, bathing everything below in red and yellow. There was a small reception cabin, next to a trash compactor and a collection of dumpsters. As she watched, an elderly man who looked Native American shuffled towards the threshold and lit a cigarette.

Adelita continued her surveillance. As she'd surmised when she woke, there was a Coke and ice machine on the concrete walkway outside her room that led down to the parking lot below. A selection of beat-up and dusty vehicles, mostly pickups and saloons, were lined up next to one another but the empty spaces showed the motel was not occupied to capacity.

Next, she looked under the bed. There was a big metal suitcase under there, as well as two tote bags. She could guess what was in them, but she pulled them out anyway. The metal suitcase had a number of guns in it, as well as silencers and ammo.

Most of them were handguns, but one was much bigger and in pieces. Adelita guessed it was a sniper's rifle, but only from a limited knowledge of thriller movies. That figured; a Sentinel agent on the run would need to be tooled up. Even so, they made Adelita shudder.

The tote bags contained more interesting fare. There was a small axe in there, with what she thought was some kind of crest burned into the handle. It looked like a letter 'B', though it could be a wave, or perhaps even a crude representation of a bird. It depended which way up it was supposed to be viewed.

There was a selection of maps and other gadgets in the bag, too. She recognised the compass and GPS tracker, but the other stuff she wasn't sure of. There were a bunch of identical phones; one of them already charging on the nightstand. Adelita also discovered Ethan had remembered to bring his standard-issue Sentinel glow-stick. She was thankful to see there was no halo in the bag.

She shoved the rest of the weapons back under the bed. In the bedside cabinet she found a laminated card that told her to enjoy her stay at the LayZ-DayZ Motel. The address was listed as West Texas. They hadn't got that far from Our Lady, then; that made her nervous. But presumably Ethan knew what he was doing.

Adelita didn't know much about Texas at all, she'd only ever seen it on TV, or from behind the walls of Our Lady. Before she'd become an unwilling Texas resident as a Legacy, Adelita had assumed the desert state would be a dry, still heat. It was as arid as she feared, but the hot winds were still an unpleasant surprise to her. With no air conditioning, they'd all sweltered at the jail. Women died of heatstroke at a usual rate of six per month, Goodys and Legacies alike. Besides the danger it posed, the endless heat made Adelita pine for New York even more. She hadn't realised that she enjoyed marking the seasons via its continental climate until she could no longer. Damn. She missed home. She hadn't seen snow in two years and wasn't sure she would even see her city again.

Stomach grumbling, Adelita perched on the bed and flicked through television channels. Unable to take in the endless vacuous game shows and rolling news, she thought briefly about escaping. She killed these thoughts off. Adelita was not a gambling woman, but she knew the odds were even more against her alone. Sentinel were bound to have airports and stations under surveillance. Even if she took a gun and a phone, she still had no clothes and no money. As much as Adelita hated to admit it, she was bound to get further with a rogue Sentinel than on her own.

The door burst inwards as she was working through these thoughts. She yelped and jumped to her feet, raising the tomahawk above her head.

'Whoa there!'

Before she could bring the axe down, her fragmented brain picked out recognisable features: blond hair; beard; split lip.

Just the rogue Sentinel. Shit. She collapsed back down on the bed, dropping the axe. He had a bulging backpack over one shoulder and a new shirt on, red and black checks.

'Nice to see you take personal security so seriously.'

'Fuck you.'

Ethan laughed. He must be used to people trying to kill him. Which was either badass or sad, depending on viewpoint. He was still pale and drawn from the bullet wound, pain etched on his face. He also still stank of bourbon, which may have accounted for his own laissez-faire attitude to life.

'Chill, Doc. Never met such an educated woman with such a foul mouth.'

Doc. Adelita rolled her eyes. This guy was a real tool. Even so, the nickname brought back memories of white corridors and scrubs, of a time when her life mattered. This thought made her angry all over again.

'Can't imagine you meet many women you don't stick in jail.'

He grinned, amiable as ever. It was like she hadn't even insulted him. He set his backpack down on the bed, pulling out some cartons and bags.

'I wasn't sure what you'd like, so I got a bunch of stuff. You're not vegetarian, are you?'

He said 'vegetarian' with a shudder, like some people say 'snakes'. Amused despite herself, Adelita looked through the selection of food and chose a sandwich and a bag of chips. She took a bite of the sandwich. It had not looked appetising, but the smoky taste of ham exploded on her tongue. She shoved a few chips in the sandwich as well. Delicious. Hunger really was the best sauce.

Ethan kept pulling other stuff from his backpack, like a magician. 'Got you some clothes. There's only a mom and pop store up the road, so wasn't much choice. Got what I could.'

He threw another checked shirt at her, some sweatpants, both in plastic wrappers. Adelita looked at him askance. The shirt was red and black, like his.

He grinned. 'His 'n' hers. Romantic, don't you think?'

She didn't rise to the bait. 'I'm getting dressed.'

Adelita retrieved her underwear from the shower rail. It was already dry. At least the unrelenting Texas heat was good for something. She slid it on, then stood up and pulled the clothes from their wrappers. The shirt was fine, but the sweatpants were far too big, even with the drawstring pulled tight. She rolled the waistband down and the legs up. She looked as if she was about to dance in a Britney Spears video circa 1999, but it would have to do.

She returned to the main part of the motel room. Ethan lay on the bed upside down, his cowboy boots on the pillows, still shovelling chips into his mouth. She hoped they would be on the road soon; she didn't want to have to lay her face where his dirty boots had been.

'So, you going to tell me where we're going yet?'

'I'm still working on it.'

'I've got family in Paraguay.'

'Paraguay is a Safeguard country.'

'I know,' Adelita said patiently, ignoring his mansplaining. 'But they don't incarcerate Legacies there, I heard. Hopefully most of my family should still be alive.'

She could feel the hope in the words, as well as her heart. Ethan's expression softened, though his words were still matter-of-fact.

'No, very bad idea. That's the first place the Sentinel will look.'

'My family tree is massive. They can't possibly know every single branch.'

'Believe me, they do.' Ethan's face was grim. 'We have to go somewhere *completely* unconnected to your past. Or mine. Just leave it with me.'

Ethan sat up and shook a carton of Kamel Reds out the bag. He opened them, offering one to her. She shook her head. Out of Sentinel uniform at last, he was really leaning into the whole cowboy thing. Ethan stood up and opened the window and lit his smoke, leaving his hand dangling out.

'Oh, I also got you this.'

He dug in his pocket with his other hand and pulled something from his jeans back pocket, chucking it on the bed. A crystal of rose quartz. It was not a seam in a pebble, like the crystal she had found in the prison, but a whole gem, about the size and shape of an egg.

Adelita felt an inexplicable joy at seeing it, like she was greeting an old friend. It wasn't anything she'd ever felt about crystals before and she caught herself, shutting the thought down

54

immediately. She still couldn't be sure she could trust this man.

'You found it lying around, huh?' Adelita raised a sceptical eyebrow.

'No. A buddy got it for me.'

'The guy on the reception?' Adelita guessed and, by the look on Ethan's face, correctly. 'Not much gets past me, *hombre*.'

'I can see that.' Ethan indicated the crystal. 'Give it a try?'

Adelita hesitated. Everyone knew Crystal witches had to work hard to gain their power – and yet her first time handling a crystal she'd managed to drop-kick two waves of Sentinel and take out the jail wall with just a seam of quartz. She could remember her mother telling Adelita how she'd been delighted to make ripples on a pond the first time she'd used Crystal magic. Going from zero to sixty like Adelita had was practically unheard of. What if Adelita held this one and went crazy with the power of it? Ethan would be right in her firing line.

But he *did* ask.

Adelita grabbed the gem, closing her fist around it. It felt smooth and cold against her palm. Unlike in the prison yard, there was no sudden flood of tingles through her body, no heightening of her senses. Perturbed, Adelita opened her palm again and rubbed the gem with her other hand, like she expected a genie to spring forth.

Again, nothing.

Ethan's shoulders seemed to deflate. With disappointment or relief, Adelita wasn't sure. He threw his cigarette butt onto the walkway and closed the window. Absurdly, Adelita felt as if she was letting Ethan down. She reminded herself she wasn't beholden to him. She hadn't asked him to break her out of jail. He must be getting something out of this screwed-up scenario. Probably redemption, for all the women he'd had a part in incarcerating and murdering. That was his issue, not hers.

'You must be out of practice.'

'I don't practise.'

'Right. You've been in jail two years. You couldn't.'

'No,' Adelita enunciated clearly, as if talking to a child, 'I couldn't practise because I had *never done* magic before yesterday.'

Ethan turned sharply towards her. 'No, that's not true. I *felt it* in you.'

'Yes, by the shower block. I remember.' Her own eyes narrowed in suspicion. 'How did you know before I did?'

Ethan raised both hands. 'Let's just back up a little. You're telling me you're *not* a Crystal witch who was masquerading as a Legacy?'

'Yes. I mean, no. This is confusing.' Adelita sighed. 'I guess I am a Crystal witch. I just didn't know it. That's what I'm saying.'

'That was the first time, in the prison yard? But you knocked those Sentinel down like bowling pins and tore down the jail wall!'

Adelita shrugged.

Ethan shook his head, as if trying to dispel this information. 'No. You're lying. You're far too old for your magic to be coming in.'

'Hey, I'm only thirty-nine,' Adelita protested.

Ethan sat on the bed and grabbed something from a bag; a square Sentinel device with a radar-like screen. Adelita recognised it immediately: a mobile iHex, a magic detection device. It measured minute changes in body temperature and blood pressure, indicating magic. There was one setting for Crystal witches and another for Elementals. The guards at Our Lady had run them over Legacy witches weekly, just in case.

He moved it towards her, but it did not beep. It was obvious why: it could not sense Adelita's magic moving within her.

'Shit,' he breathed.

There was a stunned silence. Ethan seemed more wary of

her now, antsy. Adelita felt her stomach constrict. She forced herself not to look at any of the many guns on the bed and in the room. She didn't want him to decide to cut his losses. He might snatch one of the weapons up, shoot her between the eyes and then split.

'Just a minute,' Adelita appealed, taking on the tone she'd used with unpredictable patients. 'Relax. There will be a simple explanation. Maybe it's faulty?'

'They scanned you in jail, right?'

Adelita nodded.

'So all iHexes you have ever come into contact with, for two years, were faulty?' Despite her fears, Ethan made no move towards any of the weapons in the room. 'I thought maybe you were a Crystal witch flying under the radar because you had made a deal with one of the other guards to not scan you. Shit!'

Adelita sighed. She'd had a cellmate for a while, Maggie, who'd made such a deal. There wasn't anything Maggie wouldn't do to avoid the iHex and the angel caves. Unfortunately for Maggie, about six months in, her ruse was discovered by a much more devout Sentinel guard and she'd ended up haloed after all. Guilt prickled through Adelita now: if she had known she was able to do such a thing, perhaps she could have taught her ex-cellmate how to avoid a positive scan.

'Look, I know I'm not what you thought I was.' Adelita kept her voice steady, soothing. 'I didn't know either. I can't explain it. But I won't hurt you.'

'I'm supposed to just take your word for all this?'

Adelita smiled. 'You don't have a choice.'

Ethan took this information on board. 'That's true.'

'Now answer my question,' Adelita said. 'How did you know?'

Ethan shrugged. 'I told you, I felt it in you.'

'Right, by the shower block that time.'

'No, before that.' Ethan took in her blank expression and gave a rueful smile, 'Oh, you don't remember our moment? That's disappointing, inmate.'

'I'm not an "inmate", I'm a witch,' Adelita hissed, the dark fury jumping out of her surprising her as much as Ethan. His eyes widened as he indicated something.

'Look, Doc.'

Adelita looked down. Her hand glowed hot around the gem in her palm. White light sprang up between her fingers. Her anger was like some kind of on-switch, setting her magic in motion. Tingling surged into her wrist, towards her elbow; it spiralled through her solar plexus and into her belly. It was not as intense as before, like it had been in the yard back at the jail. Even so, she could feel the power in her hand.

She shook her fist out in front of her, away from Ethan, towards the half-open door of the en suite. There was a *thunk* as her magic punched a baseball-sized hole straight through the plywood and hit the bathroom wall, cracking tiles and the mirrored cabinet inside. Ethan and Adelita stared at the damage, waiting for shouts of alarm to sound from the parking lot below. But none came.

Adelita was panting like she'd run a race. Though she was still in her magic state, it hadn't taken her over. She was aware of it this time, coursing through her veins like a thousand benevolent pinpricks. There was a quivering sensation deep inside her, working its way towards her groin. She felt a curious urge to scream but swallowed it down. The joy that burst out of her seemed to affect the rogue Sentinel, too.

Ethan grinned, triumphant. 'That was pretty awesome.'

All thoughts of Ethan being an asshole were gone. In the here and now, Adelita felt one hundred per cent connected to him, like she knew everything about him. That was why he'd known she was a witch: he was *hers*. The air crackled as Adelita's gaze locked on Ethan. He smiled, uncertain.

Still holding the gem in one hand, she placed the other on his chest and pushed him back towards the wall, pressing her mouth to his. He yielded right away, his desire jumping out of him like Adelita's anger-infused magic had moments before. She could taste the tobacco and liquor on his tongue as she teased her own between his teeth. The mix of flavours seemed masculine and made her want him more. She snaked her free hand to his crotch. He broke away from the kiss, catching her by the wrist before she could undo his fly.

'Don't,' he murmured.

Adelita blinked and dropped the rose quartz on the motel room floor. Her magic evaporated like steam. She took an exaggerated step backwards, trying to pick up her train of thought. She didn't know this man. Why did she keep acting so familiar with him? What the hell was going on?

Ethan raised both hands in surrender again. 'I just . . . can't. Not while you're like that, in that state.'

It was kind of cute he thought he was taking advantage of her, considering they both knew Adelita's magic could stop his heart beating if she wanted it to. But with his words, another flashback assaulted her brain in glorious technicolour. When they'd escaped the prison, Adelita had stuck her head out of the car window in the moving air, hooting and yelling. She'd balled up her purple overalls and thrown them out; they'd flapped across the open freeway. But she needed more, some other release. She turned and climbed over to the driver's seat, straddling Ethan, trying to kiss him.

Nearly making their car crash into a lorry coming the other way.

'Fuck, I nearly killed us on the road last night.'

Adelita didn't need Ethan's nod of confirmation, but he gave it anyway.

'Look, I'm sorry. I didn't mean to . . .'

'S'kay.'

'It's not OK. I just kissed you, against your will. Again.'

Ethan flashed her that boyband grin. 'Well. Not *completely* against my will.'

At the same time as she felt the smile growing on her face, the spectre of his Sentinel past crashed back into Adelita's thoughts again. What had he done, in the name of the State? Men like him had caught and herded her mother into an angel cave somewhere; they'd sent Adelita herself to Our Lady. Her twin sisters were out in the wind, kill orders on their heads, like all Elementals.

As the smile faded, Adelita found herself staring at Ethan. Awkward, he averted his gaze back to the floor.

The phone on the cabinet came to life, vibrating across the melamine surface. Ethan snatched it up. The words that came from his mouth next seemed like nonsense, or code. Then Adelita broke down the language; he was speaking in German. Armed with high-school Deutsch from twenty years ago, she was only able to pick out one phrase.

'*Wir sind bereit.*'

We're ready.

They were on the move.

⊙ HAPPY 🏴 SAFEGUARD DAY!

Let **23 June 2018** go down in history as the day Goodys and men broke the curse placed on us by false idols. The supposed 'religion' of witchcraft is now illegal and so are the women who practise it. Now we finally have our country back from the grasp of toxic witches, we must make one thing clear to all residents of the UK.

WE WILL NOT TOLERATE MAGIC IN ANY FORMS NOW.

Anyone caught with magical items, speaking magical words or even thinking magical thoughts better watch out! We have put up with your ways long enough, witches. You have sowed the seeds of destruction with your dark power, bringing with you the Cursed Light and killing our own. **NO MORE!** We will burn you and your kin at the stake or hang you until you die. Our gracious ally President Hopkins may have extended his hand in friendship to kitchen witches and the current amnesty may allow you to swap your cauldrons for prayer books, **BUT YOU WILL NEVER BE ONE OF US.** We don't want you. Leave now or deal with the consequences. Anyone thought to be a witch's Legacy will be reported to the Sentinel. No exceptions. Best you go now before you are found out. **BE WARNED: WE WILL FIND OUT!**

God Save the Queen, her government and all good Puritan men and women.

DEATH TO HERETIC WITCHES!!!

< @CyrusFrost has entered Pentagram >
@CyrusFrost: Hi guys... I am updating this on the go, so I gotta be quick. This means this bulletin will be only be available as a voice note until I can get a transcript on here. Apologies if you're hard of hearing. By the way, if anyone can help with transcribing, inbox me. We also need more people who can code and encrypt this channel, away from Sentinel eyes.

< < @CyrusFrost adds voice note >>

@CyrusFrost: 'As you will have seen, Death Squad activity worldwide has gone up an unbelievable four thousand per cent in the week since the Safeguard Initiative came in on June the twenty-third. Goodys and their men are going for a full slash-and-burn approach, especially outside the major cities where Sentinel presence is low. Since I'm lucky enough to be in Australia, one of the few countries without Sentinel on the ground, I will be doing as much as I can to monitor the situation and offer tips to stay safe. Make sure you hit the subscribe button for my Pentagram profile and turn your notifications on to stay up to date. My DMs are open if you need to send anonymously. I'm here for you guys.

'OK... Safeguard countries that have villages, towns and cities renowned historically for witchcraft have been hit the hardest, especially in England, Scotland, African countries such as Kenya and, of course, the United States.

'I'm hearing rumours Salem in the USA is completely gone: apparently there was some sort of riot, ending in a mass exodus over the weekend. The Sentinel have declared a media blackout, as ever, and no one has been allowed into the city since, so it's hard to verify exactly what's happened there. I'm hoping some Salem witches will log into Pentagram and let us know. I pray to the Goddess there are survivors.

'It's been just as difficult to get reliable reports of what's been going on in the other places beyond the rumours. Even so, it's probably a good idea to assume there's a real threat to witch safety in the following areas:

- Massachusetts, USA
- Valais, France
- Gujarat, India
- Sukamaland, Tanzania
- Val Camonica, Italy
- Kisii, Kenya
- Sichuan, China
- East Lothian, Scotland
- Lancashire, UK
- Devon, UK

'I will, of course, add to the list as soon as I hear of death squads happening in any other places. The situation is slightly better in non-Safeguard countries such as Russia and Germany, but it's worth remembering Elementals are banned across Europe now, as are Crystal covens. Avoid carrying anything witch-related with you and try not to travel in groups, even if you're family. Even the ordinary police are looking for any excuse to call a bunch of women together "a coven". The Sentinel are illegal in non-Safeguard countries, but that may not help ... If you are still practising on the continent, be especially careful of the FSB - that's the Russian Secret Police. Those guys HATE witches and have their own ways of dealing with them, none of them good.

'Stay safe, my witchy friends. I stand with you ... Hecate for ever.'

< @CyrusFrost has left Pentagram >

SIX

A Country Lane in Devon, UK

As night fell on the country lane, Daniel attempted to get the car started again. After turning the key half a dozen times without so much as a splutter from the engine, he got out and lifted up the bonnet. He'd known he wouldn't be able to drive it far with a cracked windscreen and broken side windows. Between that and being stranded on a country road, though, he didn't see many alternative options. Not that it mattered, when he saw what had happened.

The engine was completely frozen.

It was not just seized up, but frozen. Ice coated every pipe, bolt and nut. Icicles hung from the fan belt. Waves of cold air emitted from all of it. Daniel knew that if he grabbed anything inside, his flesh would fuse instantly to it. He had heard Water Elementals could do this kind of thing, but he had already seen green flares surge from Chloe back at the house, suggesting she had Earth magic, not Water magic. Elementals were supposed to only be able to access the power of one element. How could Chloe have two?

The floodgates of his mind finally opened. Grief, fear, panic surged through him as surely as magic must have flowed through Chloe last night. He crouched down on his haunches by the useless car and let out a low, primal howl that echoed back up the country lane.

Finally, Daniel's senses returned to him. She'd tried to kill them both, twice. She'd sent that cold sensation through him earlier, forcing him to drive too fast and then nearly crash the car. This was where it had ended up. He could not afford to dwell. They were stranded, it was the middle of the night. He was just a professor; he'd never fixed a car engine, never mind defrosted one. There was nothing he could do. He slammed the bonnet back down and clambered into the passenger seat. He had to try and get some sleep.

Adrenalin still spiking in his veins, sleep did not come. Daniel shifted in the passenger seat. He could see his breath in the frozen car. He wondered if it would have been better to sleep in the ditch, but then it was early March. Behind him, an exhausted Chloe slept on the back seat. She'd cried and cried earlier, unable to process anything he had tried to tell her. She seemed to have no memory of her magic state back in Exeter; nor could she recall what had prompted the outburst that had killed Li. Daniel couldn't blame his daughter for being unable to accept what she'd done; he couldn't either.

Daniel's exhausted mind flitted through all the knowledge he'd gleaned from spy movies and TV police procedurals. The Sentinel must know it was his home that had been destroyed by now. He also had to assume eyewitnesses would have said Chloe was the cause of it. The Sentinel would be on the lookout for his car registration, too. He briefly considered whether he should have stolen a neighbour's car, but dismissed the thought. He was no Jason Bourne, for Pete's sake.

Daniel had no frame of reference in his own life for something as huge as what was happening now. Perhaps if Li had allowed him into the secret, they could have planned for this. Maybe Li would still be alive now. Chloe would definitely have a fighting chance of evading the kill order that had almost certainly been issued on her.

The Sentinel would kill his bǎobǎo.

Daniel hadn't called Chloe by that pet name since she'd outlawed using most Chinese words around her three or four years ago. His own Mandarin was rusty; his parents had been proud of their heritage, but they'd been second generation themselves. They'd never insisted he or his sisters used the language at home.

Chloe's veto had hurt Li deeply, though. She'd seen it as a complete rejection, not just of their shared roots but of her as a mother. Of course, Daniel now understood why Chloe had changed so radically around puberty; why she'd had those attacks where she'd scratched at her skin and gone into strange fugue states. Her magic must have come in, but Li had suppressed it somehow. Which meant that Li herself must have been a Crystal witch – *at least* – to be able to do that to Chloe.

Daniel tried to distract himself from these thoughts with practicalities. Come the morning, they would need to dump the car. He didn't have his wallet or any cash on him. He didn't have his phone with him either, though that was a blessed relief as he was sure the Sentinel could have tracked them down with it. He and Chloe would walk to the nearest phone box, try his mother and his sisters, he decided. It made no sense to take Chloe up to London, where there were more CCTV cameras and Sentinel per square mile than any other city in the United Kingdom, but perhaps they could leave him some cash somewhere? At the very least they might have some ideas for him.

Hot tears sprang to his eyes. Daniel watched the grey light of dawn filter into the car, his teeth chattering. They'd spent twenty-three years together, half their lives, yet Li had never told him she had real magic. Instead she'd made a pantomime of her

Kitchen witchery, even before the Sentinel had outlawed it. She poured salt across the front door's threshold or hung up orange peel to ward off bad spirits. She met with girlfriends to see in Samhain and the solstices as well as the spring equinox, a time when witches celebrate new life and new beginnings. She'd let him think it was informal, just for fun; that she and her friends met for a glass of wine and gossip for tradition's sake.

Chloe shifted in the back seat of the car. Daniel ground the heel of one of his hands into his eyes to stop his tears falling, but his daughter only murmured something and turned over. Daniel sighed with relief. He just wanted a few more minutes to gather his thoughts. He hadn't felt like this about a sleeping child since Chloe had been in the crib, the best part of twenty years ago. He took in her sleeping form.

'What can we do, *bǎobǎo*?' he murmured.

His whole life had been books and academia, so Daniel knew from his theologian studies that some mothers muzzled their daughters' powers, in a bid to try and keep them and others safe from accidental magic outbursts. Puberty could be a hectic time, and such power could overwhelm young girls quickly. Only very powerful Crystal witches and other Elementals could perform such spells.

When the Safeguard Initiative launched two years ago, the need for muzzling spells had become even greater as a way of avoiding kill orders. The lack of magic meant the Sentinel wouldn't be able to find Elemental girls.

Whatever Li's intentions, the muzzling spell she'd imposed on Chloe had gone badly wrong. Daniel could only guess that, for some reason, Chloe's magic had not stayed bound but had backed up, before breaking free in a huge power surge. Yet Chloe was almost twenty, an adult. Li must have muzzled their daughter long before President Hopkins' emergency inauguration, before the Sentinel had arrived in Britain under the

Safeguard Initiative – a time when it was generally safe and accepted to be a witch. What on earth had his wife thought she was doing?

'Dad?'

Daniel looked at the clock on the dashboard. Half six in the morning. He turned to find Chloe sitting up, eyes half-closed, hair in her face. Her expression was pinched and drawn, her body language closed-off and lethargic. She could get like this after one of her attacks. Daniel had discovered the only way to get her out of them was to chivvy her along. Another quote popped up in his mind: *The only way out is through.* Some said Shakespeare had coined the phrase; others Robert Frost. Li had championed Alanis Morrisette as being the one who'd brought it to Joe Public's attention. Li had loved nineties post-grunge singer-songwriters.

'Morning.' He smiled.

Ignoring their rumbling stomachs, they pushed the car right off the road and into a neglected-looking field nearby. Its crop was black and wizened, like it had been rotting into the ground since the previous season. Perhaps the farmer had quit the provinces for the city like so many other families. Whether people wanted to avoid witches, or accusations of being associated with witches themselves, the Safeguard Initiative had led to a mass exodus from the country towards the cities. Now shanty towns full of displaced people could be found around major cities like London, Manchester and Bristol. Areas with historic witchcraft connections like the West Country had been the first to fall. Like so many people, Daniel had thought the situation temporary; now he was forced to reconsider his position.

Moving the car had taken a great deal of effort on Daniel's part; he wasn't a big man, or particularly strong. Pushing against the bumper pulled at his stomach and groin, threatening a hernia. It turned out Chloe wasn't much of a driver either, even with the car in neutral. Daniel spent all his time yelling to his daughter to keep her foot on the brake pedal and her hands on the steering wheel. There was one hairy moment when it seemed like the car might roll. But the vehicle limped its way into the field at last, where it couldn't be seen from the road. To be on the safe side, they covered it with as many branches, long grasses and other debris they could find.

'Now what?' said Chloe.

They walked.

They moved off the road and hugged the edges of the fields. They hadn't seen a car since the day before but didn't want to risk being seen. Two British-Chinese people covered in flora and fauna in the middle of the countryside were memorable sights. With blue skies above them, Daniel marvelled at the early foliage of the hedgerows, the green canopy overhead.

About an hour into their walk, Daniel spotted an old-fashioned bright red telephone box near the roadside on the other side of the field. It felt like it took another hour to pick their way across the hard, tilled ground, Daniel fighting the fatigue that encased his bones with every step. He left Chloe crouching in the hedgerow as he looked both ways at a small crossroads, checking more for witnesses than approaching traffic. The crossroads was small, its four roads meeting in the middle with a white signpost pointing in four directions. He wasn't as far away from civilisation as he'd thought.

Daniel crossed the road to the phone box. He wrenched open the door, trying to dredge up his mother's phone number from his memory as he did so. Then he stopped, incredulous.

'For fuck's sake!'

Daniel hardly ever swore, but he had been pushed to the limit. There was no phone in the phone box. Its cash box still hung empty on the wall, but the receiver was gone. Vandalism was not to blame. Instead, lining the floor and walls were paperback books. A polite notice Sellotaped to the glass invited him to take one. A book exchange.

'Oh, great.' Chloe's voice seemed impossibly loud behind him.

Daniel turned, angry out of all proportion with her. 'I told you to stay put! What if someone had come for me? They would have got you too,' he hissed.

Chloe's eyes bulged. She was not used to her father's anger. That figured – Daniel wasn't used to Daniel's anger, either. Remorse eclipsed it just as quickly, and he threw his arms around her. Chloe slumped against him in that way teens do, as if only tolerating the hug.

'I'm sorry.' He kissed the top of her head.

'What about there?' Her voice was muffled against his shirt. 'We could ask to use their phone?'

She broke away, pointing. Daniel followed her gaze towards the crossroads sign, where there were a couple of handwritten signs propped up against the post. One told people to close gates behind them; the other advertised a farm shop three quarters of a mile up the road. Daniel's instinct cried out against it. Exeter was a small city, but significantly more cosmopolitan than the Devon hinterlands. There was a strong chance the farmers they found out here could be New Puritans, sympathetic to the Sentinel. He tried to search his shattered mind for an alternative. He came up with nothing.

Chloe took his hand. 'Come on, Dad.'

Walking nearly a mile should have taken about twenty minutes, but the upward-sloping gradient of the road and their weary limbs slowed them down considerably. The road became a winding dirt track and darker with it, the trees overhead blocking out the sunlight. As an old Devon longhouse appeared over the crest of the hill, Daniel experienced an intense sense of relief. *Finally*.

The pair of them let themselves in through a gate with a sign that read BEWARE OF THE DOG, painted in the same red letters as the sign at the crossroads. There didn't seem to be any canines around, although a fat toad sat in the middle of the filthy yard. It lolloped off as Daniel and Chloe re-hooked the gate and made their way across the concrete.

Their eyes alighted on the deserted farm. A grain silo stood empty next to a barn with a hole in its roof. On the wooden side of the barn, there was a faded portrait of the triumvirate: virgin, mother, crone. They were crudely drawn stick women, the one in the middle the largest. Her arms extended around the other two, like a protector. Whomever had drawn it considered the mother to be the most powerful.

Over the top of the drawing someone had daubed WITCHES OUT! and FAIR IS FOUL AND FOUL IS FAIR. The dried-on red paint was smeared, like blood. Daniel's literary mind recognised it as a quote from *Macbeth*. Perhaps it was supposed to be ironic; a witch might have had the line in the Scottish play, but the graffiti artist had the final word? Too bad she or he had obviously misunderstood. The meaning of that line is that though events, things and people may seem good or bad, after careful examination, they turn out to be the opposite.

In silence, Daniel and Chloe wandered across the gravel towards the house. As they neared it, Daniel could see the windows were thick with muck. His heart plummeted. The vigilantes had probably trashed the inside of the place as well.

'The phone might still work.' Chloe's voice was small, uncertain.

Daniel moved towards the door to knock. The top of the old stable door snapped back before he had a chance to lay a hand on it. Something long and shiny poked out. As his mind finally processed what he was looking at, he shouted a warning to Chloe and swept an arm out, pushing her out of harm's way. She fell down on the gravel with a shriek.

Daniel did not dare move. The long, cylindrical object was level with his sternum. He raised both hands in the air.

It was a sawn-off shotgun.

SEVEN

Texas, USA

'We're going now?'

Adelita tried to keep her voice light, her tone undemanding, as Ethan keyed off the phone, slipping it into his jacket pocket. An alpha male type like Ethan would respond better to that, she figured. In the hospital where she'd worked as a psychiatrist, she'd come up against a million men just like him, both patients and colleagues. They needed to feel in charge, even if that authority was an illusion. Well, fine. She knew how to handle him.

But Ethan looked preoccupied. He directed her to gather all the weapons together on the bed. Adelita thought he was forgetting she was a living weapon herself, but she did as she was told and played along. She pulled the metal suitcase out from under the bed and unpacked it, lining up guns, ammo and the other weapons. Ethan shoved a load of them into one of the bags, presenting one of the handguns to Adelita.

'You know how to handle a gun, right?' His eyes narrowed. 'You weren't just bluffing me in the bathroom?'

'My dad owned a bodega.'

Ethan just blinked at this explanation.

Adelita sighed. '*Obviously* we had a gun on the premises. In case of hold-ups?'

All the same, Adelita did not take the weapon. The crystal in her pocket was enough. Ethan just nodded. 'Your dad still out there?'

Adelita shrugged, pushing the thoughts of her father away as quickly as she could. Perhaps her twin sisters were eluding their kill orders. But Ernesto Garcia would not be so lucky. Adelita knew in her heart her father would not have just accepted his wife's and daughters' arrests, as so many men had. Some had even called the authorities on their female relatives themselves; anything to stay in favour. But not Ernesto. He would have tried to stand his ground, protect his wife. Sentinel Agents would have put a bullet in her father's skull and taken her mother anyway.

'You OK?'

Adelita snapped back to reality. Ethan peered at her, concern in his blue eyes. She swallowed down the ball of pain lodged in her throat, replacing it with a forced smile instead.

'I'm fine.'

A few minutes later, Adelita had slipped her feet into her prison-issue canvas pumps and the pair of them left the motel room. It was getting light outside; there was a flurry of activity in the car park below as several motel guests left early to get a jump on the traffic. Negotiating their way across the walkway, rucksacks on their backs, they nodded to a husband-and-wife team who were ferrying sleeping children still in their pyjamas to their car.

'This way, Doc.'

Adelita fell into step with Ethan. They approached the little Portakabin reception she'd spotted last night. The elderly man was no longer there, though his smoke still hung in the air.

Overflowing ashtrays and papers littered every surface. It was the archetypical forgotten backwater motel reception; the only thing strikingly different was a collection of Native American artefacts in a locked glass cupboard on the far wall. Tribes and their clans were exempt from Safeguard as long as they kept their magical items locked away, like they were guns in cabinets. Scratch that. Guns had fewer restrictions. What a bizarre world they all lived in now.

'Ethan.' A huge guy with a broad chest, high cheekbones and a long plait snaking down his back appeared from a backroom and leant on the counter. His right arm was missing from the elbow; his shirtsleeve dangled emptily. 'Pops said you'd made it here.'

Ethan grinned. 'Jocko.'

The two men did that back-slappy hug-thing guys do. Watching them, Adelita guessed they might have served together.

'So, this is the Crystal witch, huh?' Jocko turned from his old friend, looking Adelita up and down.

'The very same.'

Under the men's scrutiny, her cheeks burned. 'Screw you guys and the horses you rode in on. Jeez.'

Jocko seemed even more impressed by this, uttering a deep laugh. 'You're right. Fire in the belly. You can see it. No wonder all that magic came shooting right out of her.'

Jocko led them through the back of the Portakabin, stopping to pick up a cup of coffee. In comparison to the front desk, his side was clean and tidy, though his grandfather's smoke had snaked its way in there too. A black cat jumped down from a chair as Adelita approached and greeted her joyfully, weaving between her legs until she crouched down and scratched its ears. Aware of the two men's gaze upon her, Adelita looked up.

'What?' she said, her tone belligerent.

Jocko gave that deep laugh again and opened the cabin door to the courtyard out back. They emerged, blinking in the morning light as their eyes readjusted.

'As you requested.' With the cup of coffee in his hand, Jocko nodded towards a vehicle parked near the dumpsters.

Adelita did a double take. It was a large motorcycle. Whether it was a good make and model, she had no idea. She knew next to nothing about them; they were always something *other people* drove. The only time she'd really formed any opinion, it was a negative one, based on a patient she'd had years ago when she was just a resident. It had been a series of random and terrible luck. He'd fallen from his bike on an easy turn, and slid backwards across a small patch of black ice. Then, his shoulder blades had slammed hard into a fence post that was leaning into the road, severing two vertebrae in his neck. He'd sustained life-changing injuries at just twenty-two.

The words were pure Julia Garcia, but Adelita's tongue still conjured them into being: 'I'm not getting on that death trap.'

Both men looked to each other and more of that laughter ripped out of them again. They seemed to think she was joking. She felt that stir of fury in her belly again. *Men.* As this thought came to life, she felt the crystal pulse in her pocket. Another flash of pins and needles swept through her body, sending a white flash of light leaping out of her. The cup in Jocko's hand exploded, showering him in lukewarm coffee.

'Fuck!' He staggered backwards, surprised.

'Oops.' Adelita smiled.

Ethan thought the turn of events hilarious; Jocko did not.

'Just get her out of here,' he snarled.

Adelita still wasn't happy about getting on the bike, but she felt the urge to get out of Jocko's way every bit as much as he wanted her gone. She pulled on her helmet.

'That guy in the Sentinel with you?'

Ethan took a last glimpse back at Jocko as he fixed his helmet on. His friend had retreated back into the Portakabin.

Ethan sniffed. 'Nah. He wasn't stupid enough.'

Adelita snapped her goggles in place. She took a deep breath to psyche herself up, then grudgingly straddled the bike and slipped her arms around Ethan's waist.

'Try not to squeeze too hard, hey,' Ethan shouted as he kick-started the engine.

She swore she could hear the smirk in his voice, even above the roar of the motorbike. *He should be so frigging lucky*.

Even so, she clutched him tight as they zoomed out of the car park. A combination of fear and exhilaration coursed through Adelita's veins almost instantly. Anxiety and adrenalin followed; it was like a low-grade version of the magic state. She knew they weren't going any quicker than she'd ever gone in a car, yet it felt twice as intense. The raw power of the machine between their legs as it zoomed along the interstate took her breath away. The long, flat road stretched out ahead of them towards the hills in the distance, yellowed scrubland flashing past them. When she chanced a look in the bike's mirror, she caught sight of Ethan's broad grin, his blue eyes hidden by his own dark goggles.

About an hour and one numb butt for her later, they arrived at their destination. It was a provincial landing strip and junk-yard, filled with the decaying metal bones of aircraft behemoths. There was no lounge, nor even a waiting area for passengers; just a control tower that looked like it was made from plywood. As they rocketed down the road that lay parallel with the runway, Adelita turned her head and saw a small aircraft take off. Various parts were different colours, obviously salvaged from other planes. Adelita felt sure that if she inspected it up close, she would find it was held together by Scotch tape. She was amazed it could make it into the sky at all.

There was no security as they thundered into the airstrip.

Adelita clambered off the bike as Ethan rolled it backwards towards the fence to park it. He swung his leg off the bike in a much more gainly fashion, the mark of an experienced rider.

Another man was waiting for them by the tower. Unlike Jacko or Ethan, this guy was tiny, with a pigeon chest and a youth's hunched gait as he smoked his roll-up. Adelita mistook him for a teenager as they approached. Seeing him up close, she saw the deep lines etched into his dark, weathered skin. He was fifty if he was a day and Adelita sensed every moment of his life until now had been hard.

'You Ethan?' The man threw his cigarette away.

Ethan proffered a hand to shake, holding it at an angle as he did so. For the first time, Adelita noticed the tattoo on the inside of his wrist. It was fully healed, but he had not had it long. The ink was still black; it hadn't turned green yet like it so often does on white boys. As she took in the design, she had an attack of déjà vu: it was that little 'B', wave or bird again.

Ethan cast an eye around the air strip. 'So where are the others?'

The other man gave an almost imperceptible shake of his head. Ethan's eyes widened; his already pale face seemed to lighten two shades.

'*None* of them made it?'

'Just you and her,' the man confirmed, grim-faced. 'Gotta be a change of plan. We had a word and Plan B is go.'

Ethan closed his eyes, as if bracing himself. 'It's a suicide mission.'

The man emitted a sharp bark of laughter. 'You mean even more so than jail-breaking witches?'

Adelita noticed Ethan clench his fists by his sides.

'You know what I mean.'

The other guy was stony-faced. 'And you know what we need to make this work.'

'Yes ... More witches.' The cowboy sighed.

The conversation clearly over, Ethan threw his motorcycle helmet down in the dirt and stalked off in the direction of the planes. Adelita smiled at the other guy, who returned the gesture by taking a step back from her as if she might explode before turning and scuttling away towards the junkyard, disappearing behind a massive, lone plane turbine.

Adelita caught up with Ethan. 'What are you planning? Who are you guys?'

'It's best if you don't know the details for now.' Ethan was looking into the distance.

'What, because I'm the toxic witch who can't be trusted?'

'No, in case we get caught. If you don't know anything, they'll just send you back. That's the best case scenario, believe me.'

Adelita grabbed Ethan's arm. 'How do I know that's not bullshit?'

She couldn't prevent Ethan ploughing forwards if she wanted to, but it was enough to make him stop. He finally turned towards her, though his gaze was still directed over her shoulder into the distance, avoiding her. She was shocked to see tears glinting in his blue eyes. It was enough to make her brain click: concern for her own plight was finally replaced by the delayed realisation.

He was meant to meet people here. People who'd broken witches out of jail, just like he had with her. But none of them had made it. His friends were either dead or in Sentinel black sites.

Oh, shit.

'I'm sorry,' Adelita muttered.

Ethan just nodded. 'Look, when we get to where we're going, I can tell you more. But for now you're just going to have to trust me.'

Another plane swam into view in the desert sun. She felt a

sharp stab of alarm course through her body like the sweep of air and thrum of engines as it landed nearby. Adelita felt she'd been a good sport so far on the journey. She'd broken out of jail under the influence of magic, been clothes-less for hours, even got on the back of a motorbike. Enough was enough.

'You have got to be kidding me.'

'Relax. We're going in that one.' As he tapped his cigarette carton into his hand, Ethan cocked his head towards a much larger freight plane on the tarmac near the chain-link fence that Adelita had somehow missed.

Adelita felt her heart rate start to slow.

'I wouldn't be too happy yet.' Ethan lit his cigarette. 'You ever been to England?'

'No.'

Ethan blew a smoke ring. 'Highest concentration of Elementals, England.'

Adelita nodded. 'The West Country.'

She wasn't sure how she knew this. She wasn't even sure she knew where or what the West Country was, exactly. Whether it was her witch heritage calling her home, or she'd just heard women in prison talking about this promised land, it didn't matter. As the pilot of the freight plane appeared, she turned back to Ethan for confirmation.

He sighed, every inch the condemned man. 'That's where we're going.'

EIGHT

Devon, UK

A lean, grubby-looking teenage girl with matted blonde hair held the sawn-off shotgun from the other side of the stable door, one-handed and steady. She had a determined yet dispassionate expression on her young face. It was clear to Daniel she'd done this before. In her other arm, she grasped a wide-eyed baby of about three or four months, resting him on her hip.

It was an incongruous sight, but Daniel had other things on his mind. He stared at the weapon, stupefied. It was level with his chest. The girl didn't say anything, but she had deadly blue eyes.

'Don't shoot,' Daniel whispered through cracked lips.

The girl answered by pulling back the safety catch.

'No!' Chloe scrabbled to her feet from the ground, where Daniel had pushed her seconds earlier. 'Please, don't! We won't hurt you or your baby.'

The girl's gaze flitted from Daniel to Chloe. She curled her lip. She clearly just wanted to blow them away. Despite this, Daniel saw something flicker in her eyes, recognising it because both he and Chloe had been through the same thing in the past twenty-four hours. Life-changing trauma.

Chloe must have recognised it too. 'We just need some help.'

'Don't we all,' the teenager countered. Her tone was flat, almost bored. She wanted them to know she wasn't fooled by their sympathies for one second.

Even so, Chloe didn't give up. 'The Sentinel are coming.'

'I'm not scared of them.' The teen girl cocked her head at the barn wall, the Macbeth quote daubed in red paint. 'You think *the Sentinel* did that?'

Her words were sharp rocks, heavy with bitterness. Despite her attempts to mask it, Daniel could see the girl's eyes were shiny with tears. But did this make her more unpredictable and likely to fire off a shot? Daniel sent a warning glance at Chloe not to come too close, but his stubborn daughter crept ever closer.

'What's your name? I'm Chloe.'

'I. Don't. Care.'

The girl did not relinquish the shotgun trained on Daniel. Daniel felt dread, as a kind of heat, flood through him next. All he could see were the two barrels of the gun, shining deadly in the sunlight.

'Let me show you something,' Chloe said.

Before the girl could reply, Chloe clapped her hands together. Daniel's eyes bulged with surprise as they came apart: a globe of spherical green light sprang up between Chloe's hands like the static of a plasma ball.

It was all so fast.

Before Daniel could work out what it was, Chloe grabbed the sphere in her fist, throwing it at the bottom of the stable door like a bouncing ball, or a cherry bomb.

Bang!

The teen girl shrieked and jumped backwards, the gun now

83

at an angle and facing upwards. She squeezed off an involuntary shot. Simultaneously, Chloe grabbed Daniel's arm, pulling him towards her. She was just in time; the pellets flew over their heads, embedding themselves in the barn door. The baby yowled in fear and burst into tears.

Daniel's senses left him and he stood there, blinking. Before the teenager could round on them and fire again, Chloe yanked her father's hand and dragged him to the side of the longhouse.

You did know about your powers, then?

The absurd thought sprang up in Daniel's brain as they both hugged the building and made their way down the longhouse. Chloe had been adamant she wasn't Elemental in the car. What the hell was going on? There was no time to ask.

'It's OK, it's OK, *ssssh* now,' they heard the teenager soothe the baby.

She was no longer in their sights, but that surely meant they were no longer in hers. Chloe and Daniel crept across the muck-spattered concrete towards an abandoned, broken-down hen house. They crouched down beside it, hiding as they heard the girl kick the bottom of the stable door open.

The baby was still crying. She kept shushing him in a distracted manner, as if she was just a harassed mum with too much on her plate.

Daniel took a chance and peeked momentarily over the old hen house. In full view for the first time, her back to him, Daniel could discern she was little more than a child. Perhaps fifteen at most. The baby on her hip, the shotgun still dangled from her right hand.

Daniel ducked down again. His thoughts whirled aimlessly, round and round. Fear was etched into Chloe's face and she looked to him as if to say, *What now?*

Don't move, he mouthed.

We have to, she'll find us! Chloe mouthed back, face twisted in furious disbelief.

Daniel could understand the logic of her words but was still at a loss for what would be best. He felt shame prickle through him. He was Chloe's father; he should be protecting *her*. But he'd stood by, inert and useless, as Chloe had saved *him*.

How could the countryside have degenerated so much in so short a time? Since the Safeguard had come in, Daniel had just kept his head down like so many people in the city, getting on with things. Thoughts of the Serbian–Croatian war in the nineties jumped into his head. Long-held grudges and injustices had simmered for decades, then war flared up and pitched neighbours against one another, practically overnight. That had all been terrible, of course, but theoretical to him. He had felt sure that could never happen in England. Yet it had.

'I'll handle this.' Chloe rolled her eyes at him as she clapped her hands together once more. From her palms, that green light glowed again.

She stood, whistling at the girl to draw her attention.

Daniel jumped up fruitlessly from his crouching position too, as if he could yank Chloe out of the line of fire. He was just in time to see the girl round towards them, the shotgun trained on them both.

The girl didn't fire straight away, thank goodness. The baby was still crying, hollering his little lungs out. Both girls faced each other down, an impasse. The air crackled between them with aggression. As young as they were, Daniel appreciated for the first time they were both alpha females, determined to win. He'd always associated this kind of clash with the animal kingdom: stags locking horns; big cats roaring their dominance. Always the male of the species, too. Now his own eyes told him he was wrong.

The girl's posture was not as rigid as before. She seemed more pensive, like she was weighing up her options.

'So, how long you been able to do *that*?' Her eye was drawn to the green spheres from Chloe's hands.

Daniel's own mind chimed in: *Yes, Chloe. How long?*

'Since I was thirteen. Couldn't do anything else then, so I thought it was just a quirk, a bit of fun. Turns out I was wrong.'

The girl ran her gaze over Chloe. 'Usually it's white lights. Not seen green ones like those before. No crystals, neither. You an Elemental?'

Chloe shrugged. 'Apparently.'

The girl finally lowered the gun. 'You better come in, then.'

Daniel was seated in the old farmhouse at a scarred wooden table. Heat emanated from an Aga; there was a bucket of firewood next to him and a blanket around his shoulders; a sour taste in the back of his throat. Had he slept? He was unsure.

At the table, Chloe drank soup from an earthenware bowl, watched by the younger teenager. The baby was seated in an old plastic highchair, banging a spoon against the tray with gusto. He had a big smile on his face now and a new T-shirt.

'He's gorgeous, Megan.'

Chloe reached over to the baby, stroking his wispy hair with her hand. Megan – as she'd introduced herself once they were all in the kitchen – smiled, but it didn't reach her eyes. Daniel felt his insides twist with sympathy for this lone young girl.

Megan indicated the horrible graffiti on the barn door, still visible through the grimy window. 'Mum was a Crystal witch. She helped everyone, my whole life. Before that, even. Never turned anyone away. Healing spells, crop spells, whatever the Goodys and their men needed.'

Chloe nodded. 'Are you a Crystal witch, too?'

Megan shook her head. 'No, I'm just a Legacy. No magic in these veins. If there had been, maybe I could have ...'

The teenager stopped, choking on her words. Chloe placed a hand on hers, to comfort her.

'Can't your dad help?'

The words jumped out of Daniel before he could think them through. Too late, he wondered if the girl's own father had led the vigilantes to their door. Lots of men had turned on their witch wives when Safeguard came in. He'd seen the lurid headlines in tabloids like the *Daily Mail* as those cretins had sold their women out: HUBBLE BUBBLE TOIL AND (MAR-RIAGE) TROUBLE: THE TRUTH ABOUT BEING MARRIED TO A WITCH.

'It was just me and Mum' – she stroked the baby's face – 'and him. The community relied on Mum. But the moment we needed help, everyone turned away.'

'Why didn't you go to the police?'

Megan met Daniel's gaze. 'What would be the point? The police have to work with the Sentinel. No one cares what happens to us, out here, anyway.'

The girl wasn't wrong. Daniel dipped his head in shame, noticing there was an empty bowl in front of him, too. There were blank spots in his memory. Recollections of the confron-tation earlier flickered through his thoughts like fragments of a half-forgotten movie, or a bad dream. As he closed his gritty eyes, Li's face appeared on the back of his eyelids.

'I need to use the phone.' Daniel's sense of purpose switched back on, abruptly. He stood, the blanket fluttering from his shoulders to the floor. 'Do you have one?'

Megan nodded. 'Aye. There's an old landline under the stairs, might still work.'

If Daniel hadn't been so single-minded in his need to call his parents and sisters, he might have considered how sad it was Megan hadn't even tried to find out herself if the phone worked. He opened the under-stairs cupboard and rummaged around amongst the mouldering wellington boots and old trainers in there.

Sure enough, he found an old rotary phone, thick with grime like everything else in the house. His hand hovered over the dial for a moment – how the hell did these things work? – then a muscle memory kicked in and he was turning the plastic dial, his parents' number at his fingertips.

'Daniel?'

His mother's breathless voice filtered down the line. How could she have known it would be him calling? In a nanosecond, he connected the dots: she'd primed herself to answer every call like this, since he and Chloe went on the run. Somehow, he knew instantly what this meant: *the Sentinel were in his parents' home, ready to trace the call.*

'Don't say anything, they're here!'

Daniel slammed the phone down without speaking. Fear sent its icy fingers through his body, making him shake. What would the Sentinel do to his family? Just twenty-four hours ago he would have thought they would let them go. But that was before. Now he was sure his mother would pay the price for her defiance. *Oh, Mama.*

Steely resolve followed as fast. His mother had always made it clear to Daniel and his sisters they owed her nothing, not even life. *Children don't ask to be born*, she'd declare; *it's why we have to do our best for them, no matter what.*

Chloe was his child. She'd already lost her mother. There was surely a kill order on her. He had to get her out of here and away from the Sentinel, no matter what. Once he had got his only child out of danger, then he could find out whether his parents were safe. There was no other alternative.

Daniel tried to collect his thoughts. Despite his mother's

efforts, the Sentinel agents might still have been able to get a location. Was it easier or harder with landlines? He had no idea. Whatever the case, he needed to find someone else to call. And quick. But who? His sisters would be too obvious; Sentinel agents would be watching over them, too.

He cast his mind back, trying to think of someone, anyone he knew who would be sympathetic to the witch cause, but who the Sentinel might have overlooked.

Tallulah.

Her face jumped into his mind, bright and vivid as a firecracker. Bright red hair, milk-white skin, sparkling green eyes. She'd been his last girlfriend, before he met Li. They'd gone out for a full term during his first year at Exeter. She'd loved and left him for a girl called Joanne, breaking his heart. But that was all water under the bridge now. Neither of them had left Exeter and the sweetness of shared nostalgia had meant he'd met Tallulah for a drink a couple of times; occasionally he'd see her in the city, or walking with her husband and twin girls along Exeter quay. Theirs was one of those relationships that were perpetually casual. They were friend*ly*, rather than friends. A sense of shared history flowed between them, innocent and yet important.

Now a nurse at Heavitree hospital, Tallulah had been a Kitchen witch when she and Daniel were together. Those years had been a much freer time for magic than now, but it was also around then that the Cursed Light had begun attacking high-profile targets: the London Stock Exchange; the Empire State Building; the Bastille. Buildings that had gone up in flames, or been destroyed by gales or floods.

Witches had begun to feel under scrutiny for their activities, some even taking to hiding them. Tallulah had been prudent enough to do so, a detail Daniel was thankful for. In fact, Tallulah wasn't even her real name – she'd always said she didn't look like a 'Helen' and Daniel was inclined to agree; like all her friends, he'd never called her this, not once. She was saved under 'Tallulah' in his phone contacts, no surname. Surely that was enough to keep the Sentinel at bay? He hoped so.

Daniel dialled the number for the operator and was put through to the hospital. A bored receptionist answered, connecting him to the nurses' station when he asked for Tallulah.

Daniel gave a fake name for himself, of course. Relief flooded through him as another nurse told him Tallulah was in today, and fetched her straight away.

'Don't tell me where you are,' Tallulah said in a low voice when she came to the phone a minute later, not even checking it was Daniel, or asking why he was calling. 'I saw the news.'

'What are they saying?' Daniel asked, for some reason keeping his voice equally low.

'They're saying you killed your wife and abducted your daughter. I know it's bollocks.'

There it was; that connection that transcended time.

'Thank you, Tallulah.'

Daniel could feel grateful tears threaten as injustice surged through him. His other friends, or colleagues at the university, would probably believe the Sentinel's story that he was a murderer and a kidnapper. Well, let them. In the grand scheme of things it was the least of his problems.

'What do you need?'

'Somewhere to go – we've got no money on us, no phone . . . '

Tallulah asked if they could make it to Taunton Deane service station today. Daniel mapped the route in his head and replied that they could – they would have to, somehow. He thanked her again.

'Don't thank me,' Tallulah said. 'This is me being selfish, for my girls. We can't let the Sentinel carry on for ever.'

Of course: Tallulah's twins were more likely to have magic – twin girls always were. They were only five, but unlike him, his old flame must be thinking ahead. Childhood disappeared in the blink of an eye; it would not be long before they reached eighteen and would fall under the Pre-emptive Strike legislation.

Putting the phone down, Daniel turned in the dark hall. Two shadows stood on the threshold of the kitchen: Chloe and Megan, the baby back on her hip. It was still daytime, but the combination of the low ceiling and the mucky windows made them silhouettes. Before Daniel could tell them what the plan was, or what they needed to enact it, Megan held something up in her hand.

A set of car keys.

'I need your help with something, first,' she said.

NINE

Over the Atlantic

In the freight plane, the cargo hold was every bit as cold as their pilot had promised. Adelita shifted in her rickety old pull-down seat, teeth chattering as she adjusted the blanket around her shoulders. They were surrounded by big metal bins of loose cat or dog biscuits and there was a musty, meaty tang in the air, mixed with chemical preservatives.

As the old plane started to taxi lazily around the airstrip, she wondered idly what Ethan had paid for their ride and who the rest of his buddies were. The metal fixtures around them shook and creaked with alarming abandon. Adelita was not a nervous flyer, but she'd never flown in such less-than-ideal conditions. If it was this bad before the wheels were even up, what the hell would it be like in the air? She glanced over at Ethan for reassurance, only to discover he'd clamped his eyes shut and was grasping hold of some empty cargo straps.

Adelita attempted to inject some gallows humour into the situation. 'You know something I don't?'

'No. Just don't like flying.' Ethan's voice was clipped; his eyes remained closed.

'But you're Sentinel. You must have flown lots of times.'

Ethan continued to wind the straps around his hands. 'What can I say? It's a new phobia.'

Keen on keeping some distance between herself and Ethan, Adelita had sat down on the end of the single row of seats but now she shifted along towards him, remembering to refasten her belt in her new seat. She grabbed his wrist, measuring his pulse. He didn't stop her. His breaths were shallow and he was tachycardic. Classic case of someone shitting himself. Brilliant. How the hell had she ended up with a rogue agent who had a phobia of pain *and* flying?

'OK. You need to breathe in through your nose and out through your mouth. Like this . . . ' Adelita grabbed his bearded chin. 'Hey, soldier. Look at me.'

Ethan's blue eyes snapped open, just as the roar of the engine kicked in. In the cargo hold, wind began to rush past the plane with the mournful, low howl of a dragon. Adelita felt the tell-tale sensation of her stomach dropping away as the wheels left the tarmac. The plane dipped to the left. One of the large bins creaked, metal against metal making an ominous moan. Ethan flinched, his hands and body shaking.

'Easy, easy. You're OK.'

They lurched forwards in their seats, their hands grasped together. He did as she told him, taking laboured breaths in, then pushing them out. He couldn't look her in the eyes, though, staring over her shoulder the whole time. As the plane climbed higher and began to stabilise, some of the banging and creaking and shaking started to ease a little. Truth be told, Adelita would be glad to reach solid ground too.

'Sorry.'

Ethan let go of her hands and sat right back in his seat, like he needed as much space between them as possible.

'It's fine,' she said, truthfully.

There was a vulnerability to Ethan she hadn't seen before, even when he'd sat in the motel bathroom, shirtless, while she patched him up.

Adelita moved back to her original seat. 'It's not just the plane, is it?'

She expected him to make some kind of wisecrack, attempt his trademark devil-may-care grin. He didn't. He looked drained, exhausted.

'Brings back some bad memories, that's all.'

'Like what?'

But the shutters came down in Ethan's eyes. 'You don't wanna know.'

'Try me.'

Ethan became aware of his chattering teeth and pulled his own blanket around his shoulders.

'It's freezing in here. Why don't you come closer? Nothing shady. Y'know, for warmth.'

Adelita smirked. 'Nice try. You're not distracting me that easily.'

'Ouch.' Ethan placed a palm to his chest, like she'd shot him through the heart. 'Who said anything about distracting you? I really am freezing. Aren't you?'

'I'm a New Yorker,' Adelita reminded him. 'We're hardier than you Califools.'

Ethan laughed, then looked startled as the plane dipped again, making their teeth snap in their skulls. The fuselage shuddered and juddered around them; their breath expelled in frosty plumes. Adelita rolled her eyes, then undid her belt and clambered along the row to sit down next to him once more. She hesitated for a second, then rested her head on his shoulder and draped her arm around his waist. Ethan's chin was on her head, his arm around her shoulders as he wrapped both their blankets around them. She knew soldiers would do this in foxholes and trenches out on the battlefield; she'd seen pictures on the Internet, a lifetime ago. As much as she hated to admit it, it was much, much warmer this way.

'Now, ain't this nice?'

He just had to spoil it. But still Adelita didn't move.

'Shut up,' she growled.

As the minutes turned to hours, Adelita felt herself zone out and let exhaustion claim her. Yet, even as she dozed, she could feel something crackling through her. It was like her body and mind were asleep, but her magic could not be switched off.

As the plane made its way across the Atlantic, she was suddenly out of her own body. Somehow she could see both Ethan and herself, huddled together, eyes closed, foreheads touching. She noted his hands were exactly where they were supposed to be, even when he was asleep.

Then she was soaring even further above. Inexplicably, she was outside the plane, above it, where the roar of the engines was all-encompassing. Lightning forks tore the black skies in two in the distance. She felt a rush of joy as the electricity made its way through the air to her.

She could determine the swirl of waves of the black sea thousands of miles beneath; she could sense shoals of fish, the leviathan bodies of whales and dolphins beneath the surface. The stars twinkled around her and she could feel the rush of air along the smooth fuselage. She matched it in speed, the icy arctic blast of air in her face.

Except it wasn't in her face, because she didn't even have a face. She was something more, something ethereal, something—

Oooooooooh shit!

Adelita started awake, slamming back into her body.

As this happened, a ball of white light burst from her, passing straight to Ethan, as nimble as a silverfish. Ethan jerked out of his chair, shocked awake, only arrested by the seatbelt around him. His eyes rolled back in his head and he slumped forwards. Adelita shrieked, sure she'd killed him.

But then Ethan raised his head. 'What the hell was that?' he groaned, a stream of drool falling from his slack mouth.

Relief flooded through Adelita as surely as the magic had moments earlier. She helped him sit back in his chair and wiped his mouth with the corner of her blanket.

'I have no idea. I'm so sorry.'

She snapped back into medic mode, taking his pulse again. Thanks to her, he was back to being tachycardic. She probably shouldn't tell him her consciousness – *or whatever it was* – had got out of her, even out of the plane somehow. It was too weird. Anyway, it was probably a weird dream, brought on by her magic. Yes. That was probably – *surely?* – it.

'I think I'm gonna throw up.'

Ethan tried to undo his belt but his hands were shaking too much. She undid it for him, instinctively stroking his hair as he sat forward and put his head between his knees.

She marvelled at how her moods around him varied so much. She felt tender towards him in that moment, rather than the pragmatic, observant psychiatrist she'd always been at work. Why? She'd known Ethan for a matter of hours. That must be her magic working through her too, Adelita decided, messing with her feelings like hormones.

'You're not like a normal Crystal witch.'

'Define "normal",' Adelita pointed out. 'I am on the run from jail, with an ex-Sentinel helping me, going to the back of beyond in England.'

'OK, you got me.'

Ethan rested his head against the seat, like his neck couldn't stand the weight. She turned his wrist over, indicated the small black tattoo scrawled there.

'You and your buddies . . . are you Cursed Light?'

'No such thing,' Ethan sighed, compelled to explain. 'Think about it. "Cursed Light" is a bit on the nose, isn't it? "Oooh, we're the baddies." But Safeguard Initiative? *Goodys*, for God's sake? It's all bullshit.'

Another piece of the puzzle clicked for Adelita. 'You're saying the government invented Cursed Light?'

'Bingo,' Ethan confirmed. His eyes were still closed. 'Keeps all the Goodys and men pliable. I fell for it myself. For a long time.'

There it was. A confession, of sorts: he'd been sucked in by anti-witch propaganda. Adelita had to admit she had been, too. The terrorist threat had been non-stop, if the media were to believed, for nigh on twenty years. Half her life. Despite her own peaceful bloodline, she'd always accepted there was a small contingent of bad witches, intent on wrecking society. It was all she'd ever known. Adelita had always thought the government's regulation and eventual ban on witchcraft was unjust, but even with her family history, she had always believed the Cursed Light terror group was real. Now here was an actual Sentinel agent confirming it was just a construct. She'd lost her family, her friends, her entire life for these filthy lies! Anger surged through her again, sending a crackle of Crystal magic flying off her fingertips like the sparks from a Zippo lighter. This time she shocked herself. Bright spots leapt up in her eyes, nausea swished in her belly.

'Oops.' Ethan echoed her from earlier with Jocko, chuckling. 'You OK?'

Adelita took some deep breaths as the wave of pins and needles receded.

'I'm fine. So, what about the assassination of President Stone?'

'That was the Sentinel, too.'

Adelita's mind swirled, this time not with magic, but with the realisation of such an audacious plan. Hopkins had enacted a daring, bloody and secret coup, using the Sentinel against the State, then the world, via the Safeguard initiative. He had always warned witches would turn on the rest of the population. Now Adelita thought about it, it was very convenient how witch attacks had upped in scale and violence with every year that passed, especially in the last two decades. Her brain couldn't compute the magnitude of it.

Ethan's blue eyes bore into Adelita's. 'Hopkins had his eye on the Senate for decades. But he was never going to get in while a president who was sympathetic to witches, like Dr Stone, was there.'

Adelita couldn't hide her horror. 'You were involved in killing her?'

Ethan shook his head. 'No. That wasn't me.'

Adelita was surprised by how relieved she felt at his assurance; at how she took him on his word, too. But what was the alternative? He'd broken her out of jail; shot his Sentinel guards colleagues for her and got her out of the country. She'd felt trapped not only in prison, but in that Texas motel room. Whatever his reasons, he was helping her and Adelita was grateful for that. She didn't want to die. If that meant going to the West Country with him, so be it.

She grabbed his wrist again, indicated the tattoo there. 'What *is* this?'

'We're called the Brotherhood.' Ethan smirked as he caught sight of her raised eyebrow. 'I know, I know. I didn't pick the name.'

'My knight in shining armour,' Adelita chuckled with him, before ambushing him: 'So, what are we going to be doing in the West Country?'

'We're going to Cornwall.' Ethan's good humour evaporated. 'We need more witches.'

'Elementals?'

Adelita wanted him to prove her hunch wrong. She'd only ever known two Elementals well: her sisters. Bella and Natasha would never have harmed her. She'd seen a few as patients at the hospital where she worked pre-Safeguard, but she wasn't friends with any. There'd been none in Our Lady, of course; with kill orders on their heads, they were executed on sight in the US. Adelita didn't mind admitting such women otherwise daunted her, even if that fear had been stoked by Sentinel propaganda. They were so powerful.

'S'right.' Ethan rested his head against the seat, barely able to keep his eyes open. 'I know some, out at a coven in Cornwall who will help us.'

Adelita couldn't keep the cynicism out of her voice. 'You, a Sentinel guard, know Elementals? How did that happen?'

Ethan's eyelids fluttered closed. '*Ex*-Sentinel.'

Before Adelita could ask any more questions, a soft snore sounded from Ethan. Tired herself, she wrapped the blanket around them again and rested her head on his shoulder. This time, her sleep was dreamless.

A burst of static woke them as the pilot called through on the intercom. He mumbled something about coming in to land and warned them to make sure they had their belts on.

Yawning, Adelita checked out a tiny side window. She could see the orange street lamps of a large city below, its streets almost visible as the plane dipped again. It was still night and the city was surrounded by blackness on one side: the sea. On the other, there were patches of darkness, fields framed by the white and red streaming lights of the freeway, or *motorway* as the British said.

They sailed straight over the big landing lights of a medium-sized airport. It seemed they would not be landing there, but overshooting it in favour of a smaller, much more anonymous airstrip beyond. Next to her Ethan shifted, stretching out like a cat.

'Where are we landing?' Adelita watched the mingling of lights create a riot in the darkened cargo hold. The plane was not juddering as much as when it took it off.

Ethan rolled his neck on his shoulders. 'Bristol.'

'Is that close to where we want to be?'

'Couple of hours.'

'By motorbike or car?'

He snorted. 'Wait and see.'

The plane landed with fewer problems than it took off with. They undid their belts and collected their things. As the loading ramp came down, Ethan turned to Adelita.

'Ready?'

In the bright lights of the airstrip, his skin looked translucent. She was shocked at how pale and reduced he seemed. How much of that was her doing? Adelita swallowed the guilt down. She'd never asked him to put his life on the line for her. She still didn't know what he wanted in return. One thing medicine had taught her, then prison had served to compound: events could turn on a dime. Control was only ever an illusion.

Adelita fixed on her game-face. 'I'm ready.'

President Michael Hopkins at The Women's Union Goody Rally, November 2016 (Transcript)

My dear women, do not be afraid of me. I am your friend. I will protect you, your daughters. My protection does not just extend to those born Goodys. I will make my assurances to you once again, so we might avoid bloodshed wherever possible. I don't want to be the president who went to war with women. I love women. I hate witches. That's the difference.

First though, the hard decisions. As most of you know, my first job in office was to draft the Pre-Emptive Strike Legislation. Elemental witches are toxic savages. They are extremists, unable to resist their base impulses. They love chaos and violence. They will not stop until they have dragged us down with them.

There is nothing we can do for these heretics except pray for their souls. I have signed kill orders on all proven Elemental females worldwide. It is not something I took lightly, I assure you. These warrants will be enacted by the Sentinel and by every member country of my proposed Safeguard Initiative.

The struggles of our forefathers to bring civilization to the savages echoes throughout eternity, from the first moments they set foot on the vast savannah of Africa; the wild jungles of India; the verdant paddy fields of the Orient. Now we must complete our mission. It is my dream to have the Sentinel bring the light of God to every dark corner of the Earth.

Kitchen witches, I will tell you once again: If you come to me and recant your right to practice magic, I will welcome you with open arms. There will be an amnesty for your cauldrons; we will take your books and family spells, no questions asked. There will be no retribution. Prove to us who you are, that you mean us no harm, and we will return this gift. Just pledge your allegiance to us, as we invest in you. Trust me. You can see I am a man of my word.

Crystal witches, we can cure you. Your Legacies need not fear us, either. But I warn you now, our patience grows thin. If you refuse to come to the angel caves any longer, I will rain down fire on your covens, bury your crystals under concrete, burn your sacred texts and artifacts, as well as separate and confine the female members of your communities. I will do whatever it takes to eradicate witchcraft from not only the United States, but from the face of the Earth.

TEN

Devon, UK

Daniel braced himself and opened the barn door, as Megan had asked him.

Two shapes were hanging from the rafters. At first, his innocent brain processed it as a stuffed bonfire guy and a sack. Then he deciphered the full horror.

As an educated man, Daniel had believed himself immune to the siren call of the rumour mill. Though he'd heard whispered stories about devout Goodys whipping up carnal bloodlust in their men, setting them against Crystal witches, in his ignorance he'd dismissed them all as old wives' tales.

Now the evidence was right in front of him: a woman and her dog were hanging from the rafters.

Megan's mother had died months ago. The woman's skin was leathery; what was left of her hair hung in wispy strands around her face. Her familiar's fur was stiff with age; the tongue that should have lolled from its mouth was small, black and curled. There was a horrible, sweet scent in the air like cured meat.

The assault of smells and images pierced Daniel's mind and sent his stomach roiling, sour saliva rising into the back of his throat. He'd been such a fool, choosing not to see. This was why Li had not shared her knowledge about Chloe's gifts with him. He'd been too blind.

'Daddy?'

Chloe's voice was small, sorrowful in the barn doorway. She'd not called him Daddy since she was ten years old. He wished she didn't have to see this – no one should.

'One moment.'

Daniel collected his thoughts. Despite a rocky start, Megan had promised to help them. She was just a girl, alone in the world. He didn't want to do this, but he had to. It was the least he could do.

'Can I help?'

Chloe arrived by his side, staring up at the bodies. If she was still shocked or upset by the sight of them, she did not show it now. Her expression was resolute and calm, so like her mother it took his breath away momentarily. He shut these thoughts down, back to practical matters, and fetched an old stepladder and sickle from a nearby bench.

'Hold on to this, so it doesn't tip over.'

Holding the sharp, curved blade, Daniel climbed the stepladder.

'You got her?' Chloe said.

Stretching as far as he could, he hacked at the thick rope the Goodys and their men had hooked up around the rafters of the barn. Dust and death tickled at his nostrils as he let a shout go, expelling his own anxiety with it. This was all so wrong. To interfere with the bodies seemed monstrous; but to leave them hanging felt awful too.

The dog fell down like a sack of potatoes, but it didn't seem right to let Megan's mother fall with such a lack of grace. Daniel braced himself and grabbed hold of the woman's skeletal body as she swung towards him before hacking through the rope. He fought the sour vomit that threatened to surge up his throat as the cloying, sweet smell of decay forced its way into his nose.

Daniel brought the blade down once, twice, three times. Finally, it made its way through the tough fibres and the taut rope slackened. Megan's mother fell into his waiting arms like a dance partner, almost slipping through the crook of his elbow. Cradling her ruined body like a lover's, Daniel brought her down the stepladder and laid her with reverent care on the earthen floor.

'Would you like to bury her?'

Megan crossed the threshold of the barn. It was clear she'd not been there since that fateful night. She carried herself with a cat's agile and watchful stance, as if ready to run. She crept forwards and stared at the bodies, the baby still on her hip.

'You don't bury witches, Dad,' Chloe chastised. 'Flames help them pass over.'

Them. Not 'us'. Not yet.

'I've got a couple of full petrol cans out back,' Megan said, her voice small.

They created a makeshift pyre of hay bales, pallets and old cardboard out in the farmyard on the concrete. Daniel laid Megan's mother and the dog on top. Megan disappeared back into the house before returning with a selection of her mother's belongings and artefacts. A leather-bound Book of Shadows went on with her, two or three wax poppets and a glass vial of something he didn't recognise. All the time Megan muttered something under her breath, too quiet for Daniel to hear.

'Protection spell,' Chloe whispered.

Daniel nodded. He wanted to tell Chloe that he already knew, that he'd studied witchcraft as a theology student, but that seemed worse somehow. He had been interested enough to read about magic, collected illegal artefacts and papers for his work. He had even been making notes for his non-fiction book. Yet he'd lacked the vision to see what was going on in his own family, or the community around him.

When Megan had finished, Daniel sloshed the contents of one of the petrol canisters over the pile. Chloe grabbed a small branch and set it to one of her green spheres; Daniel was surprised to see it catch alight right away. She presented it to Megan. Daniel took the baby as the young teenager approached the pyre, the burning branch in hand.

Megan took a deep breath, before addressing the pyre. *'I am not alone / I am connected to all / Mother, guide me and protect me / I offer myself to the light / For you, Mother.'*

It went up fast, consuming the bodies and their final resting place within minutes. Chloe's hand found her father's.

Despite Daniel's shredded nerves, the journey back up the North Devon Link Road had been uneventful in the old beat-up car Megan had given them. The girl had refused to go with them, no matter how much Chloe pleaded. Perhaps Megan wanted to stay close to her mother, or maybe the girl felt she was best off staying put, in a place she recognised, so she might stay under the radar. Daniel couldn't blame her after what she'd been through. Travelling with them would make her and her little boy conspicuous, and Daniel knew instinctively the path ahead of them was fraught with danger. He could not deny that a selfish part of him felt glad, too. Travelling with one damaged teenage girl was strenuous enough. Add another *and* a baby to the mix, he wasn't sure they could make it even as far as the motorway.

As they passed Tiverton and got back onto the M5, Chloe dozed off in the passenger seat next to him – her magic had seemed to really take it out of her. He kept an eye on his rear-view mirror all the way, just in case Sentinel – or perhaps

Tallulah herself – appeared, flashing lights at him. But he was left alone to his thoughts and the perpetual swish of traffic.

Enveloped in darkness alternating with the lights of passing vehicles, Daniel tried to calm his racing thoughts and keep his breathing steady. He had to hold it together, for Chloe's sake; he could not afford to fall apart now. He still could not believe how he'd run with her. He'd never been in trouble in his life, and now they were on the run like something from a movie. He was not equipped for a journey or responsibility of this enormity, but all he had to do was make it to Taunton Deane. That's what he told himself.

He felt a relieved sigh escape him as he spotted the signs for Taunton Deane service station. He hadn't been there since he was a little boy, when his parents had brought him and his sisters down to the coast during school holidays. Since he'd moved to the area more than twenty years ago, he'd had little need to visit local service stations. But as he flicked the indicator and turned into the medium-sized car park, memories of his family flooded through his mind. He was surprised to see the same Burger King was still there, where his younger sister Gemma had drunk her strawberry milkshake too fast and, seconds later, thrown it straight back up, bright pink and viscous down her front. Looking around, he could remember where his mother had got out of the car when she'd argued with his dad about something inconsequential. Daniel could still hear his father laugh, encouraging them to 'wave to Mummy' as she gave him the finger and they sailed past to the other side of the car park. Despite the pain in his solar plexus at the thought of what could be happening to them right now, a ghost of a smile made its way to Daniel's lips.

Parking up, he shook Chloe awake. 'We're here.'

ELEVEN

Sentinel Agent Lyle Kirby was on a break and sitting in the parking lot of Taunton Deane Services, near where the trucks were parked. Had he turned his head to the left, he would have noticed Daniel and Chloe Su's chicken-shit-smelling old car pull in and park up across the way, towards the petrol station.

But Lyle was feeling sorry for himself and trying to move his head as little as possible. He was hung-over as hell and drinking Pepto-Bismol straight out of the bottle like it was Coca-Cola. He fiddled with the iPad in his lap, trying to log on to the Sentinel intranet to access the APBs – all-points bulletins – for the day. As it was too often, the whole thing was down. Sentinel geeks blamed bad weather and poor signal strength, but Lyle suspected the fools were so secretive they even liked to keep their own agents in the dark.

Lyle threw the iPad into the footwell of the car, irritated. He rested his head against the rest, trying to still his thoughts as well as his stomach. It had been his wife Carolyn's birthday the day before. She was dead, so celebrations were out; drinking to forget was very definitely in. Now he felt like a cat had shit in his mouth then slashed the inside of his head and stomach with its claws.

Carolyn's death was why Lyle had taken the assignment in LimeyLand in the first place. He'd figured he could at least get some peace, since he didn't have to round up Legacies here. The downside was that going out drinking meant trawling dark, forgotten bars in this godforsaken backwater. He'd ended up in yet another shitty little English market town, propping up the bar with a legion of other sad middle-aged men, listening to nineteen eighties mod rock and knocking back warm watered-down ale. He'd lost count, and a chunk of his memory of the evening, after his tenth.

'. . . Any agents receiving? Goddammit.'

The sound of the Premier Sentinel agent's voice on the radio shocked Lyle out of his maudlin thoughts.

'Drones . . . currently in some Hicksville backwater . . . Is anyone fucking out there?'

Lyle made a grab for the radio.

'This is Agent Kirby, agent number 345. Receiving.'

Only crackle answered; he'd lost him again. Lyle hadn't seen Jake Pembroke since their training at the Orchid Tower, almost thirty years earlier. He'd been an insufferable prick even then, collecting kudos and commendations as easily as bag ladies harvest trash. Lyle always knew Pembroke was destined for better things than him. Now Uno had made him Premier and anointed him as the Scourge, but the rest of the recruits had called him Jake the Jerk-off, back then. Part jealousy, part truth.

The car door opened. Lyle's partner Martin Donohue sat down heavily. He manoeuvred his sizeable beer belly back into the driver's seat, making the whole car shake. Lyle groaned as a wave of seasickness made its way from his stomach, up his throat and finally ricocheted like a ping pong ball around his throbbing skull.

Martin gave Lyle a cheery grin. 'Sorry.'

Younger than Lyle by about ten years, Martin was in just as bad shape as his superior. Worse, even. His eyes were bloodshot and he had one of those goddamn hipster beards. It looked like he'd hacked at it himself with a pair of hedge clippers. They could both be poster boys for the ingrained sadness of widowers, men cut adrift from a feminine influence. Despite this, Martin was one of those 'glass half full' types, even though his wife was also dead.

'I got you an orange juice, good for hangovers.'

Lyle smiled. It was thoughtful of him. His own dead wife was all Lyle could think about these days, so he wasn't too sure why Martin wasn't constantly preoccupied by the same thing. Like Lyle, Martin had been the one who'd had to kill his. It was common ground, something that bonded them: 'The act of killing one's wife / What is uxoricide?' Lyle had learned that word on *Jeopardy*. He had scanned Carolyn with the iHex when she was sleeping and, to his horror, his hunch had been proved correct. Their wives had put them in an impossible position; practising witchcraft while married to Sentinel. He and Martin had been asked to choose between the job or their women. What were they were supposed to do? If they'd turned a blind eye, both of them would be dead too. It was just the way of things.

Back in the US, both men had enjoyed a much higher station. After their wives' deaths, no one trusted them, despite their sacrifice. Lyle could understand it. He'd been married to Carolyn for over a decade; how could he not have known she was a Crystal witch? Would he *ever* have known, had Hopkins not been elected? When the Safeguard Initiative had come in, all Sentinel agents were warned it was estimated one in twenty-five of them would discover some kind of witch amongst their female relatives. The rules were clear: should you find your wife, daughters, sisters-in-law, cousins or nieces practising *any* kind of witchcraft (including Kitchen witchery), the agent in question had to prove himself loyal to the Sentinel by dispatching her.

'Just heard the Scourge on the radio.'

Lyle's partner groaned; he was no fan of Pembroke either. Martin held up his phone. He must have got some signal outside the car or in the service station, because an APB was displayed on the screen. On it, a picture of a man in his late forties and a young woman of about twenty.

'Some Chinks are supposed to be on the road down here. A father and daughter. She's supposedly Elemental.'

Lyle scoffed. 'It'll be yet another false alarm. There haven't been any new Elementals reported in months. Someone probably pissed a Goody off and she's turned them in for revenge. You know what it's like down here.'

'You're probably right.' Martin yawned.

They peered through the dim light. The parking lot was more or less empty. Dusk had fallen at speed, just like it always did in March in the West Country. Lyle chugged back his own orange juice. Shit, maybe they better check, just to be sure.

'We could sweep the bathrooms in a minute?'

'Yeah, sure.'

Lyle shifted his numb ass. He didn't want to get out of the car. He wasn't one for rules, not really. He'd only joined the Sentinel because his father had been a decorated officer. The life had appealed to the young Lyle, the regimen of it. The money was also good. Plus there was something about putting toxic witches down. It felt good to make the world a safer place.

'Come on then.' Martin leant on the door, clambering back out. 'Fresh air will do you good, eh?'

Lyle pulled himself out of the car, joints creaking. 'Not much fresh air in a rest stop bathroom, partner.'

As he stood up, he saw a dark vehicle sail past the lorry park and towards the trees beyond. Lyle and the Sentinel vehicle were shielded from the other driver's view by a big red truck emblazoned with WALKERS, but he could see the occupants of the other vehicle clearly.

Martin stopped by the bonnet of their car. 'Hey, boss . . . ?'

Lyle held up a fist, stopping Martin in his tracks. His eyes narrowed as he took in the blond driver. He was a young guy, lean and strong like Lyle himself had been back in the academy. The guy drove too fast for a parking lot, with the assuredness of someone who could stop at split-second notice. Lyle knew the young buck would be able to slam his foot on the accelerator and peel off again just as quick. Next to him on the passenger seat was a Latina with flowing dark hair. The man behind the wheel manoeuvred their car into a parking space.

Lyle had a talent for remembering faces on the spot. He'd seen both this guy and girl before, he was sure of it. He snatched Martin's phone from his hand. His partner didn't object; he was used to his superior doing such things. The Sentinel app was still open. Lyle called up the APBs that had gone out in the past few days. He didn't have to scroll far.

There he was, bold as brass: Sentinel agent 722, Ethan Weber. Last heard of as a Sentinel penal guard at the Our Lady of Nazareth in the US, breaking goddamn Crystal witches out of jail with all those other treacherous cuck males who'd somehow lost their minds. There was a picture of the Latina, too, taken a few years back: Adelita Garcia. An involuntary smile pulled at Lyle's lips. Weber and Garcia were both on the Sentinel's *Most Wanted* list. That beat chasing yet another fake Elemental sighting any day. Something to rub in the Scourge's face at last.

'Martin, twelve o' clock,' Lyle growled.

His partner did not need telling twice. They both snatched their firearms from their jacket pockets and, keeping low, made their way through the trucks towards the fugitives.

TWELVE

Devon, UK

The Scourge looked around the grubby old English farm-house and pressed a clean handkerchief to his mouth and nose. The smell of burned meat hung in the air. He'd had to deploy the Sentinel drones over the British countryside himself that morning; none of the clueless fuckers had put any birds in the air. One had picked up the small heat bloom from the pyre that afternoon.

It was now close to five o'clock, meaning the girl had a full head start of twenty-four hours. It had taken the Scourge longer than he cared to admit to find the farmhouse. To his chagrin he discovered only some of the dirt-track lanes were covered by satellite navigation. He'd had to resort to an old-school paper map. As soon as he'd seen the anti-witch graffiti daubed on the barn door, the Scourge's gut told him he was in the right place.

The British redneck girl sat on a wooden stool, her face twisted in a furious grimace. She was little more than a child, but she had another kid resting on her lap. She was not scared of them. The Scourge couldn't work out if she was brave, or too young and stupid. She'd come out fighting when they'd drawn up outside the farmhouse, firing a shotgun in the air and yelling at them, spittle on her lips. A little hellcat madam, not ladylike at all. He would have snapped a halo on her, but it would make no difference; the iHex had revealed she was just a Legacy.

'Who's that on the pyre?'

Carter put one foot up on the chair opposite the girl, leant closer. The redneck just stared at him, an amused sneer on her face. The rookie sergeant couldn't intimidate anything; he looked like fricking Donny Osmond. He'd called for more back-up and received nothing but static. Carter had made little progress; he'd been trying to get answers out of the girl for the best part of an hour. During that time the Scourge had conducted a thorough search of the property and noted the fresh tyre tracks and space for a missing vehicle in the barn.

'Fuck off,' the girl said, for the umpteenth time.

The windows of the farmhouse were smeared with grime; literal shit had been trampled into the carpets. The Scourge was pretty sure he'd seen a mouse or rat race along the dented skirting board out of the corner of his eye a moment ago. *Jesus.* He dropped his handkerchief.

'Enough!' the Scourge hollered.

He was gratified to see the girl flinch in anticipation as he swept across the room towards her; she obviously thought he was going to backhand her. He didn't.

Instead, he grabbed the girl's child under its arms and wrenched it from her grasp. Shocked, the baby emitted a high-pitched squeal. The girl matched it, howling in fury and fear. She bared her teeth like an animal as they were separated. She jumped up, kicking out at the Scourge with her boots.

Carter caught her flailing arms and pinned one behind her back. Her whole demeanour changed; her body language slumped as she realised even an eleven-stone weakling like

Carter could best her. The two of them followed the Scourge out of the farmhouse through the front stable door.

The Scourge held the child like one might a leaking garbage bag: at arm's length, in distaste. It was a child conceived in sin, he could tell; not one of God's little angels. He should snap its neck right now and save everyone the trouble of this boy and his Lolita mother.

But he had a better idea.

'You will tell us what we want to know.' The Scourge only raised his voice as loud as he needed above the crackling of the flames on the pyre. 'You cooperate, we will leave you here, to your own devices. No child services. But if you don't ...'

He let the threat land.

The girl must have read the Scourge's intentions on his face, because her eyes bulged in horror. She renewed her struggles against Carter.

'No! No, don't!' the redneck girl screamed.

His expression blank, the Scourge held the bawling baby towards the flames. He didn't let go, but all he needed to do was simply loosen his grip. The child would pitch face-first into the pyre to join whomever was on there. He was careful to ensure he didn't hold it too close, but the baby felt the lick of heat on its skin and shrieked louder. Its face was cherry-red with the raise in temperature and exertion.

'Please, don't! I'll tell you! Whatever you want!'

'Who is on the pyre?' The proximity of the fire made the Scourge feel a little uncomfortable himself, but he did not move out of the way of the flames yet. They'd wasted enough time trying to interrogate this mini yokel.

Tears made clean tracks down the girl's face. 'My mum.'

Disappointing. The Scourge had harboured a secret hope this crazy little bitch might have shot the Sus and burned them. But that would be too neat. Oh, well.

'Who took the car from the barn?'

'Some Chinese guy,' the girl snivelled.

'British Chinese?' The Scourge needed the confirmation. He didn't give a fuck about the correct term, but the last thing he needed was a weird coincidence sending him off in the wrong direction. 'His name is Daniel Su. London accent?'

The girl shrugged. 'Yeah, whatever. He sounded like he was from upcountry. I don't know him. OK? You can't blame me for that. He just rocked up here, same as you. Him and his daughter. Now give me my baby!'

The Scourge nodded. 'One last thing. Where did they go?'

The girl took a shuddery breath as she considered her betrayal for all of a microsecond. As the Scourge had bet, it was no contest. She chose her child, like any mother would. That was what women were supposed to do. The little whore got that right, at least.

'Taunton Deane services.'

'What's that?' the Scourge barked at Carter.

Carter's eyes raised skywards as he flipped through his local knowledge. 'Rest stop on the M5.'

The Scourge was a man of his word; he finally moved the kid out of harm's way.

Carter released the girl and the Scourge dumped the baby in the girl's arms. He could feel the relief emanating off her as tangibly as he had the pyre's flames just a few minutes earlier. But he didn't process that this could mean the teen mother actually loved her baby; he didn't even look at her as she soothed him, stroking his tiny, terrified shaking limbs. The Scourge turned his back on them both and grabbed his radio.

'All receiving, this is your Sentinel Premier agent Jake Pembroke, number 656, code-name the Scourge. All available units. BOLO – wanted fugitives. Two suspects: IC5 male, late forties; IC5 female, approximately twenty years old. Considered

117

armed and dangerous, category three witch. Last seen heading towards Taunton Deane services.'

He snapped his fingers at Carter, who came running with the keys for their Sentinel vehicle. They slid into their seats, leaving the redneck girl and her baby shocked and shaking. The two youngsters stared at both officers through the windshield, but the Scourge had already forgotten about them. He continued his message.

'All responders, I will be joining you, asap. Don't fucking screw up.'

THIRTEEN

Taunton Deane, Somerset, UK

As they drove from the airstrip, Adelita dreamt she was back in jail. She was in the food hall again, lining up with the other Legacies, their purple uniforms contrasting against the Goody's orange ones. The women in orange stared at them like hungry coyotes. Even within the dream, she realised it was a real memory. Adelita had always kept herself to herself and held her fellow Legacies at arm's length, but that day she'd stood in front of the rest of them. She'd toughed it out, hollering and fronting, even as her insides turned to jelly.

In the manner of so many dreams, there was a glitch as her unconscious mind skipped the next bit. Suddenly it was bedlam; a full-on prison fight amongst the women. Elbows, knees, fingernails and teeth entered the fray. Adelita jumped on the back of a tall, angular woman with alt right tattoos on her face. The regular prison guard was gone; he'd retreated behind the grilles of the safety cage. He crouched down and yelled into his radio, his voice swallowed up by chaos as women crashed against the bars.

The alarm blared. Three sharp and short tones, one after

another, followed by a full blast: audio warfare that set all of their teeth on edge. The women were forced to desist as they made a futile attempt to block out the monstrous noise from their ears with their hands. The alarm ceased, as abruptly as it began.

All the women dropped to the floor, Adelita included. The floor tiles were filthy and crawling with stuff that was alive, both insect and germ. The rules were: face down and hands raised above heads. They'd all been instructed upon their initial induction at Our Lady and warned of the consequences if they did not comply. No one wanted to be standing upright and defiant for the next part of the drill.

Marching feet sounded in the prison food hall as a group of six men dressed head to toe in riot gear crashed through the double doors. From her vantage point on the floor, Adelita could only see highly polished boots, but she knew who they were. Everyone did. It was the prison's own Sentinel.

A man's voice filled the space above the cowering prisoners on the floor. 'Stay down, inmates . . . Anyone moves – and I mean *anyone* – you're dead! Don't give us any excuse!'

She knew it was no idle threat. Everyone lay as still as corpses. Adelita's gaze connected with another Legacy's, a few feet away. The girl looked only about eighteen and terrified. Adelita had so many teenage cousins, in her old life. They acted like they knew everything, but they were just kids, cast adrift in a hostile society. Someone as young as her shouldn't be in a hellhole like this.

Adelita wanted to reach out, take the girl's hand, but she knew she couldn't. The Sentinel could be trigger-happy; any movement, no matter how small, might be construed as an act of aggression. She couldn't watch more women die. She'd had too much taken from her as it was.

Hands grabbed her shoulders, pulling her to her feet as if she weighed as little as a child. Anger and indignation burst through her, hot and sudden like a fever. The Sentinel above her muttered a soft curse, muffled and indistinct under his protective face mask.

'I got you,' he said.

Adelita was bid to turn around – '*Slowly!*' – keeping her hands on the top of her head. She did as she was told, her eyes darting around the food hall. The teen girl was on her feet too, her face stricken. So were three other women across the room. Two of them, little and large, were next to each other and crying silent tears; the other, a middle-aged, round woman, had her eyes closed and was mouthing an unheard prayer. The rest of the Goody prisoners, all in orange, were still face down on the floor. Adelita's eyes found the Sentinel agent in front of her as she stopped turning.

'Legacy 85, clear.'

That north coast accent again. It had been him who'd yelled the warning as the Sentinel had arrived. He was not a large man like some of the other agents, but he did have the spring-like tense posture of a jaguar, ready to pounce at any moment. The other agents checked their charges for threats too. Adelita did not avert her gaze from her Sentinel, meeting his scrutiny head-on. His impassive expression gave nothing away.

Behind the mask, his eyes were bright blue.

Adelita started as Ethan shook her awake in the car.

'Hey, sleepyhead . . . Didn't you want a bathroom break?'

Blinking, she took in the parking lot, the brightly coloured trucks, the filling station across the way. She could only have been asleep mere minutes. But she didn't care about any of that. A detail from the past had snapped into place in her mind. As he leant over the gearstick to wake her, her sights connected with Ethan's blue eyes.

'It was you, in the food hall that time.'

The rogue Sentinel grinned. 'You remembered.'

121

Adelita got out of the car and stretched, joining him on his side of the vehicle. 'You like a girl who can take care of herself in a riot?'

'It has a certain appeal,' Ethan admitted, slamming the door shut. He did nothing softly.

Adelita's brow furrowed as she fell into step with him. 'It still doesn't explain how you knew I was a Crystal witch even before I did.'

'Stop right there!'

Adelita's mind rebelled at the abrupt turn in events as two Sentinel agents came running towards them, weapons drawn. One was in his early fifties, the other couldn't have been much older than her. Both were overweight and unfit, their suits rumpled and covered in stains.

'Back up!' Ethan yelled.

Confused, Adelita raised her hands in the air on instinct, struggling to take in where the two Sentinel had come from. She'd thought the parking lot had been all but deserted; just a smattering of lorries and cars on the left side, their own vehicle and weapons too far away to be of any use. The orange street lamps and white lights from the shops dappling the macadam. The gloaming hovered as a breeze whistled through the trees behind them that shielded the services from the motorway; the relentless roar of traffic drowned it out. Exhaustion had made them complacent. Damn it.

'Don't do it, son,' the bald one said.

There was movement in the corner of her eye. Adelita saw Ethan's hand go to the knife tucked in his inner jacket pocket as he rushed forwards with a bestial yell. But before the rogue Sentinel could draw his weapon out, there was the low *crack* of a gun with a suppressor going off.

Instantly, Adelita was outside her body again, just like she had been on the plane. She was high above the parking lot, seeing

122

the three men and herself, all frozen in time. Paradoxically, she could feel, see and hear everything at once. Suddenly, she realised she'd got it wrong last time – she wasn't just moving outside her body.

She was moving between time and space.

The bullet was not in slo-mo. It sped towards Ethan with deadly intent, but *she* was moving super-fast. That was why everything looked so protracted. Her consciousness or spirit – *or whatever the hell it was* – was skipping ahead.

The shooter with the beard had the efficiency and accuracy of a rooftop sniper. Adelita knew that if she didn't act, the bullet would hit Ethan straight between the eyes. She could perceive it before it even happened: hot lead punching its way through his brow bone and out the back of his skull. She could feel the horror of seeing the life leaving his body in a microsecond. She could see his knees buckle and his dead body slump to the ground. She could smell the gore in the air, mixing with fuel on the concrete.

It couldn't happen.

White light burst from her before the bullet could hit Ethan, encompassing it, intercepting it. Her magic didn't send the trajectory off at a tangent. Instead it turned the bullet back on itself. Somehow, the bullet went flying straight back at the bearded Sentinel with the same force. As she'd envisaged it hitting Ethan, it dropped the agent in the same way: brains spurted out the back of his head via the exit wound. The big man sank on his knees, already dead before he hit the ground.

Ethan didn't miss a beat. In that split second, still pitching forwards, he took full advantage of the bald Sentinel's shock and confusion as he watched his colleague's body crumple beside him. Ethan braced his weight on one foot and moved into the Sentinel's space. He brought up his right fist and slammed it straight into the agent's neck.

The bald Sentinel dropped his gun as both of his hands flew

involuntarily to his crushed trachea. But Ethan wasn't done. Almost simultaneously, his left hand yanked out his bowie knife from his inside pocket. He buried it in the agent's chest, stabbing upwards towards the heart. The bald agent's eyes bulged as he let out a strangled gurgle and dropped next to his dead partner.

In the sudden stillness, Ethan and Adelita blinked at each other.

A mixture of triumph and horror worked its way through Adelita. She'd sent white light at full force at the Sentinel during the jail break, sending them scattering like toy soldiers. She'd had to assume some of them had died, or at least been badly injured. But here, it was up close and personal, undeniable. Blood sneaked across the concrete, towards her shoes. A surge of sour saliva erupted in the back of her throat, burning her gullet. Ethan panted with effort and adrenalin, the evening gusts through the surrounding trees and the steady hum of the traffic still drowning him out. The confrontation couldn't have lasted longer than twenty or thirty seconds.

'You OK?'

Adelita nodded. Ethan seemed to notice the blood on his hands. He blotted them on his jacket, then shrugged it off altogether and stamped on it.

'Fuck!'

Anger rippled through Ethan as obviously as the magic still crackling through Adelita. She couldn't understand how he'd not faltered, confused and shocked like the bald guy, when what was supposed to happen, hadn't. He'd acted almost like he'd been able to see the situation from her point of view. But that didn't make sense. Then again, he was a trained assassin; killing was what he was supposed to do. That must be it.

'We gotta hide the bodies.' Ethan wiped blood from his face with his shirtsleeve. 'Doc? *Ada.*'

Adelita snapped back to attention. Her family had always called her Ada. Normally she bawled out anyone else who shortened her name, but for some reason it felt natural coming from him. A tiny shred of normality, comfort, amongst the butchery.

She looked at her own clothes, sprayed with blood too. 'Right.'

Adelita opened the trunk of their car and pulled out the blankets they'd used on the plane over. They weren't big enough for two such bulky bodies, but it was better than nothing. She helped Ethan roll both men onto the blankets, so they might act as slings to help drag them.

'Into the trees,' Ethan murmured.

They worked fast, hauling the men off the parking lot and onto the verge. Adelita's gaze alighted on the bright lights of the rest stop, which was still uncannily empty. It was just blind luck they'd not been seen thanks to parking beyond the lorries, though arguably they'd been ambushed because of it, too.

They rolled both bodies off the blankets and dumped them in bushes behind the trees. They brought the blankets back to the parking lot to mop up the worst of the blood on the concrete. As Ethan took a petrol canister out of the back of the vehicle and poured it on the stains, Adelita smelled the mix of gore and gasoline. She knew she'd somehow intuited the future during the shoot-out with the agents. It had been Ethan on the ground, his brains blown out. She had foreseen it and then changed the outcome.

Even the most powerful Crystal witches couldn't do that.

'I'm sorry, Doc,' Ethan said. 'I walked straight into that. It was stupid and could've got you killed.'

Adelita tilted her head as she took in his words. 'And got *you* killed, too?'

Ethan averted his gaze from hers. 'That doesn't matter.'

'It does.'

She stepped forward before he could turn away, grabbing

his wrist. As she did so, that involuntary white flash of Crystal magic passed between them. They both jumped as it sent a current of pins and needles from her to him, then back again. As it did so, that memory Adelita had seen in her dream seared through her again:

Her anger, releasing magic like a jellyfish sting as hands grabbed for her on the food hall floor. His soft curse under his mask as it struck him.

'That's how you knew.' Like on the plane, Adelita marvelled at how her moods changed around him. 'Why didn't you tell your commissioning officer?'

'Because I was looking for someone like you,' Ethan confessed. 'That's why you were able to connect with me. If I told him, I'd be telling on myself.'

Adelita struggled to understand what he meant, but there was another matter that could wait no longer.

'Sorry, I gotta press pause on this. I still need to pee.'

Ethan groaned. He had forgotten. He indicated Adelita's clothes, splashed in blood. 'You can't go inside now. You'll have to go in the trees.'

'Great.' Adelita grimaced.

'Take these with you and dump them too.'

Ethan gathered up the gory, fuel-stinking blankets they still hadn't got rid of and threw them at her. Before Adelita could consider whether it was a wise idea or not, she'd caught them. *Ugh.*

'I'll bring the car around. Get a move on.'

Adelita hurried back into the trees.

FOURTEEN

Daniel and Chloe walked through the automatic doors into the main mall, blinking as their weary eyes reacted against the fluorescent lights and the bright white floors. On the walls, the digital boards rolled through incongruous loops of messages, advertising alcohol, cereal and haemorrhoid creams.

Daniel cast a glimpse around, hoping to pick out Tallulah. Maybe twenty-five people milled about the shops and eateries: a selection of families and truckers inside the McDonald's; a couple of young women browsing books and magazines in the WH Smith; some grumpy-looking teens playing on the arcade games. Daniel noted that one gangly youth looked up and smiled at Chloe, though she wandered past, unaware. So far, Tallulah wasn't anywhere to be seen.

'Check the ladies,' Daniel instructed Chloe as they approached the toilets. 'She has bright red hair, about my age. She's tall. You won't miss her.'

Chloe nodded and disappeared into the second corridor off the main mall. Daniel traipsed into the men's, his nostrils flaring at the smell of urine and disinfectant. He peed quickly, washed his hands and drank a few handfuls of water from the tap.

As Daniel stood back up, a toilet stall door opened behind him. He flinched, forcing himself not to turn around as he caught sight of a dark sleeve in the reflection of the mirror.

It was not a Sentinel agent, as he feared. The door to the stall opened fully to reveal a burly, squat man in a civilian security uniform. He ambled towards the sinks, nodding to Daniel as he did so. Daniel acknowledged him with a tight smile, fighting the urge not to turn on his heel. If he raced out of the toilets like a dog from the trap, it would be akin to wearing a big sign reading 'FUGITIVE'.

A few steps ahead of the security guard, Daniel trudged out of the men's. He dug his hands deep in his pockets, the picture of studied nonchalance, stopping again moments later to lean against a wall near the Costa. He watched the oblivious security guard sail past him, back towards the arcade. Daniel tore his gaze away before the guard felt observed, taking in the rest of the people. Tallulah was still not there.

Watching the automatic doors, anxiety fluttered in his chest. What if she'd been picked up by the Sentinel already? He had no money and no idea what to do next. The ancient vehicle Megan had given them was running out of fuel. Worse, if they were forced to walk, he had no idea where to go or how to keep Chloe safe. Despair flooded through Daniel. Surely it was only a matter of time before they were caught? Maybe he had made it worse for Chloe when the Sentinel inevitably captured them both.

'She wasn't in there.' Chloe emerged from the ladies, next to him. 'What now, Dad?'

Her voice carried a tremor, like it had when she was a little girl and she'd wanted him to check under the bed for monsters. With the Sentinel on their tail, the monsters were real.

'She'll be here.' Daniel might be clueless, but Chloe needed him to be her father, to be strong for her. There was nothing else he could do for her at this point.

Chloe wrung her hands. 'But what if she's not?'

'We'll figure it out.' He forced an authority he didn't feel into his tone.

Chloe gave her father a ghost of a smile and leant against the wall with him. A second later a sudden blast of static overhead and a *bing-bong* of the announcement system made both of them flinch.

The advertising boards froze their banal consumerism; a familiar icon flashed up instead. A globe in the pupil of an eye, ringed by the motto *Si vis pacem, para bellum*. It was an official Sentinel message, replete with photographs of two wanted fugitives. Daniel's exhausted and horrified mind would not accept what he was seeing, like he could blink and banish it.

On all of the screens: his and Chloe's faces.

Daniel didn't have to read any of the moving ticker tape to know why. Tallulah had already told him the Sentinel were claiming he'd murdered Li and abducted Chloe. It was a copy of the photograph his parents had on their mantelpiece, back in London, though this one was emblazoned with WANTED in big red letters.

In the picture, he and Chloe faced the camera head-on, all smiles. The authorities always loved to juxtapose the 'before' narrative with tragedy and evil. Daniel had one arm around Chloe's shoulders. In the original, Li was on Chloe's other side, though the Sentinel had cropped her out. The sight of the photo, plus the fact his mother had been the one to take it, delivered a realisation with the force of a hammer-blow.

There was only him and Chloe left, now.

The security guard turned his attentions from the screens towards Daniel. He was not the only one. Several truckers and a woman in a ditsy-print dress were staring at them over their coffees, seemingly in a trance. In a service station full of white people, there could be no mistaking that the people on the boards were Chloe and Daniel.

'Daddy.' Chloe gripped Daniel's arm, her slim fingers pressing into his flesh.

With the guard in the way, they wouldn't be able to get to the automatic doors at the front of the building. There had to be a back door to this place, a service entrance or fire exit that led back out to the car park. Daniel braced himself on his back foot in readiness to run and pull Chloe after him. As he did, the security guard matched him, grabbing for his taser.

Daniel shoved his daughter behind him. 'Don't come near us, I'm warning you!'

His threat was empty, the words of a desperate man. The security guard knew it, and advanced closer. He was still about twenty feet away, still too far to make use of the taser in his hand.

'You all right, miss?' The security guard held out one arm, beckoning Chloe to him. 'Come to me. I won't let him hurt you.'

Behind him, Daniel heard Chloe snort, incredulous. Daniel's beleaguered brain struggled to catch up. The Sentinel were not telling the public Chloe was Elemental. Given the potency of Chloe's burgeoning powers, maybe they didn't want widespread panic.

Daniel matched the guard's pace, moving backwards, pushing Chloe back with him. The last thing she needed was her father tasered and convulsing on the floor. This fleeting thought reminded him of Chloe throwing one of those exploding green spheres at Megan's feet back at the farmhouse.

'Dad.'

Chloe's voice no longer had the tremor to it. Still standing in front of her, Daniel was trying to focus on the thoughts flitting through his mind. Could he really get her to throw those green spheres again? There were more people this time. Would she have enough? Even with the element of surprise, Daniel knew one or two of those big truckers would have him in a full nelson before he and Chloe could make a break for the doors. Even if Chloe managed to get away, she would never last alone on the road by herself.

'*Dad!*'

Daniel felt a rush of heat behind him, licking at the bare skin on his neck. Stupefied, he turned to see orange flames bursting from Chloe, her head crowned by them like a fiery Medusa.

His daughter was not consumed by the fire, nor was she in pain. It emanated from her like a deadly forcefield. The laminate floor beneath her shoes melted, pulling back from her shoes, a molten tide. Her brow was creased with concentration.

The security guard and all the others regarded the phenomenon, slack-jawed. A child started screaming in terror. Chloe no longer looked like the daughter he'd thought he knew so well. Now she was a stranger, her expression dark with resentment and fury. She advanced on the people, passing Daniel. Chloe raised both hands and Daniel knew immediately what her intentions were.

She was going to kill the guard and everyone else in there.

'No, don't!' Daniel bellowed.

His desperate shout seemed to turn the flames off. With a blink they were gone. She looked back at her father, fury etched on her face. Relief flooded through Daniel as he understood he'd broken her concentration. It didn't last long.

'You shouldn't have done that,' she said in a voice that didn't sound like hers.

Before he could stop her, Chloe clasped both her hands together over her head then shook them out towards the guard and the rest of the crowd. An inexplicable wind whooshed through the service station. Parents grasped their children; strangers grabbed hold of one another in an attempt to anchor themselves. It didn't work. They were swept across the floor, unable even to scream as the booming air stole their voices. The security guard tried to brace himself but fell backwards and went sliding into the bookshop. He curled into a foetal position as paperbacks crashed off the shelves.

In the eye of the storm, in the midst of the chaos, Daniel and Chloe were unaffected. Without turning back or grabbing her father's wrist, like she had at the farmhouse, Chloe walked forwards, meandering through the bedlam towards the automatic doors of the service station, the wind somehow bending around her in all directions.

Unable to do anything else, Daniel fell into step with her, trailing behind her before he could be swept away too. Watching the horror of the destruction around him as Chloe sent innocent people to the ground with silent screams of terror, it started to dawn on Daniel what had changed in his daughter. During all those years of Chloe's tantrums, her ferocious, self-inflicted episodes of violence had been directed inwards, at herself. Daniel knew that would never happen again. Now that darkness within had burst forth and was spreading outwards, towards others. Had he been right to run with her? Could he ever hope to contain Chloe? Should he? The Sentinel's message was that Elemental females were too dangerous to live. Maybe they were right.

Chloe's gale hit the automatic doors.

Adelita had her drawers round her ankles and was crouching awkwardly in the copse of trees when she heard the *boom*. Panic jumped up in her ribcage and sent iced spiders of fear skittering down her neck.

Fuck.

Whatever the noise was, it was loud, louder even than the motorway traffic and the wind whistling through the trees – loud enough to be a bomb, or at least a two-barrel shotgun. Could more Sentinel be here already?

She jumped up, pulling up her sweatpants as fast as she could. As a psychiatrist, Adelita should have questioned the reasoning behind her instinctive, physical reactions. If she was thinking with the logical part of her brain, she probably would have come to the conclusion it was better to continue hiding, especially if the boom had signalled the Sentinel's arrival, and Ethan had been killed, or taken prisoner. But logic had taken a back seat; magical intuition and primaeval instinct had taken her over again. White light erupted from her and sent her running pell-mell out of the trees, into the car park and towards the service station.

Daniel winced as the automatic doors of the service station flew open. Chloe's blast sent them rattling backwards off their runners with a smash of glass and an eruption of smoke and sparks. Chloe wandered out into the car park, spread out her arms and turned her head up at the night sky towards the moon, closing her eyes and turning in circles like a child. Daniel stumbled out into the night after her, flinching as the doors crashed shut behind him.

Overhead, one, two, three orange street lamps burst in a shower of electrical confetti, and Daniel knew the doors wouldn't be opening again – he could feel Chloe sending a surge of heat through the plastic, melting them together. He also didn't have to look behind him to know the gale inside the service station had stopped, the people inside safe from his child's rampage. Even so, he imagined them lying on the floor, shocked and mute, unable to stand, their lives forever changed.

'Chloe, what the hell was that?'

Daniel grabbed his daughter's arm, forcing her to turn

133

around and look at him, but staggered backwards, stunned and repulsed, as he took in her eyes. The beautiful, deep rich brown of her pupils was gone; so were the whites.

Her eyes were black and shiny, like the dark of the moon.

She smiled, but there was no warmth in it. It struck terror through his chest as surely as the steel of a blade.

'*You did nothing*,' she hissed, then, tapping Daniel's shoulder lightly with her palm, she sent her father spinning backwards, helpless and at speed, like a pinball across the concrete.

Adelita stumbled out of the trees just in time to see two people emerge from the service station, a young woman and an older man, both with dark hair and neither particularly tall. Father and daughter, Adelita guessed. The doors slammed behind them with a strange, unseen force.

At that moment, the girl turned face-on to Adelita. The girl's eyes were *wrong*: black, empty, deadly. But there was no time to consider what this could mean. As had happened with the agent minutes earlier, Adelita's consciousness skipped ahead.

The girl turned, and before the teenager even touched the man, Adelita knew what would happen: the girl would send him flying across the car park. The outcome, like it had been with Ethan, would be deadly: Adelita perceived the man's brains dashed out as he hit the ground head-first, a bloody halo around his smashed skull. Adelita was already heartsick from seeing so much death.

She could not let the girl do this.

Adelita pushed white light out of herself and directed it at the man just as the girl launched him through the air. His flight backwards was arrested abruptly. He hung in the air six feet above the ground, arms and legs stretched wide, a helpless puppet with its strings cut.

As she held him in place, Adelita could sense the girl's

malignant intent working against her. In that moment, she knew the girl wanted the man dead.

Adelita gritted her teeth as the girl fought against her magic. 'Stop!'

She felt the girl lock in on her now. A surge of unfamiliar magic came at Adelita. It wasn't the pins and needles of her own, but a shower of ice-cold hailstones battering her. The relentless shimmer of images of her own mind were replaced with thoughts Adelita recognised were not hers. They were the black-eyed girl's in front of her. Nails, raking brown skin and drawing blood. Her childish fists pounding her small skull; her mouth twisted in a perpetual howl. Adelita could feel the unimaginable pain and terror the girl had been in first-hand.

Sympathy and horror worked its way through Adelita as she watched the nightmare unfold inside her own brain. This girl was Elemental, but someone had muzzled her powers in the past. Adelita knew this was inflicted on Elemental girls sometimes, though her own mother had been fiercely opposed to it, when witchcraft had still been legal. Julia Garcia had spoken at covens and Goody rallies across America, sharing the message that it was better to work *with* Elemental teenagers, not against, and keep everyone safe that way. Not that it had worked.

What have they done to you, sweetheart?

Don't talk to me, bitch.

Adelita was shocked at the malevolence in the girl's tone – and at the fact she was able to reply at all to something Adelita had not said aloud. She recognised the girl, as powerful as she was, still was not in full control of her powers. Her magic was coming in fits and starts, like water through a kinked hose.

What's your name?

Get the fuck away from me!

Another surge of the girl's magic hit Adelita; this time it felt like a thousand bee stings. She clenched her jaw, letting the pain wash over her. She couldn't acknowledge it. If she did, she would be felled to the ground and the man would drop. Adelita could feel the strain of his bodyweight in her shoulders, as if she was holding him up with her hands. But just as she thought she would have to let go with her own magic, the girl's malevolent wave receded.

You don't want to hurt your old man, do you?

He hurt me.

What did he do?

Nothing. Just like always. He let her hurt me.

Your mom?

A scream from the girl echoed through Adelita's mind, making her eyes water and nausea paint the back of her throat. OK, so the girl's mother was a flashpoint. Adelita still didn't falter.

It's OK, baby. It's OK.

The girl's internal scream faltered. In the car park, she blinked, her eyes widening; they cleared, no longer black. Her gaze focused on Adelita, as if seeing her for the very first time.

Who are you?

Even inside Adelita's head, she recognised the girl's accent was British: soft vowels and rounded 'r' sounds. She was local, then.

I'm Adelita, who are you?

Chloe.

The name seemed to turn off a valve; the girl abruptly ran out of steam. Adelita staggered forward as the intense burst of her magic disappeared.

She looked behind her, surprised. She had been concentrating so hard on combating the girl's assault on her father, she'd been unaware of how she'd dug her heels into the parking lot. The concrete beneath her shoes was cracked where she'd anchored herself.

The girl said nothing more, inside their heads or out loud. She just stood there, swaying back and forth. Her father was still hanging in mid-air, though now he was clawing at it, like he could climb his way back down to solid ground. Adelita snapped her fingers and he was released slowly, falling back on his feet like a cat.

'*Bǎobǎo?*'

The girl's attentions drifted back to her father. Adelita saw confusion and fear spiral through the teenager's face as she took in her surroundings. Before Adelita could ask if the girl could remember what she had done, the girl's eyes rolled back in her head as she fainted. Adelita and the man ran forwards on instinct, both catching her and sinking to the ground together. Though Adelita and the man stared at each other, neither spoke.

Powered revs of an engine sounded across the car park, making Adelita jump. Ethan steered their car in a steep swerve towards the front of the building, screeching to a halt via a handbrake turn next to them. He leant behind the driver's seat, opening one of the passenger doors.

'Get in. All of you. Now!'

Adelita helped the man carry his daughter to the car. After bundling her unconscious form into the back seat, Adelita ran around to the passenger side and slid in beside Ethan.

'You saw?' Adelita nodded at the catatonic Chloe. She knew Ethan's feelings on the most powerful of witches. He might well be one of the good guys, but she couldn't be sure his allegiance went as far as unstable young women like Chloe.

'Yup.'

'She's Elemental.'

Ethan's expression was grim. 'I *know*.'

Before Adelita had even shut her door and put her seatbelt on, Ethan slammed his foot on the accelerator. He sent the car surging forwards at high speed out of the lot, back towards the motorway.

PART TWO

PART TWO

Interview by Lucy V. Hay for Orion Magazine, *June 2017 issue*

The Good Wife

Our first lady, Marianne Hopkins, offers her candid insights on why she feels the witch threat is far from over. Could it be only the beginning?

Marianne Hopkins is the most famous woman and New Puritan in the world. Where once feminism claimed the next generation of non-magical women, traditional values have taken their place. A self-proclaimed 'Goody' (aka *Goodwife*), the first lady has become the face of a movement. Women without magic the world over have taken up her example, defining themselves as 'Goodys' in her image.

'Tradition was once a dirty word,' the first lady observes, turning her glass around in her slim, manicured fingers. 'Now, Goodys finally understand and even take comfort in the fact they can't "have it all". Our strength comes from the home, as the New Puritans have said all along.'

We're in the first lady's suite in the Orchid Tower, New York. This has been the Sentinel's headquarters for over fifty years, though President Hopkins and his wife are the only first family to have elected to reside in the tower-slash-battle station since its construction in 1965. I've barely entered the room before I'm relieved of my coat by one Sentinel officer and patted down by another.

'Forgive the intrusion,' the first lady purrs in her velvety low voice, 'we can't take the risk, as I'm sure you can appreciate.'

I can. It was only twelve months ago previous US president, Dr Miriam Stone, was assassinated by the Cursed Light, a faction of Elemental witches dedicated to scrubbing Goodys and men alike from the face of the Earth.

The president's main suite is, as you would expect, a lavish affair filled with original artwork and statues. A lifelong movie fan, Michael Hopkins has a portrait of himself and an aged Sylvester Stallone dressed as Rocky hanging over the huge fireplace. There are heavy marble surfaces everywhere that gleam as the glow of the chandeliers hits them. A large panoramic window offers a vista of Central Park below.

'Young women are choosing marriage and children over degrees and traveling.' Marianne Hopkins grins ear to ear. 'Older women are abandoning careers and making reparations with ex-husbands and children they'd previously ignored on their crusades for personal glory.

'Ninety-four per cent of women have no innate magic. We need to remember the women who do only account for approximately *six per cent* of the female population,' she continues. I need no reminding; I have no magic myself. 'Then of course *one hundred per cent* of men have no innate magic either. Yet the non-magical population's needs have been undervalued by previous leaders. Instead they were too busy trying to appease Crystal witches and Elementals. How could that be fair? Well, no more. The majority have spoken. This is democracy, in action.'

For a woman as blessed as Marianne Hopkins, I notice she looks pale. Seated on a cream-colored couch, she's as well turned out as ever, of course. She wears Dolce & Gabbana and her face is flawlessly made up. I notice her glancing at her cell phone. When I enquire if she's all right, the first lady sighs deeply.

'I'm worried,' she taps her polished nails on the glass table that separates us, 'about the future. It's still unwritten.'

I seize on this unexpected and early opening. Does she feel the witch threat is escalating?

Marianne proffers a strained smile. 'Now, I didn't say that. But we must ensure we do not get complacent. My husband is a great man, the first to use the Sentinel to its full potential. The world has never been safer in that regard.'

But I don't have to push my previous question; Marianne abandons the party line almost immediately. Her immaculate face crumples and she grabs a tissue from an ornate box one of her Sentinel bodyguards offers her.

'Yes, the witch threat is still very real,' she admits as she dabs her eyes, careful not to smudge her makeup. 'As a mother myself, I can't help but wonder what that means for my girls.'

She means her own children, Alice and Regan. Now into their teens, the first daughters will be pursuing their own interests, potentially taking them further from the fold that kept them safe as smaller children. I feel an involuntary pang in my own chest as I regard the first lady's obvious distress. If she feels like this about her daughters when they have the literal protection of the Sentinel, how can my own children survive witch terrorism in such a chaotic world?

Marianne titters like a schoolgirl, mortified. 'Hark at me, crying already! You must think me dreadful.'

I assure her I don't. Catapulted into the public eye with her husband Michael Hopkins last year, I realize Marianne is no stranger to scrutiny herself. The daughter of eight-time Oscar-winning movie director legend Stefan Arden, the first lady spent her formative years on film sets. She mixed with stars and attended parties and awards ceremonies before she was even in high school.

'Daddy always used to take me as his plus one.' Marianne smiles, though her eyes mist over again. It's clearly still painful for her to talk about her beloved father. Arden died of an aneurism aged seventy-eight just months before her husband claimed the presidency. 'I wish he could have seen us,' she says, her voice wistful.

When I ask her more about her Hollywood roots, Marianne's expression darkens. Though I am careful not to mention Arden – or actress Ashley Rose, who accused him prior to his death of assaulting her and two actress friends in the eighties – the first lady leaps up from the couch, as though she might draw the interview to a premature close. When I splutter an apology and suggest we move toward a more mutually agreeable subject, Marianne tilts her head at me and sits back down.

'Women who don't get what they want are too quick to point the fingers of blame,' the first lady declares.

I sense she won't be drawn on what this means in detail. I reflect on this in the moment and realize growing up in the public eye cannot have been all glitz and glamor for Marianne, either.

'My whole life, I've been policed by others – especially other women,' Marianne confesses. 'It can be hard, but I tell myself it's the price one pays for success.'

A motherless girl (her supermodel mother Kristy Bright died when Marianne was just eleven), her father worked long hours as a filmmaker. This meant Marianne spent many hours with nannies, governesses and housekeepers. Not all of them were kind, she tells me.

'Young girls need the love and guidance of a strong female

role model,' Marianne asserts. 'I suppose that's why witches feel so drawn to the false idols of the triumvirate.'

The mention of witchcraft's triple goddesses – the virgin, mother and crone – intrigues me. The New Puritans call it 'the Unholy Trinity' and usually make a point of not even acknowledging it. My interest and surprise must show on my face, because Marianne laughs.

'The Power of Three,' she muses. 'We see it everywhere in our own religious icons and texts, so it makes sense witches should adopt similar. We see it with their Elementals, Crystal witches and Kitchen witches too.'

Marianne kicks off those towering, narrow Blahniks she is so famous for, stretching out her bare feet like a cat might. 'You know, it might interest Goodys that, for all their talk of equality, witches don't practice what they preach.'

I wait for her to go on.

'For twenty years now, Elementals have been whisper-ing about "The One" ... A savior type who will deliver them from evil. I suppose that evil is meant to be us – everyday, ordinary people like you and me.' She sighs, shaking her head.

'We've done all we can to smooth relations, but sadly there has been no significant progress ... And of course no sign of this special "One".' She does air quotes for emphasis.

I ask Marianne if she has ever felt a kinship with witchcraft, even though there's no magic in her veins.

'Absolutely not,' the first lady thankfully does not seem offended by my question this time, 'but it always pays to know your enemy.'

I'm surprised by her assertion, here. Though the Cursed Light have been a problem for over two decades, I'd never thought of the entire witchcraft religion as being the problem. Surely it's just the extremists – the bad apples. So, with the

Safeguard Initiative coming in soon, witches are officially our enemies now?

'I wish it weren't so, but that is the route these women have chosen,' Marianne says sadly. 'I guess you haven't been paying attention.'

(REST OF INTERVIEW MISSING)

FIFTEEN

Somewhere on the A30, UK

The Americans were arguing in low voices in the front of the car. Checking on Chloe's unconscious form next to him first, Daniel leant back against his seat, watching the cat's-eyes glint up ahead through the windscreen. Dawn light filtered into the vehicle.

Daniel's addled brain was still shell-shocked from the magic blasts, but he picked out various fragments of their rescuers' conversation as he battled the oblivion trying to claim him. He was aware he must be passing out for seconds or even minutes at a time. A lit cigarette seemed to jump from the American guy's hand to his lip without him moving it, like a glitch in a movie recording.

'What the fuck was all that last night, Doc?'

The guy behind the wheel was much younger than Daniel, whose own body was soft from a lifetime in academia. The American had the hard, lean physique of a soldier and the focus of a trained killer – a demeanour underlined by the smudge of russet-brown blood on his cheek and forehead.

'I couldn't just leave them.'

The woman had the wide-set brown eyes, button nose and dark hair of a film star. Her face was more lined and she was slender, almost bony with it.

'We've got enough trouble of our own without taking on strays,' the guy said.

'I was meant to meet her,' the woman insisted.

'Says who?'

'It's just a feeling, OK?' the woman shot back. 'I can't describe it.'

'Well, now I'm really convinced.'

· Even through Daniel's haze, he could sense the sarcasm oozing from the man's words, though it didn't seem to bother the woman. She just eyeballed him and shrugged. The man didn't seem like he could keep up his anger with her, either. He shook his head and smiled.

'Sweet Jesus, them afterclaps better be worth it.' He laughed when she grimaced, no clue what he was on about. 'Y'know, afterclaps? Whatever comes next because of picking that young witch and her daddy up.'

The woman muttered something Daniel couldn't make out. He was distracted by the double blasts of magic working their way through his body. Men and Goodys were not built for magic absorption; magic had to find its way back out, into the air. Even surviving magic blasts at impact was not a guarantee of safety. Some physicians and scientists claimed magic was toxic to men. They said it caused cancer, aneurysms and heart attacks, even years after exposure.

Daniel wasn't concerned about any of those right now, though. All he had to do was survive the next few days – and at this rate he was not sure he would. He was sweating and fatigued; his stomach roiled like a barrelful of eels. Nausea threatened to overtake him. The American woman's magic felt alien and sharp, like the teeth of a thousand microscopic piranhas working their way through his neural pathways. Chloe's was just as unpleasant, though at least more recognisable, especially after she'd sent the cold flood through his bones when she'd frozen the car engine out in the country lane. Had that been just twenty-four hours ago? Longer? He couldn't tell any more.

Daniel closed his eyes. Even feeling as horrendous as he did, he was grateful he wasn't dead. Had the American woman not shown up, he was sure he would have been. Chloe turning on him had been shocking, but not entirely unexpected. She'd killed her mother, after all. When Chloe's blast had hit him, Daniel had felt his daughter's anger, pain and confusion with the same white-hot electric power as her magic. The people in the service station must have felt it too, when she turned her magic on them. The terrible damage she had wreaked in Taunton Deane made him wonder again if he should never have run with Chloe. Perhaps he should have turned her in, like those men on the front of the *Daily Mail*? He would only have been following the law. No. He couldn't think like that. Whatever she had done or was capable of, Chloe was still his child. He had failed her up until now. He had to make this right . . . He just didn't know how.

'You OK in the back there, buddy?'

Daniel awoke again. They were not on the motorway any more. Hedgerows and trees reaching their naked boughs into the white skies zooming past the car windows. Chloe slumped forward in her own seat as they turned into a bend. She did not wake or make a sound, though Daniel was relieved to discern her chest rising and falling.

'Hey. You're not gonna die on us, are you?'

The guy behind the wheel had startlingly blue eyes; they seemed to loom at him via the rear-view mirror.

'I'm fine,' Daniel muttered, though he could hear the tremor in his voice.

The American woman turned her body around in her seat, so she was facing him. 'What's your name?'

'Daniel.'

'Hi, Daniel. I'm Adelita and this is Ethan.'

'Adelita. Means "warrior".' The words sprang to Daniel's lips. As he watched the recognition and surprise register on Adelita's face, he felt compelled to explain. 'From the folk song. I'm a professor at the university out in Exeter.'

Adelita grinned. 'I love your accent.'

Despite himself, Daniel matched her smile. 'Erm, thanks.'

'So, what's Ethan mean?' Adelita said.

'I can answer that. "Solid, enduring, firm."' Ethan chuckled as Adelita rounded on him. 'What? My mom chose it for that specific reason. She told me every single birthday for the first seventeen years of my life.'

'She change her mind or something?' Adelita teased.

The goodwill in the car evaporated as Ethan's expression fell. 'No. She died. Just before I joined the Sentinel.'

'The *Sentinel*?'

This knowledge hit home in Daniel like a thunderbolt. He sat forwards abruptly. Like a Mexican wave at a football match, Chloe did the same in tandem. Her eyes snapped open. They weren't black like at Taunton Deane, but her expression was still disconcerting. Daniel flinched as he realised, too late, what was coming. The same thing that had happened last time she'd awoken from her magically induced fugue state.

Chloe screamed.

As in Daniel's car, the back windscreen spidered with cracks, but this time the passenger and side windows blew outwards, sending chunks of glass onto the road. Adelita lifted her hands to her ears. Next to her, Ethan jumped in his seat like he'd received an electric shock. The cowboy jammed his foot on the accelerator and turned the wheel sixty degrees, taking them off-road and straight through a hedgerow. Daniel knew he wasn't able to stop himself.

Daniel grabbed for his daughter's arm. 'Chloe, no!'

Unlike at Taunton Deane, his intervention made no difference. Chloe stared ahead, despite Daniel shaking her. The car buffeted through more dead crops, the furrowed ground beneath them bumping violently against the undercarriage of the vehicle.

'Do something!' Ethan hollered.

Adelita undid her seatbelt and squeezed through the gap of the front seats. She sat down between them and held an open palm, glowing white, against Chloe's forehead.

'Chloe, stop,' she soothed. 'Stop. Please.'

Chloe blinked and looked to Adelita. She swooned again, closing her eyes, her head leaning on Adelita's shoulder. The thrum of the magic in the car dissipated, sudden and abrupt, leaving only the sting of ozone in their nostrils.

Ethan slammed on the brakes. Both he and Daniel went surging forwards, arrested by their seatbelts. The driver's airbag inflated and Ethan's head snapped back as it hit him. In contrast, Chloe didn't seem affected; nor did Adelita, despite the fact she was not wearing a belt.

There was a moment of silence as they all tried to process what had just happened.

Ethan groaned and sat back in his chair, bursting the airbag with a huge knife he pulled from his jacket pocket. As he opened the car door, Daniel could see the cowboy's nose was bleeding. Ethan tried to stand, but his legs wouldn't support him. He fell head-first onto the soil and out of their view.

'You all right out there?' Adelita called.

Ethan's muffled, pissed-off voice filtered back into the car. 'Fuckin' peachy.'

Adelita grimaced at Daniel. 'You guys aren't having much fun with us, are you?'

Daniel nodded, then regretted it. A flood of sour saliva flooded back up his gullet. Clamping a hand over his mouth, he opened his side door and collapsed out into the field, gagging and spitting next to Ethan. He hadn't eaten since the farmhouse; he barely had anything to throw up. Sitting back on his heels, he raised his face to the white sky, gulping in deep lungfuls of air. Momentarily he thought he heard the distant hum of a light aircraft in the sky, but he couldn't see anything above him. Must be his own erratic heartbeat.

'You were in the Sentinel?'

'I don't wanna talk about it,' Ethan muttered.

Daniel let himself fall forwards, onto his hands. He focused on his surroundings, noting the things around him: soil, under his fingertips. A scattering of pebbles. A black stag beetle, ambling between the dried dead grass stalks. What was the technique called? *Grounding*, right. He remembered seeing a poster or leaflet somewhere, maybe in a doctor's surgery.

As his senses returned to him, Daniel let his attention wander back to the cowboy. The American still lay on the ground, though he'd turned over onto his back. His eyes were screwed shut. Now Daniel thought about it, there was a perverse logic to a witch travelling with an ex-Sentinel agent. He would know their common enemy, help her stay one step ahead. Yet there was still one question troubling Daniel.

'Why would a Sentinel help a witch?'

Ethan opened one eye. 'We all got pieces of crazy in us, some bigger pieces than others.'

Daniel couldn't argue there. He was just as crazy, running with Chloe the way he had.

He could still feel the crackle of Chloe's magic worming through him from earlier. He hadn't felt as bad as this since his first year at university, when he'd drunk a yard of ale, followed by two undiluted shots of absinthe.

152

Adelita squatted next to Ethan, pinching both his cheeks as she checked his nose. 'Doesn't look broken to me.'

'Awesome,' Ethan growled, unenthusiastic.

'Is Chloe OK?' Daniel fretted. He wanted to raise his body off the ground and go to his daughter, but his rebelling muscles would not cooperate.

'She's still out for the count. She's totalled the car. The engine block is—'

'—frozen, right.'

Adelita flashed him a tight-lipped smile. 'She's done it before? OK. So that's water, too. I felt her air *and* fire back at the rest stop. Three elements.'

Daniel hesitated. The light he'd seen enveloping his home and that Chloe created between her palms was green, which, if Daniel was remembering correctly, signified another element. He considered keeping it to himself – having just found out the cowboy was Sentinel, albeit a Sentinel travelling with a Crystal witch – but Chloe would surely reveal it before long, by accident or on purpose, and Daniel needed the relief of voicing his suspicions out loud.

'Four,' Daniel mumbled. 'I think she's got Earth too.'

'You're kidding me.' Ethan sat up, leaning forwards. 'That's unheard of. An Elemental with all four would make her . . .'

' . . . the most powerful witch to have ever lived,' Adelita finished for them all.

There was a death-like hush as they all digested this.

'Fuck.' Ethan pulled a bent cigarette from his pocket and lit it with shaking hands. 'We are all gonna die. If the Sentinel don't kill us, she will.'

Daniel wanted to argue with him, tell the American he was wrong. But he couldn't. She'd already killed her own mother. She'd attacked him multiple times now; Ethan had got a blast as well. She would have killed everyone at the service station if he hadn't stopped her. Chloe was out of control.

'Maybe that's why I'm here?' Adelita mused. 'I've been sent, to look after Chloe.'

'Who by?'

'I don't know . . . Hecate, maybe.'

Ethan rolled his eyes. 'Then why didn't she just stop all this shit from happening in the first place? No Legacies sent to jail. No Crystal witches in the angel caves. No Elementals with kill orders. She could've surely just taken out Hopkins and the Sentinel, killed off the Safeguard. Boom.'

The *why do bad things happen* argument was familiar to Daniel. It was persuasive but failed to take free will into account. Human beings always complicated things. Too many of them enjoyed treating one another like crap. Just as many would look on at marginalisation, injustices and atrocities and call it justified, even *the Right Thing*. Just as many would refuse to acknowledge what was happening until it was too late, like Daniel himself had. Even an eternal being like Hecate could not hope to compete with the tumult of nearly eight billion people's opposing viewpoints worldwide.

Adelita helped Daniel sit up. Embarrassment seared through him as her nostrils flared; his body odour was overpowering.

'Let's get you cleaned up too,' she said.

Ten minutes later and Daniel was wearing a new red T-shirt and feeling a little more human again, even if it did read *#Caturday*, complete with a badly drawn cartoon moggy underneath. He pulled a clean fleece on over the top.

'You know how to use one of these, Prof?'

The cowboy presented Daniel with a handgun.

Daniel cast an eye over the weapon. 'Not a clue.'

Ethan sighed. 'Figured.' The new shirt Ethan was wearing suited his temperament. It read: *Spoiler alert – everyone dies.*

The American shoved the handgun into his waistband and pulled something else out of his jacket pocket. Daniel was grateful to see it wasn't the terrifying blade Ethan had fought the airbag with on his way out of the car earlier. He pressed a button and a blade flew out. A flick knife.

Daniel took it, pocketing it himself. 'Just how many weapons do you have on you?'

'A fuckton,' Adelita declared, appearing with Chloe alongside the car.

Daniel nodded. 'So, what's the plan?'

'We're on our way to Boscastle to a coven of Elementals.'

Daniel's brain refused to process this. 'Wait. Are you talking about the Gathering?'

'Oh, you know it. Good,' Ethan said.

Dread seized Daniel. He lurched forwards as he tried to gulp air into his lungs. They were going to the Gathering? The cowboy had to be insane. Everyone in the UK knew what the Gathering was: the biggest and most dangerous concentration of Elemental witches in the world. Daniel had researched this particular coven for his non-fiction book. Information about them was predictably hard to come by, but he knew the women had taken over the coastal village of Boscastle and blocked off all access. If the British gutter press's speculations were anything to go by, the Elementals who lived there were women of formidable power, and had enacted atrocities around the world.

Daniel was no stranger to acts of Elemental brutality; he'd researched many for his book. An Earth Elemental had managed to cause a mudslide that killed seven Sentinel agents in the Philippines. She'd been lying in wait outside the hotel in which they were staying. Two more in Florida had worked together, both Water and Air Elementals. They'd created a whirlwind of water so intense it grew bigger than the building they had been targeting, an old police precinct Sentinel were working out of. When the witches let it go, the water had cascaded down with such force the building was reduced to rubble in seconds.

'You think the Gathering will help us?' Daniel wheezed, the pain in his chest growing by the second.

'You think they won't?' Adelita countered. She looked to Ethan, her own concern growing. 'What the hell is the Gathering? Why is he so shit scared?'

Ethan rolled his eyes. 'Look, I don't want to go either. But I've got an in with them. Trust me.'

Both Adelita and Daniel regarded him askance. Ethan's irritated expression melted. He clapped a hand on Daniel's shoulder. The cowboy indicated Chloe, still slumped against Adelita like a rag doll.

'It'll be OK, Professor. Who better to help with the most powerful Elemental of all time than a whole bunch of them?'

He had a point. Daniel nodded. It wasn't like he had a choice. He had to trust the Americans. He was in over his head.

Ethan rolled out the map. 'We are . . . here.'

He pointed on the map.

'We're miles off Boscastle yet,' Daniel said.

'It gets better. There's a military checkpoint about ten minutes' drive from here. We're gonna need to pass it.'

'Great,' Adelita groaned.

Ethan nodded. 'We need a new vehicle. There was an abandoned filling station a kilometre or so back, we can probably boost one there. Can she manage it, though?'

Chloe's eyes were open now, though they still had that distressing vacant look. But as Adelita put one foot in front of the other, Chloe matched her, pace for pace. Daniel felt a weird mix of emotions, watching his daughter respond to this stranger. Jealousy that Adelita could get through to her with such apparent ease; then relief he didn't have to deal with her alone any more. He hadn't felt like this since his mother had lifted the infant Chloe from his arms and she'd stopped crying instantly, when he'd been trying to soothe her for hours.

Thoughts of his mother triggered another memory. In the rush of everything that had happened at Taunton Deane and with his brain getting fried by magic, Daniel had forgotten why they'd been there in the first place.

'Tallulah,' he said.

SIXTEEN

'Daniel? Oh, thank the Goddess.'

Adelita heard Tallulah's words rush together in relief over the speakerphone. Daniel had rung his old girlfriend on one of Ethan's burner phones and was struggling to get a word in edgeways.

'My guys came as fast they could. They said they missed you at Taunton Deane, by minutes. The police and the Sentinel were crawling all over it, too. They worried they might have found you. Where are you now?'

'Not far from Taunton.'

Daniel read out the coordinates Ethan gave him from the map. There was some muttering on the other end of the line as Tallulah consulted with someone.

'There's too many powerlines there,' she advised. 'Can you get to just beyond the checkpoint?'

Daniel looked to Ethan, who nodded.

'Sure. We'll be there. Thank you.'

'Daniel? I stand with you and Chloe. Don't forget that.'

Tallulah hung up. Daniel just stared at the handset,

looking like he might burst into tears. Adelita could empathise with the helplessness he must be feeling. Daniel was just an ordinary guy, suddenly cast adrift in a world that must seem unbelievably threatening. Adelita remembered those feelings only too well from when the Sentinel had arrived at the hospital to take her to jail, along with thousands of other Legacies countrywide. She'd had at least had eighteen months to get used to the reality of this world, but it was all new to Daniel.

Adelita patted his shoulder. 'You'll get through this.'

Daniel just nodded, apparently unable to answer or even look her in the eye.

They saw the closed gas station in the distance a kilometre or so back, just as Ethan had said. Adelita was glad to be travelling with someone so observant. As she caught herself thinking this, she was perturbed by her fluctuating moods around the rogue Sentinel. Anger. Tenderness. Suspicion. Admiration. And yes, desire. The thought of kissing him in the motel room in Texas still rattled through her thoughts.

Chloe trailed after Adelita and Ethan, putting as much space as she could between her and Daniel. She fished in Ethan's kit bag and pulled his carton of cigarettes out, indicating if she could take one.

'Ask your daddy.' Ethan shrugged.

'Since when did you smoke, young lady?' Daniel said.

Chloe shot Daniel a contemptuous glance. 'Seriously, you're going to ask that … After all this?'

Before Ethan could offer his lighter – or Daniel could ask him to refuse – flames danced on the ends of the teen's fingertips. She lit the cigarette, grinning in triumph, then inhaled – before spluttering like she was coughing up a lung.

'Smoking is bad for you, kid,' Ethan drawled.

Chloe scowled. Before she could throw the cigarette down in

the dirt, the cowboy wrestled it off her and placed it to his own lips. As he turned, he winked at Adelita.

'Hello, guvnor.'

'That is one lame-ass British accent. You sound like Dick Van Dyke,' Adelita laughed. 'You're not fooling me, never mind the soldiers at the checkpoint we need to pass through.'

Ethan had explained that checkpoints around the country had been brought in with the introduction of the Safeguard. Though they weren't always manned by Sentinel, checkpoints were installed in witch hotspots like the West Country to keep witches away from heavily populated areas and link roads. British soldiers might be on guard for women coming *out* of Cornwall, but Ethan was hoping they wouldn't be overly suspicious of people wanting to go in. With this in mind, it had been decided that Ethan would try and brazen it out by pretending to be British, while the rest of them would stay out of sight.

'Stone the crows. Bollocks . . . !'

From behind Adelita, Daniel spoke up, the teacher leaping out of him. 'That's not what you'd say.'

Ethan swung around, amused. 'Oh really, Obi Wan?'

'You'd just say, "All right."'

'That all?'

'Yep.'

Ethan grinned, then cleared his throat for his first attempt. 'All right?'

Daniel shook his head. 'No, too perky. No question mark at the end. Gruff. Think of it like an acknowledgement, a greeting. And maybe add a "mate" to it.'

Ethan held up a hand, as if requesting quiet so he could concentrate. 'All right, mate.'

'Better.' There was an Australian twang to Ethan's last word. 'But try the stress on the "a": *m-ay-te*.'

They practised all the way. Chloe even joined in, echoing

their words as they trekked up the country road. They discovered a battered old pickup outside the broken-down gas station. It required no magic to start, just filling up with fuel, of which there was plenty in a big tank out back.

Adelita and Ethan chucked the rucksacks into the vehicle, though not before Ethan had taken out three pistols, stashing two in his jacket and another in the glove compartment. Chloe and Daniel clambered in the back under a sheet of tarpaulin and Adelita joined them seconds later.

Ethan climbed behind the wheel. 'Everybody ready . . . You OK, Chloe?'

'All right,' Chloe said, deadpan, as the rest of them laughed.

The American turned the key in the ignition and the engine sprang to life.

Ethan was right. The checkpoint was nearby, right on the Devon–Cornwall border. Adelita couldn't see much from under the canvas in the back of the truck. In her mind she saw barbed wire and concrete, but that was a legacy of watching hundreds of World War Two movies. In reality, they were in the British countryside, surrounded only by fields and trees.

As the vehicle slowed, Ethan muttered to himself, 'Here we go.'

Adelita glimpsed an orange bollard and a red-and-white-striped barrier by Ethan's elbow as he pulled up. She heard the trudge of feet around the truck. The shadows of men fell on the vehicle. Frozen in the back, Adelita and Daniel moved as far down into the footwell as they could with Chloe, the tarpaulin still covering them all. Peeking through a gap, Adelita squinted as the late-afternoon sunlight caught the wing mirror.

At a standstill, Ethan rolled down the truck window. 'All right, mate.'

'All right.'

There was a blast of radio static as a British soldier's face swam into view in the mirror. He was a big man in his mid-forties, clean-shaven. He had the bored look of someone who'd been out in the arse-end of nowhere for ever. Just ground troops, cannon fodder, the bottom of the heap as far as Sentinel was concerned. Adelita was surprised they'd been given guns at all.

Another squaddie moved around the other side of the pickup. He was downwind of the big man, his weapon down and diagonal across his body. Adelita couldn't see his face, but his hands were small, hairless, obviously young.

'I need to see your ID.'

Up front, Ethan huffed as if to say, *Really? C'mon.*

The big one shrugged, apologetic. 'Sorry. Hand it over, mate.'

Adelita's heart made a panicked thud in her chest, fear making her magic surge like adrenalin through her veins. She heard Ethan's intake of breath as he considered his options in a nanosecond. Then she saw him nod and his hand move slowly towards his jacket pocket, like he was about to retrieve his ID.

Ethan drew his weapon.

Complacency meant the older squaddie was a second behind. The young squaddie behind gave a shout and ran up to the car, too late to do much other than raise his own gun. They were stuck in a three-way tie, an impasse.

'Sorry, *chaps*,' Ethan mocked, though there was no humour there.

'Get out of the fucking car,' the big soldier growled.

'Nah, I don't think so.' Ethan's American accent was back. 'Doc?'

In the back of the pickup, Adelita needed no further instruction. She shrugged off the tarpaulin and sat up. These guys were in their way; they had a gun pointed at Ethan. She didn't have to do much to force her anger to the surface, bringing her magic with it.

'What the . . . ?' The big soldier gaped.

In one fluid movement, she raised her fist and sent a burst of targeted power straight through the windshield, shattering it outwards. It took both unsuspecting soldiers out; they went down like skittles, stunned. One problem: their prone bodies were directly in the way of the barrier. Ethan couldn't get through without driving right over them.

'Don't you dare,' Adelita warned, thinking ahead. Ethan was ruthless, after all.

'OK,' Ethan groaned, abandoning his pistol on the passenger seat. He revved the engine, grabbed the gearstick and slammed the vehicle into reverse. 'Hold on!'

Hot lead pinged off the bodywork of the car as one of the soldiers came to and fired after them. Daniel cried out, putting his hands to his ears too late. He could see the young squaddie already on his feet, running towards them. How the hell had he recovered from Adelita's magic blast so quickly? The big man was still stupefied on the ground, so perhaps it was his youth. The squaddie had even managed to pull his superior out of the road, safe next to the checkpoint cabin.

'Get down!' Adelita yelled, lighting up again.

Daniel ducked back into the footwell, pulling Chloe with him. Outside, the squaddie dropped to one knee in the centre of the road.

'Oh no, you don't.' Ethan's voice was grim.

Ethan slammed his foot down. The Land Rover wheels squealed in protest as the American pushed the gearstick forwards and gunned the accelerator. Outside, the squaddie fired one shot after another at them as Ethan drove in an erratic zigzag at him.

The young soldier's aim was off. Perhaps his brain was more fried than his body looked. It wouldn't have mattered if he was a crack shot, though; Adelita's Crystal magic enveloped the truck, bullets bounced off it like a force field.

'Aaaah, shit!' Ethan gritted his teeth in pain as Adelita's magic worked through him like a conduit.

'He's not moving!' Daniel shouted out the pointless warning; everyone could see it.

'Then he'll get what's coming to him.' The veins on Ethan's forearms and neck stuck out.

'No!'

Adelita flicked one hand at Ethan. Against his will, the cowboy jammed his foot on the brakes and they all surged forward. Ethan rounded on Adelita as if to say, *Seriously?*

The young squaddie had the steel-eyed glare of a born soldier. Through the shattered windscreen, they could see him advance, his rifle trained on them.

'Get out. Now!'

Then the squaddie stopped dead, his posture rigid. He gawked behind them, over the car. His hands let go of his weapon; it clattered to the road. He swayed there, his body shaking like he was having an epileptic fit. Daniel, Ethan and Adelita stared at the young soldier, agog at his sudden change in demeanour.

Ethan cried out in alarm as blood erupted from the squaddie's eyes, mouth and nose. 'What the hell are you doing, Doc?'

'It's not me!'

Adelita turned towards Chloe, on the back seat beside her. The teenager was staring at the soldier. Her eyes were normal, though her face was devoid of expression. She tilted her head as if she were a scientist regarding an interesting specimen in a laboratory. Unlike with Adelita's white light, or Chloe's previous green, red, yellow or blue Elemental flares, Daniel could see nothing surging out of his daughter. She was using something else, some other kind of magic.

Horrified, Adelita watched the young man outside. 'Chloe, what are you doing? Stop it . . . Don't!'

The squaddie emitted a horrible guttural howl and fell to his knees. His hands flew to his eyes and blood leaked through his fingers. Remembering herself, Adelita did the only thing she could think of. She grabbed her rose quartz crystal in her pocket with one hand and balled up her other one, bumping it lightly against Chloe's forehead. Her fist delivered a burst of white light like an electric shock, making the teen wince and breaking her concentration.

Chloe looked to Adelita, surprised and irritated, like Adelita had only interrupted a Netflix binge. They could all feel the force of whatever Chloe had been doing lift. Out in the road, the young soldier slumped backwards, his legs still bent beneath him.

Ethan grabbed his pistol and opened the car door, his gun trained on the soldier. The squaddie did not move. The American kicked the boy's rifle out of reach. He squatted beside the youth's prone form in the road and pressed two fingers to his neck. The others got out of the Land Rover.

'He's alive,' Ethan confirmed. He stood, staggering backwards a little himself. He leant against the truck. 'What the fuck was that?'

'I have no idea,' Adelita said.

Daniel tried to prompt a response from his daughter. '. . . Chloe?'

'I don't know, do I?' The teen shrugged.

Chloe seemed more switched-on than she had earlier, but she eyeballed Adelita and Daniel with more teen belligerence. She was acting like what she'd just done was no big deal. Adelita wasn't sure if it was a defence mechanism because Chloe was afraid too, or because nearly killing someone really was nothing to her now.

Ethan sighed, leaning against the bonnet. 'That was *your* fault. None of that would have happened if you'd let me run him over.'

Adelita rolled her eyes. She checked over the young squaddie, then put him in the recovery position, followed by his superior. The older man was coming round. He groaned and waved her off, sitting up and leaning against the checkpoint cabin. He looked alarmed at the sight of the felled younger soldier, the blood on his face.

'Looks worse than it is. You're both gonna be fine,' she said.

Next, Adelita moved into Ethan's space and pulled his face closer to hers. He let her. She checked Ethan's eyes. The whites were blood red and there were pinpricks of petechiae haemorrhage along his neck, leading towards his collar. Daniel was considerably better off, but then he had not been driving, so Adelita's magic hadn't been working directly through him this time.

'How are you guys feeling, after that last magic blast?'

Ethan shrugged. 'OK. Don't feel as bad as the times before.'

'Yeah, same. Maybe repeated exposure means we don't get affected as badly?' Daniel suggested.

'Like snake venom.' Ethan ground his cigarette out in a shower of sparks on the cooled bonnet of the car. He smiled as he took their surprised faces in. 'My gramps had a ranch. He loved milking rattlers.'

'Of course he did.' A ghost of a smile tugged at Adelita's lip.

Chloe trudged off around the back of the pickup, Daniel following. Adelita turned away, taking deep breaths to steady her nerves. Ethan moved with her, grabbing her hand. He kept his voice purposefully low.

'Say the word and we leave Chloe and Daniel here, too,' he muttered.

Adelita felt her magic prickle through her, along with her anger at his words.

'We can't.'

'We can. Neither of us signed up for this.'

'Maybe we did,' Adelita challenged, 'maybe we didn't. None of that matters. What matters is that we've somehow ended up with the most powerful Elemental of all time and you want to ditch her. Seriously? I thought you were done with being "on the wrong side of history"?'

Ethan did not react as Adelita used his own words from the Texas motel room against him. His expression was as maddeningly impassive as ever. He just stared at her with those baby blues, like he had when they'd met back at the jail. Like she had then, Adelita met his scrutiny.

'OK,' he said at last, 'I got you, Doc.'

Those words echoed in her mind, too. In the food hall, she'd assumed they'd been an expression of triumph, like *Gotcha*. She'd had no other frame of reference. Now, Adelita wasn't so sure. She didn't have time to puzzle Ethan's meaning; Daniel appeared, his gaze sweeping from the rogue Sentinel back to Adelita. He couldn't have heard their conversation, but she knew he'd deduced what they'd been discussing. To reassure him, she smiled.

'We're still a few kilometres off the rendezvous,' Ethan sighed. 'Let's go.'

They all piled back in the Land Rover, leaving the stunned soldiers in their wake.

The coordinates Tallulah had given Daniel took them to the middle of a big open field, not a powerline, animal or tree in sight. Ethan turned off the engine. They all got out, looking around in the hope of seeing a vehicle coming up the long dirt track that ran parallel to the field, but there was nothing, nobody. Fear gripped Daniel all over again. Perhaps the Sentinel had discovered Tallulah's plans. Maybe her friends had been killed on their way here. An image of his old lover sliced through his mind: dead, a bullet hole in the centre of her forehead.

Daniel watched Chloe by the side of the Land Rover. She'd sunk to her knees to pick daisies, stringing them together like she was a child again. Yet her violence of the past few days weighed heavy on him: the blood pouring from the young soldier's eyes; the poor people caught in the gale at Taunton Deane; her mother's death back at the house. What was Chloe becoming? Daniel was not sure her raw power could be contained.

'You OK, Professor?'

Ethan pulled his cigarettes from his pocket and offered one to Daniel. To Ethan's evident surprise, Daniel took one and shoved it in his mouth, despite not having smoked since university. As Ethan lit it for him, Daniel inhaled deeply. He did not cough or splutter. It was like he had never stopped; he travelled backwards in time with a single intake of smoky breath.

'She's a killer.' Daniel indicated Chloe, on the grass. Adelita had joined her in picking flowers.

'There are worse things.' Ethan sniffed.

'Maybe to the likes of *you*,' Daniel spat. 'You want to redeem yourself, Mr Lone Ranger? Me, I just want out of this shit. I never asked for any of this. Nor did Chloe.'

'None of us did.' The cowboy raised an eyebrow. 'We were all born into this, no matter what part they're making us play. Everything we're on the run from: it's all legal, part of the status quo. So, we have to do what we have to do.'

'Moral relativism,' mused Daniel. Something else that had been just theory in his old life yet had crashed into his reality with the power of a landslide.

'If you say so, Gandalf. I don't know the fancy word for it.'

Their attentions were diverted as a shadow fell on them from overhead. The pulsating noise of helicopter rotor blades powered through the air, bringing with it a steady downdraught of air. Fearing the worst, Ethan grabbed his gun from the bonnet just as Daniel grasped the reason why they'd needed to be clear of power lines. He held up a hand to reassure the rogue Sentinel, his words snatched by the roar of the helicopter's engine.

'It's OK!' Daniel yelled.

'Who is that?' Ethan hollered back, though Daniel could only lip read.

'Tallulah sent them!'

It was not a Sentinel bird. A red and blue helicopter touched down in the field. On its side, in white: DEVON AIR AMBULANCE.

A blonde woman with a crew-cut opened the door. She wore the distinctive air ambulance red jumpsuit with white reflective stripes. She beckoned to them, bidding them to hurry up. Daniel gave her the thumbs up.

As Adelita and Ethan made a grab for the backpacks and supplies, Daniel fetched Chloe. She looked up at her father like she was surprised to see him. Daniel was grateful to see the belligerent, disquieting fury of moments earlier had gone. She said something, though her words disappeared in the cacophony of noise.

They ran over to the helicopter. Instinctively they ducked under the rotor blades, which were still turning. As soon as all four were inside and the door slammed behind Ethan, the pilot grabbed the controls and the bird took off again.

The blonde woman grinned at them. 'I'm Emma, this is Olivia.'

The pilot, dressed in the customary black jumpsuit, gave them a wave. There were neon threads woven through her locs, contrasting with her dark skin.

Daniel offered a hand to shake. 'We got held up at the checkpoint. Thank you for this.'

'Hecate for ever.' Emma smiled, making the sign for the Goddess. Adelita matched her.

Olivia shouted back from the front of the cab. 'Fuck the Sentinel!'

Ethan sat back in his seat and closed his eyes.

'Nervous flier?'

'You would be too, if you knew where we were going,' Ethan said.

'And where's that?' Emma enquired.

Daniel sighed. 'Boscastle, please.'

Olivia laughed. 'In that case, I'm leaving you right outside *that* hornet's nest.'

The helicopter cut through the air across the green fields and woodland, out towards the glittering blue sea of the Cornish coast.

Michael Hopkins, speaking at his Thank You Tour, December 2018 (Transcript)

Like many men, I have made it my business to study female power. They say 'know your enemy' after all . . .

(Crowd WHOOPS)

That's right, we need to know. We must protect ourselves. I have spent a lifetime studying these toxic savages and let me tell you, their strength is impressive. Awe-inspiring, you might say; I don't mind admitting it. Which is why they are so dangerous and why we must put sensible precautions in place.

First, the good news. The amnesty of magical artifacts has been very successful. Kitchen witches have voted with their feet and abandoned their heresy in droves. They have enrolled in our re-education programs. Churches up and down the USA report as much as a five hundred per cent increase in regular female worshippers. It's said this is a trend that is growing worldwide . . .

(More WHOOPS from the crowd)

. . . I know! Great! But now, the bad news. Take-up of our kindly offer of a cure to Crystal witches and their Legacies has been low. We extended the hand of friendship to these heretics and they have thrown this gesture back in our faces. They've made it clear they will not come to the angel caves voluntarily, nor will they give up their magic. They've called our efforts a 'war on women'; some of them are even in the US senate themselves. We all know who I am talking about . . .

(More HUBBUB. Clear cries of 'Geraldine NDeritu!' / 'Get back to where you come from!' / 'Crystal BITCH!')

. . . I can neither confirm nor deny. But witches walk amongst us, so it stands to reason they will be in our government too. Dr Miriam Stone was weak and it got her killed by

171

the Cursed Light. Who must it be next? Your children? Your friends? Your elderly parents? Your neighbors?

(Shouts of 'NEVER AGAIN!')

This is why, with a heavy heart, I announce that the New Puritans must extend the Pre-Emptive Strike legislation. I wanted to avoid the forced incarceration of Crystal witches in the angel caves; that is why I called on them to examine their consciences and come in voluntarily. I felt sure they would come forward to spare their Legacies jail time. But it's clear Crystal witches care as little for their kin as they do our God's traditions . . .

(Crowd HISSES)

But let me repeat myself, so we can be very clear. Women are not the enemy; it is witchcraft we are at war with. Whilst toxic witches may use their gifts against one another and against us men and – dare I say it! – even our beloved, innocent children, we must rise above their ambitions for power and bestial desires for petty revenge.

Now, we must work to correct the balance their female excesses have put out of whack. We must protect them from themselves, just as much as we must protect ourselves. In the words of our Lord, Jesus Christ: forgive them, for they know not what they do.

And now, the Sentinel. They were once the intermediaries between the magical and non-magical worlds. But in these dark times they must be the righteous guardians of all the world against what is now recognized as the female terror threat. The word of the Sentinel is thus: 'Si vis pacem, para bellum . . . If you want peace, prepare for war.'

SEVENTEEN

Near Boscastle, Cornwall, UK

The helicopter had set them down about ten minutes earlier. As they landed, Adelita had seen the field under the helicopter's floodlights was untilled and full of daisies like the one they'd taken off from back in Devon.

'This is far as I can take you,' Olivia had said. 'I'm not flying over an Elemental settlement, that's asking for trouble. Anyway, my instruments won't work.'

Adelita wanted to ask why, or what might happen if the Boscastle witches saw a bird in the air. She didn't. She was certain she would not like the answer.

As soon as the air ambulance had gone, the darkness descended on them again. Ethan's torchlight was weak, dappling the fallen leaves in the woods just a step or two ahead of them. The cowboy instructed the rest of the group to turn their lights off; they needed to get as close to Boscastle as possible without detection. If she concentrated, Adelita could just make out the *whoomph* of the helicopter's rotor blades cutting through the night air as it made its way back towards Devon.

The darkness was like a living thing. Growing up in a New

York metropolis, Adelita had seen nothing like it. There had been no such thing as true dark in her home city. Climbing out on the roof of Ernesto's bodega at night, she had been able to see twinkling lights for miles. Homes and skyscrapers; businesses and ships on the glittering waters of the Hudson. She'd always felt the presence of others nearby, both human and animal. Insects, too. Roaches and rats were everywhere, erupting from behind dry wall and beneath crawl-spaces. An involuntary smile tugged at Adelita's lip as she recalled Julia Garcia making use of Bella and Natasha's fire magic. They would close up the shop and blast vermin from every nook and cranny, Ernesto picking off any stragglers with his air rifle. They made a great team. Pain seared through her chest as their loss echoed through her.

'My mum loved Cornwall.' Daniel's whisper seemed impossibly loud in the darkness.

'When were you last here?' Adelita muttered, recognising Daniel's innate need to talk about his family.

'Not sure. Twenty-five years ago? No. Longer.' Daniel sucked a breath in over his teeth. 'I stopped going on holiday with them when I was about sixteen. Too boring, I said. If only . . . '

He trailed off. Adelita knew what he was about to say, though she didn't need magic to see the future this time. *If only I had appreciated my parents when I had the chance. If only I could go back and show them I did love them; that I did appreciate them. If only I had known life doesn't last for ever.*

Adelita uttered a murmur of sympathy. Up ahead, Ethan swept the weak torchlight over the rest of them, illuminating them momentarily as he checked they hadn't picked up any stalkers. She felt confident she would be able to sense any witch presence tracking them; Chloe standing next to her felt like a burning torch, even without her magic switched on. In contrast, the darkness felt cold. It was an empty wasteland opening up in front of them, yet also intimate and invasive, crawling on their skin and making its way into their mouths, eyes and noses. She was certain she could feel it moving and whispering as they trekked forwards through Cornish fields and woodland. She brought up the rear of their little group, Chloe and Daniel between them. Even though she knew nothing was as strong as the rose quartz in her pocket, she still carried the tomahawk by her side. The feel of it in her hand was reassuring.

'Almost there.' Ethan consulted his compass by torchlight.

They trekked through the black woodland after the rogue Sentinel. It was a steep incline down to Boscastle. In the helicopter, Ethan had described the village as nestling in a deep valley surrounded by trees, leading out to a natural harbour. A single long, winding road led into the village and out again. Before the provinces had fallen, Boscastle had been popular with tourists like most of Cornwall, welcoming thousands of visitors every year. Now its chip shop and ice cream vendors, museum, National Trust bookshop and other tourist trappings were redundant. The road into the village was blocked off by boulders and barbed wire. The women within were taking no chances. So far, it appeared the British government – and Goody vigilantes and their men – had stayed well away.

In the woodland, Daniel muttered to Chloe, 'You OK, *bǎobǎo?*'

Adelita couldn't see either of them, but she paused, surprised. What the hell was that? Her hand flew to her shoulder, but there was nothing there; not even a low-hanging branch tickling her flesh. Then she processed it; Daniel had attempted to put his hand on his daughter's shoulder. She'd even felt the teen shrug it off. *She and Chloe were connected.* Adelita trailed after the group, working through what this could mean.

'I'm fine,' Chloe replied, her tone deadpan as she added, 'Don't call me that.'

Ethan emitted a soft curse. 'We must be very near.'

175

He held up the compass under his torch, so they could gather around and see the problem. The needle was going haywire. It would be taking them no further.

'It always like that down here?' Adelita had heard about weirder technological quirks in rural areas.

'Nope. That's targeted Earth magic. A lot of it.'

Adelita's eyes widened as she watched the compass needle whizz around, a blur. 'Wow. There must be a lot of Earth witches down there.'

Ethan sighed. 'No. Only one.'

Adelita noted Ethan's fatalistic air, but didn't push it. Earth-types were the strongest of Elementals. They were able to manipulate the Earth's electrical magnetic energy. In conjunction with causing earthquakes and opening up huge craters at will, they could also jam radio frequencies, activate ley lines like natural geofences, even make planes fall from the sky. Earth-types were the rarest and most feared of all magical women.

Adelita nodded at the teenager and her father, muttering together in the darkness. 'Hey, could it be Chloe doing that to the compass?'

The cowboy shook his head. 'It was OK until a minute ago.'

Ethan handed her the torch and drew his pistol. He held it with both hands, pointing the barrel at the earth. 'All of you stay behind me.'

Adelita rolled her eyes. His weapon might make him feel like a big man, but that was the most it could do. It would be little use against a vipers' nest of Elementals. She turned to Chloe and gave her the torch, before rounding on Ethan.

'*I'll* go first.' She clenched her fist and a soft white glow erupted between her fingers.

She noted Ethan did not try to dissuade her. He must have accepted she was stronger, or perhaps he really was scared.

Adelita moved to the front of her little group and held her fist in the air like a lantern. Feeling the magic course like a shoal of fish through her arm and torso, her eyesight seemed sharper, like a cat's. She narrowed her gaze as she tried to pick out any bodies creeping about in the trees.

'Anything?' The anxiety made Ethan's voice crack.

Adelita didn't answer; she was too busy concentrating. Up ahead, she had spotted something. It was just the soft yellow dots of fireflies as they danced in lazy circles. Their dance was hypnotic, and her gaze was drawn to it, hungry to watch more. As her body stood stock-still, consumed by the dance, her mind skipped ahead. Her consciousness leapt out of her body, plummeting towards the trees as their real occupants were revealed to her.

There were no fireflies in England in March.

'Incoming!' Ethan hollered.

A flash of yellow magic erupted around all four of them in a circle, like landmines. Adelita had no time to wonder how Ethan could have caught up with her realisation so quickly. A tall, naked tattooed woman with purple hair wraps was conjured up out of the darkness next to her as if from nowhere.

'What the . . . !' Adelita yelled.

The woman's pale white skin flashed as both her hands glowed blue. She shook one of her fists at Adelita and Ethan. Freezing cold water blasted them in the face with the power of a pressure hose. Both of them fell to the ground on top of each other, shocked and breathless.

The air seemed to split apart; Adelita felt the pressure on her chest. A tiny, elfin blonde appeared next to the tattooed woman, the magic crackling around her like a portal. It was as if she'd opened a door from another dimension. She pulled the tattooed woman through, who vanished as she muscled past her. Catching sight of Daniel staring at her, his face slack with shock, the tiny blonde woman grinned at him. She grabbed him by both shoulders. Before he could resist, she pulled him in with her too.

The air seemed to collapse in on itself and they were gone again.

Chloe rushed over, snatching at the air, impotent. 'No!'

The teenager clapped her hands together. Green spheres blasted from both her open palms. Like super-powered base-balls, they spun into the trees, bursting like fireworks.

A horde of children were illuminated, small and naked. They all looked to be between six and twelve, girls and boys, their limbs smeared in mud and covered in leaves and branches like military ghillie suits. They were not frightened. The girl children glowed in various colours: red, yellow and blue. The boys were armed to the teeth, holding home-forged child-size daggers, swords and hand-whittled spears. Some hung back, pointing into the air with home-made bows.

One of the biggest yelled a war cry like something from an old John Wayne movie. The feral tweens behind the biggest girl all screamed and yelled like a rampaging army of the mini undead, running from the trees, straight at them. Arrows whis-tled up through the air towards Chloe, Ethan and Adelita on the ground. One narrowly missed Adelita as she rolled over on the woodland floor.

'Oh shit!' Ethan staggered to his feet, pulling Adelita up with him. 'Retreat!'

'I'm not leaving my dad!' yelled Chloe.

Adelita pushed Ethan behind her. '*We'll* handle this!'

She shook out two fists, sending a shockwave of white light into the first wave of tweens. They fell like skittles, though nearly all of them jumped up again immediately. It was like the residual magic energised them. What the hell? Adelita couldn't dissect it now. Beside her, Chloe clapped her hands together, but no green spheres sprang up. Her eyes bulged in surprise as her powers let her down.

'Chloe, watch out!'

The tattooed woman reappeared next to Chloe. Before she could get one of her water bombs off, Adelita sent forth a blast of white light, hitting her dead on in the chest. The older woman fell flat on her back in the dirt, uttering a grunt of surprise. She disappeared again as the air crackled around her and her blonde friend pulled her back through.

'We have to go, now!' Ethan hollered.

More war cries split the night sky. Another arrow whistled over Adelita's shoulder; she felt its feathers brush against her face. She flinched away, turning towards the rogue Sentinel and skipping ahead, seeing Ethan reloading in her mind's eye. Without seeing the rest of it, she knew he would round on the kids and empty his magazines into them all if she didn't stop him.

'They're children!' she warned him.

He held his hands open; they were empty. 'I *know* that!'

Adelita couldn't protect him so close to her. She hurriedly held up two fingers and drew a circle around him, before flicking two open palms. Ethan winced as the magic swept over him, like it had in the car when he was driving at the checkpoint soldier. White light exploded around him like a protective bubble. She was just in time; a hail of the boys' arrows came down, every single one bouncing off the protective layer. Two tween girls slam-ran into Ethan and rebounded straight off too, falling into a tangle of limbs on the ground.

Ethan let out a triumphant whoop. 'How'd you like that!'

A tween glowing yellow reached Chloe. She shrieked like a banshee and cast an open palm at Chloe, sending the teenager flying backwards like she'd been shot out of a cannon. Adelita flicked a fist out and caught her with magic as she had Daniel at the Taunton Deane parking lot.

I got this, Chloe told Adelita through the magic.

Adelita felt Chloe's green spheres before she saw them; the teenager's powers were back. She didn't freeze Chloe mid-air like she had her father at the rest stop; instead, she pulled one elbow back and pitched her through the air again, like a boomerang.

Chloe soared towards a third wave of tweens, sending out a quick succession of her green spheres like bouncing bombs. The tweens yelled, but this time there was more fear than aggression. They scattered beneath her, some of them legging it back towards the safety of the trees as Chloe landed on her feet, panther-like and roaring at them.

The sudden, pervasive, booming timbre of a long horn cut through the night air. The battle was over. Adelita felt it in her bones first; she stood where she was as it resonated through her blood and muscles.

The feral tweens froze where they were, some of them recalcitrant and angry to have their fun interrupted, though none tried to carry on the fighting. Chloe, too, stayed where she'd landed, though unlike her previous magic states she was energised, rather than drained. She bounced forwards and backwards on the balls of her feet, like a sportsman shadow-boxing.

'Where is he?'

There was another explosion of yellow sparks, like those from a welding torch; the portal or whatever it was opened again. The tattooed woman and her blonde friend appeared out of the chasm of darkness, pushing Daniel ahead of them. Chloe uttered a cry of relief and threw herself at her father. Shell-shocked, Daniel put his arms around his daughter.

'*Kernow a'gas dynnergh.*' The tattooed woman grinned, revealing a row of gold teeth.

'She says, "Welcome to Cornwall."' The blonde one's accent carried the soft burr of Scottish. 'I'm Emmeline, this is Loveday. She only speaks Cornish now. You have met the children.'

In full view for the first time, Emmeline was no bigger than any of the tweens. Both she and her tattooed sister-in-arms were unapologetically naked, though their limbs were not covered in mud or leaves like the children. Stepping in and out of the portals at will, the adults hadn't needed camouflage.

Adelita felt the crackle of her magic begin to dissipate, faster than usual. She let the bubble around Ethan evaporate into the air. She tried to ask him if he was OK after yet another magic blast, but succeeded only in falling against him, drained of energy. Ethan caught her as she sank into him, her limbs like a ragdoll's. He smiled and brushed her hair away from her face, tender like a lover.

'It's been a long time since any new witches came here. What do you want?' Emmeline enquired.

Adelita wanted to speak, but her exhausted body wouldn't obey. She leant her head against Ethan's shoulder; he held her up, his arm supporting her back, his hand resting on her hip. It had been Ethan's plan to come here anyway – his and the Brotherhood's. She could feel the quickening thud of his heartbeat. She sensed the anticipation running through him, tight like a coiled spring. He was still afraid of whatever they had come here for.

'I gotta see Tansy,' he said.

EIGHTEEN

Eager to get them home and back in bed, Emmeline took the children through the woods, all of them griping at the battle being cut short. Loveday led Adelita, Chloe, Daniel and Ethan out of the trees and onto the main road that would lead them directly into the village of Boscastle, or *Kastel Boterel* as it was known to the women.

Still drenched from Loveday's water magic, Adelita shivered in the night air. Daniel's eyes had nearly dropped out of his skull at the sight of the blithe, naked woman who was leading their way, but Adelita found it quite useful; in the gloom she could follow the Cornish woman's pale ass up ahead.

The cowboy, on the other hand, didn't even seem to notice. Clearly, he had other things on his mind. Adelita had tried to take him aside to find out what was going on, but he'd refused to be drawn any more on Tansy, saying only that she was the high witch in charge.

They'd given up trying to converse with Loveday after five minutes of walking, not that she appeared to give a damn. Loveday seemed to understand their words but, like Emmeline had said, she only answered in her native tongue, the language like a mad soup of consonants. Adelita wasn't entirely sure the Cornish woman wasn't just screwing with them, for the hell of it.

'What the hell are they doing, sending kids to protect the village?' Adelita mumbled to Ethan.

The Sentinel training in Ethan couldn't resist. 'For real? It's a genius defence move. Most people don't want to fire on young 'uns, plus Elemental kids are filled with powerful hormones as well as a ton of magic. That's a win, no matter how you chalk it up.'

'It wasn't a win at Stonehenge.' Daniel's voice was mournful.

Adelita didn't need to ask Daniel to explain. The Stonehenge atrocity had sent shockwaves around the world. When the Preemptive Strike legislation had declared all witches enemies of the State, Legacy politicians like Senator Geraldine NDeritu had tried to advocate for the curing of Elementals as well as Crystal witches at the angel caves, rather than the proposed kill orders. Nderitu and her followers had been unaware at the time that the supposed 'cure' for Crystal witches that Hopkins had been touting was bullshit. It didn't matter anyway; no Elemental witch came forward, so with such a high concentration of Elementals, the British had agreed to round up young Elemental women between eighteen and twenty-five as part of a trial curing. After the Sentinel had kidnapped and drugged them, the young women had come round ahead of schedule and escaped, ending in a bloody showdown at the old monument.

The story that President Hopkins' New Puritan government sold to the world was that the Elementals had been in the employ of the Cursed Light – only now Adelita knew the terror group didn't exist. Riots and protests had broken out regardless, until people were shown the young women had taken the Sentinel down with them. Photographs of the dead Sentinel at Stonehenge 'leaked' to the American press had helped keep

Hopkins in government. NDeritu and her Legacy colleagues were sacked from the senate, going into hiding to avoid jail time themselves. Goodys' fear of Elemental magic trumped their disgust at Sentinel methods in keeping it from their door. For now.

'Fuck the Sentinel,' Chloe growled.

At the top of the harbour, next to a couple of derelict tourist-trap shops, was a row of small white cottages. They all looked like something off the front of a chocolate box: squat and fat, with a thatched roof, whitewashed walls and rambling roses around their front doors. There was a well-tended communal lawn out the front, replete with a stone wishing well and a selection of garden gnomes in various comical poses. Kids' bikes had been abandoned by front doorsteps. It didn't look like somewhere a powerful high witch would live.

Loveday told them wordlessly to wait in the garden. She did not knock but opened the front door to the first cottage in the row and slipped inside. Tansy must have been waiting for her, because a hubbub of low voices, in Cornish, erupted through the single-pane window straight away.

Another woman's voice, in English, cut through the air as the front door of the cottage opened. '... And put some bloody clothes on!'

The woman speaking appeared on the doorstep, barefoot and in pyjamas with a teddy-bear print. Like Emmeline, she was diminutive in stature. She looked harmless, like a puff of wind could push her over. There was a forked wooden staff in her left hand. Adelita recognised it instantly as a stang. Her heart lifted at the sight of it – her mother had had one, though Julia's had the antler of a deer affixed on top. The woman in front of them now wouldn't have looked threatening at all, had it not been for the raw power emanating from her like a tidal wave. Her red hair stood on end with it, a green pulse crackling across her scalp.

There was only one person in her sights: Ethan.

The rogue Sentinel stood his ground. 'Tansy, I know, I'm—'
He got no further.

Tansy crossed the threshold, sweeping into the garden. She raised the stang in the air and slammed it down on the grass. Ethan's body reacted as if the blow had connected with his face, to the power of a hundred. He grunted in stunned pain and fell to his knees, his head snapping back on his shoulders. His eyes rolled back in his skull, then he fell forwards, collapsing onto his chest in the garden, arms and legs splayed.

White light burst from Adelita in response. Before she could make any move against the High Witch, Tansy raised a single finger to her lips, like she was bidding a child to be quiet. Adelita tried skipping ahead but was unable to; she felt the High Witch's magic flooding through her neural pathways, squeezing off her own like a kink in a wire.

Tansy pointed the stang at her. The sensation of falling coursed through Adelita, then she was *literally* plummeting backwards, windmilling her arms futilely as the High Witch's magic opened a pit in the lawn beneath her. Adelita landed in the hole, shock hitting her with the strength of Loveday's water bombs earlier. Her mind reeled with the unexpected assault. How quickly she'd become complacent, sure she could always discover what was coming next. Tansy had well and truly put her in her place.

'Stop!' Chloe said, eyes wide. A haze of magic hung over her in the darkness like a green will-o'-the-wisp. More crackled around the crown of her dark hair. 'Please, don't.'

Tansy ignored her. She wasn't finished with Ethan yet. She raised one fist in the air and the cowboy was forced back up on his knees, his body swaying like a drunk's. She circled him, her mouth turned downwards in a feral snarl of her own.

'I told you what would happen if you came back here. I should kill you now.'

Ethan's cheek was bruised, one eye swollen shut. He met her gaze with his other one, defiant. 'Do it, then.'

Tansy hissed in disgust and turned her face back to the winded Adelita, down in the hole. Though no ropes restrained Adelita, she could feel them like boa constrictors rippling around her body, the exponential pressure growing. She knew instinctively it was a muzzling spell. She was helpless. Connections fired in her brain: this was what Chloe's mother had done to her. This was what the young girl must have felt, every day, her whole life. Worse, because she wouldn't have known the reason for it, or that her mother had inflicted this on her as a child.

'I see you've brought me a Crystal witch,' Tansy peered into the pit. 'Some kind of peace offering?'

'No,' Ethan groaned, 'she's with me.'

Relief swamped through Adelita at his confirmation, but a cynical smile split Tansy's face in two.

'Of course she is. Was that the plan, Ethan? Get a witch to spellbind to you, find redemption? You didn't even tell her. Did you even give her a choice?'

Get a witch to spellbind to you.

The words interrupted the sea of pain corrupting Adelita's senses. A long-forgotten memory swirled through her mind's eye. Her mother appeared, there for her like she'd always been in life. Julia smiled and raised a finger to her lips, *Ssssh.* But it wasn't Adelita she was looking at – it was her father, Ernesto. He leant back on his elbows on their bed. He watched her take her clothes off. They were thirty years younger. Her mother's hair was still long and dark; her father was shirtless, a bashful grin on his face. Neither of her parents could see the child Adelita, peeking through the bedroom door in her nightdress, agog.

'You ready, handsome?' Julia murmured, her hands grasped around her stang.

White light crackled between Julia's fingers, making its way up her sternum, towards the nape of her neck. Ernesto nodded and closed his eyes, raising both his arms in the air. Julia grinned and pointed the stang at him, sending a shockwave of light straight into him, making him fall back and convulse on the bed. Julia raised her head to the ceiling as it bounced off her husband and back into her, a blissful smile on her face.

It was said that magic was like a lightning rod, that more than just magic could travel through it. Some believed life force, or chi, ran through it too, creating a connection. Sometimes it was temporary, other times much more long-lasting. She and Chloe had become spellbound when they'd fought at Taunton Deane. Her parents had been able to spellbind too, that much was obvious. It made sense: Ernesto and Julia had been madly in love, best friends, their main concern only each other after their precious girls. The idea that they would use Julia's magic as a conduit to grow even closer was not outrageous. Unlike so many men who were suspicious of their women deep down, Ernesto trusted Julia absolutely. Yet here was this High Witch, telling Adelita she'd somehow spellbound accidentally . . . and with a stranger? That was impossible.

Yet even as she rejected the possibility, the evidence forced Adelita to plunge from that memory of her parents straight into others.

On the plane, Ethan's arms around her for warmth. Shocking him as she woke after her consciousness had somehow got out of the plane.

At the rest stop, with the two Sentinel, when he'd known how she was going to change the outcome, before anyone else.

In the woods outside Boscastle. He'd known the tweens were about to attack at the same time she'd had the realisation herself.

How she'd tried to kiss him, yet he'd pushed her away, like he'd felt guilty.

That very first time they'd met in the prison food hall when she'd shocked him by accident. Ethan's explanation later: 'I was looking for someone like you.'

Had that been all it had taken? Was she so grateful for help – *from a man!* – that she would fall in love with him, bond with him, *just like that?*

Anger, betrayal and self-disgust at her own weakness coursed through Adelita, igniting the fire of fury in her belly. She felt the pressure of the muzzling spell crack. Her own magic burst from her like steam from a release valve. White light spiralled out of the pit, taking her with it.

She flew into the air like a corkscrew, shooting shafts of white light in all directions. She was vaguely aware of Daniel throwing himself in front of Chloe, shielding her with his own body; of the now-dressed Loveday appearing on the doorstep of Tansy's home, her jaw dropped in surprise.

Adelita wasn't aiming for any of them, though. Her light found her targets.

Tansy and Ethan.

The High Witch staggered backwards as Adelita's light struck her, square in the chest. She tried to slam the stang back into the ground to hold herself steady, but her knees buckled under her. Ethan convulsed on the ground as another hit him between the shoulder blades. Adelita felt a rush of their thoughts and emotions wash over her: Tansy's surprise and grudging respect she'd been bested; Ethan's melancholy shame that he'd been found out at last. Images whipped through her mind, one after another, too fast to make out in the moment, then ...

... Pain burst through Adelita like a million green fireworks in her brain.

The ground rushed up to meet her again, tremors of agony sweeping through her torso and limbs. Dazed and confused, she fought to lift up her head.

Chloe stood over all three of them. The contempt on her

face, looking down on Adelita, Tansy and Ethan in a heap in the garden, was unmistakable. She had one fist raised, glowing green. She'd sent a wave of Earth magic back up at Adelita, which in turn had blasted the other two.

'*Enough*,' the teenager hissed. 'You're supposed to be the adults!'

'She's got a point,' Daniel declared, shooting Chloe a nervous glance.

On the ground, all three's eyes met. Tansy looked the best, but that wasn't a surprise. She clambered to her feet, rolling her neck around her shoulders with a *crack*. Adelita rolled over, groaning. She could feel Chloe's residual magic making its way out of her body, back into the earth. Ethan got up on his hands and knees, retching.

Tansy leant on her stang. 'It's been a long night. We should all get some sleep, continue this in the morning. Costentyn!'

A bare-chested teenage youth appeared from the shadows. He was a tall, rangy, surfer-type with dark hair tied in a top knot that stood upright like a pineapple's leaves. He was also unquestionably Loveday's son and was covered in the same hand-drawn tattoos. He chewed gum, his expression blank.

'Take the males to their accommodation,' Tansy instructed.

Costentyn nodded, hauling Ethan to his feet. Ethan tried to stand, but was forced to lean against the youth, whether he liked it or not. Daniel threw an alarmed look at Adelita, grabbing Chloe and kissing her on the forehead.

'Where are they going?' Chloe demanded.

A note of panic entered her voice. Adelita didn't blame her. She may not have wanted to see Ethan right then, but Daniel was a good guy. He didn't deserve anything to happen to him.

'It'll be fine,' Daniel tried to reassure his daughter, before scuttling after the other two.

'They won't be harmed,' Tansy promised. 'Come with me.'

President Hopkins speaking at a Mother's Day pep rally for the Goody Union, May 2019 (Transcript)

I am one of you. Do you see it? Do you feel it?

(Cries of 'YES!' from the crowd)

Yeah, I know you know it, deep in your hearts. At this celebration of mothers, let's first consider one woman without whom none of this would be possible.

My mother was a strong woman, but more than that ... she knew her place. There was nowhere she would rather be than supporting her husband, my late father, Michael Hopkins Senior, in his many business ventures (God rest his soul).

She fostered high ambitions for me, her eldest child; she made many sacrifices to ensure I became the man and leader I am supposed to be. She did the same for my younger sister, tailoring her lessons to suit her gender. Now Sarah has welcomed many precious children of her own to the Hopkins fold and continues our mother's important work.

I see it too with my beautiful wife Marianne and our own two precious daughters. Everything we are, we owe to her. I love you, Mom, I know you are at God's right hand, watching over me now. You are an angel and my inspiration.

(APPLAUSE)

This is why the betrayal of witches is so abhorrent. Women are special; they carry inside them the power to create life, to care and nurture. Only women can be mothers; they must be protected. We need them, which is why the New Puritans cherish them, or we would, if we were allowed to! Witches believe chivalry to be some kind of insult ...

(LOUD klaxons drown out Hopkins' next words; the president tries to continue but BOOs and HISSING sound on the tape. Hopkins waves back his Sentinel again)

... OK. It's OK. Let the children have their tantrum. Yes, miss?

WOMAN 1 (VIA MEGAPHONE): You're a liar, Hopkins! Despot! Dictator!

WOMAN 2 (VIA MEGAPHONE): None of the Crystal witches ever come back from the angel caves ... There isn't a cure!

(The president LAUGHS)

... Ladies, please. This is just wild speculation, hysteria. If you would like to make your way to your nearest exit, my Sentinel will meet with you and take you to my office. I would be very happy to talk with you and put your minds at rest?

WOMAN 1 (VIA MEGAPHONE): This is Magicide ... He won't rest until every Elemental, Crystal witch and Legacy is dead. Then what? Do you think he will just disband the Sentinel when the job is done?

WOMAN 2 (VIA MEGAPHONE): No way! He will take anything else he wants ... How long before he comes for YOU?

(FEEDBACK SQUEALS from the microphone; the crowd winces)

Sorry, folks. Just a few technical problems there due to interference thanks to the non-regulation megaphone our protestors brought in. If we can get back to the matter in hand, I—

(FLAMES ENGULF THE STAGE. GUNSHOT SOUNDS, ALARMS, PEOPLE SCREAMING)

BLACK SCREEN.

NEWSCASTER IN STUDIO: Er ... We seem to have lost the broadcast from President Hopkins' team at the Orchid Tower, New York for the Goody Union's Mother's Day celebration. It would appear two Fire Elementals may have somehow infiltrated the crowd there. Whether they were the ones with the megaphone, we can't say at the moment. More as we get it. Join us in a prayer in the meantime for all those affected and the hope we have not lost a second president to the Cursed Light. May God protect him and all the innocents.

< @CyrusFrost entered Pentagram >

< @TwinFU1 entered Pentagram >

@CyrusFrost: I saw the news. You get him?

@TwinFU2: Negative. We were so close. But he had his human shield of expendables up around him too fast.

@CyrusFrost: Damn.

<@TwinFU2 is typing>

Hopkins is ██████████████ Why the hell do guys join the Sentinel to protect ██████████████

@CyrusFrost: Beats me. ██████████████ How is @TwinFU1?

@TwinFU2: She's fine. We got separated in the panic. She made it out the Goody Union though, same as me. We should be meeting back up in ██████████████ We're gonna need some help getting across the border, there's suits crawling around here like germs.

@CyrusFrost: Our generous sponsors can help with that. Tell me what you need and I'll make it happen.

(REST OF DOCUMENT REDACTED)

NINETEEN

Boscastle, Cornwall, UK

Adelita and Chloe were shown to a small, empty cottage a few doors down from Tansy's. It was a two-up, two-down, dark but homely, with an open fireplace like something out of a Grimm's fairy tale. After the reveal of Ethan's betrayal, Adelita was certain she would not be able to sleep as thoughts of him pinged around her head like fireworks. Her body had other ideas, though. She and Chloe fell onto the small double bed that smelled of mothballs and dust. They were asleep as soon as their heads touched the pillows.

Like in the car, Adelita was visited by another vivid dream, but this time it was not a memory she recognised. She found herself in a plush hotel room; the urban sprawl of London, the Shard and the Eye clear in the distance through a large window. The room was dominated by a king-size bed and an extra-large TV, with an empty champagne bottle in an ice bucket on the side. Through a door, she could make out an en suite bathroom with marble counters, and shiny black and chrome fittings. Even inside the dream, she was aware she'd never been in such a place. In fact, Adelita wasn't there at all;

she was just a floating presence, there and yet not, just like she'd been in the plane.

She was up at the ceiling, looking down at a man in the bed. He was naked, his modesty protected only by the Egyptian cotton sheet. She couldn't see his face, nor could she make out many details about him. But she could see his black and white suit slung over the back of a chair. Adelita knew he was Sentinel. *Ethan?*

The man lay back on his elbows, looking at someone at the foot of the bed. A shy young red-headed woman. She was thin, her skin tinged with grey; she carried with her the sickness of the streets. She took off her own clothes, averting her gaze to the floor as his eyes fell on her bee-sting breasts. He beckoned for her to join him on the bed. She smiled and clambered up there with him, pressing her soft mouth against his.

Everything changed in an instant. Like Snow White taking a bite of the poison apple, the man spasmed underneath the girl. He threw out his arms, before stiffening underneath her as the girl straddled his immobilised body on the bed.

His face was obscured by her curtain of flaming hair. This was nothing like watching her parents spellbind; Adelita knew she was seeing a man struggling to live as magic ripped its way through his body. She watched from above, horror working through her as she heard his desperate, gargled attempts to breathe. But she couldn't tear her eyes away; the dream forced her to bear witness.

Adelita awoke, gasping for breath herself.

'Bad dreams?'

In the corner of the room, Tansy was cloaked in shadows. Adelita stiffened at the sound of her voice. She swung her feet over the side of the bed. Behind her, Chloe stirred. She felt the teenager sit up. She could sense Chloe's anxiety at being alone with the High Witch and sent reassurance down their spellbind to her: *It's OK, baby.*

Tansy hauled herself to her feet. 'Morning, Chloe.'

She stood at the foot of the bed. Sunlight filtered through a crack in the curtains, hitting the crown of her head, illuminating her red hair. It gave Adelita a weird sense of déjà vu, as if Tansy had seen inside her head, into her dream.

'You're not a normal Crystal witch.'

'No,' Adelita admitted. 'Look, I feel on the back foot here. How do you know Ethan?'

Tansy appeared to mull over her words. 'It's a long story.'

'When did you meet him?'

Adelita's mind returned to her dream. Had it been Tansy who'd turned Ethan towards the witch cause? Perhaps that's what she'd seen in that plush London hotel suite. But if it had been Tansy on top of that faceless, helpless man, it had not been anything good Adelita was seeing.

The High Witch smiled, but there was no humour in it. 'You want to share something with me?'

Adelita hesitated. She had always been a woman of books-smarts and science, but since her time in jail she had started to trust her instincts. Her gut told her there was something off about Tansy. She could sense a deep antagonism emanating from her. Even if the High Witch could help Chloe, Adelita felt certain that aid would not stretch to her as well.

'Just curious.'

Tansy continued to regard Adelita for a moment, as if deciding whether to believe her or not.

'We don't normally allow Crystal witches here in Boscastle. Do you know why?'

Adelita didn't. She waited for the High Witch to go on.

'There's a theory. A powerful Crystal witch could, it's thought, steal a young, inexperienced Elemental's power.'

'Adelita would *never* . . . !' Chloe began, but Adelita put her hand on the teenager's, silencing her. *It's all right.*

She chose her next words carefully. 'I can understand why my presence here would be a concern, then.'

'Why did you bring him?'

Tansy meant Ethan.

'It's the other way around, remember? He brought me, to you.'

'Why?'

'We need more witches.'

'For what?'

Adelita threw her hands in the air. 'To stand against the Sentinel. What else!'

Tansy let loose a derisive chuckle. 'You think it is that easy? That we haven't thought of that before . . . Of all banding together and going after the senate, taking out Hopkins? The Sentinel is like a hydra. We kill Hopkins, we just get another in his place. Men are such simpletons. As are you, for believing in him.'

Adelita felt her cheeks burn. Put to the test, the Brotherhood's plan did seem unbearably macho. But it was all any of them had. If not that, what?

Tansy sighed. 'You must know what he is.'

Adelita sighed. What she'd seen in the magic blast between her, Ethan and Tansy the night before had shocked her to her core. She couldn't even find words to describe it.

'I do now.'

She had always known Ethan had done terrible things; he was Sentinel, after all. She'd even seen him kill his own men in front of her. But it was something else to see just how depraved his past was in full technicolour. Adelita could understand why Tansy was not pleased to see him; and why she wanted to kill him.

Worse, Adelita was shocked by how devastated she was at the thought Ethan was not the guy she'd thought he was. She'd only been with him a few days, yet she'd invested so much in him. The magic blast had confirmed he'd felt the same way about her, just as she'd suspected and hoped. Yet that *other* revelation had crashed between them both, ripping them asunder once again. She was finding it difficult to process it all; she had mental whiplash.

The threat appeared to evaporate, at last. Tansy rocked back on her heels, raising her face to the ceiling. Adelita could feel Chloe uncoil inside the spellbind; her own insides unclenched.

'Let me.'

Tansy came around to her side of the bed and raised her hands to Adelita's temples. She fought the urge to jerk away and bowed her head so the High Witch could do whatever it was she was checking for. Though Adelita winced in anticipation, there were no shocks or residual magic from the High Witch's fingertips. Tansy made a *hmmmm* noise in the back of her throat, but then let go. A curious anticlimax.

Tansy folded her arms as she regarded Chloe. 'And now you.'

Adelita observed Chloe raise her chin, defiant. She allowed Tansy to place hands either side of her head. The High Witch took a deep breath and closed her eyes. No one said anything. Chloe's expression was a picture; she clearly thought Tansy was crazy. Adelita awaited Tansy's verdict. The anticipation in the air was almost as electric as the magic blasts had been in the garden the night before.

Tansy opened her eyes and smiled, her expression joyful. 'We've been waiting for Chloe. She has all four elements: earth, air, fire *and* water.'

'We know,' Adelita said.

Tansy pursed her lips, forcing back a snapped reply. She kept her attentions on Chloe. 'She has an added gift, too. We call it "psyche".'

'What's that?' Adelita said, impatient.

Tansy smiled. 'You should know, Crystal witch. You have it too.'

TWENTY

Daniel woke with a groan. He was lying on an old wooden bench, covered by a thin fleece blanket. His bones creaked in protest as he sat up, his neck cracking as he rolled it round his shoulders. He turned his head and looked straight through the iron bars in front of him, raising one hand in a sardonic wave.

'Morning.'

He and Ethan were in the old Boscastle police station, with Costentyn watching over them. Illuminated by the morning light, Daniel could now see the one-storey building was not in great shape; it looked like it had been closed long before the Gathering had taken up residence. Costentyn sat in the little reception at the front. Daniel and the cowboy were in a single cell at the back, behind those cage bars. There was a small, slit-like window at the top of the cell. To the left of it, a grubby old toilet; to the right, a cleaning cupboard. A draught was coming from a hole in the roof over the communal area. An actual tree branch had grown through, extending its budding green twigs into the room.

199

Next to him, Ethan sat up on his own bench, hacking horribly. Daniel winced.

'Smoker's cough.' The cowboy shrugged.

'You should give up.'

Ethan grimaced. 'Sure, *Dad*.'

Daniel laughed.

About half an hour after they woke, Costentyn went to the police station door and collected a bag with two pints of milk in plastic bottles and some hunks of bread and butter. He presented them to both men through the bars. Ethan and Daniel ate and drank, ravenous. After that, Loveday's son bid them wordlessly to stand back from the bars. Daniel looked to Ethan, but the cowboy just shrugged again. As Costentyn bent his head to fit the iron key in the door, Daniel glimpsed blue residual water magic snaking in between the boy's matted hair.

Did you see that? Daniel mouthed.

Ethan's eyes were dull, his expression faraway. He hadn't.

Costentyn took them to a small yard behind the police station, which was surrounded by a high wall. There was an outside tap, connected to a green hose. The boy picked up a bottle left on the ground. He chucked it at Daniel, who caught it with both hands. Shower gel.

'You're joking me,' Daniel protested.

He looked behind him to see Ethan was already taking his clothes off.

'You can't deny it, Prof. We stink.'

That was true. It was also the closest Daniel had got to a shower since this whole nightmare began, so he stripped the same as the cowboy, modesty be damned.

'Aaaah, shit,' Ethan grumbled as freezing cold water cascaded over both of their naked bodies. 'I think that prick is enjoying this.'

'I reckon we could take him,' Daniel muttered as he shivered and lathered his skin.

Ethan let out a whoop. 'Dumbledore, you've changed.'

Of course, neither man made any attempt on Costentyn. Any potential victory they might have over the boy was overshadowed by the fact the rest of the Gathering would see it as a declaration of war, and ten minutes alone with Tansy, or even Loveday, was too terrifying a prospect.

Costentyn threw clean shirts and trousers at them after their 'shower'. Daniel's new shirt was a bright yellow and red tie-dye print. The cowboy now lay back on his bench, eyes closed, arms folded on his chest like he was in a coffin. He looked like a corpse too; his skin was pale and waxy, his lips cracked.

Daniel indicated one of Ethan's bags, chucked on the floor near the cleaning cupboard door. Despite his assertion to the cowboy earlier, he wanted something to do with his hands.

'Can we at least have his cigarettes?'

Costentyn ignored his request. He sat back in the half-broken chair, throwing the big iron keyring up into the air, catching it one-handed. His soles were on display as he put his bare feet up on an old desk with moss growing out of its surface.

Daniel hated twiddling his thumbs. Since an early age, he'd always found ways to occupy himself: reading, thinking, note-taking came naturally to him. It was why he'd become a professor and, more recently, started writing his book. With nothing else to do, he mulled over his observations since arriving at the Gathering. The residual magic he'd been sure he'd glimpsed in Costentyn's hair; the way all the tweens, even the boys, had jumped like monkeys, seemingly energised by Adelita's white light and Chloe's magical spheres in the battle the previous night.

Daniel decided to air his theory. 'Boys born to Elementals . . . They have to be swimming in magic in utero, wouldn't you think?'

Ethan opened one eye. Daniel took this to mean *Go on*.

'That would make them immune ... Or maybe they get used to it like snake venom, like you said.' Daniel indicated Costentyn, still watching them.

'Makes sense,' muttered Ethan. 'How does this help us?'

A good question. Daniel would have to give it some more thought. For now, he had something else on his mind.

'What happened back there?'

Though he'd heard no specifics beyond Tansy's accusations, Daniel still knew something had gone wrong between Adelita and Ethan. There was something in the Latina's eyes and posture as she'd watched both men led away. She'd not put up a fight for Ethan, either. Considering she'd stopped him being torn apart by feral tween witches half an hour before that, it didn't track.

Ethan rolled his eyes skywards. 'You don't wanna know.'

Daniel leant against the wall and instantly regretted it. The brickwork was furry and wet. Slime oozed through the back of his T-shirt, making him jump away. Like the rest of the old police station, it was being reclaimed by nature. He shuddered, doing a curious jig as ice-cold water trickled down his spine.

Ethan chuckled on the bench. 'I did that half an hour ago.'

Daniel booted Ethan's legs off the bench, making him sit up so he could sit down next to him. 'Answer my question.'

'Wow, you really *are* changing.' Ethan stretched. 'Look, sorry you're stuck in here as well, Prof. Tansy doesn't like men much.'

Daniel shrugged. In his old life, he would have been deeply upset. But now, he was a little more pragmatic. He could understand why Elemental women were not keen on the male gender, after what they'd had to deal with the past two years and even before that. That wasn't his doing, but he had not exactly stood up for women either. Not witches, not even Goodys. He hadn't picked a side at all. He might have studied witchcraft in his capacity as a theology professor, but it was just a curiosity; it had never been personal for him.

Daniel's confession leapt out of him like Chloe's magic had from her. 'My wife never told me she was a powerful Crystal witch.'

Ethan's eyes widened. 'And you didn't feel it?'

Daniel shook his head. 'No. I guess we weren't as close as I imagined. She hid it from me, right from the beginning. We were married twenty-three years. I never noticed. Not even the slightest suspicion. And now she's dead.'

'Shit. Sorry, Professor.'

There was a pause as both of them digested this.

'Chloe killed her?'

'Yes,' Daniel sighed. 'Li must've known Chloe was different, somehow. I think she must have muzzled her powers when she was just a baby. Caused unbelievable behavioural problems as they backed up. Eventually they came rushing out and . . . '

He trailed off.

Ethan gave Daniel an awkward pat on the shoulder. 'She was just trying to do her best by your kid, man.'

Daniel nodded. 'I know. But what the hell was *I* doing? I missed it all.'

'There's worse things.'

Daniel's quick brain latched on to Ethan's words. He'd heard him say this before, back at the car when Chloe had run them off the road and into the field. It was such an odd sidestep in the conversation. It was the lament of a man who heard nothing but his own internal monologue of shame, Daniel realised.

He took the plunge. 'What did you do?'

'What didn't I do,' Ethan sighed. Daylight was poking its fingers through the tall cell window. 'Maybe it's in the blood. Passed down, through the generations . . . You know, my grandfather was at Auschwitz?'

'I'm sorry—' Daniel began, before his brain caught up with what the American was *really* saying. The cowboy did not mean his bloodline had been persecuted. They had been the persecutors. Daniel felt that unfamiliar seed of horror unravel in his belly again. *Oh, God.*

'The game changed, but my family didn't. We always picked the winning side. My father was in the Sentinel. His father before him. I was trained for it, from an early age . . . And I was a good dog.'

Daniel couldn't accept this. 'No, you're remembering it wrong. Things might be going wrong now, but the Sentinel started off as noble world guardians. They were the intermediaries between the magical and non-magical worlds when your grandfather was around. We needed them.'

Ethan's blue eyes bore into Daniel's. 'Did we?'

This made Daniel doubt himself. He'd always accepted the Sentinel as not only necessary, but the only agency capable of keeping witches under control. He'd been just a little boy when women were banned from joining the Sentinel, but he'd always privately felt it was just common sense. Women were the only ones who could do magic; they had the unfair advantage over men. Men needed to be the ones in control of the Sentinel. Drawing a line in the sand between the genders was the only ethical way to try and ensure balance.

Daniel chose his next words carefully. 'But you're done with the Sentinel now?'

The American nodded. 'Not that it will do me any good. I should have known there's no redemption for guys like me. Especially not from witches.'

'Adelita loves you.' The simple truth of this seemed obvious to Daniel.

'*If* she does, she shouldn't.'

There was still something the rogue Sentinel wasn't saying.

Adelita had known Ethan was a rogue agent from the beginning. She would have understood he had done awful things in the line of duty. This had to mean it was something specific that had repelled her, back at Tansy's. Hadn't the High Witch accused the American of taking advantage of Adelita somehow?

The memory clicked. 'You spellbound with her.'

Ethan shook his head. 'I was so tired of being alone. I just wanted to be with someone so much. And Ada did too ... The moment we met, I could see it in her as her magic flashed from her to me.'

'But how did you see it, if I never saw it in Li?'

'It's hard to explain. It's like a meeting of minds; you both have to be open to it. I couldn't have done it without her consent, no matter what Tansy says.'

Another stab of grief for opportunities lost speared Daniel in the chest. If only he hadn't been so preoccupied with his own pursuits; if only she had trusted him with her secret, instead of locking it away. *Oh, Li.*

Ethan sighed. 'But now Adelita hates me anyway.'

'Why?'

The American bowed his head.

'I was at Stonehenge.'

PART THREE

TWENTY-ONE

Boscastle, Cornwall, UK

It was time for breakfast. The Gathering ate together, up at the Wellington Hotel, a large white building on the corner of the road into the village, by the bridge. A makeshift canteen had been set up in the hotel's big dining room. In one corner, trestle tables were weighed down with big pots and ladles. A couple of women and their daughters spooned porridge into waiting bowls as people lined up. Barring Tansy's own guards and sentry on duty at the police station, the woodland, the coastguard's cottage and dotted around the valley walls, everyone was there. Women and children, including boys and young men, grasped hands around tables as they said the Elemental proclamation as thanks for their food.

Such arrangements could have reminded Adelita of being incarcerated back at Our Lady in Texas. In reality, nothing could have been further from the truth. The atmosphere was welcoming and low-key; there was none of the threat or intimidation that had run like an electric current through the atmosphere, walls and floor of the prison. At the Gathering she could feel only love, trust and support surging between the women, invisible yet tangible, like the wind.

Their reputation had preceded them. Adelita and Chloe's arrival in the dining hall sent ripples around the room. Adelita averted her eyes as another woman looked up from her bowl, curious. She could feel her Crystal witch status marking her out from everyone else there. Though no Elemental or kin had expressed distrust in her other than Tansy, Adelita still felt like an intruder, or at least an outsider. While this should have been nothing new, she felt Ethan's loss keenly. After she'd spent a lifetime standing alone, to prove she could make it all by herself without the need for magic like her Elemental twin sisters, meeting him had felt like coming home, somehow.

But the Gathering was not her world; it was Chloe's. As if to underline this, a teenage Elemental with flaming red hair like Venus in a Raphael painting approached them. She was lighter in her step and much taller than her mother, and she had red, rather than green, residual magic dancing across her scalp, but there was no question whose daughter she was: Tansy's.

'I'm Gwen,' she said, grabbing Chloe's hand. 'Come sit with me?'

Chloe grinned, then looked back at Adelita, as if seeking permission.

'Go on, go.' She smiled, and watched Chloe follow Gwen across the room, leaving her standing in line on her own.

'Morning!'

Adelita jumped out of her skin as a fully dressed Emmeline appeared next to her. She could never get used to Air witches and the way they could step through the atoms of the space around them. Emmeline let rip with a suitably witchy cackle and gave Adelita's back an apologetic slap as she realised how she'd startled her.

'Does Tansy have another daughter?' Adelita collected a bowl of porridge, Emmeline queuing up beside her.

'She has many daughters.' Emmeline smiled in thanks as a

bored witch cook, obviously displeased it was her turn on the rota, ladled slop into her bowl next. 'This is a coven of many mothers and many children. But if you mean biological daughters, yes. She has twin girls as well as Gwen.'

She indicated two identical girls across the way on a bench, at a table with a couple of older boys. They were laughing and pushing each other good-naturedly. If they were tired from battling the previous night, they didn't show it. Adelita and Emmeline sat down at a table together to eat.

'No, I meant an adult daughter. Closer to Ethan's age, maybe?'

Emmeline realised what she was getting at. 'Did you see something, when you, Ethan and Tansy were connected in Chloe's magic blast last night?'

'Maybe. I'm not sure . . .'

The Air witch's interest was diverted as Loveday sidled over. The Water witch sat down next to them and kissed Emmeline on the lips with gusto. She broke away and flashed them both a mouthful of gold teeth, as if to say *What did I miss?*

'Adelita was asking about Demelza,' Emmeline explained.

Demelza. The word seemed to break something open in Adelita's brain. An image of Tansy appeared in her mind's eye, understanding unfurling with it. Demelza had been Tansy's eldest daughter, her firstborn. She'd been little more than a girl herself when she had her. The darkness Adelita had perceived in the High Witch in the bedroom that morning was not threat, but loss: *Demelza was dead.*

'She died at Stonehenge,' Emmeline confirmed.

Adelita closed her eyes. This only got worse. So that must be why Tansy hated Ethan so much, since he had been there. This realisation made something else click: she knew, deep in her gut, her strange dream had depicted an event that predated Stonehenge. The young woman was not Demelza. It was Tansy,

211

as she suspected, just much younger . . . But then who was the man in the bed? And what was Tansy doing to him?

Emmeline looked at the clock on the wall. 'Time to go.'

The three of them cleared their trays and Adelita called Chloe over. They left the hotel, stepping out into the morning sunlight. Gwen came trailing after them, uninvited, and the five of them fell into step with other women, children and teenagers swarming their way through the valley.

The Gathering was municipal; Adelita was quickly realising that everyone did everything together, for safety as well as community. A couple of teachers shepherded bright-eyed children towards the primary school building; some male youths disappeared inside the Cobweb Inn where they would be making rope and whittling spears and arrows. A small group of Elemental teen girls and young women ran up to the old tourist car park to practise their magic. They laughed and threw magic at each other until a group of stern, older Elemental women outside the broken-down community shop yelled at them in no uncertain terms to cut it out. The girls smothered grins behind their hands and walked sensibly past the women, until one of the teens yelled, 'Crones!' and they all erupted into hysterics, racing off again before the older women could retaliate.

Adelita and the others wandered down the slate path towards the natural enclosed harbour. The tide was out, leaving old fishing vessels, chains and multicoloured buoys stranded on the shoreline. The sky above them was bright blue, the March air crisp and cold, even as sun shone on the rock pools.

In the middle of the shale, Tansy stood, leaning on her stang as ever.

'Ladies,' she smiled, 'ready to train?'

'Try again.'

Tansy stood back, hands by her sides, eyes closed. Chloe and

Adelita exchanged a look. Loveday and Emmeline kicked at the shale with their boots. Gwen looked visibly bored. It had been a long, frustrating afternoon.

When nothing was forthcoming from either Chloe or Adelita, Tansy opened her eyes, exasperated. 'You can't hurt me, you know.'

Adelita wanted to beg to differ. She'd felt Tansy's shocked surprise when she'd blasted her and Ethan together shortly after their arrival in Boscastle. That said, she also knew any pain Tansy had felt was on the scale of being stung by a bee, so it probably didn't count. She slipped her hand in her pocket and gripped her rose quartz. She focused on the white light inside herself and pushed it out, straight at Tansy.

It fell short, dribbling onto the shale in a pathetic spiral.

'Maybe she should be sky-clad,' Emmeline said.

'No, that's only yours and Loveday's thing.'

Tansy's tone indicated she had fielded this suggestion from her two generals a million times before. The other women grinned. They held their bodies close together, their hands in the back pockets of each other's jeans. Adelita could see their shared history as plain as day, without the need for any witchcraft connections. They reminded Adelita of the Spartans, going into battle, their love making them even more valiant.

'Sky-clad?' Chloe realised what this meant before anyone answered. 'Ew, no.'

Adelita laughed. She actually didn't mind getting naked if it meant she could access her magic as powerfully as before. But she knew her clothes were not the issue. She tried again, but this time nothing came out of her at all.

Tansy tutted. 'You're distracted, Crystal witch. This is what happens when you let thoughts of men pollute your brain.'

Even though she was pissed at Ethan, Adelita felt irritation flush through her like a thousand pinpricks. Who the hell did

Tansy think she was? She didn't know a goddamn thing about her! *High and mighty bitch!*

A sudden burst of white light flashed out of her, stronger than before. It made Tansy step backwards, chuckling.

'Better, better. You know your problem?'

Adelita clenched her teeth. Her angry pride made her belligerent and brought her magic to life. She was glad to feel it coursing through her veins again.

'I'm sure you'll tell me.'

Tansy knocked a palm against Adelita's forehead. 'You are bound by *this* too much. Head over heart.'

Adelita tried to absorb Tansy's lesson. It was true she always preferred to take the logical approach where she could. It was why she went into medicine and hadn't been interested in magic when she was younger. But she also seemed to direct her Crystal magic with anger – surely that showed she was in touch with her emotions? And didn't her accidental spellbinding with Ethan show she was heart over head in some aspects?

'I don't understand,' she admitted.

'No. You don't.' Tansy's reply was maddening, but Adelita had no time to quiz her. The High Witch turned to Chloe. 'Now, you try.'

Chloe clapped her hands together, but no green spheres came, just like that first night against the feral tweens. Adelita felt panic burst through Chloe, bringing with it a hundred tiny flames with the power of hundreds of struck matches in one go.

The teen shrieked with surprise and fear and sent them flipping through the air. This only fed the individual fires and sent them spewing forth with the power of a flame-thrower in all directions. Loveday, Emmeline and Gwen screamed, ducking futilely for cover. When they were not barbecued, they looked up in wonder and disbelief.

Both Adelita and Tansy had created a protective bubble

around them. Adelita nodded as she made the realisation: the High Witch was skipping ahead, like her.

'You have psyche too.'

'Yes,' Tansy replied.

'I nearly killed them!'

Chloe collapsed to her knees, sobbing in the shale. Adelita followed her to the ground, placing her arms around the girl. As she made soothing noises, rocking Chloe back and forth, she became aware of more arms around them; Emmeline, Loveday and Gwen joined them on the ground, embracing Chloe too. The teenager looked up in amazement, unable to comprehend their forgiveness.

'It's OK,' Gwen said. 'You're one of us.'

Chloe looked up at Tansy for confirmation. The High Witch nodded.

'I keep hurting people, though.'

'Sometimes we have to,' Adelita said, thinking of the young soldier at the checkpoint; how Chloe had made him convulse, blood springing from his eyes and nose.

'Magic can be a powerful weapon, but that's not all of it. It's also responsibility, culpability, mental peace, aliveness. Something that connects us all.'

'Like chi,' Chloe said, catching on.

Tansy nodded, smiling. Adelita reflected on her connection to Chloe. That made sense; she felt she was supposed to be with her, whether it was fate or Hecate or random chance. She was meant to help Chloe; it made sense. She remembered what Tansy had called their shared, special magic in the cottage bedroom before breakfast this morning – psyche.

'I have a question,' Adelita said. 'When I was in prison, my magic was undetectable, even though I was scanned nearly every day. Why would that be?'

'You have a natural talent,' Tansy replied. 'You must have a very strong bloodline. It is surprising you managed to suppress it so long, even in prison. I guess that's the psyche at work.'

Adelita thought it over; it did make sense. Julia had wanted Adelita to study Crystal witchcraft with her. But she'd seen Bella and Natasha take to their innate twin fire magic as Elementals. Adelita's juvenile, jealous mind had told her it wasn't worth bothering with magic if she had to study, only to be considered half as powerful as her sisters. She'd hit the schoolbooks instead, determined to out-shine them in other ways. It had worked. Adelita had been the first in the immediate family to go to university. She wasn't the only doctor to ever come out of the Garcia family, but the only professional. The rest of her family, cousins included, were strictly blue collar. Not that any of that crap mattered now.

'Mental strength can help even otherwise normal humans develop the most extraordinary skills,' Tansy continued, as she leant on her stang, 'like divers, able to hold their breath under-water for ten minutes at a time. Shaolin monks are able to raise their body temperature with just the power of thought.'

'Psyche is like a kind of meditation.' Gwen smiled as Chloe turned towards her. 'Mum's trying to teach me to do it. Not very successfully so far.'

'You'll get there.' Tansy put her arm around her daughter. 'Just like Cally taught me.'

Adelita's ears pricked up. 'Who's Cally?'

'My own mentor. Cally has her own coven, in Moscow.' Tansy looked to Chloe. 'Tell me what you see when you go under.'

'It's like I am super-awake.' The ghost of a smile appeared on the teen's face, then her expression darkened. 'But I can't always control it. It takes me to a place I don't want to go. A dark place. I'm afraid . . . that I won't be able get out again.'

A shocking vision of Chloe with her blank, black eyes invaded Adelita's senses. She could still feel Chloe's scream from the car, like an echo in her bones. An unpleasant, prickling sensation danced across her shoulders and down her spine.

'What about you, Crystal witch?' Tansy demanded.

Adelita didn't like the way Tansy kept using that as a moniker. 'My name is Adelita.'

Tansy just stared at her, unapologetic.

Adelita sighed. 'Yeah, super-awake is a good way to describe it.'

The High Witch shot a pointed look at the other three Elementals. Gwen looked up at the sun, high in the sky above the headland: lunch time. She nodded to Chloe.

'I'm starving. Let's go eat?'

Chloe flashed Gwen a bashful smile. 'OK.'

Tansy and Adelita watched the two girls wander off; Loveday and Emmeline left too. As Adelita watched the teen go, Tansy's words *Head over heart* came boomeranging back to her. Having seen Chloe's emotional state and how her magic came in fits and starts because of it, Adelita's sharp, analytical mind finally made the connection.

'Chloe is *heart over head*, right?'

Tansy gave her that half-smile of hers. 'It would appear so. You share the same problem, in opposite ways ... Interesting. The darkness comes to you, too?'

'No,' Adelita admitted, truthfully. 'But I can see ... things.'

'You skip ahead?'

'No, more than that. I saw Ethan die. I changed it.' She took a deep breath. 'And I think I can see the past, too.'

Tansy's brow furrowed as she digested this. Another memory flash seared through Adelita's mind. When the tweens had attacked, she'd thought she'd skipped ahead and seen Ethan reloading, in readiness to fire on them. She'd been sure he would empty his magazines into them all if she didn't stop him.

They're children! she'd warned him.

I know that! he'd yelled back.

Then he'd held his hands open: empty. She'd felt his raw fear, his gritted determination and the red mist of bloodlust clouding his thoughts.

But she hadn't stopped him doing anything in that moment; it had been an echo of an event that had already happened ... At Stonehenge. As she knew now, Ethan had been part of the massacre, one of the few Sentinel agents to get out alive.

Tansy turned away and climbed upwards. Her feet scuffed against the rock and sent down a shower of shells and miniature rubble. She steadied herself as she grabbed at a huge mooring hook jutting out of the cliff, and held out a hand to Adelita.

Adelita took Tansy's proffered hand, joining her on top of the rock where she stood looking over the tops of the tall valley walls, like she was collecting her thoughts. Below, the tide was in, and the boats bobbed up and down on the undulating water. It had snuck into the harbour so stealthily, Adelita had barely noticed.

'You can't stop thinking about *him*, can you?'

Adelita didn't need to answer. They both knew she would be a liar if she tried denying it.

'You're a Crystal witch who's apparently been using psyche her whole life, consciously or subconsciously ... and you're spellbound to the strongest Elemental of all time: The One, who has access to all four elements and psyche as well. But not only that, you are spellbound to a Sentinel agent too. Can you see how that looks?'

'*Former* Sentinel agent.'

'Don't split hairs.'

Adelita gritted her teeth. 'He must have tricked me.'

'No, he didn't,' Tansy sighed. 'I would like to believe that too, but he couldn't have become spellbound with you if you hadn't allowed it. So, the real question is, why did you?'

Tansy paused, letting her words land.

'You did say I needed to reconnect with my heart.'

'Not with *him*.' Tansy shook her head. 'He's just a man.'

Irritation rippled through Adelita, but she tamped it down. Ernesto had never been a weak man, nor had he been anything but a friend to women. Adelita couldn't believe her father was the only male ally in existence. She wanted to ask Tansy where the Elementals' children had all come from, but maybe they'd only used their own men for what they wanted.

'I know about Demelza.'

Tansy reacted like Adelita had slapped her. 'Then you know what he did. What it cost me. Now he comes here, wanting us to help him? The arrogance of men knows no bounds.'

The High Witch looked out at the sea and the setting sun, her eyes glassy with tears.

'You know, Demelza wasn't much older than Chloe is now. She was an Earth Elemental, like me. The only one. The other two are fire, like Gwen . . . The Sentinel came for young witches in the night all over the West Country, snatching them from homes, bars, off the street, drugging them before they could release any magic. We weren't all together then, there was no safety in numbers. I wish I'd founded the Gathering sooner.'

She closed her eyes, before continuing. 'By the time I realised what had happened, I was too late. They tried to take them all back to London, to their Sentinel mad scientists, to see if they could "cure" them. Then the girls broke out of the buses they put them in, right outside Stonehenge. They thought they'd be safe there, that the ancient magic would protect them.'

Tansy's pain crackled off her like her magic. Adelita could feel it hanging in the air, its heavy ball lodged in her throat as she spoke. Her voice was hoarse with it.

'I'm so sorry.'

'You know Ethan was there.' Tansy picked at a thread on her skirt.

Adelita nodded.

'He slipped away and found me, walked all the way from Stonehenge to Cornwall. He told me they all fought bravely. As if I gave a shit about that, when my daughter was dead. *Murdered.* Typical male logic. I told him that if I saw him again I would kill him . . . Now he brings you here.'

'Wait.' Adelita's mind struggled to process all the new details. 'He left to find you the same day as Stonehenge . . . Is that what you're saying?'

Against her will, Adelita's memory rewound to the night they'd made it into Boscastle under darkness. Again she saw the feral tweens racing out of the trees, lit up by a shower of Chloe's green spheres. She'd turned to him and yelled that they were just children; Ethan had looked bewildered, showing her his empty hands.

I know that, he'd said.

The memory seemed to freeze, a hole burning in it like film in a projector. Underneath it: another memory, this time all Ethan's. Adelita was that floating presence again, there and yet not there; an observer. She watched Ethan grab another Sentinel's arm, manhandling him, making him look at him. The other soldier was wide-eyed and savage, itching to charge forth into battle.

You can't! Ethan hollered. *It's wrong, let them go!*

His words had no impact. The soldier shrugged him off, raised his weapon and ran. So did the others. Ethan did not advance with the other men towards the ancient monument. He stood on the sidelines in his black Sentinel uniform, watching in horror as his men lit up Stonehenge with a hail of gunfire.

Then everything changed.

From the middle, red, yellow, blue and green sparks burst like fireworks over the ancient monument. Elemental magic mixed together in one huge sphere, crackling like a plasma ball. It burst upwards; the whole thing going up like a vertical waterfall. Then it blasted outwards, taking rocks, chunks of grass and earth with it. The blast zone vaporised everything in its radius and pitched Ethan onto his back in the dirt.

On top of the harbour, relief swept through Adelita as she made the realisation. It had not been Tansy who'd turned him towards the witch cause, it had been the Sentinel themselves. It was the Stonehenge atrocity that made him start working undercover with the Brotherhood. He hadn't just spellbound with Adelita by accident at the jail, he'd been actively looking for her, just like he'd said. She could understand now, even if she didn't condone how he'd gone about it.

'He didn't fire on them, Tansy.'

'He didn't do *anything*. He just stood and watched.'

Adelita couldn't blame the High Witch; she understood only too well. Even though she'd been compelled to defend him, she was still angry with him herself. Ethan was symbolic of a system that had taken Adelita's own family and killed Tansy's beloved daughter. He'd also been one of the last to see Demelza alive; he and other Sentinel had been responsible for rounding her and the others up in the first place. Tansy's grief and hatred would only be matched by her guilt she couldn't save her precious firstborn.

Yet Adelita had also spent days spellbound to Ethan. She'd felt, deep down, what that day at Stonehenge had cost him, long before she'd known the truth of what had really happened. He had faced his fear and his own self-reproach and guilt. He'd brought Adelita – and then Chloe – to the only person he knew had the power and connections that could help overthrow the Sentinel: the Gathering, namely Tansy.

Adelita said none of this. She had negotiated with too many grief-wild patients over the years in the hospital to know any explanations would just be decoded as excuses or passing the buck.

Tansy curled her lip in contempt. 'He makes you weak.'

'No, I don't think he does.' She'd not planned to say this, but the words leapt out of her, their truth as obvious as the white flares of her Crystal magic. 'You showed me today my anger directs my magic, because your own dark pain feeds yours. But I was already using my negative emotions . . . It's what prompted me to break out of prison, get this far. You told me to trust my gut and I think he brings out the best in me. I'm stronger *with* him.'

Tansy ground the heel of her hand in her eye, stopping tears from spilling over. 'It doesn't matter, anyway. You're just a Crystal witch. Chloe is The One, she is the only one who can liberate us from all of this. She doesn't need your distractions.'

'You think I should leave her here, with you?'

'There's no think about it. We will keep her here, with us. She belongs at the Gathering. If you want to stay too, then you have a decision to make.'

Adelita was shocked at how much this proposal hurt. She didn't want to leave Chloe. She'd felt their paths were intertwined, complementary. She couldn't imagine not being with her. But now she understood she felt the same way with Ethan, too. In her previous life, Adelita had been a committed singleton; she'd had boyfriends, but only ever on her own terms. She'd never had a broken heart. Now she understood all the clichés in an instant: it *was* like a punch to the gut, a knife to the chest; it *did* take her breath away.

Tansy stood up. 'You need to choose. Chloe or Ethan.'

TWENTY-TWO

Another night and day at the Gathering rolled around and Adelita still hadn't made a decision on staying at the Gathering or leaving with Ethan, when Tansy expelled him. As Adelita joined the other witches for lunch in the Wellington Hotel, she noticed one of the witch cooks busying herself putting food cartons into an insulated bag to take to the sentries. She moved into the cook's way and flashed her a broad smile.

'I'll take the food to the prisoners, if you like.'

The purple-haired cook seemed in two minds, especially as Tansy had appeared through the dining room doors. Before Adelita could plead her case to deliver the food to the men in the old police station, the High Witch merely nodded. Satisfied, the witch cook took three cartons of food out of her insulated bag and handed them, plus napkins and wooden forks, to Adelita.

'Cheers,' the cook said. 'Could not be arsed to walk all the way up there, I tells ya.'

Adelita did not want to give Tansy any indication of what she was going to tell Ethan – she wasn't entirely sure herself yet – and didn't trust herself to meet Tansy's eye or speak to her as she left the hotel. This was unfortunate, because it dawned on her she was not at all sure where the old police station was. She hesitated on the corner by a red phone box, looking down the harbour path.

'You're the American lady.'

Adelita turned to find a prepubescent girl of about ten, her puppy fat squeezed into a gingham dress that was too tight under the arms.

'Yeah, I am. Who are you?'

'I'm Jessie.' The girl swayed side to side. She stood on one foot, the other tucked up into her dress like a flamingo.

'Why aren't you in there, with the other school kids?'

'Don't want to,' Jessie scowled. 'They're a bunch of arseholes.'

'I'm sure that's not true.'

The little girl eyeballed her. 'What would you know?'

Adelita considered the child's words. She'd always gone off by herself like Jessie; even as a child she'd been an outsider. She'd told herself she was happier alone, but the reality was she didn't want to be let down.

She smiled at the little girl. 'You're right. I don't know much. But have you tried to get along with them?'

'Yes ...' Jessie's defiant expression crumpled as she caught herself fibbing. 'No.'

'You have a great family here, kid.' Adelita's voice was soft. 'We never know how much time we have with our loved ones. Don't waste it.'

Jessie agreed to show Adelita where the old police station was. It was a five-minute walk away, past the inn, the community shop, the old tourist toilets and car park. Adelita would never have found it by herself. Situated next to the river mouth on the way into the village, it had been almost reclaimed by nature. The trees and vines had reached out and grasped the brickwork and its roof, so the building was almost perfectly camouflaged. She watched the little girl run off, towards some other kids down by the river.

Inside, Costentyn whittled a stick with a small, sharp blade. He stood as soon as he caught a whiff of the food Adelita was carrying. He muttered something Adelita couldn't quite catch; she still wasn't used to the consonant-heavy Cornish language. All the words ran together. She did however manage to identify one phrase.

'*Meur ras.*' Thank you.

Adelita grinned at the tall youth. '*Heb grev.*' No problem/You're welcome.

Costentyn raised an impressed eyebrow. When she indicated she wanted to take the other two cartons to Daniel and Ethan, he nodded, sitting down at the moss-covered desk and shovelling food into his mouth. Adelita made a nonchalant move for the iron key ring hanging on the wall nearby, but Costentyn spotted her and shook his head at her. Adelita rolled her eyes; couldn't blame a woman for trying.

She wandered over to the bars of the cell. It was pretty dark in the old police station due to the smashed strip-light overhead and the big tree branch that had crashed through the roof, overshadowing the rest of the room, and she had to narrow her eyes in the gloom.

Ethan lay on a bench towards the back of the small space, one arm flung over his face and hiding his eyes. The other trailed off the bench. He was asleep. Daniel appeared next to the bars, his cheeks covered in coarse black stubble. He smelled clean and his demeanour was lighter than she'd seen him before, like going to jail was a break for him. She almost laughed when she saw what he was wearing: a green cardigan, black T-shirt and a pair of rainbow-striped harem pants.

'Hey, Professor.' She was unable to keep the amusement out of her voice. 'They treating you well in here?'

'You like my clown trousers? I think I can pull them off.'

Daniel grinned, digging his hands in his pockets and pulling out the oversized, voluminous material.

Adelita laughed. 'Brought you guys some hot food. Chloe's just down at the dining hall eating hers.'

'Nice one.'

Adelita held the cartons up and pushed them through the bars to him. Daniel juggled both of them, kicking out with one foot, connecting lightly with Ethan's shoulder. He placed one of the cartons on the floor next to the bench.

The cowboy awoke with a start and sat up suddenly, blinking and stretching before he realised Adelita was there. He shot to his feet, staring at her.

'Hey,' Ethan said.

He wearing the clothes the Brotherhood had provided him with, though they were clean now. His previous military-style haircut was in disarray; his beard was bushier, more unkempt. He was still pale, but he looked healthier, less drawn than he'd been back at the Texas motel room. He seemed to have bene-fitted from a day of rest, too.

'Hey,' Adelita echoed.

Ethan's expression looked just like Adelita felt. Her stomach twisted with nerves. Daniel looked between her and the rogue Sentinel. It was clear from his face he would rather be anywhere else but in between them both.

'Right. I'm just gonna . . .'

Daniel trailed off; he knew they were not listening to him. He moved towards the back of the cell and sat down on the bench Ethan had been on, turning his back on both of them as he ate, trying to give them as much privacy as the cramped situation could allow.

'How are your stitches doing?' Adelita found herself saying.

Ethan blinked at her, like he had no idea what she was talking about. Then the connection fired in his brain. 'Fine.'

'No irritation, pain, temperature, anything like that?' She felt compelled to play the medic and put off the moment a little longer.

Ethan shook his head. He hesitated, then decided to fall on his sword.

'Look, I didn't kill them. I swear. I wanted to let them go ...'

'I know,' Adelita sighed. 'Tansy thinks the plan won't work.'

'She doesn't know that. Men and women have never united like this before. With enough Elementals *and* the Brotherhood, we should be able to take out Hopkins, maybe even the whole senate.'

'No,' Adelita said softly. 'Tansy will never agree to putting her witches on the front line, especially when so many of them are so young. They all have a good life here, the best they can possibly get in this fucked-up world. Why would they put that in danger?'

'Because it's the right thing to do.'

Adelita sighed. 'OK, let me put this another way ... Why would they put their lives in danger for *you*?'

Ethan digested the simple, harsh truth of Adelita's words. She could see the realisation dawn in his eyes. He was ex-Sentinel; why would his prior enemies come to his aid in overthrowing the government? The cowboy was not wrong when he said it was the right thing to do, but he was talking from a space of needing redemption for his past wrongdoings. He'd joined the Brotherhood to try and correct the balance. In contrast, Tansy and the others had done nothing wrong but exist.

'Chloe should stay here,' Adelita said. 'It's the only place she can be safe and learn how her powers work.'

The cowboy thought it over. 'Agreed.'

'Tansy says Daniel can stay too.'

'She really must want Chloe to stay, I guess. But her being here will bring Sentinel to the Gathering. Tansy ain't stupid. She knows that.'

Adelita had already argued this with the High Witch, but Tansy had turned to her generals for explanations. Emmeline told Adelita the Romans had only ever come as far as Exeter; they'd been too scared of Exmoor and Dartmoor, not to mention the Celts beyond in Cornwall, to advance much further. Nestled in the valley, with its few roads in and out and the woodland and moor beyond, Boscastle was one of the safest places in the West Country. It was why the witches had settled there in the first place. It was a tactic based in history that had served them well so far. The Gathering was the biggest concentration of Elementals in not only the West Country, but the world. No one could match their power; with Chloe residing there too, they would be nigh-on invincible.

'She says they can handle it,' Adelita said. 'Tansy is going to let you both out tomorrow . . . but she says *you* have to leave.'

Ethan pursed his lips; maybe he saw it in her eyes. The silence stretched, awkward, between them. The weight of Adelita's decision seemed to press down on both of them. Adelita didn't want to say what she had to and Ethan didn't want to hear it. Ethan rested his face against the bars of the cells.

'You want to stay here too,' he groaned.

'I don't want to. I have to. I have to stay with Chloe.'

'I get it. Really, I do. She needs you.' Ethan moved his face from the bars but not before Adelita saw the tears in his blue eyes. 'I told you, I got you, Doc. If that means it's better I go, so be it.'

Pain stabbed, knife-sharp, through her chest. 'I'm sorry.'

They both stared at each other in silence for a few moments.

'Will you be OK, here?' Ethan enquired at last. 'Tansy ain't that keen on Crystal witches neither.'

Adelita was touched by his concern for her, even in the midst of his own pain at her abandonment. 'I'll have to prove myself to her. I'll just have to show her I'm not a threat, or about to steal anyone's power.'

Ethan gave her a watery smile. 'Yeah, about stealing . . .'

'You didn't steal anything from me.' Adelita recalled Tansy's words by the harbour, 'You couldn't have spellbound with me if I hadn't allowed it.'

'Maybe not, but I'm sorry anyway.'

'We were both lonely people.' Adelita slipped her left hand through the bars and into his. His fingertips felt scratchy and worn.

'Will I see you again, before I leave?' he whispered.

'I don't know.'

Adelita moved towards the bars and Ethan did the same. With her right hand, she grabbed his chin and pressed her lips against his. Unlike before, when he'd pulled away, this time he let her. It was she who forced herself to break away, leaving a space between them. Even as she let go, she wanted to fly back across the room towards him. She forced herself to stay away as he looked at her, mournful as a caged animal in the zoo.

'I love you, Ada.'

A reply caught in her throat, as painful as a fish bone. She forced the truth back down and said instead, 'I know.'

Her vision blurred by tears, Adelita turned on her heel. She marched back out of the old police station, past the wide-eyed Costentyn. As she made it out into the trees behind the police station, she wanted to scream but couldn't bear to hear the echo of it coming back around the valley at her. Instead she let her body fold in on itself, so she was crouching down on the ground. She rocked on her heels like a child, tears coursing down her cheeks.

'You made the right choice.'

Adelita's head snapped back as she looked up. Tansy appeared from the shadows of the trees, both hands grasped around her stang. From her low vantage point, Adelita could see Tansy's feet were bare and caked in mud. Her red hair crackled with green Earth magic. It snaked down her sternum and underneath her ditsy print surf dress and home-made cable-knit cardigan. She tilted her head, offering her a hand, so she might stand up. Adelita accepted.

'I need your help with something,' the High Witch said.

Daniel's belly grumbled. The food Adelita had brought them both had been digested hours ago. Ethan hadn't touched his portion. Even congealed and cold, it looked delicious to Daniel. Ethan had pushed it towards him saying he wasn't hungry, but as much as he wanted it, Daniel had declined. It had seemed like he was profiting from Ethan's misery at Adelita cutting ties with him.

He'd attempted to talk to the cowboy about it, but Ethan had retreated deep inside himself all afternoon, so Daniel paced their small cell. Agitation coursed through his veins. Daniel had never been the active type, but he'd never been in a prison cell either. He was surprised at just how claustrophobic he was becoming; he'd never had any issues with enclosed spaces before. He couldn't understand how Ethan could stand it. Maybe it wasn't his first time locked up on this side of the bars.

'See anything?'

Ethan did not turn his way. 'Nah.'

The cowboy was standing on the bench he'd been lying on since their incarceration, peering out of the tall, slit-like window into the woodland beyond. About ten minutes earlier the rogue Sentinel's eyes had narrowed as he'd spotted a chink of light from outside dancing on the dark wall of their cell. Daniel had wondered if it was the glint of the Elementals' powers as they patrolled.

A tall shadow fell on the cell: Costentyn.

'Oh, did we wake you?'

Daniel marvelled at the sarcasm dripping off his own words. He was never normally derisive or mocking. He felt like he'd had some kind of personality transplant since this ordeal had begun. Or maybe this was his real personality, hidden under layers of bullshit obligations so-called civil society had put on him his whole life.

Costentyn rolled his eyes and made a show of pointing at his wrist where a watch would be, if he bothered to wear one. He wanted them to go to sleep. Daniel wasn't sure what time it was – there were no clocks in the old police station – but he knew in his bones it was either very, very late at night; or very, very early in the morning.

The boy spotted Ethan at the window. '*Wasson?*'

'He thought he saw something out there.'

Ethan looked at Daniel sharply for giving their jailer any information but Daniel shrugged. It was obvious what the cowboy was up to. They gained nothing by being secretive, as far as he could see.

'False alarm,' the rogue Sentinel declared.

Costentyn didn't seem concerned, anyway. He demonstrated some more basic sign language: both palms pressed together next to his cheek. It was the universal gesture between parents and small children at bedtime: *time for sleep.*

'Fuck you, kid,' Ethan growled, his attention back to the high window.

Costentyn gave him a toothy grin and the finger. He traipsed back to the moss-covered desk and the wingback chair next to it. He settled back into it and under his blanket again. Within seconds the lad was snoring softly, like someone had flipped a switch in his consciousness.

'We should try to get some sleep, too.' Daniel grabbed his own blanket.

Ethan jumped down from the bench. 'No time for that, Prof.'

The depressed and sluggish demeanour that had taken up residence in the cowboy all afternoon was gone. Now he was the Ethan who Daniel had first met when he'd careered into Taunton Deane via a handbrake turn to rescue them all before the Sentinel arrived. Spring-loaded, like a military man ready to go forth into battle.

Daniel's stomach went into free fall as he made the connection. It had not been a false alarm. Ethan had lied to Costentyn. He *had* seen something out there, in the woodland. For Ethan to snap into military mode, it had to be the Sentinel.

TWENTY-THREE

The Scourge had tracked the fugitives across the West Country, clearing up the bodies and destruction those toxic witches had left in their wake. He'd quizzed shaken-up civilians at Taunton Deane, where witnesses were insistent they'd seen a teenage girl glowing with multiple Elemental flares; that she'd fought with a Crystal witch, glowing white. He'd seen two magic flare burns on the ground himself outside the rest stop. As he suspected, his agent Lyle Kirby had been killed by someone with Sentinel training. The two soldiers at the Devon–Cornwall border confirmed they'd been accosted by an American gunman, as well as attacked by the two witches, who now appeared to be working together.

The evidence was clear: Our Lady's escapees Ethan Weber and Adelita Garcia were on British soil and helping Chloe Su and her father.

Any other Sentinel agent might have been distracted by the question of why, but not Jake Pembroke. He just itched to dispense his infamous punishment. Now the Scourge found himself in some backwater hellhole called Boscastle, staring down the valley at a coven that called itself the Gathering. He already knew from classified Sentinel briefings it was the biggest concentration of Elementals anywhere in the world. It was the British government's biggest embarrassment and the number one reason the sad little island had sought the USA's protection under Safeguard and the Sentinel.

Needless to say, he was staying well clear of the Gathering. Not because he was a pussy, but because he knew his place. He was a general, responsible for tactics; he needed to be on hand to give fall-back orders and organise help for any wounded. He had sent two teams into the coven's village, and expected a good portion of his men to not come back. The Sentinel couldn't put a stick in a hornet's nest of Elementals and not expect to get stung.

As his men advanced, the Scourge sat back at the top of the woodland with his tech guy, a monosyllabic man named Powell. Jake had briefed all his Sentinel with his plan, making clear the timings they had to play with. He'd allotted them eighteen minutes to get into the village, locate Chloe Su and spirit her away. Even assuming everything went to plan, it would be very tight. Already three minutes had rocketed by.

Fifteen minutes left.

As the Scourge watched the illuminated digits of his stop-watch count down, he soothed himself with thoughts of victory. While a stealth raid on such a large coven of Elementals had never happened before, their chances were reasonable. All the Sentinel he had rustled up were strong, highly trained Puritan men. All of them had experience with Crystal covens. They had a good selection of firepower; Elementals were not invulnerable to bullets, so that offered his Sentinel some protection.

The Scourge had to assume his men were skilled enough to get some rounds off should it all go sideways. Fire and Water Elementals were bad enough, but Air witches could open up and step between the molecules of the atmosphere. He'd heard rumours the most skilled could take others with them, whether they were witches or not. But they were a picnic in comparison to Earth Elementals. They had some kind of spooky kung fu shit going on too, seemingly able to know where people were, though the scientists at Sentinel HQ had not figured out why yet. That tidbit of information made the Scourge nervous: from the haywire GPS he knew there had to be one another Earth witch down there, as well as Chloe Su.

Could the Gathering know they were coming already, somehow?

The Scourge didn't share his fear with Uno or his men. He told himself that after what happened at Stonehenge, it was a good idea for at least one person to stay away from the potential blast zone. Unlike all the young women who'd also died at the Salisbury monument, they had no idea if Chloe Su could kill multiple Sentinel targets and survive. The Scourge suspected she could. The teenager had walked away without a scratch on her after vaporising an entire house and her own mother.

Ten minutes.

In the old police station, Ethan indicated Daniel's baggy harem trousers. 'I'm gonna need those, I'm afraid, Yoda. Just those, don't panic. I know we are technically in prison.'

Daniel's brain couldn't keep up. 'Wait ... what?'

'Just pony up and take off your pants!'

Daniel shimmied off the trousers and handed them over to Ethan. The cowboy tore the thin fabric into long strips as the confused Daniel stood watching in his boxer shorts. When it clicked what he was doing, Daniel kneeled down and gave him a hand, plaiting the pieces to make a rope. Growing up with two sisters, then a daughter of his own, Daniel was a swift hand at plaits.

'Nicely done.' Ethan nodded in approval, then indicated the door on the left beside the sleeping Costentyn. 'See the cleaning cupboard door?'

Daniel turned his head in the direction of Ethan's gaze. He had already appreciated just how observant the cowboy was; he'd identified Sentinel in the wood by a dot of light on the wall. Sure enough, the cleaning cupboard door was ajar now. A mop or broom handle inside the cupboard had fallen between the door jamb and the frame, preventing it from closing. Daniel vaguely remembered Costentyn mopping up some spilled coffee off the flagstones. Consumed with worries about Chloe and his own theorising as he tried to settle his anxious thoughts, Daniel had barely taken notice, but Ethan had.

Ethan knotted the end of their makeshift rope with his teeth. 'We need to lasso that mop handle and pull it towards us, through the bars.'

Daniel grimaced; lassos were fantasy to him, only part of John Wayne and Clint Eastwood films. Ethan grinned.

'My gramps has a ranch, remember? Anyway, that is not the hard part.'

Daniel couldn't believe his ears. 'What's the hard part?'

Before Ethan could answer, Daniel followed Ethan's sight back to the wall beside the still-sleeping Costentyn. Next to the mossy desk was one of Ethan's rucksacks, which Daniel knew was full of money, burner phones and weapons.

But Ethan wasn't looking at that. On a hook on the left wall, in a plain view, was the big iron ring with the cell door keys on it.

Daniel did a quick estimate of the mop handle's length versus the space between the cell and the wall. Even extending as much as they could, it would be a stretch. Not to mention the fact Costentyn could wake up and snatch the mop back before they could get out and retrieve Ethan's bag and guns. But they had no other option available.

Daniel shrugged. 'I guess we better not miss, then.'

It was so dark Carter could barely see his own feet as he kicked through the woodland mulch. Stomach acid still burned the back of his throat. Heart hammering, Carter attempted to concentrate, sweeping his weapon from side to side. Infrared blobs glowed to his left and right as his small team of men advanced towards the tiny village with him. All of them were counting each blob, just in case an extra one joined them; no one wanted to find themselves side by side with a witch.

Sentinel scouts had said the majority of the witches were in properties around the top of the harbour path. They'd taken over cottages, a hotel, an inn and a selection of old shops, including the old tourist information centre. This information had offended Carter mightily; those properties did not belong to the witches. They were spreading like germs or mould spores, taking root in places they had no right to. Women thought they could just take over.

Not on his watch.

Carter pulled up his night-vision goggles and squinted into the darkness, listening for any potential threats. The blackness swirled in front of his tired, gritty eyes. All he could hear were the whispering waves of the sea in the harbour beyond. He knew that beyond his sightline there were rolling hills, yet more trees. He couldn't make out any of it. There was zero light pollution and the full moon had retreated behind clouds. Everything dropped out of sight into the dark like it was the edge of the world.

Another Sentinel loomed out of the darkness, making Carter jump. He almost gave a nervous laugh; it was only Draper. A comically thin guy smeared in black paint and wearing dark clothing, only the whites of Draper's eyes were visible. He too had pulled up his night-vision goggles; it wasn't possible to read the iHex with them on, which had always struck Carter as a serious design fault by Sentinel HQ's pet geeks.

'The iHex is giving a particularly strong reading at the right-hand side of the village,' the other Sentinel muttered. 'Four different Elemental signatures, boss.'

Boss. Carter liked that. After tonight, maybe he would have his own command.

The iHex led Carter's team to a row of small, white cottages at the top of the harbour path. Carter's team approached warily, glad of the darkness as they crossed the communal gardens. The cottages' windows were small, some of them had wooden shutters. The soldiers didn't want to become targets themselves; witches could throw their magic out at them like snipers. Hell, some of them might even have guns. They had no idea if Legacies lived here too, or sympathetic Goodys. One thing Carter had learned the hard way: women were capable of anything, witch or not.

The first cottage was the one emitting the highest signal, according to the iHex. Another of his men, Symonds, moved forwards. He was a broad, muscular man with long fingers, making him the perfect lockpick. He dropped to one knee, pulling a lockpick kit from his fanny pack. But like all trained cat burglars, he tried the door handle first. To Carter's astonishment, the door opened. Symonds looked round at him, his expression unreadable underneath his camouflage paint and goggles. Even so, Carter knew he was asking if they should fall back.

Carter did not want to abort and traipse back to the Scourge, head hung low. He knew he would never live it down. His thoughts raced as he considered what the unprotected door could mean. He'd heard plenty of stories from his posting in Devon about yokels leaving their doors unlocked. It didn't seem that unlikely to imagine highly powerful witches would not place any stock in keys and locks. They were not Goodys, who had little else to protect them. Carter had to admit he'd found the total lack of activity within the coven disconcerting; he would have expected to see a light burning *somewhere*. But maybe it was all part of the witches' own security measures; could they be using the dark to cloak them, like Londoners during the Blitz? That, plus their own formidable magic, could be why they hadn't bothered locking the door.

Carter girded himself and nodded, the gesture the rest of the Sentinel were waiting for. Without a second glance at their superior officer, they all crossed the threshold single file, into the cottage. Despite its olde worlde outside, there was a modern feel within: white furniture, simple lines. It had wooden floors, but an open plan; a kitchen and dining area led straight on to two couches in front of a large flat-screen TV. Books and magazines were abandoned on the coffee table, alongside some Barbie figures. There was a computer games console amidst a tangle of cables and remote controls.

Two of his other men opened doors that led off the main area. A tiny blue bathroom and toilet, nothing behind the shower curtain. Two bedrooms. One was obviously for little girls; bunk beds, soft animals, pink curtains, clothes scattered all over the floor. The other held a double bed with a purple comforter, a bottle of gin on the nightstand. Both were empty. The cottage was clean and tidy, but lived-in. There were no booby traps that Carter could discern.

Clear.

Relief and disappointment pooled in Carter's belly. He'd wanted *his* team to be the one to take Chloe Su back to the Scourge. In his mind's eye he could already see Team B placing a halo around the girl's head, injecting her with sedatives and smuggling her back through the wood. Taking his glory.

Symonds gestured at him again, drawing Carter's eye. There was a mezzanine above them they'd missed: it was barely a room, more of an oversized shelf, surrounded by the white slats of a wooden railing, with a matching ladder. It was just wide enough for a single bed, nightstand and lamp. In the bed: the unmistakable lump of a human body, dark hair trailing across the pillow.

Chloe Su.

Carter eyed the ladder; it would take only a small man's weight. He indicated for the smallest amongst them, Garrett, to come forwards. A boy of nineteen, Garrett was skinny and short, the perfect size. The boy slung his weapon over his shoulder and accepted the halo Carter gave him. He clambered the five or six steps up to the bed, flicking his wrist forwards to connect the halo on the teen's sleeping head.

'What the . . . ?' Garrett murmured.

The duvet seemed to deflate; the girl underneath disappeared. Garrett ripped the covers back. Carter's heart leapt up in his throat; he could see a forked wooden stick in the bed instead, a high witch's stang. It had just been a spell, a magical illusion conjured via Earth magic.

Before any of them could process all of this, those tell-tale yellow sparks erupted in the corner of his eye and a flame-haired woman in her late forties stepped out of a blonde Air witch's portal. It collapsed behind her, spiriting the blonde woman away as soon as the Earth witch's feet touched the cottage's wooden floor. The redhead's fists glowed green with Earth magic. The stang flew from the bed, returning to her hand like a boomerang.

'Hello, boys,' she said, flashing the Sentinel a deadly grin.

The witch slammed the stick to the floor. A huge bubble of

magic erupted around her, then burst outwards with the power and sensation of millions of microscopic shards of glass. Directly inside the blast zone, Carter and his doomed men didn't even have enough time to scream: they were ripped apart before sound could leave their throats.

Blood painted the walls of the cottage.

TWENTY-FOUR

Tansy's cottage erupted in a geyser of green light.

On the harbour path just metres away, Adelita and Chloe raced with Loveday towards the sea. Adelita looked back over her shoulder, unable to stop herself. The beacon of green light forced its way upwards, into the sky. The powerful stink of magic came next, then the air split apart, taking Adelita's breath with it.

She stared, agog. The cottage, where she and Chloe had been sleeping just an hour earlier, was still standing, but what had happened to the men inside?

Tansy was tuned into the Earth energy that flowed through the ley lines that cross-crossed the whole valley like natural geofences. This meant the High Witch had easily detected intruders in the valley a few hours earlier as the Sentinel had crossed them, oblivious. This had allowed her to set up Adelita and Chloe's escape plan, but was Tansy still alive? Adelita hadn't thought to ask if it was a suicide mission.

She had no time to follow this thought to its conclusion. She stumbled as Tansy's shockwave rumbled beneath the harbour path, making roof slates pop up and the ground shift beneath her feet. Chloe grabbed her by the elbow, stopping her from pitching forwards onto her hands and knees.

They followed Loveday towards the harbour, where a boat was waiting to spirit both Adelita and Chloe away. Realising her plan to keep Chloe at the Gathering was based on wishful thinking, the High Witch had given Adelita instructions to go and see her own mentor, Cally, in Moscow.

'What about Dad?'

Adelita dithered. She hadn't told Chloe that Daniel wasn't coming with them, but it looked like it was beginning to dawn on her. It had been decided the men would be left behind in the jail, with the High Witch letting them out once both witches were long gone. It was safer for both Adelita and Chloe; definitely safer for Daniel.

No time, Adelita answered Chloe via the spellbind. *They'll join us later*.

Despite her anger, Chloe kept running; she knew she had no choice but to follow Adelita at this late stage. Tansy's plan had been designed that way. The teen's anger rippled through their spellbind, prickling through Adelita's nerve endings like a snake bite.

Liar!

With a burst of yellow sparks Emmeline exploded into being, falling into step on the harbour path with Adelita, Chloe and Loveday. She'd been the one to deliver the High Witch to the cottage, so Adelita's heart leapt at the sight of the Air Elemental. It sank just as quickly when she realised Tansy was not with her.

'Stealth mission,' Emmeline reported, throwing the words over her shoulder as she joined them. 'Tansy's took out one team, but she reckons there's one more. Probably coming from the left side of the valley. The Sentinel like their pincer movements.'

Adelita felt a momentary surge of gratitude as she heard Tansy was not dead. Though the valley was cloaked in darkness, she knew more witches were waiting, up and down the harbour path, beside the trees and hidden by cottages. Tweens lurked below the bridge and the banks of the river, magic and arrows and spears ready for battle. She could feel the anticipation in the air, working its way through the magic in her own veins. Running was taking too long.

'Almost there. C'mon . . . Loveday!'

Emmeline drew a door with two fingers. Yellow Air magic crackled off her like a child's sparkler. Loveday grabbed Chloe's hand, who grabbed Adelita's, in readiness, to leap through the portal to the boat waiting for them in Boscastle's natural harbour.

Pffft. Pffft. Pffft.

Too late, Adelita heard the unmistakable sound of gunshots from a weapon with a silencer attached.

'What the hell . . . ?'

They'd been attempting to hook the cell's key ring from the wall for ten minutes when it happened. As Ethan had posited, lassoing the mop handle and dragging it back through the bars had been the easy part. Ethan and then Daniel each had a try at straining their arms through the bars with the handle to grab the keys, but it was like the most infuriating hook-a-duck fun-fair game in the entire world. That was when Ethan suggested prodding Costentyn with the handle to wake him. Maybe they could persuade him to take a message to Tansy with Ethan's suspicions Sentinel had breached the Gathering's defences. If nothing else, the prick deserved a smack in the mouth with a wooden stick. Daniel could not disagree.

Just as they were about to prod the still-sleeping Costentyn with the mop handle, their cell was bathed in green light. It swooped across the walls like the beam from a lighthouse, bringing with it the stench of ozone. Ethan was forced to raise a hand to his eyes.

'That's not good.'

The cowboy always was the king of the understatement. Daniel felt a heavy weight on his chest; his heartbeat accelerated. Heat raced through his body as his vision swam not only with the blinding assault, but terror brought on by post-traumatic stress. The last time such a display had taken place, his house had been reduced to dust with his wife and child inside. The day Daniel's whole world had turned upside down; before he'd been plunged into this living nightmare.

'Chloe,' he gulped.

At the mossy desk, Costentyn awoke and sat upright, like he'd been blasted to attention. Residual magic crackled through his hair, blue like Loveday's. His eyes glinted in the darkness with it too. He sprang from the chair, his posture one of a warrior's.

'Holy shit,' Ethan breathed, 'looks like you were right about Elemental boys.'

Daniel couldn't believe the change in their jailer, either. Costentyn had always seemed like an 'odd stick', as Ethan would say, but now the youth's focus was absolute. His attentions went to the door as his hand went straight to his belt, where a large bowie knife hung.

He was leaving them.

'Wait, wait!' Daniel hollered at him in the hope it would break the young man's reverie.

It worked. Costentyn turned to Daniel, his gaze steely.

'Let us out,' Daniel commanded. 'Now.'

Costentyn capitulated and made a grab for the key ring off the wall. Ethan and Daniel held their breath as they willed him to walk towards the cell, fit the keys in the lock and let them out.

The boy moved towards them in a trance.

Costentyn froze.

Feral screams and battle cries filled the air outside the old police station. Waves of bright yellow, red, white and blue magic burst in a cacophony of colour, joining the green Earth magic that still surged all over Boscastle. It would have been quite beautiful, had Daniel not known the raw power the Elementals held and what kind of damage they could inflict.

Daniel's command over Costentyn's trance was broken. The boy appeared to forget all about them. He dropped the keys on the mossy desk instead. The boy drew his knife and uttered a bloodcurdling howl. He rushed off outside to join his brothers and sisters in battle, the big oak front door of the police station slamming behind him.

'Shit!' Daniel hit the bars with the flat of his palms in frustration.

'Don't worry about it, Prof.'

Daniel looked to the cowboy, agog. How could he be so calm? Ethan grabbed up the mop handle and demonstrated exactly why. The desk was considerably closer to the cell than the wall. The rogue Sentinel hooked the keys and made them slide all the way down the mop handle, into his waiting hand.

The cowboy held the keys up and grinned. 'Let's get outta here.'

'*Omsettya!*' Emmeline bellowed. *Attack!*

More Elemental flares erupted into the air as gunshots came down. The Air witch sent a torrent of yellow magic upwards, illuminating ten or twelve Sentinel on the opposite bank, about fifty feet away. Hoots, screams and yells came next as the children surged up the banks, teeth bared and weapons raised. Emmeline opened the door she had drawn but bounced straight back again, falling over. In her haste, she'd made a mistake.

'Fuck it!'

Emmeline scrabbled to her feet, throwing Air magic from her palms like confetti. The portal opened this time. The Air witch zoomed through to the other side and back again, causing flash burns with bursts of yellow light right next to the Sentinel.

Everything around Adelita slowed down, just as it had in the prison yard, but now *she* was the one moving in slow motion. She'd noticed her limbs felt heavy since she'd cut ties with Ethan at the old police station, but now they felt like they were made of lead. Adelita was not 'super-awake' like Chloe called it; she was not zipping forwards through time and space, like she had before. Her psyche felt sluggish; she'd not only missed the approaching threat, she wasn't responding like she normally would. It was like one of those classic nightmares where you're in danger yet can't move fast enough. Though white light had poured from her in response to Emmeline's battle cry, Adelita could feel its strength was drastically diminished. She sent white light with the tweens, though it fell short into the river in another pathetic, half-hearted spiral. Maybe she'd been right, when she'd told Tansy Ethan made her stronger. Maybe Daniel did the same for Chloe. Perhaps leaving them was a big mistake?

More bullets hit. Adelita hissed with pain as slate nipped at her hands and face like sharp teeth. Chloe's magic rattled through her, along with her fear, thanks to their spellbind: *ohnonononononono, whatdowedowhatdowedowhatdowedo?*

Stay close! she told the girl.

More shots fired.

The second team of Sentinel returned the witches' fire, but retreated into the trees, hoping the woods would give them adequate cover so they could continue their attack. Adelita saw a shirtless young man race down the other side of the harbour, whooping. He leapt like a panther on to the back of a Sentinel. It took her mind a second to catch up: Costentyn. Where were Daniel and Ethan? Had they been left alone? The boy buried his bowie knife between the soldier's shoulder blades as they both fell to the ground.

They're here because of me.

Chloe stood transfixed by the bedlam and carnage, but Adelita could still hear her thoughts, as easily if she was talking in a quiet room.

This is my fault.

Adelita had no time to persuade her otherwise or assuage the teen's misplaced guilt. She saw a boy fall: dead? She lost sight of him as he disappeared into the gaping darkness.

She had to protect Chloe.

Adelita tried drawing a protective bubble around the teenager like she had in the car near the Devon checkpoint, or Ethan the first night in Boscastle. Her powers weren't strong enough. It just popped again.

Get behind me.

Adelita pushed Chloe out of the way, shielding her with her body. In a bid to help the battle, she sent some more spirals of white light into the air. If nothing else, they acted like homing beacons, lighting the way for boys to hunt down their prey. Two young girls grasped hands and sent a ball of flame at a Sentinel, enveloping him in fire.

Loveday twirled one fist around her head like a lasso, picking up water from the river and sending it at the Sentinel like sideways fountains. Emmeline sent more yellow flares into the trees as tweens raced up the bank.

Pffft.

Loveday uttered an *unnnnh* as she was hit, falling out of sight into the darkness. There was a splash as she pitched, face-first, into the river below.

TWENTY-FIVE

'Fall back! That's an order!'

The radio only crackled in the Scourge's hand. With seven minutes left on the countdown, his fears proved true as the valley lit up in green light. Whether it was Chloe Su leading the charge or some other Earth Elemental bitch, the end result was the same: his mission was an abject failure and his men were toast. His mind jumped ahead to Uno's inevitable wrath. Could he even survive such a monumental screw-up? A few days from now, he could be in the brig at Sentinel HQ, awaiting court martial.

'Fuck!' he hollered into the night, making Powell flinch beside him.

The Scourge's reeling thoughts were halted as yet more magic jumped into the air, illuminating the valley in more hues of white, green, red, yellow and blue. Though there had been cloud cover, it was a clear night with no rain; unusual for March in the West Country. The sight would have been as beautiful as the Northern Lights, had it not been accompanied by the harsh voices of both males and females. From his high vantage point at the top of the valley, he could see only the shadowed movement of people amongst the trees, the illumination of arrows fired upwards as magic exploded like bottle rockets around them.

Shivers ran down his spine like iced water as he processed the feral war cries cutting through the air in tandem with the horrific death screams of his men. He thought he could hear children whooping and laughing, too. Christ, those toxic savages were even worse than he thought.

Goddamn them all to hell.

'What's happening down there?' the Scourge demanded.

Powell still did not answer. He just stared, muttering wordlessly and wide-eyed at his monitors as scenes of relentless horror were transmitted from the Sentinel's body cameras. The Scourge shouldered him out of the way, taking in the carnage via live feed. He followed each screen, one to the next, unable to tear his gaze away. As each Sentinel died, his feed turned to white noise. The Scourge had sent twenty-four down there in two teams of twelve; only seven cameras were still on. Shit.

Impotent and enraged, the Scourge ran his hands through his silver hair, grabbing tufts and twisting them as he attempted to process the bloodshed. It was every bit as bad down there as he had surmised: children, youths and adults were armed to the teeth with magic and weapons. They had males helping them. All of them were as feral as the women, some crackling with residual magic themselves.

What the Jesus H. Christ?

'*Mamm!*' A blood-soaked Costentyn bellowed after Loveday from the harbour path.

'No!' Chloe placed her hands over her ears like a small child.

Emmeline uttered a guttural howl of fury and appeared back on the harbour path with them. The Air witch sent another explosion of yellow sparks across the river, into the trees, keeping the remaining Sentinel at bay. Adelita held her fist in the air like a lantern. She spotted Loveday holding on to the bridge with one arm. The other was held to the wound in her shoulder. She was shivering with cold and shock, but she was alive.

'There!' Adelita pointed.

Emmeline covered Costentyn with a swirl of yellow air magic as he jumped straight into the water to retrieve his mother. As Loveday wrapped an arm around her son, more bullets ricocheted around them. Adelita felt that familiar surge of fury pool in her belly.

When were these assholes ever going to stop?

There it was. She grabbed her rage with her magic, directing it outwards and sending her Crystal magic surging forth with it. It washed over some tweens accidentally, knocking them over like bowling balls, though all jumped up again laughing and energised. A Sentinel sniper on the other side of the river was not so lucky. Adelita saw his shocked face and felt his heart stop beating. He dropped his gun and fell dead where he knelt.

Triumph brought a smile to Adelita's face, even as simultaneous horror worked its way through her. She was both elated at her win and horrified to have yet again broken her oath as a doctor to preserve life, even if it was in self-defence. Tansy's words – *head over heart* – returned to her. Her anger had delivered her magic to her once again.

They had to get to the boat.

'Chloe, we have to go . . .'

As she turned to the teenager, Adelita's stomach lurched. Like Loveday, Chloe was shivering, but unlike the Water witch, it was not with cold or shock. The teenager's eyes glinted in the darkness, inhuman and shiny, the whites completely disappeared.

Adelita made a grab for her. 'No, don't . . . !'

Chloe screamed.

*

Before the cowboy could fit the iron key in the cell door, a plaintive, primeval scream eclipsed the rest, echoing up and down the valley. It cut the rest of the battle cries dead. In its wake, an imposing hush fell down on the Gathering like a shroud over a corpse.

'What the . . . ?' Ethan said, his voice shaky.

Daniel did not answer. They both felt it first. A deep rumble, echoing up through the ground, into their bones. The ground beneath their feet shifted, making them fall to their knees. Daniel's teeth rattled in his skull, his vision spinning. They were both pinned to the floor of the cell now, like one of those gravitational-force amusement park rides. Still that dark hum rumbled on, growing louder, like a jet engine about to take off.

Too late, Daniel realised what was coming down the valley.

A deluge of water slammed into the old police station with the force of a moving vehicle. Shock and cold hit him as he was engulfed by the flood. His senses left him as his feet were pulled upwards, off the cell floor. Helpless, he somersaulted through the water, unable to stop himself.

He grabbed for solid objects to gain his bearings, kicking out his feet and arms, trying to find the top of the water. In the darkness and chaos Daniel couldn't work out which way was up. The water worked its way around him like it had a mind of its own. He knew he had to fight it, despite the treacherous voice in the back of his head that told him to give in to oblivion. There was no doubt in Daniel's mind his daughter was behind the flood. He had to get out, find Chloe. Help her, talk to her, anything.

Hot pain lanced through his chest as he ran out of air; he had to take a breath soon. Panic surged with it, but he forced it down, making himself concentrate.

There.

A tiny light dappled, catching his eye. He swam up towards

it. As he grabbed it, he felt metal; a belt buckle. Limbs and torso came next, deadweight and face-down.

Daniel broke the top of the water, gasping. 'Ethan!'

He wrestled with the cowboy's prone body, turning his face out of the water. As his face hit air, the cowboy let out a bark of explosive coughs. He was not unconscious, just stunned. A wound on his forehead trickled blood where he'd smashed his face against the stone wall when the water hit. The rogue Sentinel spat out water and lifted his face to the ceiling, taking deep breaths. Then his stupefied gaze took in the devastation around them; the water swirling angrily, threatening to tug them down into the depths like the Kraken's tentacles would merchant ships.

Ethan blinked. ' . . . Chloe?'

Daniel nodded, grim-faced. He processed the scene: the police station was filled almost to capacity; water had cascaded straight through the hole in the roof outside the cell. The building's ancient stone walls and oak door made it the perfect container. Daniel kicked out his feet. Both men supported each other, keeping their faces out of the water, up near the ceiling. Still behind bars, they knew they were going to drown if they didn't do something . . . and quickly.

'The water level's rising. You still got the keys?'

'They'll be on the bottom of the cell somewhere. Daniel . . . !'

The cowboy's words were obliterated by the water as Daniel ducked beneath it again. If he had been thinking straight, he would have pointed out it was quicker for him to look; he hadn't hit his head; time was of the essence. As it was, Daniel was not thinking at all, but operating on instinct. He really had left his old life of books and study behind. He was no longer a thinking man, but one of action now.

The water was murky, filled with mud and stones and debris. Daniel closed his eyes and sank to the bottom of the cell, feeling for the keys with the palms of his hands. He had a vague memory of seeing a police search, of men and women lining and up and thrashing through undergrowth, step by methodical step. He did the same thing, left to right, inch by agonising inch as his need for breath allowed. He was glad the cell was so small, now.

Finally, Daniel's left hand closed around that big, iron metal key ring. He grabbed it and felt for the cell door, fitting the key in the lock and turning it. He broke the surface; Ethan joined him by the bars. The cowboy helped Daniel pull the heavy door inwards; no mean feat against the flow of the water. After two false starts, the door opened.

They squeezed out, grabbing for the branches of the tree that had gone through the roof and into the vestibule. The mossy desk was demolished, but the big tree had withstood the deluge. It created a ladder out of the police station, onto what was left of the top of the building. The cowboy clambered on to its boughs, pulling Daniel out of the water after him.

Both men appeared outside, on the broken roof tiles. The pale eye of the moon appeared from behind clouds, illuminating some of the damage. The river was swollen and torrential, even though there had been no rainfall that day. The valley's steep sides acted as a funnel, sending the deluge down towards the harbour. Even without the harsh glare of daylight, Daniel knew it was bad. Timber and fallen trees floated past the old police station; mounds of mud and bricks washed up, forcing their way into homes, shops and other buildings. Daniel and the cowboy gazed in disbelief at the devastation, unable to give voice to their fears: the Sentinel were almost certainly vanquished, but it looked as if Chloe had killed everyone else along with them.

'Fuck,' Ethan said.

'Oh, *bǎobǎo*,' Daniel moaned.

TWENTY-SIX

The water hit Adelita and the others with ferocious force, scattering Gathering members in all directions. Helpless to counteract, Adelita felt her magic constrict under Chloe's guilt, distress and confusion through their spellbind. The pain of it flooded through every nerve ending as the shock of the water swept her away into the darkness.

Yet as Adelita resurfaced and the floodwaters circled around her, she could feel Earth magic cradling her from harm. She knew, instinctively, that Chloe had sent this protective power to each of the Gathering members to save them from the raging waters.

Thank you, Chloe.

Chloe's answer came down the spellbind: *You're welcome.*

Adelita's heart swelled with love for the girl, prompting white light to burst around her as she travelled through the water. Her magic's strength was no longer diminished and felt stronger than when she'd been angry. She seized its momentum and pushed the white light from herself, lifting herself out on to the riverbank. In her peripheral vision she was aware of other Elemental colours illuminating as other witches did the same.

Chloe, where are you?

No answer, this time.

'Girls!' Emmeline was calling in Cornish, though Adelita found she could understand every word as if they were in English: 'Girls, find your brothers!'

As she made this connection, Adelita's psyche switched on: she was moving fast again, spotting boys and young men in the water. No Sentinel were in the water; nor could she see any on the banks; no bodies, either. They had vanished, presumably purged from the valley by the deluge.

She joined the hunt. As Adelita found a member of the Gathering, she threw white spirals around them like life buoys, alerting other helpers to their whereabouts. She was relieved – and surprised – to see there were no serious casualties on their side. Red, blue and yellow magic flared in the darkness as witches pulled their boys and young men from the water. The little ones cried for their mothers and their sisters; the bigger ones shrugged them off and told them they were *bloody fine, get off.*

'Chloe!' Unable to rouse her in the spellbind again, Adelita called up and down the valley. But the teenager didn't show herself. Concern flip-flopped in Adelita's belly.

Adelita felt someone tug her sleeve. She looked down and saw two skinny, blonde, identical tween girls, both naked and blue with cold, teeth chattering. They hugged themselves, looking a sorry sight without their mud camouflage and Celtic-style battle dress of twigs and leaves.

'Where's our mum?' they demanded.

Adelita smiled. She recognised them as Tansy's other girls from the food hall. Even if she'd never seen them before, she'd know them in an instant. Though they did not look like Tansy, they still had the same wild and ireful look in their eyes as their mother.

A battle-weary Gwen appeared out of the darkness. 'There you are! You know how it works ... Mum will just need to recharge. Come on.'

Adelita watched Gwen take her sisters back to the Wellington. Thanks to the spellbind, Adelita knew Chloe was present; she could still feel the teen's residual magic pumping through her own muscles. She stopped and concentrated, trying to send some white light back through to the girl. She wondered if she could see Chloe's whereabouts in her mind's eye, but the teen was still blocking her. Adelita sent good vibes through the spellbind in the hope of it reaching her and bringing her back.

We love you, Chloe.

Adelita found Costentyn sitting against a wall down by the old National Trust second-hand book shop. Loveday leant against her son, her eyes half closed. She was dwarfed by him, yet he still looked like a boy, wide-eyed with concern for his mother. Another witch sat with them, holding a wad of cloth to Loveday's shoulder. She'd added more over the top as each got soaked, ripping strips from her dress. She'd wound the whole lot around the Water witch's arm, careful not to cut off the circulation.

'Good work.' Adelita knelt down next to the three of them.

'I was a nurse ... before,' the other witch replied.

'How long have you been putting pressure on the wound?'

'Since right after it happened, when she came out the water.'

'Great.' Adelita turned her attentions back to Loveday. 'Can I see?'

Loveday hissed softly with pain as Adelita bid her sit forwards so she could examine her. As she noted the red blooms of the exit wound on the other side, Adelita nodded, relieved. The Water witch would be fine. It was a through-and-through, just like Ethan's had been back in the Texas motel.

As this thought surfaced, a soaked-through Ethan appeared out of thin air, windmilling his arms. He landed on the harbour path next to Adelita, as if she herself had conjured him there. Before she could laugh in disbelief, Emmeline joined the cowboy in a blast of yellow sparks. She pulled a drenched Daniel through the portal after her.

'Look who I found on the police station roof,' the Air witch declared.

'How did you get up there?' Adelita's attentions were diverted by Daniel's bare legs. 'Where the hell are your pants?'

Both men looked to each other.

'It's a long story. Ask Costentyn,' Daniel said.

Costentyn just shrugged. Emmeline crouched down by her soulmate. He shifted his mother to Emmeline's waiting arms. She crooned to her, tucking one of Loveday's stray purple hair wraps behind her ear. Loveday smiled, though her eyes closed again with pained exhaustion.

Daniel looked around them all. 'Where's Chloe?'

Adelita shook her head. 'She's not far. I can sense it. She'll be back, when she's ready.'

Daniel took a deep breath and nodded. 'OK.'

He repeated the word a few more times, as if he was trying to persuade himself. Adelita knew he was struggling not to panic, to accept what she'd said. Ethan patted him on the shoulder, letting Daniel lean against him slightly, holding him up.

Ethan looked around the scene of devastation. 'Guess we better sort this out while we wait?'

'Good idea,' Daniel muttered.

TWENTY-SEVEN

As the roar of the water came, the Earth magic that had pinned everyone in Boscastle to the ground released its hold on the Scourge and Powell as well. Cat-like, the Scourge sprang to his feet, racing to the edge of the trees so he could bear witness to the torrent cascading down the valley below them by the light of the moon. Mud churned, ripping through buildings and taking vehicles with it, making them seem like toys. Horror and fascination surged through him in parallel with the floodwater and debris.

A glimmer of hope pierced his chest. Could this be the end of the Gathering? His men were dead, but they were done for anyway. But if the biggest Elemental coven in the world had been taken out of commission as well, then the Scourge could hide his fuck-up. He could escape Uno's wrath. He could keep looking for Chloe Su, assuming she was still alive. If she wasn't, he could claim credit for that, too. Only Powell could contradict him and the tech guy was not a problem. He could be easily despatched.

Just as the Scourge was thinking about retrieving his firearm and putting a bullet through the unsuspecting Powell's brain, lights flickered over Boscastle.

The unmistakable flares of Elementals flickered up and around the valley as witches pulled themselves from the water. Red, yellow, blue. One white. Adelita Garcia must still down there. He could discern movement, if not the actual people. He heard voices, male as well as well as female; the guttural consonants of that weird nonsense language they spoke. Most, if not all, of those bitches and their cuck male spawn and white knights must have survived. Disappointment coursed through the Scourge. When the hell was he going to catch a break in this cursed witch hunt? *Fuck.*

'. . . Sir?'

The Scourge turned to Powell, who was back by his monitors. In the corner of one screen was a wide-eyed Sentinel, surrounded by darkness. A survivor. He was a big man, but had the posture of a child, hiding in the bushes, eyes wild with fear. The Scourge searched his memory banks and dredged up a name: Franklin. He'd been part of the second team to go into the village, the one that useless fucker Carter *hadn't* been leading. Franklin had removed his body cam and was speaking directly into the lens. There was no sound.

'What the hell is he saying?' the Scourge spat.

As if he'd heard the Scourge's frustration, Franklin turned towards something by his feet. It looked like a body bag. He pulled the rubberised fabric back; there was not a Sentinel corpse inside, but something else.

A sleeping, drugged witch, the halo around her head blinking.

TWENTY-EIGHT

As daylight broke, Adelita, Ethan and the others took the walking wounded back to the old medical centre, which had escaped the worst of the floodwater too. A couple more of the witches had medical training from a previous life: one had taken St John Ambulance classes, another had been a nurse before she'd had to go into hiding to evade her kill order, like the one who had helped Loveday. After Adelita had changed out of her wet clothes and showered, washing the mud and grit from her hair, she was ready to see patients.

Adelita had been worried about being rusty, but her training came back to her quickly as she dealt with pain meds and shots; a broken thumb; a sprained ankle; various scrapes and wounds. Since he had insisted on being her medical team as well, first in line was Ethan. She shone a light in his eyes and checked him for concussion. His pupils reacted without problems. She gave him two paracetamol and stuck a Band-Aid with Tweety Pie on it over the cut on his forehead.

'How many fingers am I holding up?' Adelita flipped him the bird.

Ethan laughed and swallowed his pills dry.

The witches had been keeping the medical supplies well stocked, making Adelita's life easier; there was even an old jar of lollipops. Most of the tweens demanded a treat, which was especially amusing considering they'd run hollering into battle just hours earlier. Ethan handed them over and dispensed high fives and hugs, locating more supplies as Adelita and the others called for them.

Their last patient seen, the other nurses took their leave. Adelita still felt wired. Her brain crackled with thoughts; she felt spring-loaded. She wasn't sure whether it was adrenalin, concern for Chloe, or her magic. Maybe it was all three. As the door to the medical centre closed, Adelita indicated Ethan's side, the stitches underneath his T-shirt.

'Since we're here, I'll check your wound.'

Ethan grimaced. 'Do we have to?'

'You going to be a baby, again?'

'Get me some more bourbon and let's do it.'

'Nope. You can take it.'

Ethan rolled his eyes and pulled his shirt off. He sat down on a plastic chair he'd brought in from the waiting room. Adelita knelt beside him, a replay of when she put the stitches in. She inspected her handiwork. The wound was not raised, nor did it feel hot to the touch. The flesh had fused, a hearty pink.

'Am I gonna live, Doc?' Ethan grinned.

'I think you'll be fine.'

Still at his feet, Adelita met his gaze, her hands palm-down on the tops of his thighs. The temperature in the room seemed to go up a few degrees as the air between them crackled with anticipation. His gaze kept flitting from her eyes to her mouth.

'You're everything. You know that, right?'

Adelita smiled. She wanted to lean forwards, press her lips to his. Her head screamed against it, but her heart betrayed her. A part of her was still mad with the cowboy for spellbinding with her back at the jail, and pulling her into this mess. But then she had to be mad with herself, too: he could never have connected with her if she'd not allowed it. Adelita could also feel that tell-tale tingle working its way from the pool of her belly towards her groin. This time magic had nothing to do with it.

She wanted him.

Ethan's inscrutable expression melted. Adelita could see the indecision flicker across his face. A thought flowered in her brain – *he's scared of me* – then Ethan slid off the chair onto his knees, bringing his face to Adelita's level.

He kissed her, this time.

Adelita let him pull her to her feet. Still kissing, they crashed through the door, into a windowless back room beyond. There was a couch in there. She broke off the kiss and unbuttoned her shirt, letting it flutter to the floor. Already shirtless, Ethan yanked down his shorts so he stood naked in front of her. Adelita had seen him half-dressed before, so she knew he'd look good without anything on. All the same, she ran an appreciative eye over his body: his broad shoulders, the sinews of his arms, the blond hair on his chest getting steadily darker as her eyes dropped lower.

Moving in for another kiss, one of Ethan's hands snaked behind Adelita's back, releasing her bra in one move. Adelita pulled away, unbuttoning her skinny jeans. They only went down halfway. She was stuck. Ethan tried to give her a hand, but he didn't have as much luck this time. She laughed, surrendering as he pushed her back on the couch. Kneeling over her, a wide grin on his face, he yanked at the jeans still round her calves. They gave way with unexpected ease, making him lose his balance. He fell backwards off the couch.

'Ow!' The impact of his weight travelled across the floor and made the thin door shudder in its frame.

Adelita propped herself up. 'You OK?'

They both laughed as Ethan emerged again, between her legs. The playful tempo between them changed. His smile disappeared as he loomed over her on his elbows, his weight heavy on her chest.

His mouth clamped down on hers. He seemed to remember himself and broke off the kiss, a question in his eyes.

'Do *you* really want to?' Adelita prompted, mentally crossing her fingers.

Ethan didn't answer. He shifted his weight onto one hand, reaching for something on the floor in the narrow room. Her jeans. He pulled something from the back pocket.

Her rose quartz crystal.

She shot him a questioning glance.

'Do it,' he said softly, before adding: 'Please.'

Adelita closed her fist around her crystal as he pushed forwards, hard into her. She felt Ethan and her magic move inside her. She laced her legs around his own. That tingling, electric sensation swept through her. He gripped both her hips.

Adelita's psyche switched on. She felt that strange awareness of time and space moving apart again, like she was between two planes of existence. She was aware of the knots of muscle in Ethan's shoulders; the veins in his neck; the steady drumbeat of his heart.

They rolled over on the wide couch, so she was on top. His hands found her waist as she rocked back and forth. Her spirit or consciousness seemed to leap out of her as it had in her dream, so she was above the couch, back on the ceiling. Below, she could see the tangle of hers and Ethan's limbs.

Momentarily, there was that glitch again: the couch was gone, replaced by the bed in the plush London hotel suite. Adelita was no longer there, but the woman with red hair instead. Those desperate, gargled breaths crashed through her mind . . .

'. . . You all right?'

Ethan's voice shocked her back to reality. She'd stopped. He met her stare, bashful and uncertain. Adelita blinked; she was back in her own body, him sprawled underneath her. When she smiled, he sat up, folding his arms around her as their chests pressed together.

'I got you, remember,' he murmured.

Their lips met as they started moving again. She felt that joy surge through her: there could be no time without him. They'd always been together; they would be for ever. She couldn't imagine life without him. He was hers. She was his.

She loved him.

More images shimmered through Adelita's mind like scenery through a train window. She knew they were not her thoughts, but Ethan's. None of them were that London suite. A Californian beach in bright sunshine; the lush green grass of a park; children running after a ball. Blood on the ground; barbed wire and trains; crying children ripped from their mothers' arms. Stonehenge at sunset; a silhouette against the orange sky. Then that geyser-like blast again, turning the skies a beautiful, yet terrible mess of colour.

It made the vision burst and disappear. Bright lights popped up in front of Adelita's eyelids like pinpricks. She could feel that deep quivering sensation building within her. That familiar white light threatened to burst from her again. Her focus swirled like water down a drain as she tried to snatch hold of it, stop it from erupting.

'It's OK,' Ethan whispered in her ear. 'Let it go.'

I don't want to hurt you, Adelita tried to say.

She was too late. Her throat seized up before she could get the words out. She arched her back. White light poured from her. A combination of magic and climax ripped through her body. She was powerless to stop it.

She felt Ethan freeze, his fingertips digging into her flesh as he tried to anchor himself in her. They gripped each other tighter. Adelita didn't need to travel back to the ceiling to know both of them were enveloped by a ball of flickering white light. It illuminated the room. Above them, the light bulb blew out.

In the windowless space, they were plunged back into darkness.

The room around her swirled as Adelita lay panting. Ethan seemed to swoon, letting go of her and collapsing backwards on the couch. Alarm jumped through her, like it had on the plane over to Bristol, but her fears were short-lived. As she leant over him, she could see his chest rise and fall. He was in no pain, despite the magic blast.

Adelita pressed her lips to his. 'I love you.'

Ethan grinned. 'I know.'

Adelita laughed and slapped him on the shoulder. 'Asshole.'

They drifted off to sleep.

TWENTY-NINE

The Orchid Tower, New York, USA

Uno was excited.

There hadn't been much cause for celebration in the past six months – or since the never-ending ruinous, gaping fuck-up that was Stonehenge, come to think of it – but the Scourge's report lifted Uno's spirits, at last.

The big man appeared on the iPad screen, looking haggard and worn. There were the remnants of black camouflage paint on his temple; a couple of days' stubble on his face. Jake Pembroke's eyes always had that haunted, harried look of a man on the run from himself, but now he looked positively wild with it, like a cornered animal. The Scourge seemed every single one of his forty-nine years, plus a few more besides. Intriguing.

Stuttering and starting again, Pembroke's fluctuating emotions affected his delivery. Clicking a ballpoint pen on and off, Uno wanted to reach through the screen and slap the Scourge's bedraggled face. The Gathering must have been horrifying, even for the most stalwart of Sentinel, but empathy was not in Uno's wheelhouse.

'This witch you caught ... She's definitely Elemental?'

'Correct, boss.'

The Scourge was a prick, but a useful one. Uno had long recognised his potential for finding the witch the Elementals called 'The One'. The Sentinel had first heard whispers nearly two decades earlier. It was said the equinox had aligned and delivered a child capable of all four elements – fire, earth, water and air. March 20th had long been celebrated as a time for rebirth, so the Elementals, not to mention some Crystal covens, had delighted in this news. They'd all waited patiently to hear what would happen next.

Nothing did.

In time, The One was forgotten as modern myth, like the Millennium Bug or climate change. It didn't matter, since various other ducks had to be placed in a row first. Such as dispensing with Dr Miriam Stone. While Stone had not been a witch, or even a Legacy, she'd always had their back. It didn't help she was a holier-than-thou fugly bitch, either. It was Stone's brainpower and political nous that had put her in the position, but it seemed especially absurd to Uno that such a revolting-looking woman should be in charge of the free world. All Stone had needed was a wart on the end of her hooked nose, then she'd have even looked like a witch.

'Where is this Elemental now?'

'Being transported to Thames House, London.'

Uno's nostrils flared. Ugh. That was the MI5 building. British spooks were the literal worst, drenched in cologne in their crisp slacks, sending out passive aggression like the frigging Bat Signal. In fact, the whole of the United Kingdom blew. Tiny island full of tiny people with tiny minds. Of course, Uno didn't like anyone, but the fact such a small place had created so many goddamn natural witches meant it *had* to be a pit of depravity.

'I'll join you there. I'm leaving now.' Uno just had to see this special witch.

The Scourge's eyes bulged in surprise, but he wisely tamped his objection down. 'As you wish.'

The screen went black as the connection terminated. Pembroke was not used to being joined by the Sentinel's number one on the road. The position was usually based solely in the Orchid Tower. It had been agreed a long time ago that if Uno was to take the position, the general public – not to mention other security agencies in Safeguard countries – must not catch a glimpse of Uno in an official capacity as the Sentinel's number one.

Uno mashed a hand on the buzzer on the desk. A door opened and a Sentinel bodyguard, Riggs, opened the door, awaiting instruction.

'Get the Sentinel jet ready for me. I'm going to London.'

To his credit, Riggs did not flinch. 'Right away, boss.'

The door closed again. The vast majority of Sentinel themselves were unaware of Uno's true identity. Other than personal bodyguards, only Pembroke, the Elders, a couple of other high-ranking lieutenants and some of their pet geeks knew. Not just because of the significant conflict of interest and Uno's relationship with President Hopkins, but because of a law the Sentinel had passed some forty years ago. Women, after all, were not even supposed to be able to join the Sentinel.

They were definitely not supposed to lead it.

Uno kicked her legs back in her wheelie chair and let it transport her across her office towards her en suite. She was still in her night clothes: an old football jersey of her husband's and a pair of panties. Since she wasn't supposed to leave the Orchid Tower when conducting her duties as Uno, she didn't bother putting clothes on most days. She admired her long legs; her perfectly pedicured toes. She was fifty-three but could easily pass for her late thirties. Botox and a well-executed facelift had staved off the aging process remarkably well, especially as she'd looked young for her age in the first place.

The shower switched on; hot water cascaded down over her lean, trim body. Since she was a young girl, Uno had spent hundreds of thousands of dollars on what she called 'self-maintenance'. Cosmetic surgery, facial peels, make-up and hair, exercise and nutrition – she did it all. She'd come from money but had delighted in getting a succession of men pay for it for her, since they benefited from her efforts. Now her husband paid for her tucks and tricks; frankly it was the very least he could do.

She insisted her two daughters joined her now in doing the same, especially as they were both entering their teens. She sympathised with Regan's protestations that looks shouldn't matter; that it's what's inside that counts (a nice theory, but that's all it was; a theory). She soothed Alice's tears when she said she couldn't get those last few errant pounds off. (Yes, it was unfair.) But like her, the girls had to realise an inescapable truth: men's worth only improved with age, yet women's was destined to wither and fade. But her girls would go on to thank her, just as Uno had thanked her own mother for thinking ahead. They needed to protect their investment and their place in the pecking order.

At the top.

Uno stepped out of the shower. She caught sight of herself in the steamed mirror. A smile etched its way across her face. She knew that beauty was the mark of a powerful woman when navigating a man's world. Men were all such dogs; distraction was easy. How else could she have snatched control of the Sentinel, an environment where women had been banned for two decades?

By marrying a Senator and riding his coat-tails to the White House and becoming first lady, of course.

Marianne Hopkins had work to do.

THIRTY

Boscastle, Cornwall, UK

The Gathering set to work restoring Boscastle to its former glory. With nothing else to do but wait for Chloe, Daniel pitched in, shovelling silt and rubble away from the buildings. Even with magic at their disposal, it would be a big job for the witches. The rebuild would take months.

He had slept fitfully for a few hours but felt better for it. He wished he could do more for his daughter; that she would let him. But he understood why she'd gone off on her own. She'd had to cope alone, her whole life. Chloe's anger against her mother was justified. Though Li had never meant to torture their daughter, she'd still done Chloe a terrible wrong. The pain and anguish Chloe had been put through could never be taken back. Daniel couldn't go blundering in, saying he could fix everything for Chloe. He would have to wait for Chloe to reach out. He hoped it would be soon.

No one woke Adelita and Ethan, but the commotion brought them outside. They stumbled out of the medical centre, blinking in the light and pulling on clothes. Daniel smiled to himself; it was about time. That thought was swiftly followed by a stab of jealousy mixed with sorrow that speared him in the chest. Li's secret had made him question everything; made him feel as if he'd never known his wife at all. But their entire life had not been a lie. They'd had their problems and they'd both made mistakes; they'd been together over twenty years and had shared so much, including raising their daughter. He had loved Li and felt her love in return. Daniel needed to leave his anger behind and forgive Li for keeping her secret from him. He needed to forgive himself, too, for not seeing what was under his nose.

A shout of alarm echoed across the village. Daniel lifted the shovel into the air, brandishing it like a weapon without thinking; instinct had taken him over again. He caught sight of Ethan and the other men doing similar; Adelita and the women glowed with magic. Daniel's eyes narrowed as he tried to decipher the confusion. Something or someone was on the bend on the road into the village, further up from the bridge and the harbour path.

'Who is it?' Ethan yelled as Daniel fell into step ahead of him.

Before Daniel could answer, another Elemental flare went up. Unlike all other Elementals at the Gathering, this one was green. His heart lifted for a microsecond in the hope it was Chloe, before the realisation crashed through him. He took in the female stature, the way she lurched from side to side, her eyes fixed on the sky. Daniel's grip slackened on the shovel in his hands as he stood, transfixed and staring.

It was not his daughter.

The Elemental had been transported from Cornwall to Thames House, the MI5 building in London, on a 'need to know' basis only. Secrecy was one of the few things the British were good at, so the Scourge hoped he could contain the creature, ready for Uno's arrival in a few hours. The witch was confined to a windowless room. He waited with her, not willing to leave her for a second. He could trust no one and this was his big moment. He had finally proved himself not only to the Sentinel, but to the whole world. His name would go down in history. He would be premier in every sense of the word.

The Scourge lifted the witch's head by her hair, inspecting her face with the detached air of a scientist in a laboratory. The Elemental was strapped into the chair by her wrists and ankles. She drooled, her eyes misty and fixed ahead, the lights on her halo glowing green, flashing left to right. The combination of psychotropic drugs, the halo and a nasty head injury sustained in the flood had done the job for them. Fortune had smiled on Jake at last. Thank fuck. There was no way Uno could hang him out to dry when she got here now.

It was hard to believe the Elemental in front of the Scourge was the one he'd been haunted by for so long. Her face had been the first thing he'd seen in his mind's eye every morning; the last thing every night. Now here she was, at last, within his control. The Scourge's desire for payback knitted its way through his muscles. This unexpected bit of good luck felt like an invitation. He had to let her know he had won. Uno could have her pound of flesh later.

The Scourge slipped the halo's regulator from his pocket as he approached the chair, pressing its green button to wake the Elemental. The witch's glazed eyes cleared. She reacted against her hand and ankle restraints first, attempting to jump up from the seat. She bared her teeth with rage when the straps wouldn't budge. Her mind was as strong as her magic – but then he knew that already.

The witch looked up at him, her lip curled in a feral snarl. '*You.*'

The Scourge saw her emotions flicker across her expressive face: disbelief, anger, then finally ice-cold fear . . . Just like she'd done to him all those years ago, in London. She'd pinned him between her legs to that hotel bed with her Earth magic, her powers glowing green around him like toxic gases.

'Hello, Tansy,' the Scourge said.

Adelita muscled a slack-jawed Daniel out of the way, just in time to see Chloe's black carapace eyes as she turned towards them all. Chloe's skin was a roadmap of purple veins, her dark hair standing on end as she raised her arms in the air. Between her fingertips, green Earth magic sizzled with malevolent purpose.

'Oh no,' Adelita said.

She could feel the magnitude of the power moving within Chloe, as strongly as the quickening of her own heartbeat. That ominous, deep hum came with Chloe's dark skills, but it was louder than before. It no longer felt like a jet engine roaring overhead, but as if it originated in the centre of the earth. It brought a powerful current of air with it, stealing Adelita's breath and making her teeth rattle in her skull.

Chloe, what's happening to you?

Pulsating green light enveloped Chloe. Crackles of electricity danced over the orb surrounding the teenager as she cast those horrific, shiny black eyes at the sky. Adelita could see the molecules of Chloe's green orb surrounding her. At micro-level they seemed like tiny bomb blasts but joined together she knew they could be sent outwards, a devastating shockwave that would take with it every person, building and tree around them, leaving only smoking debris behind.

Panicked voices and shouts sounded behind Adelita as witches gathered up children, trying to get out the way of the deadly blast they were sure was coming. Only Adelita and Daniel stayed where they were. As Ethan made a grab to pull her away, Adelita sent a warning shock at him, sending him to his knees with a grunt.

She turned her attentions back to the teenager.

Don't, Chloe!

Those dark eyes fixed on Adelita at last.

But I won't hurt you, the teenager said.

Chloe stepped forward and grabbed Adelita's hands in her own.

Green light exploded around them both.

THIRTY-ONE

Thames House, MI5 Building, London, UK

'I'll kill you this time, pig.'

The Scourge showed no concern on the outside, but inside he braced himself. He still didn't know if the combined powers of the halo, the drugs and the head injury were enough to hold the High Witch at bay. Green residual magic still crackled through her hair.

Nothing happened.

The Scourge felt a smirk tug at his mouth as he watched Tansy's wicked scowl turn to disbelief as her magic did not respond to her wishes. A powerful witch like Tansy would not be used to being overcome. He could relate to that.

'Must be upsetting,' the Scourge acknowledged.

Tansy ignored the Scourge and snarled, renewing her ineffectual struggles against the restraints, spitting out cuss words and threats like a she-devil. She screwed up her face, trying to push magic from herself. The Scourge was alarmed for a microsecond when a shower of tiny green sparks jumped off her hair. They died just as quickly. Tansy sat back in her chair, panting with the effort.

'You can't escape.'

The Scourge dragged a chair over so he could sit down and rest his weary, bulky body. He still hadn't slept properly yet, only snatching forty paltry minutes of shut-eye on the helicopter ride from Boscastle to London. Pain and lethargy swarmed through him in waves.

'Fuck you.'

The witch's voice sounded different to his recollections of the redhead on top of him all those years ago. The Scourge wasn't sure if his memories had simply made her sound more evil, or maybe she'd had elocution lessons. She looked different, too. This was unsurprising given she was no longer in her early twenties, but her forties. Tansy had been a down-and-out back then; not the middle-class, middle-aged woman he could see before him now. Her skin no longer had that waxy pallor; her face and body were fuller; her teeth were fixed. Her flamed mane was just as he recalled, not a trace of grey.

'We don't have long. Numero Uno will be here by morning.'

The Scourge thought he saw another flicker of fear register on Tansy's face. She pushed it down and affected a sneer.

'How is Marianne doing?'

Confusion crashed through the Scourge.

Tansy saw this register and grinned. 'You're a stooge, Scourge. You always have been.'

The Scourge raised his hand to strike the witch but stopped himself. She was baiting him; it was what she wanted. He couldn't give her the satisfaction. There was one thing he had to know, before Uno got here and Tansy was out of his hands.

'Tell me something.' His voice was soft. 'Why did you do it?'

Tansy met his eye, smirking and defiant. 'Do what?'

The Scourge slammed his hands down on the top of a nearby cabinet, upending a metal tray of instruments that clattered to the floor with a discordant crash.

'Don't play dumb with me!'

He grabbed her by the throat, delighting in her panicked, bulging eyes; the veins that popped up in her temples. He'd waited over two decades for this. But his desire for answers bested his need for revenge. He let go before her eyes could roll back in her head and she passed out. He stood back, flexing his meaty hand as he watched her gasp for breath. He wanted her to be as afraid as he had been when she'd done the same to him, her Earth magic gripping his chest and throat, choking the life from him.

That night in the London hotel suite, twenty-five years ago.

If Adelita screamed as Chloe's bubble of Earth magic washed over her, she could not hear it. The green light blinded her and sent a horrific tidal wave of hot pain through her head, torso and limbs. Her entire body was on fire; in fact, she didn't think she had a body any more. She was that floating presence again. What was left of Adelita soared up into the sky like it had on the plane, unable to tether itself to anything. Even Chloe was gone.

Abruptly, the pain vanished, as if it had never been there.

Was she dead?

A buzzing noise, more perceived than heard, swept through Adelita next. Her hands came into focus first. She stared at her palms, then turned them over, patting her body, her face. A bright white light shone from her, illuminating the darkness. She was really there. She was alive.

Adelita intuited she was no longer in Boscastle; she was nowhere on Earth. She knew it was not some kind of manifestation of the spellbind, but something different. Wherever Chloe had taken her, it was beyond the physical plains of existence. Adelita's gut told her she had been here before; it was this spiritual space she moved through when she used her psyche to skip ahead.

'Chloe?'

At the sound of her voice, Chloe's soft green light flared in the distance. As soon as Adelita noticed it go up, she zoomed forward without the need to move her limbs. In the blink of an eye, she was standing over the teenager, who was seated cross-legged at her feet. Chloe's palms were face up, columns of green Earth magic pouring from them. They swayed back and forth, dancing from hand to hand as if Chloe was juggling.

Where are we?

Chloe looked up at Adelita. Like before, her eyes were black, oily, shiny but, unlike the previous times she'd seen the teenager in such a state, there was no anguish or pain there. Chloe was not in distress, she was laughing. Adelita felt Chloe's joy leap to her, through the Earth magic. It was this shared spiritual space that linked her and Chloe, through their shared gift of psyche. She laughed too.

The dark of the moon, Chloe said.

Another connection fired inside Adelita: the equinox. The time of the year when the sun is directly above the equator, making the day and night an equal length. Chloe's words from the beach returned to Adelita: *It takes me to a place I don't want to go. A dark place.* Every time she'd accessed this dark power before, it had sent the teenager delirious with pain and destruction.

I don't understand. Isn't this a bad place?

It can be, Chloe replied. *I get it now. It is what I make it.*

Of course. The spring equinox was a time for witches to say goodbye to winter and give thanks for new life and new beginnings. Adelita had watched her mother and sisters prepare for these celebrations when she was young, though as a woman of science she'd rarely participated as an adult. Day and night were not evil, so the dark of the moon was not inherently bad either. It was up to whomever wielded the power and how they did it.

Without warning, a woman's face swam up in the streams of magic in Chloe's hands. Her face was anguished with pain, her mouth drawn in a silent scream. Adelita knew who it was instantly, even though she'd never met her: Chloe's mother and Daniel's wife, Li. The teenager shrieked and her columns of green magic exploded outwards like a Roman Candle.

No, Chloe!

Adelita knew she couldn't let Chloe go nuclear again. She'd send her dark power racing back into the physical realm and destroy Boscastle. She pushed white light out of herself like a lantern, sending it pouring forth to the girl.

Take my hand.

Chloe grabbed for Adelita. As the girl's hand touched hers, there was another blinding flash. They left their bodies behind again and soared above that strange dark place, Adelita's Crystal magic lighting the way for them.

'Ada . . . !'

The voice seemed far off, muffled, like Adelita was underwater. Yet it acted as an anchor for her as it filtered through the dazzling white light. She knew who it was. Even though she had no body in this strange place, she felt a sense of warmth flood through her torso and limbs.

Ethan.

Like a fish on a hook, Adelita was powerless to stop his voice snaring her and pulling her to the surface. With a sudden glare of colours and noise, faces swirled around her like a kaleidoscope. Ethan loomed over her, one hand stroking her hair back from her eyes. She blinked, stunned and unable to conjure any words into being. His strained expression slackened with relief, then tightened with joy again as he realised she was back.

'You're alive.' His smile was replaced with a dark scowl. 'What the hell was that, Doc?'

Adelita attempted to lift her head, but everything around

her spun. Sharp pain stabbed her between the eyes and nausea sloshed around her belly. She couldn't recall feeling this bad in her whole life – at least, not without drinking a bottle of tequila first. Still stunned, Adelita let Ethan help her sit up. The world seemed to lurch sideways, but it was her. Ethan grabbed her, propping her back up.

'Chloe?' she murmured.

'She's OK.'

Adelita couldn't smell burning trees or any other tell-tale odours of destruction. The Gathering had not been subjected to Chloe's powers going haywire. She took in the wide-eyed stares of other witches; they were not entirely sure what had happened yet, but all of them understood it had been something momentous.

'The equinox gave her the power,' Adelita tried to explain, but spoken out loud her words came out disjointed and garbled. 'The dark moon . . . ?'

Ethan smiled, humouring her. Her eyes settled on Daniel. The professor knelt on the path cradling Chloe in his arms. As before, Chloe had passed out under the pressure of her massing powers. As he looked round, his gaze met Adelita's and she knew he had somehow seen, or perhaps felt, what she had done for Chloe when she'd managed to prevent her from exploding again.

Thank you, he mouthed.

'She's OK.'

The cowboy pulled Adelita to her feet. Her legs gave way underneath her, making her lean against him like a drunk. She slid an arm around his shoulders as he held her up by her waist.

'Don't get used to this,' she warned.

'Wouldn't dream of it.'

Adelita shuffled forwards, step by agonising step. 'Where are we going?'

'*You're* going to bed.' Ethan opened an ornate gate to the thatched cottage they'd stayed in the previous night. They staggered through the overgrown front garden.

The residual magic made Adelita wanton, just like it had back in the Texas motel room. She gave Ethan what she thought was a seductive smile. In reality, she just looked dazed and hammered.

'Come with me?' she guffawed as the double-entendre dawned on her.

Ethan grinned. 'Later.'

Peevish, Adelita let him pull her into the cottage. He took her through to the back bedroom, where there was a large double bed. Grateful at the sight, she fell back onto it with a *whoomph*. Ethan kneeled down beside the bed, pulling her shoes off one by one.

'You're an asshole.' Despite her grumbles, there was a dreamy smile on her face.

'I know.'

Ethan's tone was cheerful as he pulled the covers over her, tucking her into bed like she was a child. He leant over her and touched his lips to her forehead. Adelita could not keep her eyes open. They fluttered closed before he could pull the door shut. Just like the first words were his when she'd come round, the last words she heard were his, too.

'I got you, Ada.'

Adelita slipped back under, into a deep sleep.

THIRTY-TWO

Thames House, MI5 Building, London, UK

The Scourge had relived that night in the London hotel suite behind his eyelids every night for twenty-five years. He was thankful no other Sentinel was there with him. Shame rushed through him at the mere thought of other men thinking him weak, bested by a woman, even if she was Elemental.

Tansy spat blood on the floor. 'Fair's fair. You were going to kill me that night. Remember?'

'Untrue.'

The Scourge felt the lie weigh heavy on his tongue. The witch eyeballed him, that mocking smile still on her face. She had been there, in that room with him. She'd been able to read his deadly intentions.

'Admit it, Scourge. You got drunk with the power, killing witches in that first wave of the Sentinel's secret holy war. You thought you could do whatever you wanted. Punish any woman, for any transgression you saw fit, real or imagined.' Tansy chuckled. 'But unlucky . . . You found me instead.'

He sighed. With the benefit of hindsight, it was obvious. He'd taken Tansy's weakness at face value. Despite his military background, he had not thought to tail her, find out her real name, check her background or bloodline. The young Elemental must have smelled death on him; it was said those types could.

'We're the same, you and me,' Tansy shifted in her chair, 'two sides of the same coin, you might say.'

'I wouldn't,' the Scourge snarled.

Tansy continued her rant as if he hadn't spoken. 'You love punishing women? Well, I love punishing men like you. I can't tell you how fun it was, feeling you helpless and frozen underneath me, like the sack of toxic male shit you are.'

The Scourge's mouth twisted in renewed fury. Tansy's gaze flitted to the halo's regulator in his hand. She knew he wanted to press the red button; to send shockwaves of static electricity into her brain. He itched to do it.

He hesitated, moving his thumb away. Defiance still flickered in Tansy's eyes. The Scourge's sharp mind deciphered this; she wanted him to kill her. There had to be a reason for that ... Tansy didn't want to see Uno, but why?

'All those big muscles ... Useless, against tiny me. It's funny, really.'

The Scourge tamped down his anger, trying to clear his head. It was no use; Tansy's jibes pulled open his trauma like a gaping wound. His heart rattled in his ribcage like a trapped bird. His breath was trapped in his chest. His rebuff caught in his throat, wrapped in piercing pain.

'It doesn't matter what you think or do, Jake. It never has.'

He wanted to tell her she was wrong, but no words came to his lips. His memories of that night continued to assault him.

Jake could envisage Tansy again, leering over him, her small hands tracing his throat. He could feel her wetness as she slid onto his treacherous erection. He could still see her malicious grin as she rocked back and forth, her pelvis grinding into his, taking what she wanted. It had felt like it went on for ever.

Finally she'd shuddered deep inside, bucking against him and raising her face to the ceiling. His body betrayed him once more, orgasm sweeping through him against his will as he emptied into her.

But now, Tansy was in *his* control.

'Our time is coming, Scourge. You will lose.'

The Scourge's lip curled in a sneer. 'Never.'

He pressed the red button.

THIRTY-THREE

T ansy shrieked and bared her teeth as the halo delivered static electricity straight to her head. The Scourge was not quite as dispassionate as he had been with the Crystal witch he'd tortured back in Exeter. He'd waited a long time to find Tansy again. Pleasure rippled through him as he dispensed his longed-for punishment at last.

The Scourge took his thumb off the regulator button. Tansy's head rolled on her shoulders as she leant backwards, panting. He wanted her to plead, to tell him she was sorry; that she'd do whatever he wanted. To his increased chagrin, Tansy just let out another snicker.

'Your face is a picture. Seriously.'

The witch regarded him through half-lidded eyes. Jake was certain he had hurt her. He'd given her a much higher dose than Rita, who'd squealed like a stuck pig. Fury snaked its way through the fibre of his muscles. Why didn't this Elemental bitch know her place, even now? Her magic was hobbled; there was no escape. She had lost.

The Scourge had won.

He flicked the dial up on the regulator, pressed the button again. The green lights in the halo flashed yellow. Tansy emitted a screech and jumped around in the chair, arrested by her restraints. Her eyes rolled back in her skull as the electricity flooded through her. As he took his thumb off the button, she lurched forwards, shoulders heaving.

'Last chance, Tansy. If you ever want to see your daughters again ...'

'Oh, I will see them again.' Tansy sat up with difficulty, her tone vexingly matter-of-fact. 'With the Goddess.'

'You'd willingly abandon your daughters? Your sisters?'

'I never abandoned them; you took me. Like all witches, we know where we come from, where we are going. A witch is not afraid to die.' Tansy laughed again. 'Unlike you. You're a coward, Scourge.'

The bitch was stupid, insane, or both. He was no coward. He pressed the button again.

Tansy did not jump around this time as the halo's lights flickered from green to yellow. She sighed, inhaling deeply and closing her eyes as the static electricity flowed through her. The Scourge was perturbed; he could still see the veins on her neck and the backs of her hands standing out. It had to be hurting her, yet she was acting as if she was in a frigging yoga class.

As he peered closer, Tansy opened one eye, lips curled in a rictus grin.

'*What. Kind. Of. Witch. Am. I?*'

The Scourge's brow furrowed as he connected the dots. He realised Tansy had *earthed* the electricity, made it go to ground ... She'd been pretending to be shocked by the halo. The Sentinel had never haloed an Earth witch before, so he'd fallen into her trap. She'd been baiting him to send electricity at her via the regulator, but for what reason?

Too late, the Scourge found out.

Electricity surged back from the halo, through the regulator, into his hand and arm. He flew backwards across the room, pain obliterating his sight momentarily like a camera flash. He landed on his wide shoulders, arse in the air. Unable to beat the halo through magic alone, Tansy had been working *with* it, powering it up. She hadn't dissipated the electricity into the ground, but *herself*, storing it inside her own body.

He'd played straight into her hands.

Tansy let loose a shriek of triumph as the chair's own electrics short-circuited, releasing the metal restraints around her wrists and ankles. She tried tugging at the halo; without its key, it wouldn't budge. Out in the corridor, an alarm was sounding. The spook cavalry was just seconds away. There was the trudging of boots upstairs; the calls of more Sentinel, not to mention MI5 operatives.

Tansy looked down at the Scourge, still sprawled on the floor. The door was kicked inwards as a young, trigger-happy Sentinel with steely eyes made it through first, weapon raised. The Scourge tried to call a warning, finally understanding what Tansy's plan was.

'Get back, witch!' the steely-eyed Sentinel yelled.

Tansy tried sending a surge of Earth magic at the Sentinel guard, but it was too weak and fell short. The halo was still affecting her, and she had no electricity left after using it all on the Scourge. As he made it back up on his hands and knees, she leant down and grabbed his face between her hands.

'Bye, Jake.'

'No . . . !'

She planted a kiss on his slack lips.

Too late, Jake realised her exit strategy included him. He felt her toxic Earth magic whip from her snake-like tongue and into his mouth. It poured through his skull and down through his body, incapacitating him like it had two and a half decades before. He convulsed under its assault, his mind disappearing in a stream of coloured Elemental flares. This time he realised there could be no way back as his brain folded in on itself, unravelling as it went.

He knew he was dead meat.

Jake was vaguely aware of the sound of a gunshot and then Tansy's lips were torn from his. They hit the floor together as she fell into his arms like a lover, blood blooming in the centre of her chest like a macabre red rose.

The Scourge's head cracked back on the tiles as the life left them both.

THIRTY-FOUR

Boscastle, Cornwall, UK

Agony surged through the sleeping Adelita, shocking her awake again. She let out a shriek like a keening animal. Imagery ricocheted through her mind: a darkened room; a chair with restraints; a large white guy with silver hair in that signature Sentinel dark suit, looming and ominous. Chloe was not with her in the room, but Adelita saw the teenager sit up in her own bed, her eyes wide with pain, their minds still melded by their spellbind.

Adelita!

I know.

The door slammed back on its hinges. Ethan appeared on the threshold, his forehead creased with concern. For a second, Adelita thought she was back in that Texas motel room; that they'd never left and it had all been a weird dream. Then the room came into focus: the patchwork quilt on the bed; the floral curtains in the window; the shabby-chic dresser in the corner. She was in Boscastle, at the Gathering. It was all true.

'What's happened?'

Fear made jagged shapes of Ethan's body language. He

stepped back in confusion as he took in Adelita, sitting up all by herself in the empty room. In his hand was a revolver; he'd expected to find someone in here with her, attacking her.

Adelita tried to speak, but no words came to her lips, her voice snatched away as more agony coursed through her neural pathways. She doubled over. She could feel Chloe drop to her hands and knees, felled by that same pain.

'Oh, Jesus!' he cried. 'What's happening?'

Adelita could not answer him. She felt Ethan join her on the bed. He gathered her prone form in his arms; he could do nothing else. Her head rested against his chest; she could hear his accelerated heartbeat.

'Tansy,' she whispered.

Powerless to do anything else for her, he rocked her back and forth, stroking her hair.

'You saw it?'

The door to the bedroom opened. Chloe stood there in real life, outside the spellbind, a blanket around her shoulders. She leant against Daniel, whose own anguished expression matched Ethan's. Chloe's face was drawn and haggard, a terrible look on someone so young. Neither of the men had been party to the source of the women's pain, yet they'd felt it.

Adelita nodded. The silence Ethan had given her let her unpick what had happened. Both Chloe and Adelita had psyche; so did Tansy. Perhaps it was the residue of their spellbind from the first night in Boscastle, or perhaps Tansy had sent them some kind of mental telegram. Whatever the case, Tansy had wanted them to know what had happened to her.

She broke away from Ethan and held her arms out for Chloe. The teenager ran to Adelita, eyes full of tears, burying her face in her shoulder.

'I killed Tansy.'

Adelita kissed her forehead. 'You didn't.'

'If I hadn't sent the flood . . . ?'

'You had to. You saved everyone.'

Adelita felt Ethan get off the bed. He uttered a wordless, angry cry as he punched the door; it shuddered in its frame. 'No, this is my fault. If I hadn't brought you both to Boscastle . . . I should have known it would end like this!'

She was grateful to Daniel as he approached her cowboy. He mumbled something in a low voice to him. Ethan nodded, allowing Daniel to put a comforting arm around his shoulders and steer him into the next room.

Chloe turned back to Adelita. 'Why didn't she wait? We could have found out where she was, gone to rescue her!'

The same thought had occurred to Adelita, too. While she, Chloe, Daniel and Ethan would have had to move on, she felt sure Emmeline and some of the others could have rescued the High Witch easily. In Tansy's last moments, she had realised, the High Witch had met her fate willingly; she was going to see her beloved Demelza again. But Adelita had grasped that was a benefit, not the cause. Tansy had not meant to be taken by the Sentinel, that Adelita was sure of. The High Witch was protecting the Gathering, by taking herself out of the equation. Adelita just needed to figure out how.

'We need to tell Gwen and the others.' Adelita gave the teenager a watery smile. She wiped the tears tracking Chloe's cheeks away.

'Then do we have to leave, like we were going to last night?'

Adelita hesitated, then nodded.

Chloe exhaled. 'Everywhere I go, I hurt people.'

'No, you don't.' Adelita put her arm around the girl. 'Don't think like that. Bigger things are at work here, most of them put in motion before you were even born. You are not to blame.'

Chloe looked at her askance, not believing her. She could see only the destruction she herself had wrought. She was incapable of seeing the bigger picture; what she'd been *made* to do. Ethan had said the same to Daniel on the roadside by the checkpoint on the Devon–Cornwall border. Chloe had to forgive herself. As these words slotted into Adelita's mind, she realised she had to forgive herself, too. She might be a walking contradiction, both healer and killer, but that was the hand she had been dealt.

She kissed the teen's forehead again. 'Come on, let's do this.'

Chloe's hand curled around Adelita's.

THIRTY-FIVE

Thames House, MI5 Building, London, UK

Thames House was a hubbub of activity, unusually so for what was the HQ of glorified civil servants. Normally a first lady deigning to visit such a paltry outfit was enough to bring the sycophants out, kowtowing to her. Marianne couldn't deny it; she did like the way the Brits placed class above all things, even gender. In contrast, the United States' misogyny was baked-on so hard that Mr President's wife could get overlooked. Ludicrous.

Her escort was a beady-eyed, middle-aged spook with a giraffe neck by the name of Harper. He had been surprised to see the first lady, since there had been nothing on the schedule. She'd batted his questions away with a girlish laugh and told him some ridiculous lie about shopping in London. She claimed to have a message for the Scourge. After she'd laughed at Harper's piss-poor jokes and batted her eyelids at him half a dozen times, he agreed to take her to the Sentinel's premier agent.

Anxious to see the Elemental the Scourge had caught, Marianne missed the clamouring voices in the corridors, even the dogs employed to sniff out residual magic. She had noticed the unusual number of Sentinel gathered on the stairs and in small side rooms, but had assumed they were there because the Scourge had gathered them. He had a habit of calling his minions to him and lording it up when he was outside the Orchid Tower. Asshole.

They took a lift up to the third floor in the labyrinthine building. She was forced to come to a standstill behind the agent as he pressed the buttons of the inner door code.

Harper affected a benevolent and patronising smile at Uno. 'I'll tell the Scourge you are here, Mrs Hopkins.'

'Whatever. Fuck off.'

Harper's eyes bulged in surprise at Uno's sudden change in demeanour. Before she could enjoy it, raised voices echoed across the hall followed by two cracks of gunfire. Sentinel bodies behind her surged forward, crowding round her like a human shield. Even the MI5 agent affected the same pose. Bursts of static blasted from radios and shouts echoed up the stairwell as more troops responded.

'Enough,' Uno instructed.

The Sentinel fell away from her, obedient as ever. Only Harper stared at her, blinking and confused by the fact she wasn't frightened or freaked out, like a woman should be. Before Harper could prevent her from entering the room across the hall, Uno stalked ahead, another Sentinel taking point.

'Clear.'

The smell of gore and bodily fluids hit Marianne's flared nostrils as she crossed the threshold. She reached inside her Louis Vuitton handbag, pulling out a handkerchief to press to her nose. She never could get used to the dead pissing themselves.

Harper still attempted to follow her in. 'Mrs Hopkins, I can't allow you—'

'I told you, piss off. Now!' Uno barked.

'But—'

'I'm here as an ambassador for the leader of the free world.' Uno injected cold steel into her voice. 'I'm sure you don't want me to call my husband?'

'Ma'am.'

She did not turn as Harper retreated with her Sentinel, the door closing softly after them. She stepped towards the bodies, tilting her head to take in the scene of carnage. The first was Tansy Penrose, the Gathering's High Witch. She and Tansy had met before, of course. She'd looked a little different back then and there hadn't been a hole right through the middle of her torso. The tiny redhead had fallen onto the chest of a big man with silver hair: the Scourge. He lay on his back, his eyes open and staring vacantly at the ceiling. Marianne tutted, barely able to contain her fury at the sight of them.

'Why did you take the halo off sleeper mode?' Uno addressed the Scourge, like he was capable of answering. 'Damn it, Pembroke.'

Marianne was genuinely shocked at the Scourge's defiance of a direct order. He'd been a good dog, always doing her bidding. He hated women and he hated the fact the Sentinel was run by one, but he loved his president and Safeguard more. She'd always felt secure in that. He'd known she was travelling to see the Elemental; he must have realised she had her own reasons for needing to see Tansy. What the hell had he been playing at?

Her infuriated gaze fell on the High Witch next. 'He told you I was coming, didn't he? Or maybe you already knew. Did you guess what I was going to do when I got here?'

She rocked back on her heels, suddenly exhausted. Every time she got within spitting distance of her goal, it seemed like someone moved the goalposts.

Marianne dropped her handkerchief and dug in her bag again, drawing out the forbidden artefact she carried around in there at all times. She closed her fist around it and moved it to her heart. Comfort spread through her and she felt her disappointment start to fade. She was not one to feel sorry for herself for long. She reminded herself that the Scourge's insubordination was surprising, but the consequences were not devastating. Tansy's loss might slow her down, but the High Witch was only ever a practice subject. She was not the Elemental Uno was truly interested in: The One, who wielded all four Elements and carried the power of the dark moon inside her, too. But Uno did not want to simply destroy the girl. She wanted to steal that power for herself.

Marianne opened her hand: inside, a smooth brown and orange stone, polished to a shine. It glinted under the lights of the torture room, as majestic as the jungle feline it was named for.

A large tiger's eye crystal.

PART FOUR

THIRTY-SIX

Somewhere on the English Channel, Europe

The bonfire was still an orange dot in the darkness on the cliff edge as their boat, an old fishing trawler with the name *Lucretia My Reflection*, sped away from the Gathering. One of only three to survive Chloe's flood, it had been found beached on a large mudslide at the top of the harbour, so most of it was in good working order. Earlier that evening, Chloe had pushed it down into the water with a surge of Earth magic and a lot of encouragement from Adelita and Daniel.

Unable to put their dead matriarch on a pyre, the Gathering had built a huge fire from the debris brought by the flood instead, in honour of Tansy. Gwen had led the tributes, lighting the bonfire with her Fire magic, sending a tower of flames swirling into the air towards the pale eye of the moon. Her younger sisters Isolde and Kerensa had added their own flares, too. Since the twins were only nine, Adelita had already sought reassurance about who would look after them now their mother was gone.

'All of us,' Gwen had asserted, with typical teen directness.

Emmeline had smiled and assured Adelita that Gwen's little

sisters would join her and Loveday at the hotel with the other children. Gwen was already coming and going as she pleased with the other teens. Adelita accepted this, knowing it was what Tansy would have wanted.

As the bonfire's orange flames licked the night sky, bringing light to the harbour, the coven bore the High Witch's demise with surprising fortitude; even the small children. Only Chloe, Adelita, Ethan and Daniel had been quiet and dejected as voices, both male and female, soared through the dusk air as the flames climbed ever higher. As the notes cut through the night, Adelita recognised the song as 'The Proclamation of The Elementals'. Since she'd been a Crystal witch, Adelita's mother had been unable to provide suitable magical learning for Adelita's twin sisters. Instead, Julia had taken Natasha and Bella to an Elemental coven once a week for lessons. Adelita had eavesdropped as they practised the words up on the roof of the bodega, though they'd always pursed their lips and shut her out if she'd revealed herself.

As the words flew up in the air like embers, Adelita closed her eyes and let the familiar verse wash over her:

'We are all kernels in the earth. We are baptised by fire; fed by the water of life; powered by air. Connect us through the chain of being and bring us liberation from the ties that bind us.'

The boat was freezing, but at least it was transport. Daniel and Chloe sat out on the deck on an old bench, wrapped up warm in coats and multiple blankets, Chloe resting her head on her father's shoulder as they watched the sun sink over the horizon and Boscastle disappear behind them.

Adelita and Ethan were standing at the helm, Ethan's gloved hands on the wheel, looking out through the front windows of the boat. Was it called a windshield or windscreen, like in a car? Adelita had no idea. Again she realised how far away from her old life in the city she was, both literally and figuratively.

'Go and see Cally in Moscow,' Emmeline had suggested as they'd left the Gathering. 'She will have the witches you need.'

'Is taking Chloe and a bunch of Elementals to the Orchid Tower to confront Hopkins even the right plan, any more?' Adelita fretted. 'You heard Tansy. She was not enthusiastic about our chances.'

Chloe sighed. 'What alternative do we have?'

The teen had a point. The Brotherhood's strategy was naive, but it was the only plan they had. Tansy's scornful face in the bedroom back at Boscastle kept replaying in Adelita's mind, telling her the Sentinel were like the hydra. Chloe could kill President Hopkins, but there would be another like him to take his place. If they wanted lasting change, they had to demolish the whole system. Adelita could see she was right – the problem was, she was clueless how to go about that.

'This boat can't get us all the way there?'

Ethan's expression was grim. 'No, it will take too long, we're better off going across the continent.'

'There will be more Sentinel on land.'

'True. But we'll get more help there, too. Talking of which . . .'

Now they were out of the valley and back in signal, Ethan could make arrangements with the Brotherhood. He gestured for Adelita to take the wheel while he made calls on the phone. Adelita sighed; she couldn't argue with his logic. If they were going to get as far as Moscow, they would need the Brotherhood's help.

'I can't drive. I don't have a licence.'

'You don't drive a boat, you captain it. Anyway, you don't need a licence. It's very easy.' He pointed at the Decca navigator and track plotter. 'It's a bit dated, but this will help you. I'll be two minutes on the phone, max. Don't worry.'

She watched as Ethan took one hand off the wheel and pulled

the surviving burner phone out from his rucksack. The flood had killed the rest.

'What if I crash it?'

'Into what?'

Adelita looked out at the vast darkness, the expanse of water beyond. 'I don't know . . . A big-ass rock. Or a giant squid.'

Ethan chuckled. 'If we crashed into either of those things, it wouldn't really matter who was "driving". Now, put your god-damn hands on the wheel while I make this phone call.'

Adelita grinned, taking over at last. 'I like it when you tell me what to do.'

Ethan smiled, his blue eyes sparkling. 'I find that very hard to believe.'

They kissed as the moon peeked over the clouds out on deck.

Lucretia delivered them as far as Roscoff, a small port town in Brittany. The ground felt like it was still undulating as they made it off the boat and onto dry land at last. Feeling seasick and weary, Daniel focused on Notre-Dame de Croas Batz, the flamboyant Gothic church at the top of the town. The building had long since been stripped by New Puritans. Its derelict spire was visible for miles. He breathed in the scent of the sea and the acrid boat fuel, noticing the humidity stains on the walls of tired buildings fronting the dock.

Before long, an official-looking middle-aged man with a clip-board stalked up to them, ordering them to follow him. Heart hammering, Daniel prayed it was another of Ethan's buddies. Ethan nodded his head, bidding the women not to do anything rash. They all did as the cowboy said and fell into step with him.

The man stopped as soon as they were out of sight of security cameras and other witnesses, and revealed a tiny tattoo that matched the one Ethan had on the inside of his own wrist, before giving them some further instructions. After hitching a lift cross-country with another Brotherhood member, a huge Nordic man with a beard like a Viking, they were dropped at a small town about forty miles from the French capital, as Ethan had arranged. They were all surprised when their next lift, a VW van, careered to a standstill by the side of the road and an older woman with white hair parted in two pigtails rolled down the driver's window.

Ethan's eyes narrowed. 'You're not Brotherhood.'

Daniel looked questioningly to Chloe and Adelita.

'She's a Goody,' his daughter declared, her tone more than a little apprehensive.

'No, I am Anne-Marie,' the woman said with heavy-accented English. 'Get in!'

Anne-Marie took their suspicions in good humour, eating crisps as she drove and telling them she was there on behalf of her dead son Victor, who had been Brotherhood. His wife had been a Crystal witch, before the Sentinel had abducted her when France passed over to the Safeguard initiative. Anne-Marie told them she'd loved her daughter-in-law as much as her own child.

'Thank you for your help,' Ethan said. 'Really.'

The cramped van rumbled on, Paris passing in a blur of urban sprawl, renaissance monuments and trashed Gothic buildings, with bricked-up stained-glass windows and ruined or missing gargoyles. Like all Safeguard countries, New Puritans had demanded the Sentinel cleanse French iconic buildings of imagery they associated with witches, the occult or other religions, just like they had in London and other major British cities.

When they'd passed Notre-Dame on the way into the city, Daniel was appalled to see it had been reduced to a huge pile of rubble. The last time he'd been here was just five years ago, on a theology field trip with his students. Now flowers, poppets, candles, ouija boards and Books of Shadows were laid at the bottom of the ruined cathedral, along with a variety of signs: *Vous pouvez prendre nos sorcières mais vous ne pouvez pas prendre notre âmes. (You can take our witches but you can't take our spirit.)* Daniel knew that as quickly as Sentinel removed the items, more would replace them. Protest was the French way, as Anne-Marie had already shown them.

She dropped them at the bus station, then drove off, all waves and smiles like she was depositing a family for a planned holiday. There was only one bored-looking Sentinel at the bus station boarding desk with the ticket sellers, easy to spot in his black and gold uniform, his gun slung at an angle across his chest. Two more patrolled the terminal but, luckily for Daniel and the others, they were preoccupied with turning out a bus destined for the Netherlands. Elderly tourists stood in dejected lines as the two Sentinel sent dogs into the vehicle to sniff out the magic they were looking for. Adelita had already shared with Daniel and Ethan that psyche was a kind of mental meditation that made their magic undetectable. Even so, Daniel was grateful the agents were all the way across the terminal.

It was decided it would be better if they split up on the coach, so Daniel and Chloe sat down together a few seats away from Adelita and Ethan. Daniel allowed himself a sigh of relief as he noted their coach was under-booked. Bar a couple of old-age pensioners, the seats were occupied by students with glazed expressions. They stared at phones, plugged into headphones, not even looking up as he, Chloe, Adelita and Ethan took their seats.

Countryside and towns fell behind the coach. Road signs changed colours and languages, from French to German. The multiple lanes of the autobahn opened and their vehicle joined a large queue of traffic, a checkpoint up ahead. Daniel felt familiar prickles of anxiety work their way up from his stomach, towards his shoulders. His time locked up at Boscastle had been a relief; it had all been out of his hands. In contrast, the never-ending turmoil of life on the road felt relentless.

'Dad?'

Daniel blinked, Chloe's quiet voice crashing into his thoughts. His daughter hadn't spoken in so many hours his mind reeled for a second, telling him it had been his imagination. But as he turned his head, he found her looking up at him, wide-eyed. She looked so young, so vulnerable. He'd intuited a significant change in her at Boscastle. He hadn't been able to see what had happened between his daughter and Adelita when Chloe had returned, her eyes shiny and black with the dark of the moon, but he'd understood Chloe was no longer at the mercies of its monumental power, somehow. Adelita had helped her gain control of her powers and he would be for ever grateful.

'Yes, *bǎo*—' Daniel stopped himself. She had asked him to stop calling her that. 'Yes, Chloe?'

'When we go to the Orchid Tower, you should stay behind. To be safe.'

Daniel was touched by his daughter trying to look out for him. He wanted to tell her he would be by her side, no matter what ... But perhaps she was right. Chloe had a big job to do and he didn't want to get in her way. Daniel was trying as hard as he could, but he was out on the sidelines, a spectator in this journey. It was Chloe who was the powerful one. She needed guidance, but he already knew he wasn't the one to provide it. That was Adelita's job. Ethan was a warrior, but Daniel was not. Even so, he could not bring himself to say he would not be by her side. It seemed wrong.

'Whatever happens, you're not alone. No matter where I physically am, I'll always be with you in spirit.'

This seemed to reassure Chloe. She smiled, resting her head on his shoulder.

'Love you, *bǎobǎo*.'

It just slipped out.

Up ahead, the hydraulic doors of the bus hissed and a couple of German soldiers with magic dogs boarded the coach, calling out in their native language for any declarations.

'Here we go,' Adelita caught Ethan muttering to himself, as he always did.

Adelita watched as a nervous young woman got up, holding a set of rosary beads in the air. While they might have been considered contraband in the US, given the New Puritans had outlawed all other religions, they can't have been in Germany. The female soldier tutted and told her to sit down. A teenage boy pulled a couple of comics from his bag, each with superheroes on the front. The male soldier flipped through them haphazardly, then threw them back at the boy without care. Finally, an older man reluctantly pulled out a couple of old, leather-bound books, along with a selection of official-looking paperwork. It was clear the soldiers were much more interested in these.

'He says he's a collector, that he's brought them back to sell to an antiques shop.' Ethan translated for Adelita. 'German WASPs love that shit, apparently. It's his job.'

Adelita was agog. 'That's still allowed here?'

Ethan nodded. Adelita knew that Germany was not a Safeguard country, but it was still hard for her to believe, even when she saw the evidence in front of her own eyes. She'd known Kitchen witches in jail who had been imprisoned for crimes as small as burning sage and refusing to go to re-education classes. Germany was one of the few countries in Europe, alongside Russia, to withstand the New Puritans' initiative. That didn't mean things were easy for witches in either place; Elementals were still not tolerated, and Crystal covens were banned. But it did at least mean there would be no overt Sentinel presence on the ground. Hopkins' men could only enter Germany illegally, which would slow any pursuers down.

The female soldier looked up the gangway of the coach, her eyes settling on Adelita. Adelita smiled in return, uncertain, but whispered under her breath, 'Oh shit.'

'It's *scheisse*.' Ethan's tone was breezy. 'Just hold your nerve.'

The female soldier made her way towards Adelita's seat. '*Steh auf!*'

When Adelita didn't stand, the soldier mimed *get up* with her hand.

'Sorry. Hi there.' Adelita could feel the falseness of her own smile radiating from her. 'How can I help?'

The female soldier turned back to her colleague. '*Amerikaner.*'

The male soldier barked something into his radio. Adelita felt her stomach fall into her boots. Did this mean German authorities were on the lookout for Americans? If they were, it would not be a leap to suppose they were looking for British Chinese people too. She willed herself not to turn around and draw attention to Chloe and Daniel, sitting a few rows back. Perhaps Ethan read her mind or sensed her worry via the spellbind, because he grabbed the headrest and hauled himself to his feet next to her.

'*Wir beide sind.*' *We both are.* His demeanour was relaxed, friendly.

Ethan said something else in rapid German that Adelita didn't follow, though it seemed to impress the female soldier. Her face lit up with a big smile.

'*Herzlichen Glückwunsch.*' The female soldier pulled something from her utility belt, more apologetic now. 'Please . . . ?'

Adelita recognised it as a handheld iHex; the Germans were checking to make sure she was not Elemental. Those women were still banned here.

'Oh, sure.'

She let the soldier wave it over her. Nothing beeped. Moments later and both the soldiers and their canines had disembarked. As the coach rumbled back to life and made its way through the checkpoint, Adelita turned to Ethan.

'What did you say to her?'

Ethan flashed her that boyband smile of his. 'I told her we were newly-weds on honeymoon back in my "Fatherland".'

'Of course you did.' Adelita rolled her eyes, unable to stop herself from matching his mischievous grin.

'Wouldn't you like to?'

'. . . What?'

'Get married.'

Adelita's answer wouldn't come to her. Just like she'd thought witchcraft irrelevant to her old life, she'd thought marriage was too. Instead, she'd placed her career first and foremost. She'd heard of love at first sight; of thunderbolts coming down from the sky. Both Ernesto and Julia had spoken of it often during her childhood, but she'd written it off as romantic wish fulfilment. She'd had boyfriends when she wanted them over the years; some lasted a few months, others as long as a few years. Whenever any of them had wanted to settle down, she'd let them go. She was a bachelor girl. She liked living by herself, doing her own thing. She'd seen no reason to change for any man.

'Oh.' Ethan seemed to deflate as he took in her hesitation.

Regret speared her in the chest. 'Look, it's not you—'

'Doc, please,' Ethan interjected, 'it very much *is* me and I get why. I was on the bad guys' side too long. It's fine. Ain't like I was actually proposing or anything. Relax.'

Adelita cast her eyes at her feet as he rested his head against the window glass of the coach. She'd been heartbroken when Tansy had told her to choose between Chloe and him. She'd felt so close to him when they'd made love back in Boscastle; when he'd brought her back from the dark of the moon with Chloe. But the cowboy was right: his dark past was surely something that would always come between them.

'If I did propose, it wouldn't be on a bus that stinks of feet. Just saying.'

She looked up to find Ethan proffering a wan smile. His hand reached for hers across the seat. She took it.

Dropped at a bus stop on the outskirts of Cologne, Ethan led Adelita, Daniel and Chloe up long, graffitied streets flanked by wire fences, low-rise blocks of apartments, kiosks and car dealerships. There were no WALK/DON'T WALK signs like New York, nor even those quaint striped or beeping crossings the British favoured. Instead the crossings ticked like a clock, or a very quiet bomb. Adelita placed her hand over the yellow pad, curious.

'Weird, hey?' Ethan's body language was relaxed. It was clear he felt at home here.

They made it onto the pedestrianised shopping area around the crowded Wiener Platz. Surrounded by Germans on their way home from work, Adelita felt bodies crash into either side of her. Scared about being carried off by the throng, she held on to Ethan's sleeve with her left hand, holding Chloe's in her right, who in turn held on to Daniel with her own right. In her mind's eye she recalled seeing elephants doing the same, following one another, trunk to tail, so they didn't get separated in the wild.

A tram appeared in the station, its doors swishing open. Adelita and the others crammed into the small carriage. She looked around for a conductor to buy a ticket, but Ethan was already on it: he held up four small slips of paper. They would be meeting his next contact at Cologne Cathedral. The Brotherhood were fond of meeting in plain sight, amongst crowds of tourists. Adelita mused it was a strategy that indicated the typical arrogance of men, but it had proved an effective tactic so far.

They left the station at the Domplatte, joining yet another flow of people up the steps towards the cathedral. Cologne's Gothic architecture had fared better than Paris; away from Safeguard, there had been no Puritanical attack on its tourist attractions. Adelita craned her neck as she cast her gaze upwards at its tall twin spires. It towered into the city skyline. She'd imagined it would be small. She had never seen anything like it.

'Bit bigger than Exeter Cathedral, eh, Chloe,' Daniel said in that low-key Londoner way of his. Chloe nodded, though she stared into the distance, at the water of the Rhine and the passenger ships cutting through it towards the bridge.

It was darker inside than Adelita expected. Her eyes struggled to adjust from the bright light of the spring day as they moved between pews. The ornate religious fixtures and treasures dazzled her eyes. Before her incarceration, Adelita had barely given witchcraft a thought, despite her mother's and sisters' repeated prompts. Like so many of her generation, she'd taken it for granted as something people did, but that didn't include her. Facts and evidence seemed more appealing than the fuzzier, more introspective world of witchcraft and spirituality. Adelita had thought about other religions even less. She stopped in front of the Shrine of the Three Kings above the altar, unable to tear her gaze away. She recognised Mary and an infant Jesus from the nativity story, but the other apostles and angels were a mystery to her.

'Don't turn around,' Ethan hissed. 'We got company.'

At his words, Adelita felt her magic move inside her, her psyche switching on. She was free of her body again; she soared above it, spinning around so she might take in the huge cathedral in its entirety. At first, the swell of tourists confused her, the hum of their voices and even their thoughts interrupting her.

Then the mass of noise and faces fell away as she homed in like an arrow towards the back of the vast building.

There: Sentinel.

Two men in plain clothes. They couldn't wear the Sentinel's signature dark suits in non-Safeguard Germany as the organisation was illegal here. Even so, both agents were practically identical: tall and lean, clean shaven, neat crew-cut hair. Their beady eyes roamed every face in the vicinity. It would not be long before they spotted them, up at the front of the cathedral. Adelita's psyche took her back to her body.

'*Scheisse*,' she said for Ethan's benefit.

Ethan nodded at Chloe and Daniel. 'We need to get the hell out of here. Now.'

They were too late. One of the agents clocked them as they made their way towards some nearby doors. Ethan's hand went towards the waistband of his jeans where his gun would be, if he had one.

'Fuck.' Ethan groaned.

Single-minded, the first agent stalked down the aisle towards them. He cut a formidable sight, elbows swinging, his feet falling on the flagstones. The crowd of tourists parted in front of him like the Red Sea before Moses as he raised his handgun from his jacket pocket.

He aimed it straight at them.

Shouts of alarm and fear from tourists went up as men and women dragged children out of the way. The second agent had not been quick enough, having been identified as a threat and set upon by two large have-a-go-heroes and a couple of gangly teens before he could grab his own gun. He disappeared, hollering, into a scrum of elbows, knees and headbutts.

Before the first Sentinel could squeeze off a shot, Chloe stood in front of Ethan and the others. Yellow light burst out of her, as quick and loud as a sonic boom. It swept over the crowd. Unlike her gale at Taunton Deane, it did not send the people to the ground. Instead, the agents, Goodys and other civilians halted where they stood or fell. It was like real life was a streamed video on pause. Some of the people who were still falling defied gravity and froze mid-air.

Daniel regarded the sight, incredulous. 'How did you do that?'

Adelita noted with pride that unlike previous times she'd practised magic to save their lives, Chloe was not distressed or belligerent. She reached out, hugging the teen close. Chloe grinned at her before turning to her father.

'Honestly, I'm not sure.'

Ethan slapped her on the back. 'Well, good work, whatever it was. Come on, let's go!'

They appeared on the steps of the cathedral, blinking against the onslaught of bright light and movement. As they did, sound rushed in at Adelita; she knew the people inside the ancient building had been released from whatever hold Chloe had placed on them. Outside there were even more people, the crowd seeming to replicate every second like germs through a microscope lens.

They disappeared into the throng, leaving the two Sentinel agents behind them.

THIRTY-SEVEN

Moscow, Russia

Daniel's boots crunched in the snow and slush on the pavement. He was grateful for the warm clothes the Gathering had provided them with when they'd left Boscastle on the boat, but they were inadequate for such cold weather. The Moscow side streets were dark, with flurries of grey clouds overhead. It felt colder than Germany by at least two or three degrees. It made all the difference.

'Holy shit, this place is even colder than New York in winter.' Adelita's breath came out in frosty plumes.

A lifetime of watching Second World War movies had not prepared Daniel for the sights of the Russian capital beyond the Kremlin in the Red Square and the onion-like domes of St Basil's Cathedral in the distance. The skyline was decorated with skyscrapers in polished glass and chrome, not to mention concrete high-rise apartment buildings, just like London. He was surprised by the never-ending flow of traffic, the sirens and pollution in the air.

Russia was as snowy as Daniel had assumed. Despite his jacket and gloves, he could feel the icy air creeping its way between the layers of clothing, into his solar plexus. He wanted to fold in on himself, draw his knees up to his chest to keep warm.

'How do you think *I* feel?' Ethan said in a gloomy voice. 'We're a long way from California. I reckon all my extremities will snap off.'

'Well, there's only one I'm interested in,' Adelita said with a lecherous grin.

They'd laughed, except for Chloe, who'd grimaced and declared them all 'gross' and 'immature'. Daniel smiled to himself, remembering how he'd thought adults were all tedious and sex-obsessed when he was the same age. He couldn't imagine enjoying travelling with three back when he was a teenager either.

After they'd shaken off the Sentinel agents in the cathedral, another of Ethan's buddies had met them on the steps, as if he'd been conjured by magic himself. The Brother was full of apologies for being late, explaining in stilted English that he'd had to lose a tail himself. Then he'd conversed in low tones with Ethan in German as they'd all woven their way towards a taxi rank with a fleet of white vehicles. Before they got in, his friend gave him new passports, some train tickets and a new phone. All four of them ended up on the Berlin sleeper train to Warsaw, changing there for Moscow.

The train had taken over twenty-four hours of travel, minus the inevitable wait between connections; the journey had allowed them to get some kip. Daniel doubted he would ever feel truly well rested in his life again, but all the travelling in the last few days had at least helped ease the aching in his bones. They'd arrived in the capital a few hours earlier, with instructions to meet their next contact, who had agreed to take them to Cally. Ethan broke it to Daniel they'd run out of Brotherhood contacts – Russia's secret service, the FSB, were way too effective

316

at making them disappear – which meant their guide would not be a man this time, but a witch.

Daniel tried to still the lurch in his chest. The Gathering had been accommodating, but there was no reason to assume it would be plain sailing with Moscow witches too. There was a possibility of being double-crossed, especially if Cally's coven had a score to settle with the Sentinel. Ethan's presence in their group might put them in danger. Tansy had not made good on her threat to kill the cowboy, but Cally might be better at follow-through.

'I can protect us,' Chloe declared, her expression grim.

Daniel grinned as he detected that steadfast resolution in his daughter again. He draped an arm around her shoulder. He was gratified when Chloe did not immediately shrug his contact off. This time she let his arm rest on her for about thirty seconds: a record.

Like in Germany, Daniel could sense the lack of Hopkins' Safeguard measures around Moscow. Though Ethan had warned them all witchcraft was still mostly unwelcome in Russia's capital as it had been in Cologne, there was a more relaxed atmosphere. Daniel had seen street traders with tarot decks and poppets laid out on blankets, and noticed signs for the Goddess daubed on walls: a minimalist tag of three slashes, a circle around them. Most of all, he could sense Chloe unwinding, breathing a little easier. The Sentinel may still be on their tail, but there was no denying Eastern Europe's lack of engagement with Safeguard made them all feel safer.

'What about this one?'

They stood outside an old derelict Soviet cinema. One wall was daubed with colourful skater graffiti, the other side was completely gone, its brickwork crumbling. Another Moscow resident trudged past, looking at them curiously. Every person they'd seen in Moscow so far had been white. It was like the

317

West Country, but to the power of a million. Daniel almost met the man's eye out of defiant habit, but Ethan gave him an imperceptible shake of his head, the meaning clear: *Don't draw attention to yourself.*

Ethan waited until the Muscovite had gone, then consulted his map. He indicated a sign of the Goddess in black marker pen on one of the old, broken doors. Before he could reply, a moving bundle of rags appeared on the threshold. Ethan was not quick enough in drawing his weapon. The rags seemed to spring down the steps like a jack-in-the-box, landing next to the cowboy. A young woman not much older than Chloe pulled back her hood, revealing bright green hair and a round, pale moon-face streaked with dirt.

Daniel's brain caught up. 'Air witch.'

The Elemental had a different way of moving through the air than Emmeline. With a blink she seemed to jump through the space around them. She zipped about, appearing in front, behind and to the side of them all. Finally she came to a stand-still next to Ethan.

Adelita turned to Chloe. 'She's quite the show-off, isn't she?'

'I am Evgenia. You are Brotherhood, yes?' She poked one finger in Ethan's ribs, punctuating her words.

The rogue Sentinel pursed his lips, irritated. 'That's right.'

They watched as the young woman took an abrupt turn on her heel. She marched three or four purposeful steps away from them before stopping and turning, exasperated when she did not hear their boots on the snow following her.

'People! Come now, please!' She clapped her hands together in command.

'Well, this is going to get old quickly,' Ethan muttered to Daniel.

Daniel nodded. 'Kids, eh.'

'Oi,' Chloe complained.

Up ahead, Evgenia was doing some kind of jig, kicking her boots up in the air like the chimney sweep in *Mary Poppins*. Adelita laughed and turned to the three of them, shrugging.

'OK, she is annoying,' Chloe relented.

They all followed the Air witch.

THIRTY-EIGHT

The Orchid Tower, New York, USA

Uno was restless. She paced her palatial suite like a caged animal. As necessary as it was to her power and standing, she hated the tower. She should be in the Hamptons right now, cocktail in hand with a little parasol, not at the battle station of Sentinel HQ. She hated the sounds of boots on the stairwells; the smell of men in its corridors; their beady eyes on her wherever she went. None of them would dare meet her eye, never mind speak to her or touch her.

Marianne did not hate the Sentinel for their part in incarcerating or murdering the sisterhood. She hated all other witches every bit as much as any man. Uno had not taken hold first of Michael, then his shadowy Sentinel cabal, to save her sisters. She wanted to annihilate them all.

It was the only way to become the best, most powerful one of all time.

'Hello, darling. I was wondering when you'd got back from London.'

Michael wandered in from an interconnecting door, wearing his workout gear. He'd been in the gym downstairs, running on the machine for fifty minutes. Like he did every day between four ten and five p.m. He was so predictable.

Marianne smiled through gritted teeth. 'I've been back hours. *Sweetie.*'

Uno allowed him a chaste kiss on her cheek, fighting the urge to shudder as she felt beads of sweat transfer from his face to hers. Despite his commitment to fitness and heart health, he was still middle-aged and bald, with an addiction to Haribo that would make a fourth-grader blush. He'd been good-looking in his youth, square-jawed and tall like Ryan Reynolds. Like so many men, Michael had stopped taking care of himself long ago. He didn't have to bother; power made him look good to most people.

Marianne watched her husband undress on his way to the shower. He threw his clothes in a heap by the doorway to the en suite like he expected her to pick them up and put them in the laundry basket.

'The Scourge is dead.'

'Oh, really?' Michael reacted as if the news was mere local gossip, not a matter of national security. 'That is a shame. He was a good soldier.'

Marianne cast her eye down her husband's naked body. Sweat glistened on the greying chest hair that curled around his paunch; on the damp pubes around his smaller-than-average, flaccid penis. He'd never known what to do with *that*, even when he was young and virile.

'Yes, I guess age finally caught up with him.'

Michael smiled in an absent fashion; he wasn't listening to her. He disappeared inside the en suite. As the shower turned on, Marianne collapsed in an armchair, kicking back and extending her feet in the air in a random yoga pose. She still had it. Unlike Michael, fat sweaty fuck that he was.

There was one thing she was lacking, though. Marianne had

never forgotten the possibility there was a witch out there with everything she had ever coveted. She had never forgiven her own lineage for not giving her the Elemental power she craved; she'd had to study for it like a regular Crystal chump. Her hard work may have trumped most natural talent, but the fact remained there was a *little fucking girl* out there who could potentially reduce Marianne to ashes, even when she was at her strongest. It made her sick to her stomach with envy and fury.

Over the resulting two decades, Marianne had gone all out to find The One, coming across a young, rogue Tansy Penrose to help her at the beginning of her search. Tansy had taught Marianne to access some mind control technique she called psyche. The Cornish witch was on the streets in those days, lost and lonely. Marianne had been mistaken in not dispatching her right away, before Tansy had a chance to set up the Gathering. At the time, Marianne had only just married Michael, just a baby politician at the start of his career. Misandrist that she was, Tansy had hated the thought of a man knowing their secret, but Marianne swore to the High Witch she could control Michael. She would make him her puppet and help witches, by making the senate understand.

Of course, Marianne was lying. She never had any intention of sharing any clandestine power she gained in the senate with anyone. By the time Tansy realised how she'd given the enemy a powerful weapon, she was on the Sentinel's Most Wanted List worldwide. No one would listen to the accusations of a toxic savage like her.

Despite her wealth, then her never-ending resources via the Sentinel, Uno had been nowhere close to discovering who this elusive child could be until just a couple of weeks ago, when Chloe Su had lit up like Hiroshima in that backwater English town. It was hard to believe the child's mother had been so successful at muzzling the girl's powers so long, never mind ensuring no one knew where or who she was. Each resulting equinox over the last two decades must have broken down the mother's defences, one by one. As the girl's powers massed, her mother could not withstand them.

'What a day, I'm beat.' Michael padded out of the shower. 'Non-stop meetings!'

'You poor thing.' Marianne's tone was deadpan.

She doubted very much that the hours her husband spent listening to the briefings of Sentinel underlings could hold a candle to her crappy day, the Scourge and Tansy dead at her feet in Thames House. Marianne could feel her plans and dreams unravelling, moving farther from her grasp.

Michael did not appear to notice her angst, continuing to towel himself dry. 'How about an early night, darling?'

Marianne knew what that was code for.

'What a lovely idea ... ' Marianne slipped her hand in her pocket, clasping her chunk of tiger's eye crystal. She touched her husband's shoulder, her demeanour changing on a dime: 'But since you couldn't find my clitoris with a goddamn map and torch, how about no, you boring, inept douchebag?'

Michael blinked as her magic swept through him, taking control of him. He'd become used to its strength years ago; he no longer thrashed around like he was having an epileptic fit. Her ability to control Michael had been a pleasing side development and a useful secret to have. A couple of years ago Sentinel geeks made the same discovery in their creepy angel cave experiments on Crystal witches and male convicts. Some Mengele-type had been delighted as he'd made his report to her. Weirdo. Uno had given him a heart attack where he stood, then redacted all of that shit too, not just from official documents but all nineteen of the remaining Sentinel geeks' memories. It was hard work, presiding over all those freaks.

Uno watched as her husband put on his pyjamas like the meat

323

puppet he was and got into bed. He pulled the covers up to his chin, his eyes closing as soon as he lay down. Within seconds, sleep overcame him.

'Good dog,' she said.

THIRTY-NINE

Moscow, Russia

As they followed the pale girl and backstreet after backstreet fell behind them, Adelita became increasingly nervous. She wasn't convinced Ethan could find his way back; she and Daniel certainly couldn't. Her anxiety was at peak level by the time they'd been walking nearly fifteen minutes and had reached a seemingly endless, dingy alleyway lined with trash cans and with rows of washing lines overhead.

'How long now?' Ethan shouted ahead to the Air witch.

'Quiet please, mister penis-head man!' Evgenia shouted back.

'I swear I'm gonna kill her,' Ethan mumbled to himself.

With a sudden *zoom*, Evgenia was right next to the cowboy, making him jump. Before he could stop the young woman, she bashed one fist lightly against his shoulder. Her yellow Air Elemental flare sent him flying backwards. There was a metal *clang* as he collided with a couple of trash cans.

Behind them, Ethan rolled over, winded. '... Ow.'

Evgenia looked to Chloe. 'Little tap. Men are always whining, Godssake.'

Chloe nodded, unable to stop the impressed grin spreading

across her face. Evgenia's brow furrowed as she took Daniel in, like she was challenging him to have a go, too. Chloe's father raised his hands in the air as if to say, *I don't want any trouble.*

Residual yellow magic crackled across Ethan's torso and shoulder as he sat up, groaning. He flapped his arms in a futile manner, like he could make it dissipate quicker. Adelita helped him to his feet.

Another couple of minutes of walking – or staggering, in Ethan's case – revealed an open-fronted bladesmith workshop at the end of the alleyway. Sparks flew as two middle-aged male twins in overalls pounded metal and baked it white-hot in a forge that was fed by a young, bored-looking Fire Elemental. The men were huge biker-types, replete with bushy beards and bandanas. There were no bellows in the forge; apparently they were not needed. Another Air witch sent flares of yellow magic into her sister's flames. The heat billowed out of the forge like the fire of Hades.

The men and the forge witches looked up, muttering greetings as Evgenia skipped past them. The teenager took zero notice or interest in any of them, making her way to a spiral staircase that began at the top of the royal blue building.

'*Mama!*' Evgenia bellowed.

Adelita watched as a white woman about her own age appeared in the blink of an eye at the top of the stairs. She had the same round moon-face and bore more than a passing resemblance to Evgenia. The older woman's lined face creased even more at the sight of her errant child. She started to shout at the girl, her gestures telling Adelita what she was asking: *Where the hell have you been?* Evgenia took this in her stride, shouting back with gusto. The argument appeared to cease as swiftly as it had begun.

'*Gde Kelli, Mama?*'

A machine started grinding in the forge below, obliterating

Evgenia's mom's reply. Adelita didn't have to guess the meaning, because the older woman mimed, too: *She's down there.* Following the gesture, Adelita noticed for the first time the building did not end at pavement level. Now her eyes had adjusted to the shadows and the wavering heat, she could see there were more steps leading down towards a door with a sliding peephole, like a speakeasy straight out of the prohibition era. The peephole slid back as soon as Evgenia banged on the door. The teenager wasn't asked for a password.

A tall, black woman with box braids and the angular, lean physique of a Zulu warrior opened the door. Everything about her was accessorised to the max, from her purple silk robe down to her long purple nails and fluffy purple booty slippers.

To Evgenia's obvious chagrin, the woman was not looking at her, but at Adelita and Chloe. The tall witch's bright purple lips curved in a delighted smile. The grinding noise stopped, and in smooth American tones, she spoke.

'I've been waiting for you,' Cally said.

In a wink, Evgenia was gone before any of them could say goodbye. As Adelita had assumed, there was a bar behind the big vintage door. If she'd been able to read Russian, she would have known the establishment was called THE FORGE, just like the workshop upstairs.

Cally led them into the dark cellar room. As she settled into the booth the Forge witch had directed them to, Adelita let her gaze wander. The bar had a purposefully shabby interior, complete with a vinyl music station. There was a wide selection of spirits, as well as a coffee pot on a bar top made of reclaimed oak. Empty bottles acted as drip candles, cold wax spilling down their glass exteriors. Swords and blades hung for decor on the walls.

'Got a thing for warriors?' Adelita enquired.

Cally raised a perfectly arched eyebrow. 'Don't you?'

Adelita and Ethan's eyes met across the table. It was like Cally had read her mind.

'I meant, it's very different to Boscastle,' Adelita said. 'Why weren't you at the Gathering?'

Cally's playful smile disappeared. 'Tansy and I had a difference of opinion.'

Adelita recognised the words Cally *wasn't* saying. 'She's a pretty tough broad.'

The Forge witch sighed. 'Yes. She was.'

Her use of the past tense caught Adelita's attention. 'Then you know . . . ?'

Cally nodded quickly. 'I got her deathgram too.'

There was a moment as they all cast their eyes downwards, remembering the High Witch. She may have been a difficult, anguished woman but there was no doubt she'd left a massive hole behind her.

'Can I get anyone a drink?' Cally finally said.

The Forge witch poured them beverages – black coffee for everyone but the two men – before retiring to a back room to get dressed. Ethan opted for three fingers of bourbon, with Daniel following his example. The cowboy eyed Daniel with amusement.

'Damn, Professor, it's not even ten a.m., Moscow time.'

Daniel grinned and lifted his glass. 'Cheers.'

Cally appeared again from behind the bar, having shrugged on a faded Metallica T-shirt and a pair of ripped grey skinny jeans. Evidently she dressed for daytime with less care than for bed. She'd kept her fluffy slippers on, though.

'Nice place, by the way,' the cowboy said.

'Thank you, Ethan Weber.' Tansy's mentor joined them at the table. 'So, you're the rogue Sentinel cowboy who swapped sides and spellbound with a Crystal witch?'

Tansy's mentor laughed as Ethan's eyes widened in surprise. She watched as he put two and two together: Cally had psyche. Like Tansy, this meant the Forge witch had access to information other witches did not. Adelita wondered if Cally's psyche could 'soar' like hers between time and space, or whether the Forge witch was more like Chloe, capable of driving men to their knees, blood pouring from their eyes and ears.

'It's different in everyone.' Cally answered Adelita's query without her voicing it. 'In my case, I guess the easiest way of describing it would be "mind-reader", though I prefer "truth-teller". I can see past the barriers people put up within and around themselves; I can see past the lies and falsehoods all around us. Make the connections others can't ... Or won't.'

Cally sat down next to Chloe, placing an arm around the teenager. Chloe flinched, but did not remove herself from the tall woman's embrace.

'You're The One.' Cally's voice was warm, sympathetic. 'Lot of pressure, huh?'

Chloe averted her eyes, both rueful and embarrassed.

Cally pulled her closer, cupping the girl's cheeks with her hands. 'You are stronger than you know, Chloe. Never forget that.'

Cally took the rest of them in. 'I saw you all, back in Boscastle. You too, Daniel.'

'I don't have psyche,' the professor said. 'I'm nobody.'

'No, you're much more than that. As a man; as Chloe's father. You're everything to her. Family ties can be like natural spell-binds. She needs you.'

'But I didn't see what her mother was hiding ... I was so blind.'

'But you're not any more.' Cally let this sink in. 'You thought everything would be OK if you ignored it. You were like a lobster, oblivious as the water heated up around you. We have to be connected with the world, to change the world. No one person is an island, right?'

Daniel's literary mind got Cally's allusion to John Donne straight away.

'"Any man's death diminishes me, because I am involved in mankind."'

Cally grinned, 'Well, I'd say *person's*, but yes, exactly.' She looked to the rest of them. 'Tansy sent you here?'

Ethan set his empty glass on the table. 'Kind of.'

'I know what you did, when you were still with the Sentinel.'

Ethan's face was stricken. Adelita's hand sneaked under the table, her fingers intertwining with his. Their conversation on the coach came rolling back to her. He'd been wrong; she hadn't hesitated because he'd been with the bad guys too long. It was because she'd been alone so long. She'd never realised she could be anything else until he slammed into her life.

I know that wasn't the real you, she said in the spellbind.

He gave Adelita a watery smile. 'I can't take any of it back. I know that. But I swear I will do whatever it takes to help the witch cause.'

'I know that's true,' Cally said. 'You know, a lot of people are like you were. Angry and alone, they want to make the world pay for their pain. They don't realise it's a contradiction. They have to look inside themselves, be vulnerable, to connect with others.'

'Like Tansy,' Ethan muttered.

'She wasn't very fond of you,' Cally said. 'That wasn't your fault. She was so lost. I wish I could have reached her, but she was too damaged.'

Adelita could feel the truth in Cally's words. Talking with the High Witch in the harbour herself, Adelita had sensed an inherent sadness in Tansy that went beyond losing her precious Demelza. Via Tansy's deathgram back in the Boscastle cottage, Adelita had intuited something else: a bitter darkness that was missing in Ethan. He'd left his in the past. The horrors he'd seen and enacted had chipped away at him, until he'd made his breakthrough after Stonehenge. He couldn't work against his conscience any longer. He had gone looking for a way to right the balance that had been twisted in his favour too long.

'Tansy did good things.' Cally picked at a splinter on the old table with one of her long nails. 'She raised her daughters better than she'd been raised. And she gave her life for all of you in this room.'

'What do you mean?' Chloe asked.

'Tansy was a powerful Earth witch, but she knew she'd be weakened as the Sentinel's prisoner. Someone there was going to try and steal her powers, to practise stealing yours, Chloe. If it had worked, it would have made taking yours so much easier.' Cally's eyes were glassy with tears. 'But she went to Hecate before that could happen.'

There was a moment as they all digested the High Witch's sacrifice.

Cally continued. 'But it's not about doing good to make up for the bad.'

Adelita's mind refused to process this. She'd taken comfort in the fact she'd been a doctor before her life blew up, that she was more good than bad. Now Cally was saying that didn't even count. Adelita knew she'd killed and maimed since breaking out of jail; she'd stood by and watched as Chloe, Ethan and others had done the same. Her cowboy might be on their side now, but what was the *real* difference between his actions now and then, if what Cally was saying was true?

'Tansy was never able to let go of her fear and rage,' Cally continued. 'It's not all her fault, either. Her Earth magic was very potent. When it came in she was just a little girl, only six; far too young for such strong powers. She was alone a long time; saw things she shouldn't have. It sent her down the wrong path.'

'Like me,' Chloe said, eyes downcast. 'What I did to Mum—'

'That wasn't your fault,' Daniel cut in, automatic.

Cally put one hand on his. 'You're right, it wasn't. But Chloe is the one who did it, so she alone is the one who must bear the guilt. You can't fix everything for her. That's not your job.'

Chloe nodded, relieved to have her feelings validated at last. Adelita could see Daniel's confusion written all over his face. It was obvious he couldn't bear for her to blame herself. It had been Li who'd muzzled Chloe's powers in babyhood; it had been him who'd failed to see what was going on, right under his nose in his own family.

Chloe's voice was quiet. 'So, what am I supposed to do as The One?'

'Your powers have been massing towards something, correct?'

'They're hard to control,' Chloe confirmed. 'They come out in bursts. They've been getting stronger and stronger each time since that first time. I can feel it.'

'When did this start?'

Chloe's brow furrowed. 'It's hard to say. I went to bed, I felt really awful, like everything was weighing on me. I knew something bad was going to happen. I had these terrible nightmares. I was trapped in this weird place, where I took you, Adelita . . .'

'The dark of the moon,' Adelita confirmed.

'Right. I saw fire, but they weren't real flames, they were green. I could feel it burning me, ripping out of me, making my bones disintegrate. But even though I wasn't there any more, I was still here . . . and capable of this terrible power; I could destroy everything. But then I woke up in the car, with Dad, in the middle of nowhere.'

There was a pause as they took in the teen's words. Chloe's

eyes were haunted; her simple explanation made them all shudder. Ethan leant forward.

'The Brotherhood coordinated all the witch jailbreaks for Friday March sixth.'

'Yes,' Daniel said, 'it was a Friday. The day Li . . . '

He let his words dwindle away as they contemplated the date all their lives had changed for ever. Cally's gaze fell on a block calendar on a shelf behind the bar; it read *15 MARTA*. Adelita did a double-take as she took in the date. How could they have been on the road less than ten days? How could she have known Ethan, Chloe and Daniel less than a fortnight? When so much had happened since Adelita's jail break, it felt like both for ever and no time at all.

'Take my hand.' Cally held out a palm each to Adelita and Chloe. She grinned at Daniel and Ethan, eyes sparkling with amusement: 'You probably want to stand back a bit, gentlemen . . . Unless you don't mind being in the blast zone?'

Neither Ethan or Daniel needed telling twice. Both men drew their chairs right back from the table. Adelita took Cally's hand without hesitation. Across the table, Chloe regarded them both with wide eyes, her apprehension etched across her face.

It's OK, baby.

The voice echoed through the spellbind, but it was not her own. Adelita blinked, looking to Cally, who chuckled.

Do you trust me? Cally asked Chloe.

The teenager pursed her lips, resolve replacing her hesitation. She took the Forge witch's hand.

Bright light sprang up around them. Adelita's psyche switched on; this time she was aware of both Chloe and Cally's presence with her. Chloe's multiple elemental flares mixed with white from Adelita; red from Cally.

So, she's a Fire witch too, like my sisters.

Adelita's thoughts were snatched from her head. All three

333

of them swirled into what felt like a technicolour whirlpool of beliefs, experiences and memories. Without opening her eyes, Adelita knew a huge bubble was enveloping them, like Chloe's huge green sphere of destruction she'd had to nullify. Unlike that time, she could sense joy and warmth; she felt like she was home. She knew Chloe did too.

Like the glowing white-hot end of a sparkler, Adelita's memory came first. She saw Bella and Natasha sending plumes of black smoke into the air. They laughed with Julia in the kitchen as Adelita watched from another doorway. Always on the outside.

Then the image popped. A green flare whirled, signalling Chloe's turn. A much younger Chloe, about ten years old, gouged at her own eyes. A woman who looked just like her appeared, her hair crackling with residual magic. Chloe's mother grabbed the child's hooked fingers and prised them away from her face. They fell to the ground together, stunned.

The image flared red, next. Adelita saw a teenage Cally reflected in a steamy mirror. She held up both hands in the foggy glass, gazing down in wonder as flames danced on every fingertip. Somehow, Adelita knew this was not the whole story. She could intuit something else, like reaching for a word on the tip of her tongue. She wanted to see Cally beyond the mirror.

She was too late. The mirror cracked and fell away. All three of them descended with the pieces, which melted on the ground like mercury. The reflective liquid undulated like the ocean, more images shimmering up from its depths.

First, a baby girl, swaddled in a pink blanket. An exhausted woman in a hospital gown in her mid-twenties cradled the child. Chloe's mother again; a much younger Daniel joined her at the bedside. His face beamed with pride.

Adelita shimmered to the surface next. A cake bedecked with twenty candles, its frosting pink and white striped. Inside the magic blast Adelita was sure she laughed. She recognised the cake. Her mother had made it for her twentieth's celebrations, staying up all night to decorate it. They'd cut it, only to discover the exhausted Julia had somehow put salt in the cake batter instead of sugar.

'My birthday.'

The words pulled Adelita's psyche back to her body, but they weren't hers. It was Chloe who'd spoken.

'Mine too,' Adelita said. 'March twentieth.'

Cally clapped her hands together. 'Right. March twentieth is the spring equinox. A time of rebirth, new beginnings.'

'The dark of the moon,' Adelita and Chloe said, in unison.

Ethan and Daniel looked on, puzzled.

'Chloe showed me, back at Boscastle,' Adelita explained again. 'Her powers come from the dark moon.'

Ethan continued to look blank, unsure of the significance, but Daniel smiled; he got it.

'Equinox is from the Latin, "equality of night and day",' he explained. 'It's when the sun moves across the celestial equator. For witches, it symbolises new beginnings. This year it's on the twentieth of March.'

'Right,' Adelita said. 'So it makes sense that Chloe's powers are massing towards the spring equinox. She's a new start for us. I can't believe I forgot what date it was.'

The cowboy nodded, looking to Cally. 'It can't be an accident they were born on the same day?'

'You're right, it's not,' Cally agreed. 'They are linked by psyche, but also by the time and date they were born. Hecate made it so. Adelita is Chloe's guide ... A kind of midwife if you like, delivering her towards her destiny.'

The teen grimaced, still perturbed. 'What do I have to do?'

'My best guess is, your powers need to link with the equinox, with all witches. It should have happened a long time ago, but first you had to work your way through the muzzling spell your mother placed on you.'

'How do I do that, though?'

Cally looked to Adelita.

'How am I supposed to know?'

Adelita's mind swirled at this new information. If she'd known what to do, or how to do it, she would have told Chloe by now. There was still a big piece of the puzzle missing. She needed to figure it out.

Cally didn't argue with this. 'Like I said, there's someone who wants to steal Chloe's powers.'

'So, what Tansy said was true,' Adelita replied. 'A Crystal witch is after Chloe?'

'We'll keep her safe . . . From the Sentinel, too,' Ethan added.

Cally shook her head. 'You don't understand, the one after Chloe is both. That's why she has to face her.'

'Face who?'

'Marianne Hopkins. She has the president and the Sentinel in her pocket.' Cally shook her head. 'Tansy told me. She met Marianne a long time ago, before the Gathering, but after she met me.'

The Forge witch let this sink in. They all stared at one another in disbelief. Marianne Hopkins was a benign kind of celebrity, writing newspaper columns and doing charity work. She was a favourite amongst Goody voters, holding candlelit vigils and appearing at Pray-A-Thons for peace amongst the magical and non-magical worlds, even before Safeguard came in. Adelita understood what Cally was hinting at.

'Tansy taught her psyche,' Adelita groaned, recalling their session on the beach, how Gwen had excitedly mentioned that Tansy was teaching her the practice. 'That's why Crystal witches aren't normally allowed in Boscastle!'

'Fuck,' Ethan muttered.

336

'No. No way,' Daniel breathed. 'Marianne Hopkins can't be a Crystal witch *and* Sentinel leader. Women haven't been allowed to serve for over forty years.'

Cally shrugged. 'I've shown you nothing but the truth since you got here. I don't have time to argue this. She is who she is.'

'I saw you *before*.' Chloe drew a sharp look from Cally. 'When our psyches melded together, I mean.'

The teen's words triggered something. That weird sensation Adelita had perceived when seeing Cally's memory unfurled and opened up. More images rushed in at her. She saw the pieces of the broken mirror jump back up off the floor, returning whole again to the wall of that steamy bathroom, like an old VCR tape in reverse.

In the mirror's reflection, the teenage Cally again, flames on her fingertips. Adelita could appreciate the angle of the vision was different this time, though; she was no longer looking just at the girl's reflection. The image seemed to widen, like Adelita could step back so she might take in more information. That was when she realised what she was seeing didn't make sense. Someone else, not Cally, was in front of the mirror. A teenage boy. Another realisation swam up in Adelita's consciousness.

Cally was transgender.

'That sad boy was never the real me.' The Forge witch smiled, indicating herself. '*This* is who I really am. It always has been.'

Chloe was confused. 'But aren't only women able to do magic?'

'Yes – and that's why I can do it,' Cally explained. 'It's always been thought magic is connected to biology, the XX chromosome. This is half right. It's biological, as thought ... But even Crystal witches can access it because it's connected to Estra; oestrogen amplifies it. Witchcraft is part of the hypothalamus, the only part of the brain that's gendered. So *female brain* equals magic, which is why you get trans witches like me, too.'

She hugged the teen. 'The power, quite literally, is inside you, Chloe. You need to send it out there. You can do this.'

'What about Costentyn?'

Adelita could see Ethan's memory via their spellbind: Loveday's boy, blue residual magic snaking through his hair. He'd carried it with him somehow; his mothers and sisters had called him into battle with it. Adelita had seen the other children too, felled by hers and Chloe's magic at Boscastle. They'd jumped up, not only unharmed but *energised* by it, males and females alike.

Daniel leant forward on the table, keen to put his theory forward again. 'That's right. It seems to me that men can't create magic by themselves, but they can harness their mothers' and sisters' powers. Boys born to Elementals have an obvious head start, since they're literally borne from witches. But in reality *anyone* with a powerful connection to a witch can do it.'

Ethan squeezed her hand. Adelita didn't need the spellbind to understand her cowboy was thinking about how he'd acted as her conduit in the car, driving at the soldier at the checkpoint on the Devon–Cornwall border, or the white light that had surrounded them when they'd made love.

Cally nodded. 'This used to be common knowledge, but the Sentinel have been working to divide us all a long time. This predates Safeguard and President Hopkins; or even when the Sentinel outlawed women joining its ranks. The people in charge have always tried to pit the magical and non-magical worlds against each other for their own ends; it keeps us weak. Goodys don't realise magic has never been anything to fear; it's not toxic. It's an effort to get used to it, like all things worth doing are. But it's easier to be scared, to call us all toxic savages and terrorists. To sow the seeds of doubt, misinformation, fear.'

It all slotted into place for Adelita at last. The endless fight between worlds had never been about gender. It was why politicians like Michael Hopkins had sought to divide and conquer; why the Sentinel had done everything they could to keep Elementals and Crystal witches isolated from one another; why Marianne Hopkins wanted Chloe's magic for herself.

This witch hunt had always been about power.

'Can you tell me why I ended up spellbound to Chloe?'

Cally dashed her hopes. 'No, sorry, I can't. If I could, I would – but that's for you to figure out. You are part of a strong bloodline, though, that much is clear.'

'Tansy said the same.'

'Then perhaps start with our ancestors?'

The Forge witch's point landed, but Adelita was still disappointed. She'd felt certain Cally would have the answers she needed to help Chloe. Even with psyche as part of the package, Adelita not using her magic until she was almost forty was still weird. It was odd that Hecate had chosen such an inexperienced, virgin witch for the important job of protecting The One.

Cally turned to Ethan. 'So, you want to take as many witches as you can to the Orchid Tower for the equinox, to destroy the Sentinel?'

'That was the plan,' Ethan said, 'but maybe we have everything we need in Chloe. The rest of us are back-up.'

Chloe looked stricken. 'I still don't know what it is I'm supposed to do when I get there. Not exactly.'

'Yes, you do,' Cally smiled, 'you have to face Marianne Hopkins and use the power of the dark moon to bring the Sentinel down. Your psyche will guide you. So will Adelita.'

They had no time to absorb this. Evgenia blinked back into existence next to the table, nearly making Ethan fall off his stool. The green-haired young woman grinned, dancing on the balls of her feet.

'Bad menz here.' She vanished again.

Adelita perceived a huge crash upstairs, though she knew it

hadn't happened yet. Her psyche had switched on, sending her soaring up through the ceiling and into the forge above. As she expected, half a dozen Sentinel had swooped on the building. Like in Boscastle, they were dressed like black-clad storm-troopers with their helmets and goggles.

She watched as Elemental flares exploded over the forge. Evgenia's mom exploded into being, grabbing one of the twins and kissing him on the lips. He roared as her yellow Air magic poured through him, and grabbed the large quench tank. The young Fire Elemental sent a jet of fire at it and Evgenia, appearing next to her, fed the flames with her Air magic. The heat didn't seem to affect the huge man as he pushed it over, dumping its scalding contents over the two Sentinel at the front, the force of the water sending them to the ground, scream-ing in agony.

Back in the cellar bar Adelita opened her eyes, falling back into her body as if she'd never left. She panicked for a moment, thinking they were trapped below the fight.

Cally seemed unconcerned. The Forge witch stood, gesturing them all towards a large wall hanging of the triple goddess by the bar. She pulled it aside, revealing a door. When she pulled it open, an underground catacomb yawned behind it like the minotaur's lair.

The Forge witch dug in her jeans pocket, pulling out a phone. 'Take this. Look up Cyrus Frost on Pentagram. He'll help you get out of Russia. It's waterproof, too.'

She pressed the handset into Adelita's hand, who shoved the phone in her own pocket. She didn't have time to ask Cally what the hell she was talking about. The rogue Sentinel hesitated. 'We should help your guys upstairs.'

Cally shook her head. 'They can handle it.'

Adelita knew Cally spoke the truth. As she'd said, she'd told them nothing but.

'Will we see you at the Orchid Tower for the Equinox?'

Cally smiled. 'Try and stop us.'

Keeping Chloe close behind her, Adelita went first in the catacombs, glowing white in the darkness. Daniel came next, Ethan on their six.

Cally closed the door after them.

FORTY

The Orchid Tower, New York, USA

Uno discovered her Sentinel's failure in Moscow when the director of the fucking Federal'naya Sluzhba Bezopasnosti called her in the middle of the night on the restricted line. She awoke to find Riggs hovering over her, holding the phone in his gloved hands like it was a prize catch. Marianne sat up and snatched it from him, dismissing him with a flick of her hand. Her bodyguard was only too happy to oblige.

She swiped a finger across the screen, remembering to ensure her camera was off and the Tongue Box app was operational. It would not do to reveal her true female voice to the head of FSB. That would be a gift to Sentinel enemies.

'This better be good, Aleks.'

Aleksandra Vasiliev was one of the few female intelligence leaders Uno had regular contact with. Uno had a grudging respect for her. It was too bad Russia had resisted all attempts by the United States to come on board with Safeguard, especially as their expert hackers could have made short work of Pentagram, the world witch web. Even the Sentinel's cyber geeks still had trouble decrypting and deciphering that shit.

'Uno, we have problem.'

Marianne rolled her eyes as Vasiliev outlined the issue: the surviving Sentinel had been apprehended trying to sneak back across the Russian border, having entered the country illegally. The team leader, Franklin, was unhurt other than a magic flare to the shoulder; the other three had suffered severe flash burns, one to his face. Upon investigation, the FSB had discovered two more badly scalded Sentinel bodies in a landfill site just outside the city. Uno's men were refusing to tell the FSB the names of the witches they had been fighting, or why.

As Vasiliev spoke, Uno shuddered; she was well aware of the FSB's cruel and invasive tactics for extracting information. Though maybe it would teach them to be more careful next time. Idiots.

She affected a bored tone to her fake voice. 'What can I do to make this go away?'

'Tell us what they were looking for, of course.'

Uno started as Michael emitted a sudden explosive snore in his sleep, beside her. She poked him viciously in the side. He turned over onto his front without waking.

'Pick again, Aleks.'

Turning her attentions back to her call, Marianne raised her eyes towards the ceiling.

'I hear interesting rumours.' Vasiliev sounded just as jaded by their conversation. 'Chatter on Pentagram says The One finally surfaces?'

'News to me.'

Uno could sense Vasiliev was fronting: *Can't kid a kidder.* She knew full well the FSB had been monitoring the Forge witches. So far those tedious creatures had managed to cloak their magical operations behind their businesses very effectively.

'How about this ... If you are kind enough to release my men, I can assure you I will share any intel we get on The One.'

Vasiliev went silent as she considered the offer. 'Very well.'
The line went dead.

Marianne groaned as she realised she was now fully awake. Her eye wandered to the clock on her phone: just before five in the morning. Her husband's sleeping form still lay face down in the pillow.

She loomed over him, whispering in his ear. 'I'm going to kill you.'

Predictable as ever, Michael did not stir. Uno got out of bed to go to the suite's kitchenette to make coffee, taking the iPad with her. It was a waiting game. Her agents knew the score now she'd dug them out of the shit. Franklin needed to get a move on and call in with a report. He better have something good for her, otherwise she'd been telling the FSB where to pick him up again.

Three hours later and the expected call came in. Franklin's bedraggled form appeared on the iPad screen. She'd promoted him to acting premier agent after Boscastle, since he was the one who'd brought Tansy in. He'd been the only Sentinel who hadn't fucked up. Like with Vasiliev, Uno was careful to ensure her camera was off and the Tongue Box app was on. She always preferred to reveal her real identity in person, especially as she normally used her powers on the men as she did so. As strong as her Crystal magic was, it didn't work via an iPad screen, more's the pity.

Franklin was about thirty-five, dark-haired, with a rugby player's squashed nose and cauliflower ears. Though not quite as muscle-bound as the Scourge had been, he was still a big man. So many of them overcompensated for their soul weakness. His first assignment as patrol leader had been a real baptism of fire. His face was devoid of colour, bar the purple bruises to his cheekbone and jaw where he'd taken multiple fists. His left eye was swollen, almost closed. Dried blood had pooled in the corner of his mouth and temple. He held his arm around his ribs; his shoulders heaved with fatigue and pain.

'So, the Forge witches received The One and her little coven?' Uno enquired.

'That is correct,' Franklin confirmed. 'Plus I ran into Kesha Makorovich.'

Now the agent had Uno's attention. 'Tell me more.'

Franklin's time in the Lubyanka Building the night before with the FSB had been interesting in more ways than one. As well as his side order of torture, Franklin had managed to get some information from an FSB operative going by the name of Kesha Makorovich, who was really a Sentinel double agent. Real name Trey Delaney, he'd infiltrated the FSB years ago, long before Uno's time. In truth, she'd forgotten all about him. He had been watching the Forge witches on behalf of the FSB, particularly the one calling herself 'Cally'. It was Delaney/Makorovich's belief she had access to some kind of special magic the Sentinel had not seen before, one that helped her read minds and see things ordinary Elementals could not. Psyche, in other words.

Marianne already knew this, of course, having accessed it thanks to Tansy Penrose twenty years ago. Delaney had also reported to Franklin that Cally was American, like Ethan Weber and Garcia. It was Delaney's theory that Cally had met the Boscastle witches, and The One's powers were something to do with the spring equinox on March 20th, just four days from now. He was also of the belief they would be returning to confront the Sentinel, probably via an attack on Michael and the New Puritans. This was because the FSB had recently captured two members of that freakish white knight cult calling themselves the Brotherhood. The two traitors had been trying to smuggle Crystal witches out of the country. Both had given up the secret plan of murdering the senate with witches. They'd been put up against the wall and shot.

Uno absorbed all this from Franklin, impressed. She, too, had thought the equinox had something to do with Chloe Su's sudden explosion into witchdom; but then Uno did have an added, secret advantage, being a Crystal witch herself. It was logical, not to mention true, to suppose Cally had known Tansy Penrose, as well. Her forgotten soldier was obviously a good agent. Too good.

Of course, Delaney could not possibly realise that mad bitch Tansy Penrose would have told Cally about her mistake in teaching psyche to Marianne. Ethan Weber and his curious little coven would now know she wanted to steal Chloe's powers. Presumably that meant they would be on their way to confront her at the Orchid Tower. That was irritating, but not a major problem. She could tweak her own final plans for the spring equinox a little to accommodate that.

Before she forgot about Delaney again, Uno wrote a note to self on a Post-it in eyeliner pencil, reminding herself to call in her double agent when this palaver was all over. She would give him some guff about wanting to reward him for his years out in the cold, then give him a little heart-bomb or aneurysm instead. Introducing a little time-release magic to a man's bloodstream was always thrilling. It was also the perfect murder, since residual magic would work its way out of the corpse by the time an overworked pathologist could autopsy it. *Daddy Dearest* had discovered that when he wouldn't stop fooling around with the damn casting couch, putting her plans for Michael's emergency presidency in jeopardy.

'Well done, Franklin. Get yourself and your men to the evac zone.'

Uno's tone was begrudging; there was a part of her who'd have loved to leave him and his surviving brothers in arms stranded in Moscow. But it appeared he still had his uses: she needed to get her hands on Chloe Su and sending Franklin and his men after them would facilitate that. She would prefer having The One on her own terms, rather than let her turn up of her own accord right in the middle of the goddamned equinox.

Marianne swiped off and Franklin vanished from the iPad screen. She raised her coffee cup to her lips. The coffee was cold, but it still tasted like victory.

FORTY-ONE

Moscow, Russia

'No, my extended family is in Paraguay,' Adelita whispered. '*Our* ancestors, Cally said.'

They were in Sheremetyevo International Airport. Daniel leant back in the hard plastic of the airport chair, straining his ears to hear what Chloe was doing. He had his back to them, on the opposite row a few seats away, as if travelling separately. He knew his daughter had Cally's phone in her hands and that Adelita sat next to her. Ethan was across the terminal floor, near a ticket booth, standing under a big bulletin board as if watching for news of his flight. In reality, the rogue Sentinel's beady eyes were on the crowded hall, watching for potential threats.

'Like *all* witch ancestors?' Chloe mused. 'But we're all different people, from different places. That makes no sense.'

'I know.'

As Daniel and the others had descended into the tunnel beyond the Forge bar, they'd soon discovered it wasn't part of a catacomb, as such, but a labyrinth of what appeared at first to be storm drains. As they edged through the arched tunnel, Daniel shuddered as he spotted rats and cockroaches under the soft torch-like glow of Adelita's magic. There was no sign of sewage, so Daniel was thankful it didn't smell of shit; only the odour of damp walls and dirty rainwater tickled his nostrils. There was a slight murmur of traffic in the distance, which morphed into something else as they walked on: another distant, thunderous roar, like a dragon in a cave.

'What the hell is *that*?' Ethan's voice was weary.

Adelita forced a smile. 'It'll be fine.'

As they had emerged on a main conduit, a river appeared, raging straight through the middle, swollen with winter rainwater and melted snow. There was no way they could get through; the tunnel was completely impassable.

'Oh, great.' Ethan threw his hands in the air. 'Fucking great!'

'The Neglinnaya River!' There was a big grin on Chloe's face. 'She'll take us where we need to go.'

Chloe was glowing blue, and Daniel understood her Water Elemental power had told his daughter the river's name. He also realised, without the need for magic, what Chloe was going to do before she did it. He'd felt her reconnecting with the world, gaining in confidence and shedding a good portion of her prior angst as the equinox drew closer. With a whoop, Chloe had taken a run straight off the adjoining tunnel and landed with an almighty splash in the river. She was swept away before Daniel could even get a word out to stop her.

'You heard the girl.' Adelita held her nose and jumped in after Chloe.

Ethan shot Daniel a long-suffering look. It wasn't their first rodeo with raging waters that week. Despite his reticence, Daniel could feel something shift inside him. He realised it was excitement. He'd spent so long on the sidelines, studying and observing. It had been a good life, but there was something enthralling about being mixed up in the middle of things.

Ethan was right; he *had* changed. Like the boys at Boscastle, he felt re-energised.

'After you,' the rogue Sentinel said.

Knowing he could never jump in face first, Daniel gave a joyful yell like Chloe and flung out his arms. He toppled backwards into the river as if he was bungee jumping.

With a resigned 'Fuck!' the cowboy leapt in after him.

As Chloe had promised, the river spat them out near a derelict metro platform. They dragged themselves up onto the concrete, blue-lipped and freezing cold. Ethan's survival training kicked in: he told them to shed their wet clothes to ensure the soaking fabric did not conduct heat away from their bodies. It made sense; they didn't need to get hypothermia.

Only Chloe was reluctant to get naked. 'I don't need to.'

To prove her point, she lit up with fire magic. There was a damp smell of cooked fibres, like a jumper left on a radiator, as steam poured off her. As it cleared, her soaking garments were dry; so was her hair and skin. Then she shrugged, as if to say, *see?* Fifteen minutes later, Chloe had dried all their clothes, shoes and underwear. Adelita remembered the iPhone in her pocket when she slid her jeans back on.

'Waterproof.' Her face had cracked in a wide smile when she saw it still worked. Thankfully Chloe had not melted it. 'Cally knew we'd have to jump in the river.'

Fully dressed, Ethan took it from her hands. 'What was the name of the guy on Pentagram we have to contact to get out of here?'

Daniel had studied redacted transcripts from Pentagram in his research for his non-fiction book. 'Pentagram' had been the joke name courtesy of the press for the world witch web, which had somehow stuck. It was darker than the dark web and just as difficult to get into, the virtual equivalent of Fort Knox. The Sentinel could get in, but files and messages were heavily encrypted and full of code words that changed constantly.

'Cyrus Frost,' Adelita said. 'You know how to get on Pentagram?'

'Nope, I'm useless with this shit,' Ethan admitted.

'Don't look at me.' Daniel was more at home in a real library than an online one; he didn't even have a Facebook profile or Twitter account. He didn't see the point.

I'll do it.' Chloe snatched the phone out of the cowboy's hands. She felt Daniel's incredulous stare. 'What? Everyone *young* knows how.'

That told them.

Ten minutes after that, Cyrus had found them on Pentagram. He pulled Chloe into a heavily defended chatroom, telling her he'd been on the lookout for Cally's signal. He was already aware of what they needed: money for plane tickets, plus US dollars for the other side; new passports; as well as safe passage through the airport face-recog scanners so the Sentinel didn't spot them in crowds. Did they need him to jam the iHex as well?

'I like this guy,' Ethan said.

Where are you going? Cyrus typed.

That was the question. Adelita still hadn't decided. They all accepted Cally's point that Chloe needed to take back the power from Marianne Hopkins and the Sentinel; the problem was *how*. Adelita had already rejected Ethan's idea of storming the senate with the Brotherhood, but she didn't have a new plan. With the equinox just a few days away, the Crystal witch needed to find out why she'd been chosen by Hecate as Chloe's guide.

As Daniel drained the dregs of his coffee from a paper cup, something occurred to him. He turned slowly, rather than catch Adelita's eye straight away. He didn't want anyone sitting near him on the plastic chairs to understand what he was he going to say. White people rarely spoke his grandparents' native tongue, but there was one person in the airport who did.

'*Měinǚ, nín yǒu shíjiān ma?*' *Excuse me, miss: do you have the time?*

Adelita shoved Chloe in the ribs, who glanced over at her father, understanding his ruse straight away. She rolled her eyes and handed over the phone, as if to let him look at the LCD clock. As he glanced at the screen, Daniel quickly typed something to Cyrus Frost.

His reply was almost immediate: *Sorting that now for you.*

Daniel handed it back to Chloe. '*Duo xiè.*' *Thank you very much.*

Daniel gave Ethan an almost imperceptible nod across the terminal, indicating it was sorted and they would be going soon. He kicked back in his chair, waiting for their flight to flash up on the screen.

Cally had said '*our* ancestors', meaning all witches, just as Adelita had supposed. As part of the research he'd carried out for the book he'd been writing on witchcraft, Daniel knew Exeter was the first and last place to hang a witch in England. The fact that The One was born there couldn't be a coincidence, just like the fact that both Chloe and Adelita were born on the spring equinox, twenty years apart. So, what other places beyond the UK's West Country came to mind when people thought of witches?

That was easy.

PART FIVE

FORTY-TWO

The Orchid Tower, New York, USA

The Sus, Ethan Weber and Adelita Garcia were in Salem.

Unfortunately, it was Wednesday mid-morning on March 18th before Uno realised she had missed them all making it back to American soil. With less than forty-eight hours to go before the spring equinox, Marianne had been mainlining more coffee and enough uppers to kill a bull elephant. Her eyes felt grainy and sore from wading through reports and screens. When it turned out someone else's incompetence had wasted her efforts, Marianne scrolled through the Sentinel logs to see who'd fucked up. They would be going on her shit list as well as Trey Delaney.

Marianne discovered an undercover Sentinel air marshal-in-training had spotted two British Chinese faces on a flight out of Moscow to Boston late Monday night, but he was so wet behind the ears he screwed up not only his location ID, but his call sign numbers. This meant the Sentinel operative at the Orchid Tower filed the sighting under a 657 on a flight to New Jersey airport; 657s were 'MUI' – 'magic under the influence'. There hadn't been a single MUI reported in the USA since the Safeguard

Initiative had come in, for obvious reasons. That alone should have raised alarm bells for Sentinel HQ. Instead, the mistake was only revealed when a very surprised East Asian Goody who was *not* drunk was arrested at Newark Liberty International as she attempted to visit relatives with her new baby.

The significance that her quarries were in Massachusetts was not lost on Uno. Despite her bone-crunching fatigue, a smirk played at her lips. Perhaps they hoped to gain information, or to draw strength from hallowed Salem ground somehow. Before Safeguard, Crystal witches would journey there every Hallowe'en like it was Mecca. As a student, Marianne had gone herself once. Magical tourism had been a thing back then; witch boutiques sold their wares on every street. Witchy icons could be found in every logo, even the schools, university and police cars. The museums boasted interactive witch trial experiences; there was even a large statue of Samantha from that shitty old TV show *Bewitched* outside the Essex Street pedestrian mall. Differing to her Crystal sisters, Uno had found the place rather twee and embarrassing.

Feeling a smidgen better, Uno fell into bed. Hopefully, by the time she woke up, Chloe Su would be captured and in the brig at the Orchid Tower.

Just where she wanted her.

FORTY-THREE

Salem, Massachusetts, USA

Norway maples lined every street in Salem, lifting their naked boughs into the white, overcast sky. Leaf mulch and mud had been trekked through the wide streets, and the town's colonial history could be seen in the architecture of the large buildings that were still standing; its first-wave Puritan roots, too. wooden, plain, no nonsense. Georgian duplex homes stood alongside Greek and Italian revival style. It might have been beautiful, had it not been for the debris that littered every available space: concrete rubble, glass, burned timber.

Adelita meandered after Daniel, Ethan and Chloe, casting her gaze around the abandoned coastal city. It felt strange and disconcerting to be back in her home country, the place that had incarcerated her and ripped her family away from her, just for the virtue of belonging to a witch bloodline. She'd thought keeping her head down and being a useful contributor to society would be enough. But Safeguard coming in had shown her the USA built its foundations on the blood of its own people. It always had.

Cyrus Frost had warned them all something had gone down

in Salem, though he didn't have any details to share with them. It wasn't difficult to see why he'd received zero eyewitness reports: the whole place was like a ghost town. The evidence of the mob was everywhere: shop windows were broken; roofs were missing from homes and shops, burned and collapsed. The various museums had been burned almost to ash and the *Bewitched* statue had a chain round her mid-section where she'd been pulled from her plinth. She was also missing her head, while still sitting jauntily on her broomstick.

A soft moan of horror caught in the back of Adelita's throat as she saw the remains of a giant bonfire in the square. She'd heard rumours in prison of travelling death squads made up of Goodys and their men, roaming from place to place, unencumbered by the law. Daniel had told her how he and Chloe had seen that poor Crystal witch and her familiar hanging from the rafters in that rural Devon barn. But this was on a whole other level.

In the bonfire's deadly nest of twigs and timber, Adelita could make out the blackened bones beneath. Arms and hands, rising up out of the ashes like they were praying for mercy; skulls cracked by the heat, their mouths open in silent screams. How many of her witch sisters had come here, desperate for sanctuary after Safeguard, only to be confronted by murderous mobs? Surely hundreds, at least. Horror and sorrow surged up inside her as she fought to control her psyche, to prevent it from taking her back and showing her for real.

Salem's harbour was still, its smaller vessels sunk and overturned, their colourful bows peeking above the sea like neon icebergs. The tide was in, and the smell of fuel wafted off the top of the water, a slick running out of Derby Wharf. A ghost ship like the *Marie Celeste* was out further, its broken hull beached near the lighthouse, its once-magnificent sails tatters in the breeze. The rest of it was submerged beneath the water.

Perhaps Adelita had thought some kind of awakening would

crash through her when she set foot on Salem soil. As they made their way into the forgotten town, all she felt was hopelessness and a resigned frustration.

'This place . . .' Chloe had no words for it; her eyes were wild with the horror of it. 'How could they *do* this?'

As the girl looked to her, panic burst through Adelita's chest. She was meant to guide Chloe, but she had no answers for her.

'I can't do this.'

Ethan stopped next to her, nodding at Daniel and Chloe to wander a few steps ahead. Ethan's benevolent words echoed through the spellbind. The nausea receded as she fixed on the sound of them. She inhaled, trying to steady herself. She pushed her psyche down, envisaging herself forcing white light into a box and slamming the lid. As she did so, Adelita realised that was what she'd done her entire life.

Ethan rested his forehead against Adelita's, his hands on her waist. She pressed her lips against his, as if to draw strength from him.

You can do this, Doc. We are all here with you.

He was right. She remembered Cally's words back at the Forge bar about needing to be connected. Adelita had set herself on a lonely path of her own making, years ago; she'd cast herself in the role of the outsider. She'd so badly wanted to be independent; to stand on her own two feet; to prove she had what it took, no matter what anyone said. Adelita had repressed that magical part of herself; the part that was spontaneous, fun-loving, linked with others. She'd been so focused, so single-minded, she'd never let herself look inside that box; even when she had wanted to, she'd denied herself.

Back in Boscastle, Tansy had told Adelita that Ethan made her weaker. The High Witch had been adamant Ethan was 'just' a man and that he was distracting Adelita, at best. But Tansy had been wrong. Anger and vengeance had been Tansy's path to walk alone, but that was not Adelita's. Her magic channelled through love, joy, companionship. With Ethan, she was no longer the outsider, disconnected from others. Adelita's initial feelings had been right: he did make her stronger.

I got you.

Ethan grinned at her, but for once he didn't make one of his quips. 'Always.'

They found Daniel and Chloe further up the road, in the old elementary school. It had fared no better than the other buildings. Its main roof had caved in; most of its hallways and classrooms wrecked first by arson, then months of rain. The whole place still stank of bonfire.

Chloe and Daniel were in one of the few classrooms with all four walls, though its windows on both sides were missing. It had once been a library or quiet reading area; now decaying ceiling tiles and old strip-lighting hung down from yet another hole in the roof. Colourful paper bulletin boards and posters were white with age; books were swollen with water. Chloe held a big cloth wall hanging that had survived the weather. Though it had clearly been painted by the children, it resembled the one Cally had hanging over the secret door into the tunnels from the Forge bar.

'The triple goddess,' Adelita said. 'The virgin, mother and crone.'

Daniel looked up as Adelita and Ethan appeared in the doorway of the classroom.

'One of them's you . . . '

'Hey, I'm not that old!' Adelita objected. 'What is it with men always throwing women on the trash heap when they get near forty?'

Daniel chortled. 'As if I would. Will you let me finish? Over there.'

The professor pointed to the wall he was facing. Adelita

and Ethan hadn't seen it as they entered, and turned to look at a huge portrait of a woman, done entirely in tiny pieces of coloured glass like a mosaic. She wore a red dress, a red choker around her throat. She had the same wide-set, deep brown eyes, button nose, light brown skin and long, flowing hair. It was an uncanny resemblance.

The mosaic woman looked just like Adelita.

'Whoa,' Ethan breathed.

Mesmerised, Adelita approached the picture. On the left-hand side, a small plaque was signed by the artist. Its title read *Tituba, 1692; she cheated death by using her witchcraft confession against her accusers.* Underneath, there was a short summary about Tituba and her husband John, believed to be Native American. She was thought to have been brought to Salem in 1680, possibly from South America (though her origins are debated), bought as a slave by Samuel Parris. The plaque also revealed that historians believed Tituba confessed to witchcraft and implicated others as revenge against Parris. She protected her own interests – and John – and played on the religious fervour of the Puritans, manipulating an entire village to free herself and her husband. Ethan appeared behind Adelita, reading the information over her shoulder.

'Wow, they shouldn't have messed with her.'

'Shouldn't have messed with *us*.' Adelita indicated the triple goddess cloth in Chloe's hands. 'It's all connected, like Cally said.'

'Someone's gonna need to catch me up,' Ethan said.

The professor nodded, pointing to the first woman on the wall hanging, the virgin or maiden. 'This is Chloe. The virgin is the girl who is yet to awaken. She is full of youthful enthusiasm, a new beginning, associated with the moon growing from dark to full.'

Chloe grimaced at her father's description of her, though

Adelita could sense the logic of it. She knew from Boscastle that Chloe's fight with the darkness had never been about evil at all. Her black, carapace eyes were symbolic instead of rejecting the dark of the moon. Her journey was about embracing the true light of her powers.

'Then there's the Mother, who is represented by the full moon,' Daniel continued. 'She is about fertility, growth, the gaining of knowledge. She is about fulfilment: social, emotional, sexual . . . '

Adelita cast a glance at Ethan as Daniel continued talking. The cowboy winked at her and she stifled an involuntary laugh. She was thankful neither the professor nor Chloe had noticed. What Daniel was saying made sense, though, in all parts. She'd needed to reconnect to the world, in her own way. As Tansy had said, she'd been *head over heart* far too long.

' . . . She doesn't have to have biological children, by the way,' Daniel finished.

'That's a relief.' Adelita had never wanted kids of her own. She met Ethan's amused gaze again; he also seemed quite relieved. 'Unless I'm the crone?'

'Actually, you shouldn't be offended at that possibility,' Daniel said. 'The crone is a wise woman, represented by the waning moon. You said it yourself; it's the world of men who discredited her as an old hag, as something to fear and be reviled. She's not.'

Adelita raised an eyebrow. 'So I *am* the crone?'

Daniel laughed. 'No. It's like you thought . . . Hecate sent you to Chloe. The goddess is the crone, the third one in your trinity.'

'And you know what this means,' Ethan prompted Chloe.

The teenager nodded, resolute. 'Now we both know who we are, we can take on Marianne Hopkins and the Sentinel.'

It still felt like there was something Adelita was missing. That curious sensation she'd felt when she'd seen the younger

Cally in the steamed mirror was back. Like she could perceive something just out of reach. Something to do with Marianne and how she'd been conducting her Crystal witch powers in plain sight all this time.

Before Adelita could follow this tantalising thread, her psyche switched on.

'*A-da . . . ?*' Ethan's voice deepened, slowing down like an old cassette tape.

That feeling of moving between the planes of existence came over her again as everything went into slow motion. Ethan, Chloe and Daniel blurred in her vision as she focused on something dancing on the rubble near her feet.

A red laser dot.

She could see every mote of light in the red beam. She could follow it as if it were solid tape. It went straight across the crumbling bricks of the wall and through the broken glass window at a right angle. Her spirit body leaped out ahead of herself, soaring towards a copse of trees beyond the elementary school. There was a flash of field glasses and goggles.

A Sentinel sniper.

That weird sensation she'd felt at Taunton Deane when she'd seen Ethan die coursed through Adelita, cold like iced water. Again she saw a bullet smash through a skull and bury itself in the wall with deadly accuracy.

' . . . Chloe!'

Adelita fell back into her body a nanosecond before the shot really came in through the window. Everything sped up; Ethan yelled something else she couldn't make out. Chloe lit up with a yellow Elemental flare: Air magic.

Yes. Move, Chloe!

Adelita made a snatch for the bullet with her magic as Chloe blinked across the room. The bullet sailed through the ethereal fist Adelita made to intercept it: she'd missed. Too late, the

Crystal witch understood immediately why; it had never been meant for the teenager.

No. NoNoNoNoNoNoNoNo . . . !

Chloe's voice shrieked through the spellbind with Adelita's. Horrified, they watched as the bullet connected, making a head snap back on its neck. Bone and blood flew before he could move out of the bullet's trajectory. He collapsed to his knees, then his front, on the library floor, his life-force leaving him in an instant.

'Daniel!'

The cowboy gave a futile holler, raising his own weapon. Chloe stared at her father's fallen body, her eyes glued to his corpse. A guttural cry of rage and grief exploded from Adelita. White light forced its way out of her whole body like lightning.

As she powered up, she became aware of something else buzzing through the air, like a drone but super-fast. It sliced through the window on the other side of the library and hit her from behind, before she could even turn around.

Everything went black.

FORTY-FOUR

The Dark Side of the Moon

Daddy?
NoNoNoNoNoNoNoNoNo
This can't be happening
I need you
Don't leave me!
How can I do this without you?

Ssssh Chloe
Listen . . .
We haven't gone anywhere
Your mum and me . . . we will always be with you
I promise
(Remember what Cally said:
The power is in you)
Just listen
You can do this
Love you, bǎobǎo

FORTY-FIVE

Salem, Massachusetts, USA

In the bloody mêlée, Ethan's reeling mind could not keep up. He perceived, rather than saw, the shot through the front window of the library. As the professor crumpled next to him, Ethan felt Daniel's lights go out, as tangible as a room plunged into darkness. A tumult of distress, anger, frustration and hopelessness coursed through the cowboy next, as sure as the white light flooding through Adelita.

The rogue Sentinel raised his own weapon towards the window to deal with the bastard who'd taken his friend out. Before he could, he felt the updraught of something spinning through the air, entering the library via the back window. Ethan had seen them used and deployed them himself enough times to know what was coming. Heat-seeking, it was so fast. Ethan had no time to warn Adelita, even in the spellbind. It hit her from behind and snapped around her head like a deadly crown, its lights winking like malevolent eyes.

A flying halo.

Too late, Ethan understood the Sentinel plan: distraction first via a kill, followed by *hoop-a-witch*. It's what he would have done. Hell, he *had* done just that in Crystal witch covens across Europe in his twenties. He watched in horror as Adelita slumped to her knees in the rubble, head bowed like she was praying. Her magic snapped off as the Sentinel-induced lethargy shut all her faculties down.

'Doc . . . No!'

Ethan fell to his knees next to her, pulling her head up, so he might look into her eyes. Adelita stared ahead, unresponsive, her face vacant. She lolled against him, her body slack as he grappled with the halo and tried to pull it off. He knew it was a useless endeavour without the key; they were designed to constrict around the shape of the individual witch's skull. But the thought of his precious Ada, reduced by such a wicked thing, was too much to bear. He would never let her go to the angel caves. He would put a bullet in her himself first.

More hot lead peppered the walls at head height, plaster erupting in showers of powder around them. A shelf collapsed, spilling yet more paper and books. The cowboy closed his eyes and calmed his breathing, just as he'd been taught in the Orchid Tower. If he was going to defeat the Sentinel outside, he had think like one.

More flying halos flew through the air, looking for their next victim: Chloe. He had no idea if haloes even worked on Elementals; he guessed the agents outside didn't either. If Ethan were still Sentinel, he would have judged it as worth the risk with such a powerful witch present. But where the hell was she?

There.

The teenager was lying on the ground next to her father, her head resting on his chest. Blood pooled around them both, Chloe's hands covered in gore. Her eyes had not turned black but were clear. She was so still she looked dead herself.

Ethan let Adelita sprawl on the ground. It was the safest place for her as more bullets flew overhead. He crawled on his hands and knees, praying no strays took him out. Peril skewed his perspective; the three or four feet to Chloe and Daniel felt like miles. The teen did not react as the cowboy drew level with her.

'Chloe . . . Chloe!'

Ethan grabbed her, pulling her towards him. He made her look at him. Chloe lifted her head with difficulty. Her face was almost as expressionless as it would be had a halo snapped around her head already. It sent a shudder down the rogue Sentinel's spine.

'We're dead.'

Her voice was monotone, like it had been when he first met her. Like the others, Ethan had seen her reconnect with the world as she gained more control of both her emotions and her powers. They had come so far. He felt wrath flower within him at the unfairness of what was happening to her; to all of them. He'd told Cally he owed the witch cause, after everything he had taken from it. A burgeoning idea sprang up in his quick mind. It was risky and he wasn't certain he could survive it, but if he saved Chloe and Ada, it would be worth it.

'Not yet, we're not.'

Ethan shook Chloe as her eyes wandered towards the fallen Adelita.

'I need you to do something for me, Chloe. Are you listening?'

'Hold your fire . . . We'll come out!'

Weber's voice was hoarse and weary with it. Franklin was pleased to hear the lack of hope in the rogue Sentinel. He'd had a hell of a few days and was still pissed about Moscow, especially after the carnage at Boscastle. He was relieved to see no white light emanate from the school library; he felt fairly sure one of his twelve men had haloed Garcia, though he could not be sure. The Crystal witch was a credible threat, but a bigger concern was the teenager. As The One, Chloe Su could rain four kinds of Elemental magic on all of them. The fact she hadn't was intriguing. They must have hooped both women and pinned Weber down in the old school. If true, Franklin could go back to Uno with his head held high.

'We need proof both witches are neutralised.' One of his Sentinel, a squat toad of a man called Capstone, shouted through the megaphone.

Afraid of trigger-happy Sentinel, there was a tinkling crash as the traitor chucked a piece of rubble through the remaining glass of the window first. Franklin held up a fist, signalling his men not to fire. When no bullets came, Weber appeared at the window, holding Garcia's prone body in his arms, her head lolling back like she was his corpse bride.

Franklin plucked the megaphone from Capstone's hands. 'And The One?'

Weber ducked away from the window. He reappeared, this time holding Chloe Su, her arm around his shoulders as if she were drunk. The teen slumped against him, the unmistakable lights of a halo blinking on her head.

A huge, triumphant grin split Franklin's face in two as relief engulfed him. He had them. Uno would surely reward him. He might even get his own special handle like his previous idol, the Scourge, though he'd fallen from his pedestal in Franklin's mind. He'd delivered Tansy Penrose practically gift-wrapped to that weak fucker.

Weber bobbed out of sight again with the two witches. 'If I bring The One out, I need your word . . . You won't shoot me or Garcia?'

Franklin rolled his eyes. Uno was only interested in The One. Garcia had been of fleeting interest, but that was long gone now. Weber was expendable. Franklin had his own plans for the rogue Sentinel, right there on Salem ground. He was going to enjoy it, too; he was owed it after the pasting he'd got from the FSB. But first the traitor could bring the women out to them.

Franklin forced sincerity into his voice. 'You have my word.'

Quiet reigned for thirty seconds or more as Franklin and his men waited. Just as impatience rose like heat in Franklin's neck, there was a flash of blue jeans across the window inside the elementary school as someone ran the length of the room inside. His brow furrowed as he watched Weber race towards the back window, his witches abandoned. He vaulted over the window sill like Starsky and Hutch across a car bonnet. The traitor's cowboy boots hit the tarmac outside as he raced off in the direction of the harbour.

Franklin pressed his radio button. 'Don't shoot, he's mine.'

He gestured to his men to advance on the elementary school to collect the witches while he rounded the building and went after Weber, drawing a knife from his utility belt as he ran. He threw it after the rogue sentinel, another trick Weber would know of old. The blade hit him right where Franklin wanted it to: in the calf, just below back of the knee. It was not deep, but a move designed to disable and deliver maximum pain. The rogue Sentinel fell on his palms, swearing.

On instinct, Weber grabbed the blade from his own leg and swiped it upwards, as Franklin loomed over him. He blocked it easily, knocking it from the rogue's hand and across the macadam, out of both of their reach.

'Ethan Weber, agent 722.' Franklin was breathless. 'Pleased to meet you.'

Franklin landed a hefty kick in Ethan's ribs as he spoke. Next he threw a punch, his fist connecting with Weber's jaw, and blood spurted from the traitor's mouth onto the road.

Weber curled up in a foetal position, protecting his head. Franklin landed some more kicks, letting savagery overcome him. He felt something give in the traitor's side; a rib maybe.

A deep satisfaction bloomed in Franklin's chest. The rogue Sentinel had led them all on a merry dance across the world, with witches in tow. What kind of man aligned himself with women or witchcraft anyway? He pulled a handgun from his belt and yanked back its safety.

'Any last words, cuck?'

Ethan's voice was muffled. 'Yeah. Fuck the Sentinel!'

Before Franklin could squeeze off a shot into the back of Weber's skull, a commotion arose from the elementary school behind them. There was a cacophony of alarmed male voices, then gunfire went off in disorganised and ineffectual bursts like firecrackers. Before he even looked around, his quick mind saw through Weber's ruse. The rogue had only ever been a diversion. Franklin knew what he would see.

Green light, welling up like a bubble around the school.

'But . . .'

Franklin had seen the girl, the halo around her head. Before the question was fully formed, the answer came to him: *Earth magic.* Those Elemental cunts could manipulate and bewitch men, make them see all kinds of things that weren't there until it was too late.

'There she blows,' Ethan declared, grim pride in his voice.

Inside the library, Chloe screamed.

Green light burst upwards like a geyser, like it had in Boscastle, obliterating the building with it. It travelled outwards in an epic shockwave, pitching Franklin on to his back. Both men were propelled down the road by the force of the magic blast.

A rapid assault of magic coursed through Franklin, bringing nausea with it and making white spots jump behind his eyes. The traitor seemed to fare much better, struggling to his feet even before the Earth magic had receded. He held up a hand to shield his eyes as magic swirled around him, as if it was protecting him, *re-energising* him. It was like watching those male Elemental savages he'd seen at Boscastle. But Franklin's brain had to be playing tricks on him again; everyone knew magic was toxic to men.

Through sheer willpower alone, he grabbed hold of something else from his utility belt. He pulled it free. Against the force of the magic blast, fighting it every step of the way, Franklin had to concentrate to push his own arm out in front of him. In his hand: a stun gun.

He pressed the button.

The weapon's two barbed darts flew out, towards Weber. Through luck rather than judgement, it hit the turncoat in the back of the thigh. The rogue Sentinel stiffened as the electricity flowed through him. His eyes rolled into the back of his head as he fell, convulsing, back to the ground.

Gritting his teeth, Franklin struggled to his feet as the magic blast dissipated. Shell-shocked, he stared ahead at the building, hands on top of his head. Nothing moved within the elementary school. He knew it was pointless to look for survivors; all his men were dead. They'd been too close to the epicentre: Chloe Su.

Black wings fluttered overhead as crows flew from the branches above. There was an ominous silence over Salem, broken only by Weber's groans as he started to come back round. Before he could, Franklin yanked his medical kit out of his Sentinel-issue vest pocket. He found a syringe of sedative and plucked its rubber plug off, plunging it into Weber's neck in one deft movement. Franklin could still save his own bacon, by taking the traitor back with him.

'You're my ticket to the next level,' the Sentinel agent murmured.

The big man grinned as he saw Weber's eyelids flutter, falling unconscious again.

FORTY-SIX

The Dark Side of the Moon

> *Adelita, it's me, Chloe. Come back. Please.*
> *They've taken Ethan, he's gone. What do we do?*
> *Adelita!*
> *I can't do any of this by myself.*
> *I'm not strong enough.*

That's not true.

> *. . . Who said that?*

It's me. Tell Doc it's OK.

> *Ethan?*

Yeah. Surprise. You have to go through with the plan and link with the equinox tomorrow, like Cally said. Forget about me. You can't come and rescue me, OK? That's what they want.

> *You don't know that.*

I do, it's what I would have done.
Promise me you won't?

I can't do that.

FORTY-SEVEN

The Orchid Tower, New York, USA

The klaxon blared, one, two, three times from the top of the Anther Cap.

Uno waited below on the lead glass petals at the top of the Orchid Tower with Michael and the other Sentinel. The bird set down on the helipad, the Scourge and Ethan Weber inside. As the rotor blades thundered overhead, Marianne could feel the ripple of dark anticipation through the ten Sentinel waiting for the helicopter's door to open. Bored, she yawned as she listened to Michael give one of his speeches to them about honour, integrity and the re-education of deserters.

Uno was not present in her official capacity, just as first lady. To the Sentinel officers, Uno wasn't present at all. She hated the pomp and ceremony of returning traitors to Sentinel HQ, though she always enjoyed seeing them run the gauntlet of their furious brothers and their electrified batons. Marianne was disappointed Franklin had let her down in Salem but was delighted to hear he'd managed to capture the rogue Sentinel, Ethan Weber. She had already issued Franklin with orders not to let his men kill him. There would be no blows to the back of the head; nor were they to get carried away. She'd limited them to three blows each with their glow-sticks and no electric shocks.

Chloe Su and that Crystal witch of hers would undoubtedly want to rescue Weber's sorry butt. With the equinox less than thirty hours away, Uno knew the two women would be coming to the tower and Weber was just the juicy bait to keep things on her own terms.

The door to the helicopter opened. Franklin stepped out, pushing Weber ahead of him. The rogue Sentinel lurched forwards, limping, his hands tied in front of him. He was favouring his right side, his face bloody and dark with bruises. Franklin hadn't been able to resist; he'd already had some fun with him. Shame. Uno had already looked up Weber's file and he was exactly the kind of guy she usually liked: broad-shouldered, strong but lean. Not a squishy gorilla like Michael; or a muscle-bound freak overcompensating for a small penis like Franklin and so many of the others. Oh, well.

Weber lifted his head to stare at the two rows of Sentinel facing each other. Uno knew he would have participated in the gauntlet himself from the other side. He would have beaten on his brothers; maybe even killed them, depending on the offence. He must be wondering if it was the end of the line for him; he had no way of knowing for sure. Uno expected to see fear, but was not surprised when a broad, defensive smile cracked the rogue's face instead. One of his front teeth was missing.

'You're all drones,' Weber said.

The klaxon blared again and Franklin pushed him between the rows. Blows rained down on Weber. He raised his bound hands as he ran, making futile attempts to protect himself. He was quite the alley cat, elbowing his ex-brothers, clouting them back. At least one of the blows landed; Marianne was impressed as one of the other Sentinel fell to his knees, stunned. Another stepped forward and brought his baton down over Weber's shoulders, sending him to the ground. In contrast to his wife's broad smile, Michael flinched each time he saw blows rain down, his countenance painted in a ferocious grimace. Before bloodlust could overtake the men, Michael held up a hand.

'Enough!' Franklin bellowed.

The Sentinel fell back straight away, rolling their shoulders and massaging limbs where they'd been hit. Michael started congratulating them all, telling them they'd done a fine job. Uno stayed where she was and watched the fallen rogue Sentinel.

Weber groaned, crawling commando-style in slo-mo across the lead-glass floor of the helipad towards her. He stopped as he reached Uno's feet and he realised where he was. He took in her red satin Blahniks, incongruous next to black shined shoes of his ex-brothers in arms. He could barely hold his head up. Marianne knelt down to his level.

'I know what you are.' His words rasped in his throat.

Uno smirked. 'And there's absolutely nothing you can do about it.'

Hands grabbed Weber and dragged him off to the brig.

FORTY-EIGHT

Salem, Massachusetts, USA

Life rushed in again like an electric shock; just as it had at the beginning, back in that Texas motel. Adelita surfaced from the dark depths the halo had inflicted on her, jumping to her feet with the nimbleness of a cat. She raised both fists in the air, only to falter as the absence of battle dawned on her.

The air was quiet; Adelita could hear no gunfire nor could she feel the shadowy intentions of the enemy, or the *whizz* of flying haloes through the air. She forced her mind to focus and her gaze locked on the fallen body near her feet, the blood on the rubble.

Daniel. Oh, no. Not the professor.

A sob caught in Adelita's throat. His glassy eyes stared up at the ceiling, his limbs sprawled at awkward angles, like he was running. Daniel was a good man. He'd been a great father to Chloe and a good ally to both Adelita and to all witches. He'd been plunged into a situation he barely understood, yet he'd come through for them and helped them wherever he could. He'd never deserved any of this.

Still shell-shocked, Adelita took in the multiple fallen Sentinel bodies around them, residual Earth magic crawling across their chests where Chloe had stopped their hearts. Adelita pressed her hands against her own body in wonder. How had she survived? And where was Ethan?

Next into focus came Chloe, sitting back on her haunches, staring up at Adelita. The teenager's face was stricken, her cheeks tracked with tears. The flying halo was in her hands, in two broken pieces. Adelita could feel the sting of a minor burn on her forehead and by her left ear; Chloe must have made the halo expand and snap with heat from her fire magic.

Relieved, Adelita crouched down and flung her arms around her. Chloe's cheeks were wet against her neck. As their bodies touched, Adelita's psyche switched on again and she received a vision of Chloe doing the same in reverse. She saw Sentinel advancing on Chloe. The teenager knelt in the rubble, next to her father's dead body. Adelita, prone and haloed, lay next to him. Chloe grabbed Adelita's ragdoll form, pulling her close. The teenager screamed, a green bubble of Earth magic exploding around both of them. But they were in the eye of the storm; the blast magic swelled outwards, washing over the Sentinel, taking them out where they stood. Their lifeless forms fell to the ground in unison.

'He's dead. He's gone.'

Pain surged through Adelita at Daniel's loss. It seemed unthinkable the professor was gone, but they had no choice but to grieve for him later. She could see the sun sinking over the Salem skyline. The spring equinox was less than a day away.

'I know, baby. I'm so sorry.'

As she held Chloe tight, Adelita closed her eyes and searched for her cowboy in the spellbind, but he was conspicuous by his absence. What did that mean? Dread pierced Adelita's heart. He couldn't be dead, too. *Please, Goddess.*

'Listen, where's Ethan?'

Chloe pulled away. 'I told you. Gone.'

'Dead?'

Chloe shook her head. Relief washed over Adelita.

'They took him. Back to Sentinel HQ.'

'The Orchid Tower.'

As the words sprang to Adelita's lips, so did another vision. She saw Ethan staggering between two rows of Sentinel under the force of multiple blows. He fell forwards, onto his front, glass beneath his palms. Next to his bound hands: red shoes.

The images vanished. Ethan's voice echoed down the spellbind, his voice maddeningly quiet.

I don't think so, Doc.

You're blocking me?

It's for your own good.

Adelita strained against Ethan's barrier. How was he doing it? She could see nothing; feel nothing. It was like he'd put the phone down on her, but there wasn't even the comforting finality of a dial tone. All she could perceive was nothingness. Abandonment and panic coursed through her. What was she meant to do next? How could she do this without him? What the hell was he thinking?

What happened to 'you got me'?

No answer.

'He thinks we should proceed as planned, linking with the equinox and all witches.' Chloe wiped a tear from her face. 'He says not to rescue him.'

'*What?*' Adelita could not countenance this. 'We have to.'

'He's bait.'

Of course he was. But he was Ethan. They'd already lost Daniel; he'd been snatched from them, right in front of them, before they even had a chance to react. They couldn't stand back and let Ethan go the same way. Anyway, she'd told him this sort of macho lone-wolf bullshit was no good. She had to get him back, so she could kick his ass next.

'There must be a way.'

The Crystal witch was screwed if she could think of what the way was, but she felt certainty as well as magic move within her. So, what the hell was the answer? She knew the Orchid Tower well from growing up in New York – she'd walked past where it stood near Central Park on the way to and from work twice a day for years. Gleaming glass and chrome, the Orchid Tower had claimed the title of tallest building in the city. It was crowned by multiple rounded lead-glass petals at the top, just like the flower it was named after. One of the petals was where helicopters landed. The hospital Adelita had worked in was directly under their flightpath; she'd watched them approach the magnificent building from the huge plate glass windows of the break room as she had her coffee.

Adelita's mind returned to the last vision she'd had of her cowboy, his bound hands falling onto the thick floor of the helipad. She saw his reflection staring back at him from the glass floor underneath him, the fear and resolve there. He was prepared to die; she knew that. He felt he ought to, after everything he had done. She knew that, too, had felt it through the spellbind and when they'd made love, her white light enveloping them.

He says to proceed as planned, linking to the equinox and all witches.

The significance of what Chloe had said moments ago finally dawned on Adelita.

'Wait – when did Ethan tell you not to rescue him? Before he was taken?'

'No, in the spellbind. When you were haloed.'

'But *you're* not spellbound to him – I am.'

Chloe opened her mouth to reply, then realised she didn't have an answer for this curiosity. She shrugged.

'You ever spoken to him before, in the spellbind?'

Chloe shook her head.

Adelita felt that odd sensation again; it was as if there was an itch on the inside of her brain, like she was on the brink of an important realisation. Her gaze fell on the mosaic of Tituba across the library. Chunks of glass were missing now, where bullets had gouged them from the wall. Its little metal plaque was hanging at an angle, its words obscured by bullet holes so it read: *cheated death . . . witchcraft . . . against her accusers.*

She grinned. It felt like a message from Hecate herself. Maybe it was. The professor's last act in bringing them all to Salem had paid off. Daniel had facilitated Adelita's understanding and given his precious Chloe the fighting chance she needed against the Sentinel. It was their best option for rescuing Ethan, too.

Adelita knew what they had to do.

< @Forged1NF1re entered Pentagram >

@Forged1NF1re – Paging Dr Frost. I need a prescription.

< @CyrusFrost entered Pentagram >

@CyrusFrost – paging?? Soooooo 90s

@Forged1NF1re – Yup. Told that to 'you-no-who'

@CyrusFrost – Yeah, I get it. Wait a sec while I make sure this line is secure

@Forged1NF1re – It doesn't matter

< @CyrusFrost is typing …

@Forged1NF1re – oi come back … typing …

… typing >

@CyrusFrost OK done. What can I do for you?

@Forged1NF1re – You can unencrypt all of Pentagram.

@CyrusFrost – Wait, what?? Sentinel will see, Chloe!!!

@Forged1NF1re – So let them see. We need everyone to see. If Sentinel can = witches can. We need as many as possible @ Orchid Tower = the equinox. Brotherhood too, if you can get them.

@CyrusFrost – Is this a trick? How do I know I'm not talking to Sentinel right now?

@Forged1NF1re – 1 sec

< @Forged1NF1re is typing …>

@Forged1NF1re – Cyrus, this is Adelita. I'm going to ask you one question, don't answer it. If you understand, then delete this thread and open up Pentagram, OK?

< @CyrusFrost – NO ANSWER … >

@Forged1NF1re – Cyrus?

383

< @CyrusFrost - is typing . . . >

@CyrusFrost - No promises.

@Forged1NF1re - What're the petals on top of the Orchid Tower made of?

@CyrusFrost -What's that got to do with anything???

Forged1InF1re - Just think about it for a moment

< @CyrusFrost - is typing . . .

. . . typing . . .

. . . typing >

@CyrusFrost - OK. I get it . . . FML. I must be mad

@Forged1NF1re - You'll do it?

@CyrusFrost - I'll do it. Shit.

@Forged1NF1re - See you on the other side.

< @ForgedinF1re has left Pentagram >

384

NOTE: *THIS IS A RUSH TRANSCRIPT AND MAY STILL BE UPDATED. VIEW OUR WEBSITE AND SOCIAL MEDIA ACCOUNTS FOR REAL-TIME UPDATES.*

NEWS ANCHOR # 1: Hello, I'm Becky Buchanan. I'd like to first start by welcoming our viewers here in the USA and from all around the world via our web channel. We begin with today's breaking news.

Right now, we are reporting live from the Orchid Tower, New York. Sentinel sources are telling us that very early this morning, an Elemental witch broke into the presidential suite and murdered President Michael Hopkins, with the attack witnessed by our First Lady Marianne Hopkins. This follows the attempt on his life by Fire Elementals at his Thank You tour, plus of course the assassination of Dr Miriam Stone, which catapulted Hopkins to the White House two and a half years ago. But it's been a busy night, because that's not all that's been happening, is it Chad?

NEWS ANCHOR # 2: No it is not, Becky. Sentinel also tell us they captured a rogue agent yesterday in Salem, Massachusetts, travelling with two very powerful witches. It's thought that one of these creatures was attempting to rescue the rogue agent and that she is also behind the murder of our beloved president. To have two of our supreme leaders killed within five years of each other by witches . . .

NEWS ANCHOR # 1: I know, it's just awful. I'm sorry . . . I just— (*SHE DISSOLVES INTO TEARS; WAVES AT CAMERA; CAMERA SWAPS TO # 2*)

NEWS ANCHOR # 2: Sentinel are all on high alert, they are trained exactly for this type of situation. The brave Marianne Hopkins is expected to address the nation later this afternoon. We are going live to our correspondent in Central Park, Stacey Davis. Stacey, what are you hearing and learning?

CORRESPONDENT ON THE GROUND: Well, Chad, this is still very much a developing situation. And as you reported and as we're hearing from our sister networks, we've got reports of said Elemental killing the President and somehow vanishing from the Orchid Tower, despite there being over a thousand Sentinel stationed there.

NEWS ANCHOR # 2: That's highly unusual, isn't it, Stacey?

CORRESPONDENT: Absolutely, Chad. The Sentinel are highly trained men when it comes to witchcraft, so the fact an Elemental assassin could slip in and out of the Orchid Tower apparently unnoticed is very, very troubling.

NEWS ANCHOR # 2: Let's talk about some more about assassins ... What have you learned about the rogue Sentinel agent?

CORRESPONDENT: The Orchid Tower is obviously on lockdown, but I have managed to talk to a couple of Sentinel who didn't want to be identified ... They have confirmed the rogue agent as being Ethan Weber, thirty-one years old, previously a highly decorated officer with an immaculate record. He is thought to be part of an uprising on March sixth, when groups of men tried to free witch felons from angel caves and prisons. Weber and a Crystal witch, Adelita Garcia, were the only survivors from those synchronized jail breaks, escaping from Our Lady of Nazareth, Texas.

NEWS ANCHOR # 1: Extraordinary acts of bravery by both the Sentinel and the US penal guards in putting down those treasonous, coordinated attacks two weeks ago.

CORRESPONDENT: Indeed, Chad. (*CAMERA SHOT WIDENS*) As you can see behind me, there's a lot of activity in Central Park right now. Marianne Hopkins will be making her address from the Orchid Tower as she hands over emergency presidential powers to Sentinel elders just before three this afternoon, New York time. Sentinel are currently sweeping the area for potential terrorist threats because it's thought Sentinel HQ will be making an example of the rogue agent Ethan Weber to mark the occasion.

(*CAMERA PANS TO MEN PILING WOOD ON A PYRE BUILT AROUND A STAKE*)

CORRESPONDENT: They say 'live by the sword, die by the sword' ... It seems Ethan Weber has been living with witches, so he will die like one this afternoon. I know I feel a lot safer already! Back to you in the studio, Chad.

Sentinel HQ1: Red Knight, are you receiving? We got some kinda fucked-up shit going down on Pentagram.

Sentinel HQ2: Goddammit T-Bone, will you at least *try* to use the correct lingo and call signs? We've had enough of this crap lately . . . Over.

Sentinel HQ1: I think the time for correctiquette is gone, Old Timer. The cyber geeks in IT say the witches tore down all the encryption on Pentagram. They aren't even attempting to hide their messages or signals. It's like they don't give a shit we can see. They've sent out an SOS to witches all around the world.

Sentinel HQ2: So what? They're just women. We've got bigger problems. The president is dead, in case you forgot.

Sentinel HQ1: It gets worse, buddy. The geeks say they're seeing wall-to-wall calls to arms from witches all over the world. They are talking about taking on the Sentinel, together somehow.

Sentinel HQ2: Hah, they wish. Stupid bitches. You're talking crap.

Sentinel HQ1: Am I? Their plans are real detailed. Crystal witches are talking about remote magic with Earth Elementals. Fire Elementals are threatening to band together so they can try and bring fucking lava up through Central Park. We got Air witches saying they will try and get as many women as they can, as far as they can, through portals. Water

Elementals are talking about parting the fucking oceans so women can walk across the goddamn seabed. Even if that's all puffed-up bullshit, we've got witches coming to the Orchid Tower. No doubt about it.

Sentinel HQ2: How many?

Sentinel HQ1: . . . All of them.

Sentinel HQ2: Fuck.

FORTY-NINE

The Orchid Tower, New York, USA

Marianne checked the clock: not long now before her big speech and the start of the new world order. She would smile bravely, her precious girls Regan and Alice by her side. No one in the Orchid Tower knew it yet, but once the equinox hit, just before three o'clock, Marianne would not be handing emergency powers over to Sentinel elders as planned. She would be keeping hold of the reins of the United States, as well as taking The One's powers for herself when Chloe Su finally arrived.

Today, Marianne Hopkins would become the strongest witch of all time.

It hadn't been difficult to murder Michael. Her meat puppet of a husband had so much latent magic swimming in his veins, all she had to do was set it off like a well-timed bomb. More difficult had been 'persuading' Sentinel guard outside their suite she'd seen an Elemental scaling the tower. She'd tied the Orchid Tower up in multiple spellbinds a long time ago. Men who signed up to the Sentinel were always looking for answers, someone to take their pain and confusion with the world away; spellbinding with them was easy.

But as bad luck would have it, her usual bodyguard Riggs had been off sick last night, and there had been a hairy moment when the new guy, Quinn, had resisted. Luckily the situation had turned on a dime and he'd capitulated, so she hadn't had to kill him as well. That would have been super-awkward, not to mention tedious.

Marianne peered at her reflection in the mirror, checking her hair was mussed, her skin was pale and her eyes red and puffy. It half-killed her to go on live television looking like a soccer mom who'd rolled out of bed late for the school run, but she could not look too perfect. Her husband had just been killed. Women were judged constantly; this prejudice was never clearer than during times of crisis. If she appeared at the main, middle sepal of the Orchid Tower to make her address looking too 'with it', she would lose the crowd. She didn't need even the tiniest thing throwing her plans for that afternoon off.

Next, Marianne visited Ethan Weber in the holding cells. The rogue agent was pacing, as so many of them did before execution. He did not stop when he saw her, refusing even to look her in the eye.

The original plan had been to parade Ethan Weber through the park and tie him to the stake just before her last speech as first lady. Sentinel on the ground had nixed this idea when it was revealed a small but vocal number of women claiming to be Goodys had needed to be kettled on the Westside, up near the Museum of Natural History. Marianne was disquieted that some Goodys were apparently sympathetic to the witch cause now. But they must be exceptions to the rule; she'd never had any problems with the prols before. Anyway, they had been dealt with.

'Hello, Ethan.'

Weber stopped pacing, against his will. He snarled as he watched his own feet turn towards the cell door. They brought him straight to her, whether he liked it or not. He did not. Marianne smiled as he drew nearer, only the bars of the cell between them.

'You're making your last hours needlessly painful for yourself.'

She spoke the truth: he'd refused a last meal; sent the chaplain away; got tasered when he'd thrown a punch at one of his guards. Yes, she liked Weber a lot. It was such a shame he had to be barbecued.

'Open the cell door.'

The Sentinel on guard could not betray his alarm. 'But Mrs Hopkins . . . ?'

'Do it.'

The Sentinel's eyes dulled again as Marianne's influence washed over him. He pulled a key card out and opened the door, holding it for her like it was an elevator. The Sentinel turned his back and retreated down the hall out of sight, leaving the door wide open.

She strode in, peeling her gloves off. Weber made no effort to escape. He knew he would never find his way out of the tower without any of his witch friends. Marianne beckoned the rogue to her with one finger.

The veins surfaced in Weber's neck and arms as he rocked back on his heels, attempting to withstand her magic. Marianne smiled, impressed as his resistance snapped back at her, stinging her mind's eye like a rubber band. He was strong.

Marianne turned her magic up another notch. 'You are beholden to me.'

'No . . . I . . . am . . . not.'

The rogue agent's hands cradled his temples. Marianne perceived flashes of Stonehenge and crying women. Weber still resisted. Interesting. He really was something else. Now Michael was dispatched, this young man could have been her new pet. They might have had some fun. She could have put a love spell on him and he would follow her around like a lost puppy. But there was no sport in that.

'Yield.'

Ethan shuddered with the exertion. 'Never.'

White light flashed between them like lightning. Marianne was so surprised she almost jumped backwards, before she realised it was within her magic flow; something had cracked inside Weber. It was peeking through, even as he tried to shove it back inside.

'That's it,' Marianne said, 'give it to me.'

Ethan ground his teeth and squeezed his eyes shut, as if physical effort alone could contain whatever he was keeping from her. More images washed over Marianne: barbed wire and trains; blood on the ground. Damn it, she was out of practice in retrieving information straight out of men's heads like this. Another reminder of her inferior Crystal magic. If she was an Earth witch, she'd be able to pluck Weber's thoughts like nimble silver fishes from a fast-flowing stream.

Snarling with irritation, Marianne reached out, placing a palm on his forehead. The rogue Sentinel cried out. He fell to one knee, arms now by his sides, convulsing like she'd electro-shocked him. His eyes rolled back in his head.

That white light enveloped them both inside the magic flow. They were no longer separate people; they were no longer people. Just psyche. Swirling around one another like embers on a bonfire. More white light came; it flashed like a lightning storm illuminating a room within.

Flash – brown eyes, long dark hair

Flash – Ethan, staggering between the rows of the gauntlet

Flash – spirals of white Crystal magic, blasting outwards

Flash – a glass portrait of a Latina woman in a red dress

Flash – Ethan's hands on the glass of the helipad floor

Flash – Ethan's hands again, this time gripping a woman's hips, their lips touching as a white bubble exploded around them . . .

... Marianne blinked. He'd thrown her out again. No matter. The spellbind had been temporary, but she'd got what she wanted. Weber had thought he'd managed to hide everything from that other Crystal witch he'd escaped Our Lady with, but he hadn't been able to completely turn his love off. Marianne had been able to snatch at the thread and unravel it. She knew what they knew. Marianne would be ready for them.

She looked down. Ethan Weber lay at her feet on his side, staring at the wall, stupefied, a single tear tracking down his bristled cheek. She knew it would take a while for him to recover his senses. The flow of her magic – perhaps the only giving side she even possessed – made her crouch down and stroke his blond hair.

'Good dog,' she crooned.

FIFTY

Central Park, New York, USA

S he knows.

Adelita lurched to a standstill, her breath snatched from her lungs. Chloe's fingers curled around her arm. The teen stared up at her: *All OK?* Adelita gave her a hasty nod. She felt Ethan's block on the spellbind lift momentarily; she could see what he'd been forced to show that bitch Marianne Hopkins.

I tried to keep her out. I'm sorry, Doc.

Adelita had guessed from the offset Marianne would make him reveal their plan. She had control over everything that happened in the Orchid Tower, thanks to the lead glass it was made of. Ethan had realised the moment he'd fallen after the gauntlet; that's why he'd worked so hard to block Adelita, in case Marianne took control of him. He was trying to protect her and Chloe, but he was the one who needed help.

It's OK, babe. We're coming for you.

Their strategy was a good one; Chloe could still link with the equinox as planned and Adelita could still rescue Ethan from the pyre. They could still win. Adelita pushed away her own doubts and sent that message down the spellbind to Ethan.

No. Abort. Get out now.

Not going to happen, Adelita told her cowboy.

Their conversation was interrupted as a tall man with an angular nose and a long plait stopped beside Adelita, hands in his pockets. Chloe tilted her head at him, curious.

'Fancy seeing you here.'

Adelita's face cracked in a wide grin. 'Jocko.'

The Brotherhood was not on Pentagram, for obvious reasons. Adelita had had to go old school and call the operator. Stuck in Salem, she'd got put through to Jocko's pop's motel from a regular payphone that stank of dog pee. People were still not staying at the LayZ-DayZ, so Jocko had answered on the second ring. They'd parted on bad terms back in Texas, so Adelita had worried he might put the phone down on her. Jocko had just laughed, though, and told her she could buy him a new mug to replace the one she'd smashed with her Crystal magic.

He'd been less cheerful when she'd outlined their plan. Jocko had told her she was mad, just like Cyrus Frost had. He reminded her Ethan was a cowboy, a rogue, a lone wolf. He wouldn't want rescuing from the tower like a pretty princess.

'That might have been true before, but he's changed. You don't know him like I do.'

Jocko went so quiet on the end of the line, she thought he'd abandoned the receiver.

'C'mon, no man left behind?' Adelita crossed her fingers.

Jocko let out a loud *harrumph* that told her he was going against his better judgement.

'I'll call around the guys.'

He'd sent a small crop duster for them, which had deposited them on the outskirts of New York. Now, Adelita looked across Central Park. They were on the Great Lawn, near Croton Reservoir. Across the water, the glass and chrome building of the Orchid Tower grew up like the gigantic, poisonous alien triffid it was. Towards its front, Adelita could make out the huge pyre of wood the Sentinel planned to execute Ethan on, by burning him at the stake. She'd wanted so badly to be home when she was at Our Lady, but the New York she saw now was very different to her vision of it growing up.

She and Chloe had their hoods up, their faces covered in the cold, biting March rain like so many. Across the way, another familiar face swam up in the crowd. There was a flash of purple and box braids as Cally swept by. The Forge witch had kept her promise and snuck into the country, bringing more witches with her. Kill drones buzzed overhead, their lights twinkling like deadly eyes. They only carried a certain number of bullets, but one was too many. They were fitted with iHexes too, to identify and kill witches in crowds, but Adelita's, Cally's and Chloe's psyche meant their magic would go undetected.

Adelita could see the beady eyes of half a dozen Brotherhood in the vicinity; she knew there were even more up towards the tower and near every exit. Jocko hadn't said how many he'd brought, but she guessed it was several hundred. That wasn't many compared to the thousands of Goodys and their men gathering for Marianne Hopkins' speech, but it was all they needed. The Brotherhood were there to help get witches into the park and past the kill drones.

They'd also brought sympathetic Goodys with them to create a diversion. It was working. They were still yelling slogans, waving signs and throwing missiles at Sentinel and a lot of extra manpower was being deployed and redirected to keep them under control. That suited the Brotherhood just fine. Another man, a boy really, stopped beside Jocko.

'This is EJ. He'll help get Chloe into the tower.'

EJ flashed them both a toothy grin. He was about twenty-one, thin and rangy with a burst of freckles all over his pale face. He looked like a ginger Just William from the front of the books Ernesto used to read Adelita and her sisters every night when they were kids.

Jocko must have sensed her apprehension, because he grinned. 'This fucker looks like a puff of wind will knock him over, but *he* is the tornado. Nothing can get in his way. He's British, too. Mad dogs and Englishmen; they're crazy bastards.'

EJ seemed flattered by this description, tipping Jocko an imaginary hat. His eyes alighted on his watch, then Chloe. 'You ready?'

'Wait a sec.' Adelita turned away, huddling with the teenager. She could feel anxiety flushing through Chloe; it bristled through their spellbind. 'Baby, look at me.'

Chloe's gaze locked with Adelita's: *I can't do this.*

You can. You are so strong. Just remember the plan.

Marianne has had her whole life to prepare! I've had fourteen days.

That's all true. But you are Elemental; she is a Crystal witch.

She has psyche too. Look what you can do. She could be stronger.

But you are The One.

Chloe's eyes shone with tears. She looked away from Adelita across the crowd. In the throng, Adelita caught sight of Cally again up ahead. It was as if the Forge witch somehow knew what they were talking about, even from a distance. She probably did.

Beside Adelita, Chloe sighed. *What if Marianne manages to steal my powers?*

What if she doesn't?

Chloe nodded, taking deep breaths. She hugged Adelita, throwing her arms around her and kissing her cheek like a little child. Without another word or looking back, Chloe took EJ's proffered elbow and they vanished into the crowd. Adelita felt a strange pang in her chest as she watched her go. She sent another message down the spellbind after Chloe.

Happy birthday, baby.

Out of sight already, Chloe answered from somewhere in

the crowd.

Happy birthday, Adelita.

'Proud mommy, huh.'

Adelita watched as Jocko blithely unscrewed his home-adapted prosthetic hand and threw it away like trash. He unzipped his jacket and shrugged it off, revealing a baldric underneath. In the sling, a wide-bladed parang.

Adelita couldn't believe her eyes. 'How the hell did you get that through the metal detectors?'

Jocko looked at her like she was mad. 'Made of ceramic, of course.'

'Of course,' Adelita said. 'You gonna be OK?'

An incredulous chuckle escaped him. 'Why, cos I only have one arm? Wow, Adelita. I would have thought you had a little more about you than *ableism.*'

Adelita laughed. 'I meant when all the witches turn up? I know they freak you out.'

'Oh.' The outraged wind went out of Jocko's sails. 'I will admit it's not my favourite thing to do on a Friday afternoon. But you gotta do what you gotta do and all that shit.'

Across the water, the klaxon on the Anther Cap, the pinnacle of the Orchid Tower, blared. It filtered through the big speakers, harsh soundwaves travelling throughout the park. A cacophony of human voices followed as Goodys' and men's cheers surged through the air.

On the big screens that had been erected either side of the tower, Marianne Hopkins stood, shoulders hunched in supposed grief, both her teenage daughters blank-faced next to her like mannequins. They were beamed all around the United States and the rest of the world. Camera phones took pictures, uploading to social media in seconds.

Anticipation flooded through Adelita. They would be bringing her cowboy out to the pyre any second now.

'Here we go,' Jocko said.

Just like Ethan always did, before it all kicked off. Adelita's mouth tugged in a smirk.

That was you, wasn't it?

This time he didn't block her. Even inside the spellbind, her cowboy seemed exasperated, as well as fearful.

I can't dissuade you from this, can I?

Nope.

See you soon, Doc.

FIFTY-ONE

The Orchid Tower/Central Park, New York, USA

A carpet of faces could be seen below the sepal, stretching across the whole of Central Park and beyond the reservoir. They were all there to see her.

That's what Marianne had to remember. She was the driving force behind not only the Sentinel, but the whole United States of America. Just moments from now, she would take what was rightfully hers and reveal herself as the proud ruler of both the magical and non-magical worlds.

'Like Dr Miriam Stone, my husband gave his life to keep us safe.'

Marianne paused, lurching forwards and leaning on the mike stand. A Sentinel came running, both hands splayed as if to catch her. This drew a sympathetic *aaaah* from the crowd. Mission accomplished, she waved him away.

'. . . Thank you, but I can do this. I have to honour my husband. He was a great man.'

Those words almost stuck in her throat. Marianne reminded herself that she had already taken calls from some of the remaining non-Safeguard countries, expressing interest in further

401

discussions. It would not be long before she would have her men on the ground in every nation on Earth. No one would be able to touch her. She could take her rightful place, unchallenged, as the most powerful witch *and* leader of the world.

But first, she would need Chloe Su. Marianne gave a surreptitious glance at her watch as she finished her speech: 2:44 p.m., EDT. The crowd erupted with rapturous applause below, followed by hisses and boos as the rogue Sentinel was brought up to the pyre.

The One was mere minutes away.

Ethan stumbled as he passed the executioner, who was preparing the tinder and torches below. The agent escorting him grabbed him by his shirt collar, wrenching the cowboy to his feet and half strangling him in the process.

'Careful with the merchandise, everyone's come for the show,' Ethan choked.

'Shut up, cuck.'

It was the same agent who'd captured him in Salem; he'd heard others call him Franklin. He looked like all the others. He pushed him up the scaffold steps, making the cowboy fall to his hands and knees. Behind them, rain spat down a fine mist onto the water of the reservoir. The crowd was penned behind it, a decent way back from the Orchid Tower. Irritated by the lack of pace, Franklin grabbed Ethan by the shoulders. The cowboy let his body go slack, forcing the agent to grapple with his deadweight as they made it to the stake.

'Uno won't do right by you. You're just cannon fodder. She'll put you in the brig eventually. She doesn't give a shit about any of you guys.'

'She?' Franklin's mouth fell open in a hearty chuckle. 'Yeah, OK.'

'Oh, you don't know either?' Ethan wrenched his hands away

as Franklin attempted to tie them to the stake. 'All this is a lie. I mean, I knew it was, but it's so much worse than your tiny brain can comprehend. She's been using all of you.'

The broad smile did not leave Franklin's lips as he delivered a kidney punch to the cowboy's lower back. The pain of the blow made Ethan fold over, hissing like a burst tyre.

'You're done, traitor.'

Franklin wound the leather cord around the cowboy's hands to the stake, sure to tie it in a strong bowline like a good boy scout.

Ethan breathed through the pain, 'You can't win.'

Franklin shrugged. 'Already have, from where I'm standing.'

'You're on the wrong side.'

'If you say so. I hope it was worth it, traitor.'

It was pointless. This guy had drunk so much of the Kool Aid, he was drowning in it. Ethan raised his head to the sky, letting the rain wash over his upturned face. As he did so, a flash of white light seared through his mind and he saw Adelita's face again. If he died here today, he knew one thing.

'Yeah. It was worth it.'

Up on the Anther Cap, the klaxon blared again.

Down in Central Park, as the klaxon sounded to signal the lighting of the pyre, Jocko and hundreds of his brothers hollered like warriors and targeted the kill drones hovering overhead. Batons, baseball bats – and ceramic-bladed swords – cut through the air. A good sixty per cent of them connected before the Sentinel drone operators could react and buzz them back up out of reach. From the others came the crack of gunfire and bursts of bullets.

Bystanders' screams cut through the air as they scattered, running for park exits. The Sentinel had been on high alert, but they were still unprepared for such bedlam. There was a primeval piquancy as Brothers descended on nearby Sentinel and anyone else who dared challenge them. The kettled Goodys linked arms and surged forward at Sentinel, using their wooden signs as both shields and weapons.

As all this went on, Cally and Adelita sent corkscrews of white light and flashes of fire magic into the air like pyrotechnics, hitting unfortunate Sentinel in their way and at the same time obscuring the crowd from the view of any kill drones still in play.

'Stay behind me!' yelled Jocko.

'I've got this,' Adelita scoffed.

Elemental flares crackled all over Central Park.

Jocko gulped. 'Ah, crap.'

An explosion of yellow sparks came first; Air witches appeared in the blink of an eye like Evgenia, or through portals like Emmeline. They brought Earth witches with them, who sent their green spheres into the air as they arrived. The smell of burned plastic and wiring filled the air as their workings scrambled. Any remaining kill drones roaring overhead died, falling from the air to the mud, where they were set upon by waiting Brothers.

Before she could send white light at a Sentinel bearing down on them, Jocko pitched in front of her. He sliced his sword across the agent's neck and chest. The Sentinel fell into the mud, trying to hold his flesh together in vain, blood pouring between his fingers. Adelita sent a flash of white light around them as they raced towards the reservoir.

From the middle of the crowd, Cally sent some more columns of fire upwards, joined by her fiery sisters from the Forge. Evgenia and her mother shrieked like banshees, sending the jets of fire towards advancing Sentinel, making them fall back. The klaxon resounded from the Anther Cap again. The fighting did not stop. No senator's voice boomed from the Orchid Tower.

Instead, a voice Adelita had never heard before filtered through the sound system – not American, nor British either. It was an Australian voice, the intonation at the end of the sentences almost turning them into questions:

'This is a takeover . . . It's been divide and conquer too long! See what happens when we join together . . . It doesn't matter what side we've been on, but that we stand up against the Sentinel!'

Adelita figured it was one of the Brothers, and kept running for the reservoir. Up ahead, the water was undulating like the ocean . . . waves gathered in the middle and sent a column of water up towards the sky. It was the work of ten Water witches who were now lining the reservoir banks, their fists in the air and working together. She grabbed Jocko by the wrist. He groaned.

'I'm not going to like this next bit, am I?'

Adelita smirked as yellow sparks showered, a portal opening up next to them. A sky-clad Emmeline appeared. Loveday was with her, her only piece of clothing the sling around her injured shoulder. They both waved like they were seeing Adelita on a routine trip to the park. Adelita grabbed Jocko and pushed him ahead of her.

The portal collapsed behind them. Yellow air magic swirled around them, taking her breath away and snatching Jocko's surprised yell from his lips. She was aware of moving forwards, her mind insisting it was her body, though her heart told her it was something else. It was ferocious in its intensity, making her feel both nauseous and exhilarated, like a fairground ride. It lasted for ever yet in the blink of an eye it was over, delivering her, Jocko and the two Boscastle witches to their agreed destination.

The top of the pyre.

After persuading Regan and Alice to go back to the presidential suite, which was on lockdown, Marianne let herself be swept along corridors by her Sentinel underlings. She'd already seen Chloe and her little ginger pet on her iPad, beamed up from Sentinel CCTV. With the girl's formidable magic and the boy's fighting skills, the pair of them had had no trouble gaining entrance or making their way up the tower. Marianne hadn't thought they would.

'Enough.'

She snapped her fingers. The spellbind kicked in and her men fell away, leaving her in peace at last. Marianne's high heels clicked on the frosted glass of the corridor floors; her face reflected back at her from the walls of the glass elevator as it climbed the tower. The glass lift doors opened and she tottered out onto the platform. The girl hadn't made it here yet. Marianne checked her watch: 2:52 p.m., EDT. Marianne was not foolish enough to hope the child would not make it in time. She knew she would.

Six minutes until the equinox.

Marianne didn't normally go as high as the Anther Cap. It was home to the klaxon, but not much else beyond the anther itself. Below, she could see the glass petals and its sepal on the platforms below. New York itself was so far down, the people on the street did not look like ants, but bacteria.

Marianne caressed the anther. It was not a true orchid stamen, but a glass ball. The size of a large beach ball, it had been her secret weapon since the day she'd had it put in, when she and Michael had moved into the tower. It conducted her magic for her, sending it into the hearts and minds of everyone in the tower, sending it through the glass walls and floors as definitively as light through mirrors. She'd used it to enact spellbinds on all her men, making them beholden to her. The anther had cloaked, facilitated and enabled Marianne to take whatever she wanted. She'd made everyone forget one simple fact, over and over and over again, since the day the tower had been built and the anther cap had been put in: the Orchid Tower was indeed made of glass. Lead glass.

Also known as *crystal*.

The doors of the elevator opened. The boy came out first. He was just a baby savage, blood smeared on his pale face and forearms. He carried two sais, one in each fist. Even with the dark violence rippling through the young Celt, he was no threat whatsoever to Marianne. No man ever had been. Nevertheless, she could also tell the boy was the type who never knew when he was beaten. Cute.

The girl joined him, eyes wild and resolute. She edged in front of the boy, green Earth magic crackling through her like electricity. Marianne could see the child was powering up in readiness for the equinox. That was more problematic. She looked to her watch: 2:53 p.m.

'It's over. Stand aside,' the ginger boy instructed Marianne.

The first lady tilted her head. 'I don't think so.'

White light burst from Marianne's palm as she flicked her hand to the left. The Celt hollered as Marianne's magic swept him off the platform and pitched him backwards into the void. He would be falling for a good while before the ground rushed up to pulp his flesh and bones. She smiled at the shocked Chloe, who stared at the space where the boy had been.

'Let's talk,' Marianne said.

Before the klaxon blare had receded, Franklin heard the feral yells of men below. *What the hell?* Then he saw the first wave of kill drones get taken out, only some of them quick enough to get shots off. Multiple Elemental flares sprang to life all over Central Park. Gunfire exploded from non-Sentinel-issue firearms.

Franklin's mind rattled around his skull with questions: How had so many witches gotten into the park? What the actual fuck was going on? There was no time to answer. Yellow sparks burst

407

right next to him. The traitor raised his bound hands in the air, shielding his eyes as best as he could from the magic conjured right next to them. Before he could react, white light poured through the opening portal like lightning. It powered Franklin backwards, dropping him onto his back on the platform.

'What took you so long?' Weber grinned.

Stunned, Franklin flipped over to his front. Adelita Garcia and a one-armed redskin dropped from the portal. Garcia kissed Weber on the lips like she was Robin Hood.

'I got you,' she said.

Weber laughed. His head still swimming, Franklin tried to stand, but fell to his knees again.

Garcia's shadow loomed over him. 'Don't move, pig.'

Franklin complied; he had no choice. The woman was glowing white with Crystal magic. He was shocked to see two naked witches hanging back in the portal, too. Did none of these toxic savages have at least some modesty? He watched as the Indian sliced through Weber's bonds with a vicious-looking parang.

'So, you needed rescuing by a girl, huh?' the one-armed man teased.

Ethan chuckled as he pulled the leather cord from his wrists, released from the stake. 'She's no girl, she's a witch.'

Franklin's lip curled in a sneer. The traitor had that right, at least. Why did he sound so impressed? That bitch was dangerous.

Garcia checked her watch. 'Four minutes till the equinox. We gotta go.'

Franklin flinched and squeezed his eyes shut. He was sure she would send a flood of white light into his body and stop his heart. That sense of the air splitting apart came instead, making his stomach lurch. The smell of burning ozone burst through his sinuses. In wonder, he opened his eyes: the fugitives had stepped back into the portal and vanished into thin air, leaving him behind. He was alive. Gratitude and confusion swirled through him as he wondered why they'd spared him.

Another shadow fell on the scaffold as Franklin staggered to his feet.

A gigantic column of water was whirling up from the reservoir towards the sky. The Water witches had used every litre available. He could see the mud and detritus below; the litter that had sunk and stuck there. The column loomed over the unlit pyre, huge and ominous in its power. Franklin knew if he looked down, he would see the executioner at the bottom of the scaffold on his knees, realising his fate and appealing to his maker to spare him. Franklin braced himself, inhaling a futile deep breath as he did so.

The deluge came down and swept the Sentinel agent and the whole pyre away.

FIFTY-TWO

Chloe Su ignored Marianne's request to talk. The first lady watched as the teenager released a shower of yellow Air magic, sending it off the platform after the red-headed boy.

It swirled down like curling ribbons, surrounding the soldier as he fell, gaining in speed. In a blink, the Air magic disappeared, taking the boy with it.

It was an impressive trick. Before Marianne could congratulate the child, Chloe conjured up small green spheres of Earth magic between both palms.

'You're in my way,' the teenager said.

Emmeline delivered Adelita, Ethan and Jocko back to the action in the midst of Central Park. They poured out of the portal, faltering as they took in the battle still going on around them. Elemental flares and flashes of white light from Crystal witches lit up the park. Muzzle flashes from Sentinel and Brotherhood weapons. Ethan ducked as an axe flew overhead, burying itself in the trunk of a nearby tree. They were in the wrong place.

'Fuck it!' Emmeline said, realising her mistake.

She raised two hands again, but her yellow Air magic wavered. She was exhausted; she was taking longer than usual to power up. Loveday rested her chin on her soulmate's shoulder, stroking her back. Emmeline hung her head, anguished and pissed.

'It's OK, just focus. You can do this,' Ethan said.

They all jumped as more yellow sparks burst next to them that had nothing to do with Emmeline. There was a shout and a streak of orange. EJ came flying through another portal, arms and legs snatching at the air. He landed face down, splat in the mud. None of them needed to ask who'd delivered him to safety: Chloe.

Jocko grabbed the stunned boy, lifting him to his feet. 'Holy shit, are you OK?'

Stunned, EJ just stared at both Jocko and Ethan, catatonic with shock. Then his face cracked into a wide grin and he howled like a wolf. Ethan joined him. Despite himself, Jocko gave an accompanying warrior-like whoop as they all raised fists in the air.

'When you're quite finished, boys.' Adelita looked at her watch, then up at the Orchid Tower and its Anther Cap. 'Three minutes to go.'

Beside her, Emmeline's fists exploded with yellow Air magic.

The first lady didn't like the dismissal in The One's tone. She was in her way? Perhaps Chloe Su thought Marianne was not a worthy opponent. But she'd spent a lifetime – *longer than Chloe had even been alive!* – planning and preparing for this showdown. She had endured hardships unnumbered in the past twenty years. The least the little Elemental bitch could do was acknowledge that. Marianne's ego could not withstand her doing anything else.

Chloe's green spheres danced on the end of her fingertips. *Please move.*

Marianne's blood-red lips curled in a snarl.

Never. This whole kingdom is mine. I've worked too hard to step aside now.

It's not yours. It's all of ours!

Marianne could sense the girl's strong conviction. She intended to link with the equinox and send her power to all witches. Well, not on her watch. The One's power was hers. She hadn't come this far to fall at the final hurdle.

I don't want to hurt you, but I will if I have to.

You are nothing, Marianne jeered.

We both know that's not true.

Chloe sent her Earth magic at Marianne. The spheres cascaded outwards across the platform like bouncing balls. Surprised, Marianne winced in pain as the first two or three hit her, making her slide backwards across the glass. She stamped her foot and drew herself to a halt before she could fall.

Stop that!

Irritated, the Crystal witch clenched her fist around her trusty tiger's eye. The green spheres dissipated in an instant, popping like soap bubbles. Chloe sent a wave of water across the glass platform, designed to wash Marianne off the edge. It never reached as far as the first lady. She rolled her eyes and made it turn to ice. Marianne made short work of the gale Chloe sent next towards her, too. Watching the teen's shoulders heave with the effort, derision coursed through the older woman.

That can't be all you have, surely?

Chloe met Marianne's eye. She didn't like the defiance in the teen's face.

I'm not here for you.

Chloe rushed forwards, towards the big glass ball of the anther that stood between them. The older woman smiled.

Oh, I know what you're here for . . .

On her wrist, her watch read 2:56 p.m. She had one hundred

and twenty seconds to stop The One from linking with the equinox and all witches worldwide. Marianne slammed her open palm down on the anther, just as Chloe reached it, placing her own hands on its smooth, round surface.

. . . But you won't get it.

Emmeline's portal opened again. That stink of ozone came with it, along with that sense of the air weighing on Adelita's chest. But as it split apart, something prompted Adelita's psyche to switch on. She did not fight it, even though time was at a premium; she knew better now than to resist her heart's impulses.

She soared above the battle below. Ethan and the others slowed down as they moved towards the portal. Moving between the planes of existence, Adelita could see Sentinel agents blundering about in their black suits and stormtrooper gear, locked in combat with the Brotherhood. Witches, Elemental and Crystal, sent flares and white light into the clashes. Faces she knew jumped out of the throng like Where's Waldo. None of them needed Adelita's help. Cally and her sisters from the Forge surrounded themselves with a wall of flames, blasting their enemies back. Blades between their teeth, Costentyn and two of his Boscastle brothers ran the length of the meadow, leaping on three Sentinel who didn't stand a chance. It was then she saw him.

Another Sentinel agent, running straight at her group like the one in Cologne Cathedral, weapon raised. Only this time, Chloe was not with them to help by freezing him in his tracks. Adelita fell back into her body just as the crack of gunfire sounded. She knew she wouldn't have time to intercept his bullet.

But Ethan was standing right next to her.

She pushed white light from herself, enveloping her cowboy, Jocko and EJ with him. She blasted them forwards, out of the bullet's path. All three men went down like dominoes as

Adelita fired a shoot of Crystal magic straight at the Sentinel agent, taking him out. He flew backwards, into the mud, not moving. Adelita moved out of the pathway of the bullet herself, watching it sail in slo-mo over her head as she zoomed between the planes of existence.

But the cause and effect of Adelita's Crystal magic blast did not stop there. Emmeline shrieked a warning to Loveday, pulling her soulmate out of harm's way back into the portal. The Air magic collapsed around them in the mêlée, taking both Boscastle witches with it.

Too late, Adelita realised her error: she had stumbled directly into the line of fire of some Water Elementals who were controlling the angry torrent of water from the reservoir. She was wide open and in the path of their angry torrent.

Before she could move, the water hit her, full-on.

White light emanated from Marianne, through her palm and into the lead glass. The anther acted like a plasma ball, the first lady's magic striking through it like fork lightning. Chloe lit up with Earth magic, a column of it pouring from her, upwards towards the sky. The Orchid Tower gave an ominous moan as magic thundered its way through the steel girders that held it up, down to its foundations and the park below. Glass spidered under their feet. The building shuddered, a dying behemoth.

Look what you're doing! You're going to destroy everything.

The teen met Marianne's gaze. *No, that was all you.*

Marianne gritted her teeth. She did not like to admit to herself it was harder work withstanding the girl's magic through the anther. It worked its way through her forearm, into her joints. Stinging agony like electric shocks made its way through her elbow, into her shoulder and spine. It coursed through her pelvis and legs, to her feet. Her whole body sang with pain.

You want everything for yourself.

These words caused genuine surprise in Marianne.

Doesn't everyone?

No. Some of us want equality, to share.

Inside the spellbind, Marianne laughed. This child was so naive, blinded by the idealism of youth. No one really cared about anyone else, it was all lip service. Sure, people had their favourites, but in real terms no one really cared beyond looking after number one. It made sense: if you looked after yourself, those closest to you would also benefit. When Marianne became the strongest witch in the world, her girls Regan and Alice would be protected. That was just common sense.

Your girls only ever wanted your love. Instead you left them alone and murdered their father, all so you could take what isn't rightfully yours.

Marianne gaped in shock; The One was as strong as she'd feared. The teenager had snatched her thoughts and fears from her head and exposed them with ease. Like any normal working mother, she *had* always worried about Regan and Alice being raised by a succession of nannies. Taking over the world was not normal work, but she'd thought her actions and ambitions were a worthwhile trade-off on their behalf. But what if they weren't? What if her girls hated her for it? What if they came for her for killing their father, like Electra and Orestes had for Clytemnestra?

Oh no you don't. You know nothing of parenthood, girl.

Marianne tamped down Chloe's taunt, before it could unravel her.

I am not taunting you. I speak the truth.

Chloe Su's was a natural talent. It was raw and unpolluted. It was also one Marianne would never be able to achieve, even with a lifetime of study. She shut down the doubts before they could take root. She didn't need to study. She was here to take The One's power, straight out of the eye of the equinox. What

Marianne lacked in magical strength, she could make up for with her own mental acuity.

As imagery continued to flood between them, Marianne homed in on two faces amidst the blur. A man and a woman; both in their mid-forties with a strong familial resemblance, she knew immediately they were the girl's parents. Both existences swirled around and around. They were alive and then snuffed out, on a loop.

You killed your mother and father.

The girl's gaze did not waver, but her magic did. The pain of The One's magic abated a little, like the teen's focus had stumbled. Marianne's scarlet lips fixed in a rictus grin. This was the child's own Achilles heel; she could feel it. Certainty filled Marianne's belly as she pushed up her Crystal magic through the anther at Chloe Su.

It's your fault they're dead.

No. Your Sentinel killed my father.

Your mother, then. You killed her all by yourself, didn't you?

That was an accident.

There it was. The conviction in Chloe's voice in the spellbind wavered and became quieter. A flash of the girl's mother's face loomed between them: she ran through a door, palms up, desperate and pleading. Like now, a green column of Earth magic was bursting from the teenager. It deluged towards her mother and swirled around the woman like a boa constrictor. Chloe's mother screamed as the teen's magic forced its way into her flesh, making her body crumple and implode in a shower of dust. Green light exploded outwards with the deadly power of a meteor strike.

I didn't know what I was doing. I never meant to do it!

Marianne could feel Chloe's distress flow with it, but also something else. A dark force, ebbing from the teen.

You were angry with her.

No. I loved her.

But you also hated her. She muzzled your powers. And you wanted to make her pay.

I DID MAKE THE BITCH PAY!

Chloe's voice changed inside the spellbind. Marianne's heart leapt with malevolent pleasure as the tables turned. The girl was becoming consumed by thoughts of vengeance; she could feel it. If Marianne could ensure the teen sent these dark thoughts through the anther as she linked to the equinox, The One's powers would be hers.

Your mother took everything from you.

WHY DID SHE HURT ME?

She was jealous of what you were. She wanted to ensure you couldn't be more powerful than her.

The girl's darkness faltered as Marianne said this; she'd over-reached, though she couldn't imagine how. Obviously the girl's mother didn't want to be outdone; who would? No mother liked her daughters overtaking them in youth, looks, or magic. Before she could lose her hold on Chloe, Marianne doubled down, dredging up more words of supposed sympathy for her to pull her into the trap.

She made you lose yourself, so you never knew who or what you were. She made you live with pain and confusion every day of your life. She was scared, so she hurt you.

SHE HURT ME SO MUCH.

The girl's tortured howl chucked Marianne out of the spell-bind for a split second. Light, noise and ozone invaded her senses. The first lady screamed through clenched teeth, her eyes watering as she fought pain and the urge to tear her hand away from the anther. She knew the equinox was less than ten seconds away. If Marianne could just hold on, Chloe would send her darkness through the spellbind, conducted through the Orchid Tower straight to Marianne. She would have all of The One's Elemental power, at last.

That's it. Give it to me.

Marianne would be the most powerful witch of all time. She could feel the dark of the moon taking over The One. She was moments from snatching the equinox's raw power out of the teenager's head.

Before her, Chloe's eyes turned shiny and black, like oil.

FIFTY-THREE

Everything sped up again as the flood punched into Adelita, forcing her body forwards like a crash-test dummy. As it did so, Adelita's Crystal magic burst out of her. Whether it counteracted the Water magic, or served as a distress flare to the Water Elementals who'd sent it, the impetus of the deluge disappeared almost immediately, like a shower or hose turning off. The water moved harmlessly around her, but its damage was done. Dazed, Adelita swayed from side to side, then fell onto her back in the mud.

'No!' Ethan hollered, from somewhere above her.

The white sky spiralled above Adelita as she blinked in confusion. Her mind was not able to catch on to what had happened to her body. Her brain reeled as a deep, throbbing pain that was somehow numb at the same time bloomed outwards from her chest.

HURT

Adelita could visualise it like a red arrow from her sternum. Broken? She tried to raise her left arm to touch her chest. She couldn't. It sent an explosion of agony through her, as well as blood into her mouth. She gagged, hacking a horrible, wet cough.

'Oh no no no.' Ethan was beside her, looming over her. 'Ada!'

I'm OK, Adelita tried to say through the spellbind, but even that was too much for her. Her thoughts seemed to glitch, like her mind was receiving radio interference.

HURT SO MUCH

Jocko swam into view with EJ, his brow knitted with concern. He said something to Ethan, but Adelita couldn't understand or hear the words falling from his lips. She could still hear the sounds of battle behind them, the explosion of Elemental flares and the cries of the injured and dying drowning the men out, even though they were right next to her.

The three of them all nodded to one another, shifting their arms underneath her prone body. They were going to move her. Something flickered in the back of Adelita's mind. But they mustn't; they couldn't move her . . . For some reason. What was it? Yellow sparks burst next to them as Emmeline rematerialised with Loveday, her face stricken with guilt. She beckoned them over, to bring Adelita to safety. Ethan and the others picked Adelita up.

A red sea of pain flooded through her and she screamed. The agony brought clarity with it, echoing up the spellbind, from Adelita's injured body to the top of the Orchid Tower. She could feel the Crystal and Earth magic at war, smell the stench of ozone swirling around Marianne and Chloe. She could see the teenager's black, beetle-carapace eyes as she struggled against the dark side of the moon.

CHLOE, NO!

The equinox was maybe seconds away, but Adelita was badly injured. She didn't have the words or ability to stop the teen from self-destructing. She couldn't stop her from transmitting her powers straight into the master manipulator Marianne through the conductor of the anther.

But there was one person who could go in her place, as her conduit.

Ethan staggered forwards, letting go of Adelita. The other two stumbled, almost dropping her and causing another horrendous wave of pain. She didn't care. Ethan stared at his hands in disbelief as white residual Crystal magic snaked through his body, transmitted from Adelita to him. He was in no pain. He was used to her power in his veins now, like Costentyn had been to Loveday's and his sisters'. Cally's words echoed back from the Forge: . . . *anyone with a powerful connection to a witch can do it.* Ethan was Adelita's; she was his; they were one.

Go, Adelita instructed.

Without looking back at her, Ethan muscled towards the Orchid Tower through the crowd, which parted around him like lines of ants. Witches looked on in amazement as they saw him pass, a *man* glowing with Crystal magic. Brothers and Sentinel alike stared, pausing in the fighting as their brains refused to take in the bizarre sight.

Ethan pressed both palms against the glass base of the Orchid Tower.

As Adelita's magic exploded upwards, towards the anther, other witches in the vicinity understood what they needed to do. Crystal witches and Elementals alike abandoned the skirmish, pouring towards the tower. Emmeline and Loveday ran from the portal, beckoning Costentyn and the other Elemental boys with them. Evgenia's mother's biker boyfriend joined the race towards the huge lead-glass building, yellow residual Air magic snaking through his bushy beard. Cally and the Forge witches sent up more flames in their wake, driving any remaining Sentinel back before running at the tower themselves.

'Cover them!' Jocko hollered.

The Brotherhood forced themselves between the tower and the diminished Sentinel. The agents knew they were beaten.

They fell back, compelled to watch slack-jawed as multicoloured magic flares lit up the tower. White, green, yellow, blue and red surged through the lead glass, up towards Chloe, Marianne and the Anther Cap at the top. Strength in numbers. Below, Adelita concentrated, gripping on to consciousness and EJ; she could feel the grip of the dark of the moon descend.

The equinox was here.

At the top of the Orchid Tower, Chloe's eyes cleared. Frustrated, Marianne felt the teenager's superior powers flood back through the spellbind, swamping her own as the equinox hit. The pain of The One's magic was total this time, surging through the first lady's veins and sending her eyes rolling back in her head.

'Everything is not all for you,' the teen said.

FIFTY-FOUR

The Dark Side of the Moon

My people are here
Here's what you don't understand, Marianne . . .

. . . No person is an island
Just like my dad said.

But you thought you could take it all, didn't you?
The old world was built on greed and self-interest, in keeping the
downtrodden down and the privileged at the top of the tree.

Well, no more.

Equality is true power; generosity, too.
Everything is not all for you.
That's not what true power is about.

We are one.

FIFTY-FIVE

E than came to with a gasp. Bright spots sprang up in front of his eyes as he sat up, Central Park spinning in lazy circles around him. He had no memory of being knocked unconscious but he knew that, whatever had happened, it had been the dark of the moon and Chloe's magic that had pinned them all to the ground.

Around him, the cowboy could see witches, Goodys, Brotherhood and even Sentinel stagger to their feet, shell-shocked. Multicoloured magic flares were dancing everywhere overhead like the Northern Lights. He turned to look to the top of the tower, where lights still flashed: white, green, yellow, blue and red. They lacked the urgency of the magic blast minutes – or was it hours? – earlier. Instead they twinkled, iridescent, round and round like carnival glass.

Ethan could feel Adelita's residual magic still moving within his solar plexus, skittering down his spine like feathers. Where was she?

There.

He tried to stand but fell onto his knees again. With his legs refusing to support him, he scrabbled along the ground in the mud to where she lay, gathering his love in his arms. Her eyes were still closed. For one paralysing second, he thought she was gone.

Not dead yet, hombre. Also, ow. Be careful.

Relief coursed through him as he pulled her close. He leant down and kissed her cold lips.

I got you.

We got each other, she said, *always.*

Glancing up, he noticed something moving within the tower, his brain slow to make sense of it. Then he realised: it was the glass elevator coming down. At the base, the doors opened, and Chloe appeared, pushing Marianne ahead of her. The first lady wandered out, swaying from side to side, almost like she was a dancing child.

'Not using Air magic?' Ethan said.

Chloe shrugged. 'I can't. Something's changed.'

'What?'

'I'm not sure.'

EJ moved forward, taking the president's wife from Chloe. She capitulated, making no effort to break free. She seemed completely vacant, her eyes black with the dark of the moon. Ethan understood Chloe had trapped the older woman there, inside herself. The first lady was no longer a threat.

Chloe grinned at the young redhead. 'You're OK then.'

'Thanks to you,' EJ said, bashful.

The teen looked around at the remnants of the battle, at the survivors gathering round her in wonder, as if surprised to see them. Cally, Evgenia, Jocko, Emmeline, Loveday, Costentyn and the others appeared, eyes wide. All wanted to hug Chloe, congratulate her.

'Er, guys?' Jocko stared at his hand. His fist glowed with residual magic. He looked terrified, impressed and quizzical, all at once. 'What the hell is happening?'

The whole park lit up, Elemental, Crystal witch, Goody and man alike. As Ethan hugged Adelita closer, the pair of them glowed softly, their love feeding the beams flooding out of them.

Adelita's eyelids fluttered. *So, our girl came through for us?*

She did, her cowboy said.

Chloe smiled and knelt down by Ethan and Adelita. Ethan pulled the teen towards them, so his arms were around both women. The light flooded out of all three in a vertical column, up towards the night sky.

They were all witches now.

FIFTY-SIX

Sydney, Australia

Ethan looked out across the glittering water of Sydney Harbour. It was one of the few places he'd not travelled with the Sentinel. The cowboy picked out all the iconic sights: the bridge, the opera house, the waterways alive with cruise boats, ferries and kayaks. It was very different to the sombre and dead Salem Harbor they'd seen just a few weeks before. He looked over to Adelita and Chloe, standing beside him by the edge of the water; he knew they were thinking the same. Adelita leant on a stang, which doubled as a walking stick. He could feel her pain through the spellbind. Even so, he thanked God or Hecate or chance; *whomever* or *whatever* had spared his precious Ada.

Her gaze met his, her expression soft as she took in his eyes, glassy with tears.

So much for being a tough guy. She smiled, reminding him of their words in that Texas motel room, back when it all started.

I never said I was a tough guy.

Their lips met.

Ugh, get a room, you guys.

Ethan grinned at Chloe. It was hard to believe she was the

same tortured, mixed-up girl he'd met on the road at Taunton Deane. The loss of Daniel and her mother cut deep, of course; it always would. She was only at the beginning of processing her bereavement. They all were. Ethan missed the professor's pragmaticism and acceptance of the incredible; his stoic commitment to fatherhood and to his daughter had been humbling. It would be a long road for all of them in getting used to Daniel not being there.

I miss him too.

Chloe nodded, looking back out at the water.

I know you do.

Adelita placed an arm around the teenager's shoulders. Everything had changed beyond recognition, but this also meant Chloe had been released from the never-ending torment her mother had imposed on her. She was no longer a lost girl; that terrible darkness had been pulled from her like a veil. It was like she could see and feel the world with new eyes and optimism, even while dealing with her grief.

'You guys looking for Cyrus Frost?'

An indigenous woman in a nurse's uniform appeared by the waterfront, putting air quotes around the name as she spoke. Her wavy hair was tied in a high ponytail on top of her head. The sunlight glinted off her pocket watch. She seemed pissed off, yet cheery with it. A weird combo.

Ethan gave her an uncertain smile. 'That you?'

The woman rolled her eyes. 'Nah. I'm Jedda. I can't believe he was getting involved in all this while I was earning a crust at work. Here he is, the little bugger.'

They followed her gaze. A few yards behind her was a boy of about seventeen or eighteen, wearing a T-shirt with a Superman logo. A wheelchair user, an iPad rested on his knees.

'Hi.' He grinned at them and waved, a little awkward. 'I'm Arthur.'

Ethan recognised his voice at once. Arthur had not only de-encrypted the world witch web, but also declared the takeover in Central Park.

Chloe raised an eyebrow. 'I told you, everyone *young* can get on Pentagram.'

Ethan laughed, watching as Adelita and Chloe joined Arthur and his mum to thank him for his help, laughing and hugging.

Ethan envied them; he felt as if the darkness the Sentinel had put in him would stain his soul for ever. When he closed his eyes, he could still see barbed wire and trains; blood on the ground. He could still feel the horror of his Sentinel actions weighing down every cell in his body. He was sure he had not done enough to redeem the sins of his past. He felt as if he could spend a lifetime trying to make up for what he'd done to witches, to women, to the world, and he would not scratch the surface. The new magic coursing through his veins reminded him of this, day and night. The only thing he could do now was love Ada and Chloe and let them love him back, while they all kept each other safe. He'd been alone a long time, but no more.

They were their own coven: family.

EPILOGUE

Miss Leonora Smart is twenty-five years old and it's her first academic year in her first teaching job. When she was given the position she was delighted, envisaging a school full of kids desperate to learn. What she actually got was a bunch of recalcitrant teens who'd rather scroll through Insta, Snapchat or YouTube than do almost anything else. This is OK, though; she likes a challenge.

Today, Leonora – Nora to her friends – is dressed in a black pencil skirt, black patent Rockabilly shoes and a black slimline shirt that strains a little on the bust. She's put a little weight on since she bought it, so was planning to wear her looser white one instead. Then the cat startled her at breakfast while Nora was drinking her coffee, and you can guess the rest.

'Hello, everyone, if we could try and keep questions to a minimum today, I would appreciate it,' she trills.

Thirty blank teenage faces stare back at her. Correction: twenty-eight. Two of them – Justine Harrison and Bella Lewis – are striking what Nora calls 'the pose'. Heads tilted towards the

430

floor, one foot outstretched, one arm under the table. No doubt about it, both girls are on their phones. Sigh.

'Justine, Bella! Put your phones away or they come and live on my desk for the rest of the day. Thank you.'

Both girls jump to attention in their chairs as if they've received a bolt of Crystal magic. Muttering under their breaths, both teens slide their phones into their bags and zip them up. As they do this, Nora writes the date on the whiteboard: 16 April, 2021.

'OK, we have a lot to get through today in our GCSE Origins of Witchcraft class.' She clasps both her small hands together as she turns back towards her charges. 'With mock exams around the corner we really need . . . Yes, Justine?'

The girl mutters something barely intelligible only a trained teacher like Nora can decipher. At teacher training college they stressed the importance of lip reading, otherwise you'd go mad asking teenagers to repeat themselves.

'Just open your exercise book and do the best you can.'

Nora slips her glasses on and consults the worksheet in front of her. 'Now, where was I . . . Ah, yes. At 2:58 p.m., on Friday the twentieth March 2020, the entire human race ceased to function for approximately two minutes. There were no uploads to social media, radio stations went dark; it was said that everything and everyone simply . . . stopped. This includes me and all of you in this room. Can any of you tell me why?'

The usual suspects – Ben Kennedy, Lilian Murphy and Rebecca Wilson, the swots, nerds and boffins of the class, in other words – raise their hands. Nora stares over them towards the others in the class, her smile frozen on her face, in the hope someone else might take the lead for once. No dice. Trying to avoid looking frustrated, she bestows a nod at the nearest girl with her hand in the air.

'We assume it was a magic blast, miss.'

Rebecca shoots a triumphant look at the other two. Ben makes a rude hand gesture in response, almost making Nora smile. She'd underestimated him; he does have a personality.

'That's absolutely correct. Now, we don't know for sure, but what we do know is down to television and CCTV footage recovered later, not to mention live feeds of the Battle of Central Park. These appear to show everyone – witch, Goody, man and child – falling to the ground, enveloped by multicoloured lights. This happened in the United Kingdom and all around the world. Experts later concluded the blast originated at the top of the Orchid Tower, New York ... Yes, Ben?'

The boy puffs up his chest. 'We only *assume* everyone on earth was affected.'

Nora stops her prepared spiel in its tracks as she considers this contribution. This is why she got into teaching: alternative viewpoints and ways of looking at the world, direct from the next generation. Nice.

'That's actually a great observation, Ben, well done. Yes, we only *assume* it was the entire human race that was felled by the magic blast. There are, of course, places without technology, so we cannot be one hundred per cent sure that every single human being on Earth was affected.'

Nora swallows down a laugh as she sees Rebecca shoot Ben daggers.

'That said, given the lack of eyewitnesses anywhere on the globe, experts have a fair idea the event on Equinox Day was total. No one fully knows exactly what caused this phenomenon, though there are theories. Can anyone name any?'

There's a cacophony of noise behind her as students start calling out random theories, ideas and notions. Only some of them are what they've been studying. Nora does her best to keep up, writing on the board as quickly as she can.

'Yes, very good, Lilian! Some experts do believe it was some kind of solar flare that coincidentally happened to strike at the time of the equinox ... They believe the witches we once called "Elementals" somehow jacked into this power for some reason, which if you ask me seems a little far-fetched.'

A male voice that isn't Ben's booms through the room. Nora doesn't have to turn around to know it's Alex Hinton, the six foot five fifteen-year-old rugby team captain who locked her in the stationery cupboard the first month she'd started at the school. He'd been on an internal exclusion for a week for that. He continues listing possibilities, each of them as ludicrous as the last.

'... Zombie President Hopkins, Alex? Erm, he was a strange man, but even if that were possible, I think that was probably against that Puritan religion of his. Aliens? OK, you're being absurd now.'

The room laughs at Alex's theories, but not at Nora. Phew. Congratulating herself on defusing the situation, Nora finally hears the answer she is seeking from a quiet redhead down the front of the classroom. The girl doesn't look up from her doodling as Nora addresses her.

'Thank you, Madeleine, that was the answer I wanted to hear. You're right: most experts believe the witch known as "The One" sent the magic blast across the world, using the Orchid Tower as a kind of giant conductor, uniting all existing witches together. Does anyone know her name?'

The hubbub in the classroom ceases abruptly. Nora smiles as she watches the students search for the answer; some flip through exercise books and leaf through worksheets.

'Well, I'd be surprised if any of you lot did, because no one knows who The One is. Trick question! Sorry, guys!'

Nora laughs and holds her hands in the air in surrender as the students proffer good-natured complaints. After that dies down, she continues.

'After the Orchid Tower fell and the Sentinel were disbanded, it was revealed all records pertaining to "The One" had been wiped. Some claim she never even existed! So, how do we have *any* information about her?'

Madeleine down the front of the classroom holds something up. Nora nods and encourages her to show it to the rest of the class. It's a hardback book with red letters on a black cover. On the back, a black and white photograph of a smiling British-Chinese man in his late forties or early fifties. It's not on the official GCSE reading list because it's far too advanced, plus it was only published about six weeks ago. Nora had been first in line to buy it at Waterstones, even before it had smashed through the *New York Times* Bestsellers List. On the front, the title reads: *The Science of Witchcraft, by Daniel Su.*

'Daniel Su worked up at Exeter University in the theology department; some of you may have mums and dads who knew him. Unfortunately, we don't know what happened to him, or why; he seems to have disappeared somewhere around Equinox Day. What we do know is that Daniel Su was very interested in witchcraft, especially Elementals. His colleagues at the university parcelled up all his notes and essays and this book is the result. He had been collecting transcripts, leaflets and other materials for years. This was very dangerous, because no one was supposed to study witchcraft after ... well, after what, class?'

'The Safeguard Initiative!' a bunch of teens chorus in unison.

Nora savours her victory; they *are* listening. 'Good. That was the legislation President Hopkins drew up to make witchcraft – and witches – illegal. But all of that is pointless now. Can anyone tell me why ... What happened to everyone on Equinox Day?'

Another surge of correct answers washes over Nora.

'Excellent, that's right, class. We ALL became witches. It would seem "The One" gave us ALL a piece of her power ...

Elemental, Crystal witch, Goody or man, we all ended up with magic! It's not known whether she fully meant to do this, or whether it was an accident. I like to think "The One" did it on purpose. It's genius, if you think about it: if everyone starts on an equal footing, then this will change everything. And it has, for the most part.

'Obviously there are teething problems; some people are daunted by their new magic. Not everyone likes having their original power reduced. But we come together, to try and ensure this transition period goes smoothly. It's why we have classes like this: to understand and process what has happened to us all and ensure we learn a lesson from history. We are not one hundred per cent there yet, but change is coming.'

The bell rings, prompting almost every student to make a grab for their belongings. Frustration surges through Nora again, just like it had at the beginning of the lesson. White light crackles out of her, making her hair stand up like static electricity. She coughs, embarrassed, thinking relaxing thoughts about coffee and the birthday cake for another teacher waiting in the staffroom for break time.

'The bell is for me, not for you! You don't go until I dismiss you. Now, for homework . . .'

All the kids groan.

Lizzie Fry is the pseudonym of an internationally acclaimed author and script editor. As well as working with numerous film production companies, she is a core member of the London Screenwriters' Festival board.

Acknowledgements

Growing up in Devon, witchcraft was never far from the fringes of my life. As a child and teenager I was obsessed with the idea of magic, always searching it out. I met many real-life witches who took me into their confidence, plus I visited local witch spots and read about them whenever I could.

One such place was the plaque at Rougemont Castle in Heavitree, Exeter. I came across this one accidentally. I was working as an English language teacher at a school around the corner. I discovered Exeter is known as the first and last place to hang a witch: Temperance Lloyd, Susannah Edwards and Mary Trembles (aka 'The Bideford Witches') were hanged at Exeter Prison in 1682.

The women were convicted on the basis of hearsay evidence and probably tortured into confessing. The plaque commemorating the witches' deaths reads at the bottom: *In the hope of an end to persecution and intolerance.* With misogyny so rife in the twenty-first century, this optimism gave me pause.

In addition, as a child of the eighties and nineties, I grew up on *Buffy* and *Charmed*, as well as classic witch movies like *The*

Craft and quest narratives like *Labyrinth, Willow, Ulysses 31* and *The Dark Crystal*. I felt sure I would write a thriller about witches one day, with strong feminist themes.

So *The Coven* is the kind of story I have always wanted to write: an allegorical tale with fantastical elements, combining high-octane action with nuanced characterisation. I hope I pulled it off!

As ever, the journey a book and its writer undergo is varied and I have lots of people to thank for helping me on my way.

First up, many thanks to the wonderful witches, spiritualists and experts who advised me on this magical voyage: Sara Amanda; Emma Martin; Jade Bokhari and Vered Neta. Thanks also to Steve Simmonds and The Boscastle Museum of Witchcraft, especially in helping me work out where Boscastle's old police station could be!

I'd also like to thank Mark and Tracey Norman – your expertise was invaluable in working out where to begin! Thanks also to the many #witchesofinstagram and those posting over on Pinterest, your content was a real inspiration and gave me a lot to think about.

Thanks to all my 'Bang2writers' who answered all my queries and musings about 'Chosen One' narratives and The Hero's Journey. You also helped me immeasurably in my musings on the intersection of witchcraft with politics, religion, feminism and race on Twitter and Facebook. Major appreciation points to my friends Bethany Black and Amy Coop who helped me pinpoint how 'biological magic' could work.

I'd also like to thank my 'international crew' who gave me pointers on various cultures, locations and languages, including Bob Schultz; Carolin Grosse Hellmann; Kent DuFault for asking his lovely wife for me; Olivia Brennan; Maja Bodenstein; Daniel York Loh; Deirdre Statham and Rose Su Cawsey.

Thanks also to my screenwriting buddies, who helped me envisage the visuals in this book, especially the set pieces. You know who you are! Special thanks to film producer Iain Smith, who kindly talked me through the thematics of *Mad Max: Fury Road* and inspired my notion of the male characters being able to 'carry magic' when they connect and work with female witches, instead of fighting them. Thanks also to the multi-talented Eric Heisserer whose fantastic female lead Louise in *Arrival* helped inspire so many of the female characters here, especially Adelita.

Thanks also to Maddie West, Darcy Nicholson, Thalia Proctor, Francesca Banks and Abby Parsons at Sphere Books. I loved working with you all.

As ever, undying gratitude to my agent Hattie Grunewald, as well as my beta readers, accountability partners and cheerleaders JK Amalou, Emma Pullar, Jenny Kane, Debbie Moon and Elinor Perry-Smith. Couldn't do this without you guys!

To Mr C and the children: thanks for bearing with me as I wrote this book. I got more than a little preoccupied with it and dragged you all to a LOT of drowning pools, hanging sites and other connected places! You never complained, even when I ended up writing a good chunk of the book right through a family holiday. I am a very, very lucky writer to have you all and have my foibles and failings accepted.

Finally, thanks for reading! This might be my first outing as 'Lizzie Fry', but as always I appreciate each and every reader. I hope you enjoyed it as much I loved writing it.

Hecate For Ever (and fuck The Sentinel!),

Lizzie x